Duets™

**Two brand-new stories in every volume...
twice a month!**

Duets Vol. #83

Royalty makes an appearance in the line this month
with a fun-filled Double Duets by fan favorite
Carrie Alexander. Look for the sexy, sassy
RED-HOT ROYALS miniseries from this author
whom *Romantic Times* says is "a gifted writer,
with a fresh distinctive voice." The regal miniseries
continues next month with Jill Shalvis!

Duets Vol. #84

Bonnie Tucker and Holly Jacobs team up this month
to write about disastrous weddings. Bonnie's
The Great Bridal Escape features a runaway bride
who elopes with the best man. Holly follows with a
quirky story, *How To Catch a Groom,* about a hunky
hero left at the altar with only the gorgeous wedding
coordinator to console him. Enjoy all the matrimonial
antics with this dynamite writing duo!

Be sure to pick up both Duets volumes today!

"Ooh, my blouse is all damp," *Lili said.*

She peeled off her pink jacket and reached to unbutton the blouse. The wet silk had gone transparent, clinging to the curves of her breasts.

Good God! Simon thought. Breasts! Naked! Lucky, lucky man!

Then: Bodyguard! Royal outrage! Disgrace!

Worth it!

"Do you have a hair dryer?" Lili asked.

"There are hand dryers in the lavatories. I'll take your things, if you like."

His brain had lost too much blood for him to think straight. Staring at the ceiling, he reached out a blind hand, hoping she'd put the clothes into it.

"I'll do it." She stood suddenly.

Simon got a handful of breast instead.

The princess gasped.

Lili looked at him with bright, inquisitive eyes, her clothing clutched to her chest. "Now that you've touched my breast, you practically *have* to take me on a date."

He hesitated. "Would I get to touch the other breast?"

For more, turn to page 9

"I know nothing about the stolen pearls."

"And the rest?" Henry lifted a paper off his desk. "We have two wallets, one money clip and a lady's compact missing."

Jana looked at her clasped hands. "I didn't take them, I swear to you. But what if I knew where to find them? Would that be enough to make amends?"

He leaned toward her. "If you know where the stolen goods are, you'd best confess it now before I—"

"Before you what?" she said, her eyes blazing.

"Before I—" He swallowed. "Before I kiss you." He swore his heart skipped a beat when the words fell out of his mouth.

Jana's eyes widened, but she didn't retreat. "You wouldn't dare."

Oh, yes, he would. "I've never been a coward."

They were both brash and combative and too stubborn to back down. Jana's lashes fell as he covered the last bit of space between them and touched his mouth against hers.

For more, turn to page 197

HARLEQUIN DUETS

ISBN 0-373-44149-5

Copyright in the collection:
Copyright © 2002 by Harlequin Books S.A.

The publisher acknowledges the copyright holder
of the individual works as follows:

ONCE UPON A TIARA
Copyright © 2002 by Carrie Antilla

HENRY EVER AFTER
Copyright © 2002 by Carrie Antilla

This edition published by arrangement with Harlequin Books S.A.

® and TM are trademarks of the publisher. Trademarks indicated with ® are registered in the United States Patent and Trademark Office, the Canadian Trade Marks Office and in other countries.

Visit us at www.eHarlequin.com

Printed in U.S.A.

Once Upon a Tiara

Carrie Alexander

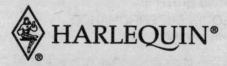

HARLEQUIN®

TORONTO • NEW YORK • LONDON
AMSTERDAM • PARIS • SYDNEY • HAMBURG
STOCKHOLM • ATHENS • TOKYO • MILAN • MADRID
PRAGUE • WARSAW • BUDAPEST • AUCKLAND

Dear Reader,

I had such fun writing for the RED-HOT ROYALS miniseries. I'm never going to be a princess—and, honestly, I wouldn't want to be—but occasionally it's a treat to indulge in the fantasy world of ball gowns, tiaras and fairy godmothers. Of course, since this is the wild and wacky world of Duets, I also threw in a few less perfect elements: bee stings, bad dates, pickpockets and a Gypsy curse. To say nothing of two rather improbable Prince Charmings...

Please enjoy the intertwined stories of my two princesses, Lili and Jana. One's not quite as royal as the other—except to her hero. That's as it should be. Because we're all princesses where it counts!

Yours, with a sprinkle of fairy dust,

Carrie Alexander

P.S. Amelia Grundy isn't finished yet. Remember to look for Lili's sisters' stories, *A Royal Mess* and *Her Knight To Remember* by Jill Shalvis, next month.

Books by Carrie Alexander

HARLEQUIN TEMPTATION
839—SMOOTH MOVES
869—RISKY MOVES

HARLEQUIN BLAZE
20—PLAYING WITH FIRE

HARLEQUIN SUPERROMANCE
1042—THE MAVERICK

Don't miss any of our special offers. Write to us at the following address for information on our newest releases.

Harlequin Reader Service
U.S.: 3010 Walden Ave., P.O. Box 1325, Buffalo, NY 14269
Canadian: P.O. Box 609, Fort Erie, Ont. L2A 5X3

To Susan Sheppard,
a final pearl for the true pearl

Thanks for everything,
"Clam"

1

"PEANUT BUTTER," Lili said to herself, gazing beyond the wisps of vaporous clouds. The airplane was beginning its descent.

Soon, she, Liliane Brunner, Her Serene Highness of Grunberg—*oh, my, my. La-di-da!*—would have her first taste of genuine American peanut butter. To be excited over such a silly little thing was not at all grown-up or sophisticated. Even though Lili had sworn to her family that she'd behave on this trip, at the moment she didn't give a fig about what a proper princess would do. There were peanut butter jars to explore! Childish or not, she'd wanted to stick her finger into a jar of Skippy or Jif ever since she'd heard of the exotic brands.

And grab a handful of M&M's, she added silently, leaning closer to the small window to get a glimpse of land. *Oh, and I mustn't forget hot dogs, slathered in mustard and ketchup and relish and sauerkraut and pickles and five-alarm chili...*

Perhaps it would be best not to try it *all* at once!

Lili smiled, propping a fist beneath her chin in a gesture left over from her storybook childhood, when life at the royal castle in Spitzenstein had been one grand entertainment after another. Her mother's death in an avalanche in the Swiss Alps had changed all that. Lili had been nine. Her father had grieved deeply, withdrawing from the world for several years. Afterward, he'd become far more restrictive about what he allowed for his three young daughters. Lili and her two older sisters, Natalia and Andrea, had grown up as sheltered as possible in the modern day.

Despite her mother's tragic demise, Lili's optimism and outgoing personality could not be stifled. She tried to be good to please her father—especially since Natalia, the eldest, had grown into a rebel, while Andrea played the nonconformist—but being good was terribly boring. Lili loved life—all of it! She wanted to experience *everything*. This was her first trip to America as an adult, and she was practically light-headed, her anticipation so fizzy it was as if she'd been guzzling expensive champagne straight from the bottle.

Lili nipped the tip of her tongue to quell an eruption of sheer excitement. If she let it out, she might not be able to stop…and it wasn't very princessy to giggle in first class.

Then again, why should only *she* have to behave? Prince Franz, her father, was spending a weekend in Cap d'Antibes with his va-va-voom mistress—though Lili wasn't supposed to know that—while Andrea, the tomboy, and Natalia, who was Lili's role model for *mis*-behavior, completed preparations to attend a wedding in the American Southwest. They had been enlisted to lecture Lili about the importance of maintaining proper royal comportment, but *really*… Was she seriously expected to take instruction from Natalia, with her leather miniskirts and bite-my-heinie attitude? Or Annie, who knew her own mind and spoke it frequently?

Lili was the baby at twenty-two. Old enough, in her opinion.

Her father had another, however. She was considered too capricious to handle vital duties. For her first overseas outing as a solo representative of the royal family, the opening of an exhibition of the royal jewels in a diddly-squat museum in Middle America was as safe and insignificant an assignment as Prince Franz could find. Lili didn't mind. She'd been waiting for *any* opportunity to strike out on her own.

At her first glimpse of land, Lili nearly bounced out of her seat. She'd spotted green trees and golden-hued fields far below. Those had to be the "amber waves of grain"—a phrase that had piqued her curiosity far more than "purple mountains majesty." She'd seen plenty of *those* in her homeland, a pocket-sized principality tucked between the Swiss Alps and the Austrian border. America was a thousand times the size of Grunberg, whose citizens were so stuck upon their traditions they didn't even have the Golden Arches.

Too thrilled to keep silent, Lili turned to her traveling companion, Mrs. Amelia Grundy. "This is the most exciting thing that's ever happened to me."

Mrs. Grundy, a solid British sort not given to hyperbole, shook her head at the young princess. "Surely, sweet child, it's not better than the time the sheikh from Abu Dibadinia offered Prince Franz two hundred camels and a sixty-carat ruby for your hand in marriage."

Lili let out a huge smile. "Oh, much better. You know red's not my color. Besides, he offered *three* hundred camels for Natalia. I was highly insulted."

"What about when you ran off with the young Scottish laird of Kirkgordon to the topless beach in Monaco?" Mrs. Grundy had heartily disapproved of the escapade, even though her eyes had twinkled while she'd scolded the young princess. Lili was certain that she brought it up now only to remind the princess of past transgressions.

"That *should* have been exciting," Lili mused, her lips curving into a reminiscent smile, "but poor Johnnie, with his unfortunate red hair and all those freckles—he wasn't prepared for the hot sun of the Riviera."

"And a lucky sunburn it was for you, young lady. Because of the lad's solar allergy you made it off the beach in the nick of time. The papparazzi arrived a full five minutes before the palace bodyguards."

Lili put on a pretend pout. "I never even got to take my top off."

Mrs. Grundy rolled her eyes heavenward. "Goodness, no. Remember, my dear, you promised. There will be no mischief on this trip."

Lili opened her mouth. *How very dull that sounded!* "But—"

"No *ifs, ands* or *buts* about it, Your Serene Highness. You know what I always say—"

"Not to worry." Lili interrupted before the dear woman repeated one of her favorite expressions. It was always a bad sign when Amelia Grundy launched into the Your-Serene-Highness song and dance.

Lili glanced sidelong with a foxy smile. "I hear that Americans still emulate the Puritans when it comes to nudity…and other regards. It's extremely unlikely that Blue Cloud, Pennsylvania, will offer me a single opportunity for naked shenanigans." She gave an airy sigh. "What a pity."

"If I didn't know that you're teasing me…"

Lili gripped the older woman's hand. "Of course, I am, Amelia. I remain as pure as the driven snow." *In spite of my best attempts.*

Amelia Grundy's stern but kindly face crinkled into dubious speculation. She was sixtyish, rather tall and formidable, built as round and solid as a ski mogul, with keen blue eyes and silvered hair she wore on top of her head in a pouf. A widow, she'd been with the royal family since before Lili was born, acting first as the three sisters' nanny, then—when the princesses chafed at being overseen by someone who bore such an old-fashioned term—as their combination escort, companion, social secretary and lady-in-waiting.

"Perhaps you are pure in deed," Amelia said, "but not, I fear, in thought or intent."

Lili scrunched her nose. How true! She never could manage to fool old Grundy, who had an almost mystical omniscience when it came to the three princesses. Many a time she'd shown up where least expected, just at the right moment to stop one of their wild adventures or dangerous stunts. Or facilitate a dignified exit when none seemed possible. The sisters had come to accept, and even rely upon, their former nanny's more "magical" abilities.

Now that Lili was an adult, Amelia's way of knowing what was on her mind—often before she knew it herself—could be as annoying as it was helpful. When a girl was trying to lose her virginity, it didn't help to have a nanny overseeing her. Transcendentally or not!

"It's the twenty-first century, Mrs. Grundy. These days, no girl stays a virgin until marriage."

"Unless she is the daughter of His Serene Highness, Prince Franz Albert Rudolf of Grunberg, and subject to public scrutiny in all that she does." Amelia nodded complacently, as if the subject was settled, and reopened the romance novel she'd been reading all the way across the Atlantic.

Lili sighed to herself. Upon their official debut into European society, she and her sisters had become known in the tabloids as The Three Jewels. Although their country was small and inconsequential and their father avoided the press whenever possible, much attention—and not a little speculation—had been devoted to the sisters' love lives.

Or lack thereof, Lili thought, squirming against the restraint of the safety belt as she peered out the window. They were circling the airport now. She was mere minutes away from freedom. Or as close to freedom as she could get with both Amelia Grundy and Rodger Wilhelm, the bodyguard her father had insisted she take along, watching her backside as if it were spun from glass and subject to shatter at the merest touch. Natalia and Annie were better off; they'd been granted permission to travel on their own. As the youngest, Lili was babied more than she liked.

But no more. She was determined about that. This trip would be the start of something tremendous for her. She could sense it.

Peanut butter, M&M's, hot dogs and hamburgers, Lili chanted to herself. America was so diverse, so raw, so much an adventure-in-waiting. *Hip-hop, bebop, shop till you drop. Drive-ins, push-ups, hoedowns and take-outs!*

As the plane dropped toward the runway, anticipation rang in Lili's ears. This was her chance. She would have herself an authentic American experience or her name wasn't Liliane Marja Mae Graf Brunner.

Why, she wouldn't even say no to a daring whirlwind fling with a dashing American playboy!

"WITH ALL THAT'S going on at the museum," Simon Tremayne said as he waited for the first passengers to disembark, "meeting a spoiled princess from some backward little European country no one but us has ever heard of is the last thing I have time for.''

"Take off your glasses,'' said Cornelia Applewhite, the mayor of Blue Cloud, who had a tendency to ignore all complaints, which made it easier to bulldoze her constituency. "You'll look less like a nerd and more like a dignitary.''

Simon did so, pretending there was a smudge. After he'd finished wiping the lenses with the end of his tie, he slipped the glasses into the breast pocket of his suit coat. Who knew why? It couldn't have been because in photographs the princess was young, blond and cute as a buttercup.

"I suppose I have to kiss her hand?'' he said, making sure to sound long-suffering.

"Didn't you read the protocol report I faxed over to the museum?''

"I intended to.'' *It was on his list, right after Put On Clean Underwear.*

"Si-mon!'' the mayor pealed.

He winced. Cornelia—you had to remember to pronounce it Cor-*nell*-ia, and saints preserve the person who shortened it to Corny—was a short woman with a voice and figure like Foghorn Leghorn. Speaking in a normal tone made her vibrate. When she turned it on full blast to give orders—and she lived to give orders—her entire body swayed with the effort, from the tassels on her pumps to the rooster fringe of her upswept hairdo. Simon wondered if it was considered good protocol to megaphone greetings forceful enough to puncture the princess's eardrums.

"They're coming,'' Cornelia said to the small group of Blue Cloud VIPs she'd recruited to greet the princess. "Look sharp, people. Pretend you know what you're doing. And you, Simon, tuck in your tie." She took a closer look. "King *Tut?* Couldn't you have gone for a nice sedate blue or gray?"

"Too late now," he said, tucking Tut in. The greeters murmured with excitement. The princess and her entourage had naturally been deplaned first. Between the on-coming phalanx of tall, stern people in dark blue suits, all Simon caught of the princess was a flash of pink and a glimpse of ruffled corn-silk hair.

The blond head bobbed. Several times. He chuckled. The petite princess was on springs.

Cornelia said "Shush," to him in her normal tone—loud—just as the princess's plaintive voice announced, "But I can't *see* anything!"

Everyone hushed.

A small feminine hand appeared on the broad shoulder of the closest bodyguard. Next, a blond head with short hair going in six different directions pushed past the woolen sleeve of a woman who looked as starched as her collar. The princess peeped out at the group from Blue Cloud. She blinked several times. Long spidery lashes curled back from her eyes like stamens.

The greeters returned the stare in complete silence.

"My goodness," she said. "I do hope you weren't shushing *me.* I haven't been shushed since boarding school, even though I suppose there were plenty who might have liked to."

She smiled, very prettily.

And Simon's heartstrings went *zing.*

Fortunately, Cornelia began booming her practiced welcome speech, and he was able to classify the electric thrumming in his veins as sound-wave reverberation. Corny's reverb had been known to register on the Richter scale.

He had neither the time nor the inclination for dallying with princesses, even when they were cuddly little blondes built for the boudoir. The very idea was absurd, particularly when he remembered who he was: Simon Stafford Tremayne, boy genius, college egghead, museum wonk. Before he'd learned to keep activities that required tuxedos and courtliness permanently outside of his comfort zone, his greatest success with the opposite sex was slow-dancing with Valerie Wingate at his high school prom, and that had happened only because she was mad at her quarterback boyfriend and had grabbed the nearest nerd at hand for revenge. That one dance had earned Simon a broken nose, and it hadn't even been worth it. Valerie Wingate had been so vapid, not even the chance to look down her cleavage was compensation. At least, not after the first thousand or so mental slow-motion replays.

The older woman with the bulk and the bulging leather satchel was shaking each of their hands, taking names, and introducing them to the princess. "Mrs. Amelia Grundy," she said to Simon.

He gave his hand. "No, it's Simon Tremayne, actually."

Her lips crimped. No sense of humor. She gripped his hand a beat too long, staring straight into his eyes. Damned if he didn't feel the *zing* again. Well, that was good. That meant the feeling could be anything—static electricity from the carpet or maybe indigestion. He'd inhaled a spicy burrito at lunch. Give him a Tums and he'd be safe from all manner of embarrassing eruptions. Burps to bolts from the blue.

"Cor-nell-eee-yah," Princess Buttercup was saying, with an ill-concealed mischievous glitter to her eyes.

"Cornelia Applewhite. My, that's too long a name. I shall call you…"

She glanced at Simon. He arched a brow.

"Nell," she said. "You look like a Nell to me, born and bred among the amber waves of grain on a wholesome American farm."

Simon barely withheld his laugh. Cornelia, for once, was too flustered to bluster. She was hugely and loudly proud of her venerable family background, but contradicting princesses was undoubtedly against protocol.

The stern Englishwoman glanced sidelong, her mouth pinched into a disapproving knot.

The princess saw the look and sobered so suddenly it was comical. She drew herself up, tipping the saucy royal chin into the air and taking on a formal tone. "That is, unless you prefer Mayor? Or would it be Madam Mayor?"

The British battleship returned her attention to Simon. "And you are?"

"Boggled."

Mrs. Grundy frowned. "Is that a distasteful American slang term?"

"No, it's the Queen's English." He'd never been so irreverent in his life, but there was a certain gaiety in the air and he couldn't resist. "Its definition is to be overwhelmed with fright or amazement."

"Ah, that sort of boggled." She looked him over. "You're not cowering…"

His gaze strayed to the princess, who'd relaxed as soon as Grundy wasn't looking. She was charming Corny's cravat off despite the farm-girl nickname. "Maybe I'm amazed."

"Wings," Mrs. Grundy said, surprising him. "Paul McCartney. A Liverpool lad." Simon tore his attention off the princess and refocused on the Mistress of Starch. Amelia Grundy's eyes were Atlantic blue, and not nearly as humorless as he'd first assumed.

"I'm the curator of the Princess Adelaide and Horace P. Applewhite Memorial Museum," he said. It was a terrible mouthful; the townspeople had already shortened the museum's name to "The Addy-Appy." "We are most honored to host the debut exhibition of the Brunner family jewels."

Usually the term *family jewels* provoked a grin or a snicker—Blue Cloud wasn't a bastion of sophistication despite Corny's pretentions—but all he got from Grundy was a stiff nod. "As is the princess to be your guest of honor," she said.

"Indubitably," Simon said, because it sounded very British.

Mrs. Grundy's lips twitched as she passed him over to the princess, introducing him by name and occupation. "Mr. Tremayne," she continued, "may I introduce Her Serene Highness, Princess Liliane Brunner of the sovereign principality of Grunberg."

You may indeed.

The princess placed her hand lightly in his, palm down. He found himself succumbing to a deep bow, propelled by some instinct he hadn't known he possessed, his lips hovering above the smooth skin on her delicate hand. Her scent suited the season—spring fresh, green and sweet as tender rosebuds.

Gather them while ye may, he thought, one hairbreadth away from a courtly kiss when his suit coat gaped. His glasses fell out, landing on the princess's toes. She trilled a startled "Oh, my!" and gave a little backward hop. Her big, jowly bodyguard moved in swiftly, crunching Simon's glasses beneath his heel before Grundy could wave him off.

Princess Liliane patted the mastiff's arm. "It's quite all right, Rodger."

The guard swung around to glare at Simon. *Crackle.*

"Dear me, your glasses," said the princess.

She and Simon knelt at the same moment. "Please, let me." She lifted the mangled wire-framed spectacles in both hands as if she were cradling a bird with a broken wing. "I'm afraid they're ruined."

He plucked them off her palm. Tiny cracks spiderwebbed through one of the lenses. "I have another pair at the museum, Your Royal…uh, Your Serene Princess—"

"Please call me Lili." She looked into his eyes.

"Lili," he said, blinking.

"Are you nearsighted?"

No, just boggled. "Farsighted."

"Then I'm too close…" she whispered, bringing her face another millimeter nearer nonetheless.

"For what?"

Her face was youthfully round, her skin like buttermilk. Her smile was generously wide and unaffected, but it was her lips that stole his breath away—they were full and pink and utterly, undeniably kissable. "For you to see me clearly," she said, suddenly turning her face up and her delectable smile down when Mrs. Grundy reached between them and pulled the princess unceremoniously to her feet, bracing Lili on a protective, sturdy arm as if the young woman were an invalid.

Simon also rose, the glasses dangling from his fingertips. He didn't need them to see that he was more than boggled. He was enchanted.

What a pain in the patoot.

WITH ALL THE FAWNING and milling around, it took Simon several minutes to sort out that the princess's entourage, which consisted of a large portion of airline personnel and only two official watchdogs: Amelia Grundy and Rodger Wilhelm, the heavyset middle-aged bodyguard, who kept shooting suspicious glances at Simon, as if museum curators were high on the dangerous-kook list.

Kooks, yes, he conceded, thinking of a colleague who'd paid a cool million for a fake Rembrandt or the poor sot who'd had a scarab stolen out from beneath his nose. Kooks, but not dangerous kooks.

The assemblage moved toward the exit. The princess's head was on a swivel, as if the small municipal airport was a fascinating tourist site. Simon overheard her telling "Nell" that she'd hadn't been to America since she was a child. Apparently, her father considered the country an immoral wasteland filled with mobsters, cowboys, homeboys and decadent Hollywood movie stars.

"Well, my goodness, that's just ridiculous," Corny said, forgetting that it was bad etiquette to deprecate princely opinions—even those belonging to the ruler of a mostly overlooked sliver of a country that had produced nothing of consequence for the last three or four hundred years of his family's monarchy. "Your grandmother was an American."

"Hot dogs!" the princess said.

What a scatterbrain, Simon thought, certain his eyes were glued to her as they'd be to a train wreck. She trotted to the airport restaurant, where a half-dozen shriveled wieners rotated on spits around a feeble warming bulb. They were withered, like an old man's... finger.

And she was in raptures. "I've always wanted to taste a genuine American hot dog, not the pale European imitation. Please, may I have one?"

"Of course," said Corny, with less than her usual gusto. Doubtless, she was thinking of the tea-and-cake tent reception planned for the princess's arrival in Blue Cloud.

Simon stepped in. "Trust me, Princess Liliane, you don't want one of those. We can get better hot dogs at the Blue Cloud drive-in."

"A drive-in restaurant? Like the one in *American Graffiti?*" Lili's eyes widened. They were exotically almond-shaped. Brown, almost black—the color of semisweet chocolate. "Do you promise?"

Before Simon could make the date—protocol demanded it—Grundy interrupted. "We must follow the schedule, Princess." She literally said *"shedjul,"* but only Simon seemed to notice. He pressed his lips together, holding back a smile.

"Yes, you're right." Lili quickly conceded, allowing them to hustle her away even though she threw a longing glance over her shoulder. At the hot dogs, alas, and not him.

Simon shrugged. There must be hot dogs in Grunberg. The country was a stone's throw from Germany, home of the bratwurst. In the days of the World Wide Web and supersonic air travel, even a sheltered, pampered princess couldn't be *that* naive. Going by the diamonds in her elfin ears, the pale pink designer suit wrapped around her luscious curves and, particularly, her easy charm—well-schooled, perhaps—she had to be more sophisticated than her bubbly personality would have him believe.

It's because she's only twenty-two, practically a

child, he thought, with all the wisdom and maturity of his twenty-nine years. *A bright, enthusiastic child. You can't have a crush on a child.*

Even one packaged in a hoochie-mama body.

"IT LOOKS LIKE a picture postcard," Lili said as they drove past the rolling green-and-gold fields, quilted by white fences and mounds of trees that grew medievally thick. She was enjoying herself again, after being momentarily distracted by disappointment when only the mayor and a bald, beady-eyed man named Spotsky had accompanied her, Grundy and Rodger in the limousine from the airport. The oddball museum guy with the flashy tie and the quiet chuckle had been left at the curb along with the rest of the greeters.

She'd been subjected to Nell's running discourse on the history of the town ever since. If the oddball had come along, he would have smirked, devilishly. His eyes would have twinkled and one brow would have arched high on his even higher forehead, and Lili might have gotten the little hitch in her throat again. He wasn't knock-your-socks-off handsome, not in that awful tie and the terribly wrinkled suit, but there were his intelligent eyes to consider, and the cowlick that distracted from his receding hairline, and the adorable way the two sides of his face didn't quite match up…

Simon Tremayne, she thought. Not a solid All-American name like Chip or Hank or Dave, but it suited him. She liked him instinctively, even if he wasn't what she'd expected. Or hoped for.

Lili tuned in to the mayor, who was saying, "My esteemed grandfather, Horace P. Applewhite, founded the Society of Concerned Citizens, putting into action the preservation of the…"

She tuned her out again, careful to maintain a wide-eyed look of interest. It was a talent she'd developed when stuffy state dinners became de rigeur, quickly followed by de trop. Mrs. Grundy would fill her in on the highlights later. If there were any.

Lili let her gaze stray to the window. Despite her longing to emulate her sisters and quit trying to conform to her father's expectations, it seemed to her that she was always looking at the world out of windows, from a distance. Was it so wrong of her to want to experience her life instead of only observing it in a dull and stately manner? She wasn't blunt like Annie, nor gutsy like Natalia. All she wanted was a bit of fun now and then.

The limo was entering the town. Lili was delighted by what she saw, even if it was through a pane of glass. Blue Cloud appeared to be the quintessential small American town. There was a spare white church with a steeple on one corner, a stone post office with an American flag on the other. The car passed through a bustling downtown—with parking meters!—populated by gift shops and tourists, who pointed and took photos of the limo. She glimpsed something called a Freezee Treat, a redoubtable bank with pillars and stone lions and an old-fashioned brick schoolhouse—with a crossing guard!—and then they were cruising through tree-lined streets of quaint bungalows and wood-frame houses as upright as Puritans.

Lili pressed the toggle to roll down the window. "Prin-*cess*," cautioned Mrs. Grundy, but Lili went ahead anyway and thrust her face into the wind, not caring a whit that she would probably be mistaken for a Pomeranian with its head hanging out the car window. Her hair fluttered against her cheeks and forehead, just like the little flags at the front of the car. Wonderful!

Bright sun, the rush of wind, the smell of blacktop and hot brick and—

Rodger tugged her back inside. The occupants of the car stared at her, smiles wavering. Nell had actually stopped talking. So it hadn't been the wind in Lili's ears drowning her out. *Good,* she thought. *Good. I don't want to be a jewel, refined and polished to perfection.* There was nothing more boring than perfection.

An immense sea of cars shining in the sun caught Lili's eye. "Oh," she cried, "I want to shop *there.*" The limo had passed through town and was cruising along a busy boulevard. Cars surrounded a building that looked like a cement bunker. A plasticky sign in primary colors—so American—read: Salemart.

"But that's the Salemart," the mayor said, aghast. "It's cheap and tacky."

Lili beamed. "Perfect." She wanted a pair of flip-flops, a T-shirt with a silly slogan and one of those fluorescent-colored beverage concoctions that was so giant, it looked as if you'd stuck your straw in a bucket.

The limo was slowing to turn into a glade of green so emerald it made Lili squint and miss what the discreet signpost read. A mass of trees shimmered against the blue and white of the sky. The razor-edged curve of lawn was as plush as carpeting. She would dance on it in her bare feet, given the chance....

Suddenly there were people everywhere, scattered across the tarmac road, parting to make way for the limo, then moving in to surround them as they cruised to a stop. A red-and-white striped tent was set up on the lawn, against the backdrop of shade trees. There was also the museum building, but Lili didn't have time to look at it. She was smoothing and rebuttoning, preparing herself for display.

Showtime.

"This is it! The Princess Adelaide and Horace P. Applewhite Memorial Museum," the mayor announced proudly, before Rodger extended an arm and pulled her out of the car, along with the town's car repair-shop owner, Rockford Spotsky, who hadn't said a word the entire trip, only stared bug-eyed at Lili until she'd wanted to hand him a magnifying glass.

Mrs. Grundy pulled a handkerchief out of the breast pocket of her woolen traveling suit and dabbed at a spot on Lili's cheek. "Now, remember, my girl. You are representing not only the royal family, but your country, as well."

Suddenly Lili was nervous. "Are there reporters? Cameras?" What if she tripped or stammered or peed in her fancy silk drawers the way she had when she was six and invited to take part in the Assumption Day pageant?

"There are always cameras."

Not always, thought Lili. She'd escaped on occasion, sometimes tagging along after Annie and Natalia and sometimes completely on her own. Brief, memorable occasions.

With a murmur of reassurance, Mrs. Grundy left the car.

Lili looked out her window. So many smiling faces, soon to be focused exclusively on her. You'd think she'd be accustomed to the attention, but it seemed there was benefit in being the youngest of three sisters after all. Or demurring to the powerful presence of her father.

You wanted this, Princess, she said silently.

Rodger opened her door.

No, I wanted peanut butter.

Mayor Cornelia Applewhite stood nearby, ready and waiting. "Ladies and gentleman, I present to you..."

The polite applause began as soon as Lili emerged from the limo. "...Her Serene Highness, Princess Liliane of Grunberg."

Lili stood. Shutters clicked. Flashbulbs popped. The applause grew, peppered with "oohs" and "aahs" as if she were an especially impressive roadside attraction.

She gave a friendly wave to acknowledge the cheers, but her smile felt awkward and fake. Then she saw Simon Tremayne, standing beside the silent, staring Spotsky, and a warmth spread inside her. Only inside. Her silk drawers were safe...for now.

A child came forward to present her with flowers. Lili spoke to the girl, thanking her by name, then straightened and lifted the extravagant bouquet of sweet freesia to her face. She took a deep breath, momentarily losing herself in the scent.

Her lips parted with a sigh of pleasure. She dropped her nose into the fresh blossoms for a second, even deeper whiff, then popped back up, startled by a strange sensation. Something was buzzing inside her mouth, bumping against the back of her throat.

She'd inhaled a bee.

Lili motioned frantically to Amelia, her eyes bulging. Should she keep her mouth closed? Should she spit? Was it better to swallow? Could she swallow a bee even if she wanted to?

A sharp sting on her tongue settled the question.

With a howl of pain, Lili's mouth opened wide.

And the bee flew out.

2

"AM AW WIDE," the princess said.

"She's all right," Mrs. Grundy translated.

"I'b nod awwergick."

"She's not allergic."

"Got that one," Simon said. He'd hustled Lili into the museum to tend to her, leaving the mayor outside to marshal her forces and continue the tea party without the guest of honor. Lili had insisted, smiling a brave smile even though there were tears in her eyes.

"Here we are," said Edward Ebelard, who was an RN at the Blue Cloud Medical Clinic and had accompanied them to Simon's office. He held up an ice pack made from a plastic bag and two pounds of ice chips taken out of the soft-drink machine in the museum snack bar. "Stick out your tongue, dearie." Edward was thirty, six-three, two-fifty, bearded; to compensate, he spoke like a nurse of the old school.

Lili stared up at the towering RN with big dark eyes. She looked at Simon. He shot her a thumbs-up. She gave a watery hitch of her chest, then squeezed her eyes shut and stuck out her tongue. The tip was fiery red and swollen to twice its normal size. Or at least what Simon assumed to be its normal size.

Edward tsk-tsked as he peered at the tongue, poking it with a pencil he'd liberated from the holder on Simon's desk. He plopped the ice pack on Lili's tongue.

Her head wobbled under the sudden weight. "There we are. That will soon take the swelling down, Princess. We'll be better in no time."

Mrs. Grundy grabbed the bag of ice and applied it more gingerly to the princess's tongue. Lili whimpered softly.

"Is that all you can do?" Simon asked the RN.

Edward shrugged. "Yes. Unless she wants to go to the clinic for a shot. But you really only need that if you're allergic."

Lili waved a hand, the lower half of her face obscured by the lumpy bag of ice. "No shaw. No shaw."

"No shot," Simon and Grundy said in unison.

"She's not awwergick," Simon added. The princess crinkled her eyes at him.

"It will be sore for a few hours, but there should be no lasting effect," Edward said as Simon showed him out. "I could stay, just in case. I'd be happy to. It's not every day I have a princess for a patient."

"I'll handle it from here." Simon shook Edward's hand. "Thanks for all your help." He lowered his voice, imagining the lewd spin the tabloid reporters could put on a story about the princess's red, naked, swollen tongue. "If the reporters ask, you can tell them she was stung by a bee, but keep the details to yourself."

Edward inhaled. "Of course. I do have my professional ethics, you know."

"Indeed."

The RN looked with reverence at the pencil in his hand, the one he'd used on the royal tongue. "Mind if I keep this?" He put it in his shirt pocket. "For a souvenir."

"Help yourself." Simon thanked Edward again, then closed the door behind him and turned back to Princess

Lili. She sat on the couch placed against the paneled wall of his office, her head thrown back against the cushions as Mrs. Grundy applied the ice-chip pack to her open mouth. It was already melting. Droplets of water leaked onto her white lace collar, spreading in a large wet patch. There had to be a better way.

He got a paper cup and plastic spoon from over by the coffee machine in the reception area. Lili was pushing the ice pack away when he returned. "Maw howe mowf—"

"Your whole mouth is frozen," Simon said, sitting beside her. "Let's try this." He scooped some of the melting ice chips into the cup and fed Lili a spoonful.

She opened her lips as obediently as a baby bird, looking at him with glistening eyes. "Thank ooh."

"You're welcome. Hold the ice against your tongue until it melts. Is the sting still painful?"

"Naw so much."

"Will you be able to return to the reception, Princess?" Mrs. Grundy asked. "There are a hundred guests waiting to be greeted."

Lili nodded dutifully.

"Give her fifteen minutes," Simon said. He looked at the older woman, nudging her along with a head bob. "Maybe you could go and report to the mayor? I'm sure Cornelia can delay the program for another fifteen minutes."

Mrs. Grundy glanced from one to the other, squinting a skeptical eye. "Princess?"

Lili shooed her.

She hesitated. "Rodger's right outside if you should need his assistance."

Simon fed Lili another spoonful of ice chips. "I'm a

mild-mannered museum wonk. I assure you, the princess is safe with me.'' Grundy, mollified, finally left.

Lili looked at him and smiled through the ice melting on her tongue. ''They thay ith alwayth the quiet one.''

He waggled his brows, knowing no one with a cowlick and a metallic King Tut tie could ever look dangerous. ''You're talking better. Swelling going down?''

''Yeth.''

''More ice?''

''No, thank you. Already feel like an iceberg.''

''Would that make me the *Titanic?*''

She blinked. ''How?''

''We've had one encounter and already you've torn off a vital piece of my heart.''

She was quite fetching when she giggled—her eyes slitted, her cheeks plumped, her wide smile infectious. ''Is that a line that works on American girls?''

''I wouldn't know, being a museum wonk.'' He'd never tried an idiotic line like that on a girl in his life. When it came to hitting on women, his batting average was too dismal to account. He'd even come to the conclusion that associating with the female gender was dangerous to his welfare. Too bad about the biological urges he was having more and more trouble supressing. Thoughts of swollen body parts and how they meshed kept popping into his head. Definitely not on the how-to-treat-a-princess list.

''Then you're not married?''

He managed to cover his surprise, telling himself that she was polite, not interested. ''Only to my work. The sarcophaguses—sarcophagi?—would get jealous otherwise.''

She smiled as he fed her more ice. ''You're very amusing.''

"I practiced my act special for you."

"Ooh, I'm all damp," she said, and for an instant he was nonplussed by the idea of *damp* swollen body parts, before he realized she was referring to her clothing. She peeled off the pink jacket and reached under her lace jabot to unbutton the blouse. The wet silk had gone transparent, clinging to the curves of her breasts, outlining the plunging neckline of her undergarment.

She kept unbuttoning. He pulled his gaze away, rising from the couch. "Hold on. I'll step outside."

"Don't bother. We Europeans are accustomed to going topless."

Good God! Simon risked a quick glance and saw that she was taking off her blouse entirely. He spun around, keeping his back to her, every synapse firing. Breasts! Naked! Lucky, lucky man!

Then: Bodyguard! Royal outrage! Scandal! Disgrace! *Worth it!*

He clenched his hands. Naked breasts were also surely against Corny's protocol. "Uh, Princess, I really don't think this is—"

"Oh, it's all right, you silly man. I was only joking with you. I'm wearing a camisole."

He glanced over his shoulder. The camisole was soft, silky, loose-fitting. It covered about as much flesh as a tank top. The fabric tented over her round breasts, held up—rather flimsily—by narrow satin straps. Even at a glance, it was obvious that the princess possessed a nice set of erect nipples. They were properly positioned and everything.

And everything.

He tore his gaze away a second time. It had taken the *Titanic* hours to go down, and here he was, sunk in mere minutes. "Could you put on your jacket?" he asked the ceiling.

"It's damp, too. Do you have a hair dryer?"

Self-consciously, he passed a hand over his hair. It was clipped close to his skull despite an excess of forehead and temple. He figured he'd be bald by the time he was forty, so why fight it? "There are hot-air hand dryers in the lavatories."

"Would you?" she said, holding out her blouse and the pink jacket. "Please?"

He sidled closer, still not sure that he should look directly at her, as if she were the sun. The sun, with breasts that shifted beneath the silk camisole every time she moved. His brain had lost too much blood for him to think straight *and* maintain willpower, so it would be best if he left the room as quickly as possible.

He reached out a blind hand, hoping she'd put the items of clothing into it.

She's royal, she's privileged, she thinks of me as a handy servant, he told himself. *A valet. There's nothing for me to see because in her eyes I barely even count as a person.*

Ha! Nice try, but no go. This princess was no snob.

"I'll do it," she said, standing at the same time as he reached again for the clothes.

He got a handful of breast instead.

Sliding silk. Plump, firm breast. Taut nipple.

The princess gasped.

"Sorry," he said, whipping around and pulling his hand away as if it had been burned.

Her face had gone as pink as her tongue. "My fault."

"No, mine. I'm clumsy."

She narrowed her eyes. "Shouldn't a museum wonk be good with his hands and eyes? All that detail work."

Every detail of her breast was carved into his brain. Sparks were still shooting up his arm. "Clumsy socially," he clarified. "I'm no good once you take me out of the museum."

She patted his hand, and he realized it still hung in the air between them. He let it drop.

"You're doing fine." She sighed. "I'm the one who's fouling everything up."

"You couldn't have anticipated a bee in the bouquet."

"Maybe not, but it doesn't matter. These things always happen to me when I make public appearances. My father won't let me out of the castle till I'm forty if I turn this event into a fiasco."

"You're an adult, aren't you? You can do as you please."

She shook her head. "I'm twenty-two, but they still treat me like a child. Ours is a traditional, hidebound monarchy, you see, and my father became very strict after my mother died. I know he's only worried about his responsibility to me and my sisters, seeing that we have a proper upbringing, but it's very hard to—" Lili stopped. "Listen to me. Complaining about life in the castle. You must think I'm a spoiled brat."

"No..."

"You do. Admit it."

"I don't know you well enough to judge."

She looked at him with bright, inquisitive eyes, her clothing clutched to her chest. "Now that you've touched my breast, you practically *have* to take me on a date."

His eyeballs were on the verge of popping out and rolling across the floor like marbles. "A *date?*"

"The hot dogs," she said. "You promised."

He hesitated. "Would I get to touch the other breast?"

For a moment, she looked as stunned as he. Her mouth dropped open—the sight of the tender, red, swollen tip of her tongue made him feel curiously protective—and then she burst into laughter.

He shook his head, relieved by her reaction, but still appalled at himself. "I can't believe I just said that to Her Serene Highness of Grunberg."

She lowered the hand she'd clapped over her mouth. "Honestly, I'm glad you did."

His brow went up.

"I didn't mean…not because of…" Her lashes fluttered. "Or maybe I did." She cozied up to him, one hand tucked into the crook of his arm. "You see, this is my first time out on my own. It's my chance to assert my independence. I was hoping to meet a dashing American playboy, but perhaps you'll do."

He was feeling pretty good, up until the last several words. They made him snap to attention.

He'd do, as a means to an end.

Story of his life. From Valerie Wingate to Paula Manthey, the grad student who'd faked a romantic interest in hopes of securing herself a cushy position on his team of researchers, women would far rather use him than amuse him. They saw him as a social misfit, an egghead scholar desperate enough to accept any female advance, whatever its motive. Sometimes, he even thought that way about himself. Which was why he was better off spending all his time with museum artifacts. Women were a species not even a man with an advanced degree could understand.

And Princess Buttercup was potentially more trouble than all the rest put together.

He'd take her for hot dogs if she insisted, but he'd definitely be ignoring the annoying little *zings* of his heartstrings.

Because if he didn't, the beautiful young princess would soon be playing him like a violin. Just like all the rest.

"WOULD YOU LIKE to see the tiara?" Simon asked, after she'd dried her blouse and jacket and he'd met her outside his jumble of an office. They were returning to the outdoors reception. The museum was spacious and silent. Their footsteps echoed as they descended a wide stone staircase to the double-height first-floor entrance hall. Large arched openings on either side led to the exhibition rooms. Everything but the exhibits themselves was new and clean and shining. Lili was accustomed to old and crumbling and venerable.

Worrying the tip of her sore tongue against her teeth, she stopped in the center of a design inlaid on the marble floor. She'd said or done the wrong thing, back in the office. Suddenly Simon had lost his irreverence. He was being stiff and formal with her, like all the rest.

Certainly, they'd been too familiar. If she'd seen what had happened, Mrs. Grundy would have gone into a stuffy British form of apoplexy and probably have put Lili on the next plane home. But Lili hadn't come to America to play it safe. She'd come for an adventure.

She tossed her head at Simon. "Why not?"

"This way, Princess," he said, his fingers nearly, but not quite, touching her elbow.

She practiced her royally reserved face as they walked through a room lined with glass cases. Placed on velvet and satin backdrops, lit by subtle spotlights, all the finest pieces from the royal jewels of the Brunner monarchy were on display. Despite her position, Lili seldom had the opportunity to examine the jewels. On formal occasions, the three sisters might be allowed to wear one of the valuable pieces, but that was rare. She wasn't particularly interested, either. Who wanted to be draped in history so valuable and weighty you had to be escorted by six guards and armed with an emergency panic button?

"It's in here," Simon said, exchanging a word with a uniformed security guard before entering a second, smaller room. A case with a glass dome had been set up in the center of the room to capitalize on the "Ah!" factor.

Despite her training, Lili wasn't very skilled at curtailing her natural reactions. When she saw the famous tiara, nestled on a hillock of watered blue satin, she stopped and gave the obligatory exclamation.

Simon shoved his hands into his trouser pockets. He looked pleased with himself. "It's something, isn't it?"

Lili was in awe, as well as *ah*. "Yes, it's something."

"Have a closer look."

She approached slowly. She'd seen the bridal tiara only twice before, at similar exhibitions in London and Spitzenstein, their capital city. Both times, she'd been a child, enchanted by the story of the long-ago prince who had so loved his betrothed, he'd commissioned the greatest jeweler in all the land to create a bridal tiara with the Vargas diamond, a gem of somewhat mysterious origins, as its centerpiece. Ever since, the tiara was only worn at royal weddings. Each new Brunner bride was given the honor, including Lili's American grandmother, Adelaide, a simple country girl from Blue Cloud, Pennsylvania, who had married the crown prince of Grunberg exactly fifty years ago.

"It's beautiful." A delicately wrought construction of platinum and many tiny diamonds in addition to the spectacular center gem, the tiara was truly a work of art. Lili walked slowly around the case, looking at the piece from all angles. There was a thick velvet rope set up to keep onlookers out of touching distance, but that was mainly a psychological barrier.

She gave a little laugh. "How's security?"

Simon's face grew even more serious. He motioned around the dimly lit room. Lili realized that there were two more security guards, positioned in shadowed niches. "The case is alarmed, as well," he explained. "Breathe upon the glass—it's shatterproof, of course—and the entire museum will go into lockdown mode, alarms blaring."

"I see how you were able to persuade my father to let the royal jewels out of the country for their first American exhibition."

"Our museum is state of the art," Simon said with pride.

"It's new?"

"Brand-new. Cornelia Applewhite's family provided a large portion of the funding, hence the unwieldy name."

"I wonder what my grandmother would have thought about being celebrated in such a way." Oversized blow-up portraits of Princess Adelaide had been placed here and there as decoration. She'd been a beautiful, kind and graceful woman, but not one who'd enjoyed the spotlight, a vestige of her humble Pennsylvania origins. She had passed away from illness at sixty-one, when Lili was only six, followed in death three years later by her daughter-in-law, who'd perished in the skiing-vacation tragedy. All of Grunberg had mourned the losses.

"Blue Cloud is very proud of Princess Adelaide," Simon said. "She's their one claim to fame. The town officials are hoping that a museum dedicated to her memory will pull in the tourists."

Lili understood. Her country was in much the same position. Her father's advisors had even mentioned how beneficial a royal wedding would be to the economy. "And what about you?"

"Me?"

"How did you come to be the curator? Are you a scholar of royalty?"

"Not in particular. My field of specialty was—is— Egyptology."

Simon had put on a second pair of wire-framed glasses, but they did not disguise the evasive shift of his eyes. Lili grew more curious. "Then why are you here in Blue Cloud…?"

"It's a fine job." He pulled his hands out of his pockets and tucked in the gaudy gold-and-blue King Tut tie. "Should we return to the reception?"

"There are many things we *should* do," she answered in all solemnity. "Are you an eat-all-your-vegetables kind of guy?"

"No, I'm a burrito-takeout kind of guy."

"When was the last time you had hot dogs?"

"Wednesday."

"Is this evening too soon to have them again?"

"Tonight? Are princesses allowed to run away from their responsibilities on a whim? Don't you have a *shed-jul* to keep?"

"Mrs. Grundy has one. I don't."

"And the responsibilities?"

Lili sighed. "You *are* an eat-all-your-vegetables kind of guy."

"I can't be responsible for—"

She cocked her head. "I'm responsible for myself!"

"Then why do you have a bodyguard and a— What is Mrs. Grundy? Your baby-sitter?"

"Close," Lili said, feeling a tiny bit snippety. "She's my nanny."

Simon put out his hands, as if he'd been knocked off balance. The velvet rope swung. "Your nanny?"

"She *was* my nanny. Now she's my traveling companion."

"You have a nanny."

"No. She's my social secretary."

"A *nanny*."

Lili narrowed her eyes. Had she thought Simon was amusing? He wasn't. He was irritating. "My lady-in-waiting."

"Jeez," he said, running a hand through his mouse-colored hair. It was too short to stand up on end, except for the strands of the cowlick where his part ended in a swirl that showed a little too much scalp. "You live in a fairy tale."

"I *am* a princess. I have a certain duty to my homeland. An image to maintain." Regardless of her yearnings to be free.

"It's difficult for Americans to conceive of such a thing. We're an independent, egalitarian society."

"I know. That's why I was so excited to come here. There's so much I want to see and do and taste and touch—" She stopped suddenly. If that was so, why she was wasting time with a self-described museum wonk? The adventure of her lifetime wasn't in here, among the static displays. Artifacts might satisfy Simon Tremayne, but they'd never be enough for her.

"Don't bother yourself about the hot dogs," she said, giving him a brisk pat on the arm as she moved past him. "I'll find my own way to them." Her heels tap-tap-tapped across the polished floors as she hurried away.

"Wait," Simon called, catching up. "I didn't say I wouldn't take you." He held open the wide front door for her and she swept through with her head held high, as befitted a woman of royal blood.

"I'm sure I'll manage on my own." She looked over the animated crowd, the men in light-colored summer-weight suits, the women in hats and pretty dresses. A few of them had actually worn white gloves. Not even Amelia expected to put Lili in white gloves. "Perhaps I'll find a dashing playboy among the guests to act as my escort."

Simon muttered a response, but the mayor had spotted them and was shouting a hello, her arms in sema-phore mode. Lili waved back.

"There'll probably be a reception line," Simon said, sounding as though he dreaded it as much as she. "Is your tongue up to it?"

"I won't be kissing any babies." She poked it out at him.

"Still swollen. Does it hurt?"

"Thum." She closed her lips. "It hurts, but the ice helped a lot. Thank you for that."

"You're welcome."

She studied his cockeyed face. One brow was tilted higher than the other, his high-bridged nose was crooked, his lips were lopsided. Even the glasses sat slightly canted. But there was something about him—

the warmth in his eyes, the smile creases that ran from his nose to his mouth—that made him attractive. He was the kind of man who wasn't exciting, but who was strong and capable and quirky and kind. It would never be dull, talking to him. It might even be interesting to kiss him....

"If you're recovered, Princess," Mrs. Grundy said, from several steps away, "your public is waiting."

"May we begin the introductions?" Mayor Applewhite intoned with a bit of an edgy chuckle. "The cakes are cut and the tea leaves are suitably steeped."

Lili winked at Simon as she turned away. She gracefully descended the steps, her throbbing tongue curled against the roof of her mouth, her smile dutifully intact. The guests responded with a smattering of applause.

"Stay away from the flower beds," she heard Simon say as the mayor swept her into the eager, pressing crowd.

SIMON DREADED this part of his job. There were curators who developed a slick schmooze, who knew how to curry favor with the right people to secure grants and gifts for their institutions. He couldn't even identify the right people from the wrong, though anyone from Cornelia Applewhite's lengthy guest list was a good bet. If it wasn't for Corny's exclusive Platinum Patron list, Simon would have raised no more cash than a pauper on the street.

Basically, he'd lucked into the Royal Jewels of Grunberg exhibition. A friend from grad school knew a translator who knew an attaché to the Swiss ambassador who oversaw the tiny neighboring principality. It hadn't hurt that a couple of Princess Adelaide's Blue Cloud cousins still lived on the family farm, either. Corny had worked the two old ladies like a bagpipe, huffing and puffing over the honor and privilege of the new museum hosting the exhibition on the fiftieth anniversary of Princess Adelaide's marriage until whatever influence the Wolf sisters had with the royal family was brought to bear.

However it had happened, securing the go-ahead from the palace had been a coup for Simon. One he sorely needed, considering the ignominious past that had landed him here in the first place. He'd been "asked" to leave his previous job—his dream job—after he'd let the wrong woman cloud his judgment. Sticky-fingered Traylor Bickett had been the last straw in a short lineup of users masquerading as girlfriends. He'd promised himself never to be so gullible again. Unfortunately, all but one of his subsequent job applications had been refused.

Which was why he was stuck here. Curating an exhibit that was a royal pain.

The security setup was a nightmare, blowing his budget right off the start because he'd had to overcompensate for the previous mistake: one tiny scarab stolen from under his nose. Given Simon's track record, the Grunberg officials had insisted on tripling normal security. Luckily, Corny had hosted a Platinum Patron party and persuaded her wealthy friends to pull out their checkbooks. With the influx of funds, Simon had been able to correct glitches in the system and hire another guard.

Even so, there were a thousand details to handle before the official grand opening tomorrow afternoon. The last thing Simon needed was to become preoccupied with the visiting princess.

Yet here he stood, drinking strong tea and popping tiny frosted cakes by the handful, watching as Lili greeted guest after guest after guest. Her smile never wavered. But it was a professional smile. Already he could tell the difference between it and the naughty little twitch of her lips that preceded her mischievous moments. For now, she was on her best behavior.

Alas.

Simon scanned the crowd. Socially inept or not, even he recognized that the party could use some livening up. He supposed it was proceeding exactly as the mayor had envisioned. That was the trouble. Corny prided herself on her old-world stodginess.

Lili's laughter drew Simon's attention. Darned if she wasn't up on her toes, reaching a hand to the top of an overgrown young man's lofty head. The Tower lowered his chin obediently. Her hand sank into his thick, curly hair. Thick? It was as dense as a jungle. The guy had twice as much hair as he needed. He could donate half of it to Charles Barkley and have enough left over to weave himself a hair shirt.

Simon edged closer. What *was* Lili doing?

"I heard they grew them tall in America," she said admiringly. "Are you a basketball player, Mr. Stone?"

Simon missed the man's response. His voice was a low rumble, an avalanche on a mountain. Figured.

"Ever since I saw Dallas play in the Super Bowl when I was a little girl, I wanted to be a Dallas Cowboys cheerleader. The boots, the pompons—such fun." Lili tilted her head back, listening to the Tower. Another peal of delighted laughter. "Oh, that's football? And what about baseball? How *do* you keep all your odd sports straight?" She tapped him on the chest. "You Americans are so healthy and vigorous."

Simon grabbed the shoulder of Blue Cloud's solid, tenacious police chief, Henry Russell, as he walked by.

Henry was also a bachelor, only a few years older than Simon, though he was more of the plainspoken base-ball-and-bowling type. They'd become well acquainted while coordinating their efforts to secure the safety of the jewels. Simon admired the man. There would be no screwups if Henry, who was in charge of the town's small but well-run police department, had anything to say about it.

"Who's that guy?" Simon asked. Henry knew every blade of grass and leaf of marijuana in Blue Cloud. You couldn't filch a plastic jewel from a gum-ball machine without him hot on your trail.

Henry lifted the brim of his hat as if that would give him a better look. Simon had already seen the man's blink-of-an-eye assessment.

"Tourist," the sheriff said. "We've got a lot of them in town this weekend."

"Are you sure?"

"Sure I'm sure."

"He doesn't look suspicious to you?"

Henry's eyes narrowed. His lantern jaw bulged. "Everyone looks suspicious to me."

"He's too slick, don't you think?" The Tower was dressed in Amana or whatever they called that sort of unrumpled designer tailoring. Definitely the dashing playboy type.

Henry wasn't perturbed at all. He scanned the crowd swarming in and out of the tent instead of keeping an eye on the suspicious snake who was charming Lili. "The princess seems to approve."

Simon scowled. The stranger was holding up the receiving line. As they talked, Lili glancingly touched his arm, his shoulder...hell, she even flipped up the end of the guy's subdued maroon silk tie and giggled a little.

The Tower put his hands on her waist, bent down, said something about her being a "tiny little package," and squeezed. Simon's face got hot. He wasn't a violent man, but suddenly he wanted to use his fists like sledge-hammers.

"Stone," he remembered. "His name's Stone."

"Ah."

"Does that mean anything to you?"

"Nope," Henry said.

"Can't you run the name through your, uh, system? I don't like him." *He has too much hair. He has too many white teeth. He has too many hands on Lili.*

"I'll keep an eye on him," Henry pledged. But his eyes were elsewhere, following a woman's dark head through the crowd. Simon was too distracted by his own fixation to give more than a fleeting notice to the chief's.

Until a sharp cry rose above the babble of the crowd. *"Pickpocket!"*

3

EVEN BEFORE Simon turned, Chief Russell was gone, shooting through the crowd toward the disturbance. A woman in a feathered hat warbled like a particularly high-pitched ghost: "Oo-oo-oo-oo-oooh!"

Her squat husband was the one raising the ruckus. "Pickpocket! Pickpocket! They got into Dora's purse." He patted his behind. "Sonovabiscuit. My wallet's gone, too."

A shrill panic overtook the guests, with everyone checking their purses and pockets for missing valuables. A shout went up about another missing wallet. The chief and his force of one officer quickly took control, calming the crowd as they herded them under the tent like cattle.

Simon looked for Lili. She was fine, attended by the royal bodyguard. Her face was animated, sympathetic in expression, but with lively eyes and a high color in her cheeks. It figured that she'd enjoy the excitement.

The mayor spread loud platitudes, assuring the attendees that Chief Russell would take care of the "minor disturbance." Mrs. Grundy and Wilhelm tried to coax the princess into the museum, away from harm. Lili, patting the distraught feather-woman's hand, refused to go.

The guests milled around, gabbling and fussing. Despite instructions, a number were slipping away, heading off to the parked cars. Henry left the other officer in charge and went to round up the renegades.

Out of suspicion—or maybe mere curiosity—Simon looked around for the Tower of Hair who'd charmed Lili. Nowhere in sight. That was interesting…possibly.

Simon had begun to make his way forward to aid the police officer with crowd control when a plump woman in head-to-toe polka dots let out a squawk. She clutched at her throat. "My pearls," she said, and fainted dead away—straight into Simon's arms.

"Oof," he said, catching her under the armpits. She was no bantamweight. Nor a middleweight. He nudged a knee into the small of her back to help hold her up.

"Oh, dear, poor Elspeth," said a companion, tearing off the collapsed woman's straw hat to fan her flushed face. "The pearls are a family heirloom," she told the crowd, flapping. "Worth a pretty penny."

"Somebody," Simon choked out, jostling the woman's sagging weight. "Help."

A man grabbed Elspeth's ankles and another wrapped his arms around her hips. They lugged her toward the tables. Simon meant to sit her upright in a chair, but the fellows holding the rest of Elspeth heaved her onto one of the abandoned tables. *Splat*—her polka-dotted rump landed in a plate of petits fours. A plastic cup of punch fell over, staining the paper tablecloth red as the spill crept toward the inert woman.

Cornelia was frantic. She whipped out a lace-edged handkerchief to sop up the encroaching flow of punch. Simon recognized the invalid at last. Elspeth Hess was tops on the Platinum Patron list. Losing her good graces would be disaster for the museum's donor fund.

Corny looked at Simon and sputtered unintelligibly. "Watch over Mrs. Hess," he said, not adverse to taking advantage of the mayor's momentary loss for words to make his getaway. "I'll go and see what's happening."

Henry had rounded up the defectors—the man named Stone among them—and was issuing commands and restoring order, directing the crowd to quiet down, to take seats and wait to be interviewed about the apparent pickpocketing incidents. He had an angry young woman by the elbow and wasn't letting her go. She stood quite still, her chin tipped up in the air, a yellow flyer that matched the ones that were scattered about the grounds clutched in her fist. She was holding equally tight to her temper, but she looked ready to shoot sparks.

Simon approached cautiously. "I'm going to take the princess into the museum, if that's all right with you, Chief Russell."

Henry nodded. "That would be best."

"If you need my help…"

"Not necessary. I've got another officer on the way to manage the crowd. We'll have to take names and do as many interviews as we can on the spot." The chief looked significantly at his captive. "I expect one of them will have seen something suspicious enough to warrant a body search. With any luck, we'll find the stolen goods before the day is out."

"A body search!" With a swish of her glossy hair and long loose skirt, the woman tossed her head. She set her hands on her hips. "Just you try it," she said through thinned lips, her voice seething with haughty insult. Although her demeanor was all fiery outrage whereas Lili's was sweet and fluffy as cotton candy, there was something about the pair of opposites that struck Simon as similar. Perhaps the quick tongue—too much of it in both cases.

"Body search," the woman snapped at Henry. "I'll give you a *body search,* Chief Russell."

Henry was unperturbed, though Simon noticed how white his knuckles were where they clenched on his captive's elbow. "Thanks for the offer, Ms. Vargas." Henry's mouth made a grim, flat line, betrayed by an infinitesimal twitch at one corner. "I can take care of the search. You only have to provide the body."

The woman's cheeks flamed. Henry kept his eyes on her face, but Simon did not. It was obvious that she had a one hell of body, all right, even hidden beneath her fringed shawl, a loose blouse and long, layered skirt, cinched by a bright green sash that showed off her slender waist. She wore sandals and much jewelry, as flashy as the Emperors nightingale, right down to the rings on her toes. Not your average, everyday Pennsylvanian, but Simon wasn't making any guesses. Maybe the Gypsy look was fashionable, for all he knew.

"Harassment," the woman hissed.

"Not yet," Henry said threateningly.

"Are you threatening me?"

Perceptive woman, Simon thought.

A muscle jumped in the sheriff's jaw. "Depends whether or not your cohort slipped away with the goods."

She inhaled. "My *cohort?*"

"The young man you were looking for in the crowd. Possibly working with."

"I wasn't. I told you. I'm here alone."

"We'll see."

"What about Stone?" Simon said, interrupting the pair's mutual glare. "He's a stranger in town *and* he tried to get away when you told everyone to stay put. That's suspicious, isn't it?"

The woman shot Simon a grateful look.

"So did Reverend Anderson and Tommy Finch, the paperboy," Henry said. "Don't worry, Simon. I know how to do my job."

"Of course," Simon conceded. He had no good reason to suspect Stone. Or to be resentful. All there was between himself and Lili was a suspended hot dog date.

"If there's anything you need," he offered, before stepping away to search for Lili.

"There may be." The police chief indicated his prisoner. His grip hadn't loosened a notch. "I'd like a room to stash my suspect in."

She smiled poisonously. "Why don't you just handcuff me in the town square and let the townsfolk pelt me with rotten fruit?"

Simon snorted with laughter.

Even Henry had to smile. "I'm saving that for after the trial."

"How nice to know I won't be summarily executed without one."

There it was again. Simon took another look at her. That thing—what was it? Peppery pride, scrappiness, inborn spirit?

"I'll set you up with a room," he said to Henry, more than eager to get back to the princess, his own sparring partner.

"Preferably one that's secure, private and—" Henry scowled at his prisoner "—far away from the jewels."

Simon went to Lili, which wasn't easy because she was buttressed by her nanny and bodyguard. "How are you?" His glance skipped over Grundy and Wilhelm. "Everything okay here?"

Lili's eyes sparkled. "What a to-do! I thought small towns were supposed to be boring."

"Not this weekend."

"We must move the princess away from the riffraff," Mrs. Grundy said. A camera flash made her lips pucker. "Even more importantly, away from the photographers and reporters."

Simon realized that a small number of media were circling like sharks, grabbing hold of the incident for what would no doubt be sensationalized stories and photos. The museum board had hoped for enough publicity to put their new facility on the map. Looked like they had it in spades.

"We can take her back to my office," he offered.

"I *am* here," Lili protested. "Don't talk over my head as if I'm a child."

Simon looked down at her. "Sorry."

Her smile flickered from polite to genuine. "Apology accepted."

"Form a wedge," Wilhelm instructed. "We must move quickly." Mrs. Grundy opened her satchel and removed a folding umbrella. With a snap, she opened it to full length, leaving the spokes and fabric furled. She dug the sharp tip into the ground, squared her shoulders and threaded an arm through the princess's.

Simon took the other elbow. "Off we go, then," he said cheerily. He was quite happy to be leaving the Tower behind, subject to interrogation, sans princess.

"No talking. No stopping." Wilhelm took the lead position, parting the crowd like the prow of a ship. "No deterrence."

"Damn the torpedoes, full speed ahead," Simon whispered to Lili as they quickly moved out from beneath the tent and across the tarmac road.

She tittered. "Grunberg doesn't have a Navy. We're landlocked." The reporters closed in on them, but were no match for Lili's bodyguard. Mrs. Grundy's bulk effectively blocked the photographers from getting good angles on the princess. When they pressed too close, she jabbed at them with the umbrella. The quartet swept up the steps and into the museum.

Henry and the woman, who was apparently his prime suspect, arrived on their heels. After assuring the security guards that all was under control, Simon made introductions. "Princess Lili, this is Henry Russell, the main man in Blue Cloud's police department. He's in charge."

"Pleased to meet you, Chief Russell." Lili offered him her hand. "Even if it is under trying circumstances. Was there honestly a pickpocket loose among the guests?"

"It looks like it. We have two missing wallets and one ransacked purse. Possibly a stolen necklace. My officers will be searching the grounds thoroughly."

Lili's eyes widened. "Are the royal jewels safe?"

Henry and Simon exchanged a glance before the chief responded in an official tone. "I apologize, Your Highness, but I can't give a one-hundred percent guarantee. In my estimation, today's criminals are no more than petty thieves, out to take advantage of the holiday crowds. Only a sophisticated burglar could successfully lift the jewels." He looked at Simon, who nodded in agreement. Henry relaxed—slightly. "Nothing for you to worry about, Princess."

The chief's suspect glowered at him from beneath a sheaf of dark, silky hair. A leaf clung to the disheveled tresses. Henry picked it off.

Tilting her head, Lili regarded the woman with interest. They were as opposite as Simon had assumed— one fair, the other dark; one well-dressed, polite and poised, the other brazen and belligerent in her flashy ornaments and cheap silks. And yet...there was that common bond. The moments of regal hauteur, ameliorated by an obvious zest for life.

Lili held out her hand. "Hello. I'm Princess Lili of Grunberg."

"Oh, I know who you are." The captive's top lip lifted into the slightest of sneers as she swept her gaze up and down the blond princess. She clasped the royal hand, every inch the queen herself, despite her outer dishevelment. "I am Jana Vargas."

Lili gasped. "Vargas?"

A nod.

"How peculiar, considering that the Brunner bridal tiara is set with the *Vargas* diamond! Have you ever been to Grunberg? Could you be related to someone who owned the diamond previous to my family?"

"No, I've never been to Grunberg. But some of my people were there...a long time ago."

"Would I know of them?" the princess asked.

Jana dismissed the possibility with a small, ironic smile. "Not very likely. Romany folk don't get invited to the castle for formal dress balls."

Henry and Simon exchanged a second look. A confused one, for Simon's part. Romany? Was Jana Vargas a true Gypsy, or simply playing the part for her own devices?

"Romany," breathed Mrs. Grundy, under her breath. Her keen eyes clouded. For the first time, Simon saw her less than sure of herself. Perhaps even taken aback.

Lili must have noticed, too. "Amelia?" she asked. "Do you know how the Vargas diamond came by its name?" She looked at the others. "There's quite a legend associated with the tiara, but I don't recall why it's called the Vargas diamond.''

Grundy's expression closed. "I couldn't say."

"I *could*," Jana Vargas said. She handed Lili the colored paper that had been crumpled in her left fist. "If you care to learn the truth..."

Lili glanced at the wrinkled flyer. Her face lighted. "A Gypsy carnival? Ooh, with fortune-telling!"

Grundy went pale.

Wilhelm put out a meaty hand, inserting it between the two young women. "Princess, I must insist."

Grundy recovered. She moved deliberately in front of Jana, nudging the princess along after she'd snatched away the flyer. It fluttered to the floor. "Shall we go upstairs to regroup?" she said, a steely non-question. "Rodger, you may call for the car. We've had quite a day. It's time we retired to our hotel. We shall send regrets to Madam Mayor."

"Just when events were getting interesting," Lili protested, although she allowed herself to be shepherded up the stairs.

"You may use the museum snack shop," Simon told Henry as they followed, noticing that the chief had retrieved the paper and was examining it closely. "It's empty and quiet. Three doors, but we're keeping everything locked up tight, so they're all inaccessible. Here's the key." He slipped a key from the ring he carried in his pocket. The same master key opened several doors in the working areas of the museum: storage, kitchen, supplies, lavatories. No state secrets there.

"I'll get this back to you as soon as we've finished. I want to stash Ms. Vargas, here—" Henry still hadn't let go of the woman's arm "—while I oversee procedures outdoors."

"Stash me?" Jana said. "I'm a human being, not a piece of luggage. You can't detain me for no good reason."

"I have reason. You may be a conspirator in the pickpocketing scheme, which means it's well within my bounds of authority to hold you for questioning. For the time being, consider yourself in police custody, Ms. Vargas. You will remain so until my suspicions are proved."

"Or disproved," she retorted with a double helping of sarcasm.

A troubled sympathy shone from Lili's eyes when she looked back over her shoulder. Wilhelm and Grundy hustled her into the reception area of Simon's office.

The princess was a soft touch, Simon deduced. He remembered the weight and curve of her breast. *Very soft.*

"I'm perfectly fine," Lili was saying to Mrs. Grundy when he entered the inner sanctum of his office. She brushed aside the woman's solicitations. "Please stop fussing. No one came near me." Lili's eyes sought Simon's. They danced with a saucy, provocative humor. "*Alas,* as Simon would say," she added, lifting her brows at him.

"Princess!" Grundy aimed a narrow look at Simon. "Really, my dear, you'll give Mr. Tremayne the wrong impression."

She laughed. "Oh, I do hope so." She clapped her hands. "And now, I'd like to freshen up. Mr. Tremayne, sir, I hate to be a bother, but would you please unlock the ladies' room for me—again?"

Simon bowed. "Your wish is my command. After you, Princess."

Lili stopped the older pair from following her. "I'll be quite all right. Simon will stand guard."

He patted his pocket. "I gave the key to Henry. Just a moment." He rummaged in his desk. "Here's a spare."

The princess whipped the key from his fingers when he held it up. "Thank you, kind sir." She put her nose in the air and swept from the office, stepping along the corridor with a sassy rhythm to her shoulders and hips. He was amused, knowing she was putting on the grand lady act for his benefit.

"I'll do it," she said when he tried to take the key from her. She turned it in the lock, then palmed it. Watching his face, she pushed open the swinging door to the lavatory with her backside. "I can wipe my bottom by myself, too."

He nearly choked, recovering only as the door was swinging shut. "There's a limit to my servitude, Princess," he called after her, hoping for her Tinkerbell laugh. She did not disappoint. He closed his eyes and took a deep breath, making a small gesture of triumph with his clenched fists. He might not make her swoon, but at least he could make her laugh.

He cracked an eye open. *Oops.* At the other end of the hallway, Grundy and Wilhelm were peering from the office door. Simon shrugged somewhat sheepishly and thrust his hands in his pockets. The party was a disaster and the museum's funds were at serious risk. Didn't matter.

One laugh from the princess and he felt like a million bucks.

Unfortunately, Simon couldn't quite sustain his exhilaration when Lili still hadn't emerged thirteen minutes later—he knew the time exactly because he'd been checking his watch. He paced the width of the corridor, counting under his breath. Another three minutes went by, excruciatingly slowly. Neither Grundy nor Wilhelm had budged. In fact, they were beginning to glare, as if *he'd* done something to delay the princess.

He went to the door and knocked. "Princess?"

No answer.

He put his ear to it. Silence—not even running water. The princess's attendants were coming toward him now, craning their necks to hear. "Princess Lili?" he called, pushing the door open an inch. "Are you doing okay?"

There came a thud, then a crash. A female grunt. "Fiddlesticks!"

"Lili?" Simon burst into the room, followed by Wilhelm and Grundy. His first shocking sight of the princess sent him skidding to a stop, with the other two piling up behind him.

Mrs. Grundy pushed by. "Princess, what *have* you done now?"

"I think my foot is stuck," Lili said. She was sprawled on the tile floor with her tight skirt rucked up around her hips, showing a good portion of a rounded, wriggling, panty-clad backside. One foot was trapped in a swivel-lid trash can, which lay on its side, a number of crumpled tissues spewing from its maw.

"Shall I call an ambulance?" Wilhelm said.

"Heavens, no!" Lili stopped wriggling and lifted her head and shoulders off the floor, her hands splayed on the tiles. She looked up at them with big, dark, glistening eyes, like an innocent baby seal. "Nothing's broken. Just help me pull my leg out of here, for pity's sake."

Mrs. Grundy knelt awkwardly and tugged Lili's skirt down a few inches. "However did you...?"

"It was an accident."

Wilhelm crouched, his big hands outspread, hesitating to place them on the exposed royal thigh. He went for the trash can instead, giving it a wrench. Lili winced, twisting partway onto her side. "Ooh! Ouch! Wait!" Her gaze rose to beseech Simon. "Would you? Please? The lid is pinching the back of my thigh."

"All right," he said, kneeling beside her. He examined the...uh, situation. Grundy huffed at the insult, hurriedly unbuttoning her jacket. She threw it across Lili's lower half.

Simon put his hand on her leg—on *top* of the scratchy tweed covering. Somehow, the princess had managed to insert her leg all the way down inside the can, but they should be able to maneuver it out easily enough. "Another fine predicament you've gotten us into," he murmured to distract them all as he slid his hand beneath the jacket. Lili tensed as he reached around her warm thigh, his fingers gently probing. He pushed his flattened hand between her thigh and the lid, easing its bite on her tender flesh.

She sighed with relief. "That's better."

He smiled at her. "Mrs. Grundy? Could you reach in here and push the lid down to make more room? I'm sure I'll be able to help Lili pull her leg free if we have another inch of space."

Grundy pinched her lips tight and reached down. While the bodyguard held the can steady, Simon gripped Lili's leg and slowly eased it out, trying not to look as she parted her thighs even wider to squirm free.

Grundy let go and the lid snapped back in place. She and the bodyguard were immediately at the princess's side, helping her to her feet. Simon saw that Lili had lost both shoes, so he set the can on end and fished inside. No shoes.

He spotted them on a ledge by the sink. Odd. He retrieved them, wondering why she'd taken them off in the first place. "Your slippers, Cinderella."

Grundy snatched the shoes away. "Let me help you into them, Princess." She knelt.

Lili murmured her thanks, balancing herself with one hand on Wilhelm's arm as she lifted her feet for Grundy. She looked at Simon. She was blushing. "I apologize, Mr. Tremayne. I didn't intend to destroy your washroom. I was—" Her eyes flitted. "Well, you see, I was…"

"No explanations necessary," Simon put in. He'd seen the open window, high up on the wall. "My museum is your museum."

"You're very understanding."

"I make special allowances for royalty."

She had the grace to look abashed. "It seems that I demand plenty. I *will* try to be on my best behavior tomorrow."

He inclined his head. "We're happy to have you on any behavior, Your Serene Highness."

Her eyes rolled. "Oh, please. We're *definitely* past that stuck-up claptrap. If you can't remember to call me Lili, I won't be able to eat hot dogs with you."

"Then it's a date?" he said quickly, refraining from adding an *"Again?"*

Lili tilted her tousled head. "Why not?"

Grundy cleared her throat as she stood. "What about the schedule?"

"The *shedjul* will survive, Amelia." Lili stamped her newly shod feet, intercepting Simon's amused glance. "You may be a prince of a guy, Mr. Tremayne, but I'm not allowed to surrender my feet to just anyone."

He chuckled. *A prince?* Impossible. He'd always been the frog.

Mrs. Grundy took Lili's arm, not unlike the way Henry Russell had taken Jana Vargas's. "Enough of that, Princess. We really must be on our way."

"Yes, we must." Lili cast a lingering parting glance at Simon. "See you soon?"

He swallowed. "Indubitably."

She stopped, pulling the key from an inside pocket of her short pink jacket. "I almost forgot."

He took it, surprised that she still possessed it. Maybe his suspicions were wrong?

Had she fallen into the trash on her way out the window, or on the way in? Either way, he'd better go and find the chief. Henry should be told immediately that it was very possible the princess of Grunberg had been conspiring with a pickpocketing suspect. Simon could think of no other reason for Lili to have deliberately taken her shoes off and climbed through the window. Since she still had the key, she must not have been able to successfully pass it to Jana Vargas, in the snack shop next door.

THE LIMO AWAITED.

Lili stopped short, preventing Wilhelm from opening the door for her. "I wonder if you'd mind…" This was going to be delicate. "It's been such an eventful day. I'd like a few moments of…quiet time." She smiled hopefully at Mrs. Grundy, cutting her eyes in the direction of the front seat.

The older woman maintained a stony face. "As you wish, Princess Lili."

Lili knew she wasn't fooling Amelia for a second. But that didn't matter, as long as she wasn't betrayed to the authorities. For all of the former nanny's lectures and reprimands, Amelia put the princesses' desires above any other concern. She could be trusted with the most precious of secrets.

"You can scold me later," Lili said, as Amelia joined the driver in the front seat. Wilhelm insisted on opening the door, but Lili stepped inside quickly so he wouldn't see much of the interior. Fortunately, the limo was commodious enough to hold a marching band.

Wilhelm and the driver boarded the vehicle, shutting the doors behind them. *Thunk. Thunk.* The solid black privacy panel was in place, giving Lili complete solitude.

The car pulled away from the museum, moving slowly past the disordered remains of the reception. As they rounded the bend, Lili turned to watch through the back window. Simon Tremayne was loping down the steps in his gangly, loose-limbed way, his ridiculous Egyptian tie flapping in the breeze.

Lili knew he'd figured it out. And that he would tell. But that was okay. He was too late for the police chief to stop their getaway.

"Well," she said to her passenger as she settled in. "You made it."

Considering that she was a fugitive taking a limo ride in the company of a princess, Jana Vargas looked remarkably at ease. "Yes," she said. "Nothing to it."

4

LILI AGREED. She'd done the most difficult part—hoisting herself up and stepping along the brick ledge between the windows. A crazy impulse. When she'd realized that the key to the ladies' room could set Jana free, she hadn't been able to resist offering the Romany woman a chance to get away from the handsome, but awfully stern, police chief. So she'd gone out the window, sidled along the ledge to the next window and passed the key to Jana in the snack shop, who'd unlocked her door and then given the key back.

Stepping into the trash can had worked marvelously as a distraction, although Lili certainly hadn't planned it that way.

"How did you manage to get into the limo without my driver noticing?" she asked Jana.

The Gypsy snapped her fingers. "Nothing to it. He—and everyone else—was watching the pandemonium under the tent."

"And none of the museum guards saw you?"

"I'm adroit. Besides, they're not looking for a person stealing *out* of the museum."

"Chief Russell?"

"Him." Jana's brows drew together. "He's going to hunt me down first thing, you know. Our little escape means nothing."

"I know." Lili shrugged. "It won't matter in the end,

since you're innocent.'' She didn't know why, but she believed Jana was honest. Mutual circumstances had created an immediate sisterhood between them. ''At least you're free for now.'' She opened the limo's small built-in refrigerated compartment. ''Aha. Champagne?''

Jana sat silently while Lili poured them each a glass. Lili checked the windows—there wasn't much time to spare before their arrival at the hotel—then clinked flutes. ''To us, for putting one over on the men, however briefly. I love a good caper.''

Jana sipped, continuing to watch Lili warily. Finally she blurted, ''Why did you do this? Why did you help me?''

''I don't know. Sympathy, I suppose.''

''But I could be guilty as sin. I might even steal *your* jewelry, right here, right now.''

''Phooey.'' Lili couldn't pretend to be a perfect judge of character; after all, she'd nearly let Lars Krunkel sweep her off her feet when she was eighteen, and *he'd* turned out to be the biggest two-timer in Spitzenstein. She'd always been susceptible to a handsome face and a smooth line. ''You're innocent. Mrs. Grundy wouldn't have let me get in the limo with you otherwise.''

One side of Jana's mouth quirked into a reluctant smile. ''How would Mrs. Grundy know?''

''That's what my sisters and I often wonder! But she does. She *always* knows.'' Lili shrugged. ''It's the strangest thing. There's something almost…*magical* about her. Like a fairy godmother.'' Lili laughed a little to show how silly that was. Even though it wasn't, really.

Strangely, Jana seemed accepting of the absurdity. She nodded at the privacy panel. ''If that's the case, then she knows I'm back here right now. She might be arranging for the police chief to meet us at your hotel.''

"Don't worry.'' Lili pressed the switch that opened her side window. "Mrs. Grundy wouldn't do that to either of us.''

Jana didn't look convinced, but she let it go. "You haven't answered my question.''

Lili emptied her champagne out the window. She took Jana's flute and did the same. "Swill,'' she said, raising the window.

"Sympathy isn't reason enough.''

"Perhaps it was…freedom.'' Lili lifted the empty glasses as if she meant to toss them out the window, but then returned them to their fitted niche instead. She gave a soft sigh. "You see? I'm too well trained. I have my moments, but in the end I'm always dutiful to my position. That's why I envy your lack of responsibility. Your total freedom.''

"Oh, please.'' Jana folded her arms, looking cynical, except for the sympathetic rapport that Lili had already discerned beneath the brunette's brittle shell. Lili was certain that if they could forget their "stations'' and apparent clashing family histories, they would be great friends.

"I know. Poor me, subjected to first-class luxury and limos on demand, albeit ones stocked with domestic swill.'' She shrugged, aware that the car were slowing and turning as they made their way through the downtown area. The hotel was moments away—the mayor had proudly pointed it out earlier. "But it's true, Jana. What I wouldn't give to be you for the night, a Gypsy, free to go where I want, when I want. To dance, to sing, to travel…''

"To spend the night in Chief Russell's jail cell.''

"But you're innocent!"

"That means very little when you're a Roma. Our reputation precedes us."

Impulsively, Lili reached out and squeezed Jana's hands. "What can I do?"

"Nothing. I will handle Chief Russell."

Lili grinned. The police chief was one handsome hunk of man. "I'm sure." She checked their progress. No time left, and she had so much to ask! "Can you tell me what you know about the Vargas diamond? I'm sensing there's more to the story of the bridal tiara than I've been told."

"My family's side of it isn't fit for the official version." Jana regarded Lili steadily. "You've been protected...."

Lili made a face. "It shows?"

"Sometimes that's a good thing." Jana turned her face away. "You should probably ask Mrs. Grundy for the entire story. I'm sure *she* knows it."

"But what if she won't tell me!" The car had stopped at a traffic light in downtown Blue Cloud. "When can I see you again, Jana? I know. I'll come to the carnival."

"We're camping outside of town," Jana said. "You're welcome anytime." She hesitated. "At least by me." Before Lili could respond, Jana whispered, "Thank you," opened the door and slid out, as elusive as water trickling from a palm. Lili threw herself across the seat to catch the door, hoping for a last word, but the mysterious Gypsy was gone, moving swiftly away from the car, lost among the pedestrians.

After a long moment of inner struggle, Lili resisted the urge to follow. She pulled the door shut, resting her head against it. Oh, to succumb to the temptation of escaping her schedule, if only for one night!

The intercom telephone trilled. Lili bolted upright and picked it up.

"Princess?" said Rodger Wilhelm. "Are you still back there?"

"Yes, certainly, of course I am." *Where else?* On cue, the limo accelerated through the intersection. Lili looked behind them with a sigh, searching for Jana Vargas, who didn't know how lucky she was. Although Lili's day had been full of misadventure, nothing had changed. Not really. She was still looking at life from behind a pane of glass.

AT TEN, Amelia Grundy appeared in Lili's room at the hotel. She was in curlers and a white terry-cloth robe that belted tightly around her waist, making her middle section look like a marshmallow in a rubber band. A film of chunky oatmeal gook covered her face; she was quite proud of her English Rose complexion and maintained it rigorously.

Lili pulled the bed covers up to her chin. "I certainly hope you haven't come to tuck me in."

"*Tch, tch,* Princess. You're too old for that."

"One would think so," Lili said darkly.

Mrs. Grundy's brows arched, opening cracks in the stiffening oatmeal mask. "One should *know* so."

Lili made a face. Amelia had a point, but...why shouldn't she be allowed some fun before she settled into a lifetime of royal duty? Her father was such a traditionalist, he probably wouldn't be happy until he'd married her off to a scion of one of the stuffy old Grunberg families who could trace their ancestors back to the Great Flood.

"I might be willing to listen to a bedtime story," Lili said with a light laugh, looking hopefully at her former nanny. She'd asked Amelia about what she knew of the Vargas diamond and how it could possibly be connected to Jana's Romany clan. Amelia had scoffed, claiming the name must be a coincidence. The diamond's provenance had always been a mystery, she'd insisted, dismissing the subject. Lili knew she wasn't getting the entire story. For some reason, Amelia wouldn't reveal the truth—a rare occurence.

"No stories for you, child," Amelia said, smoothly avoiding the subject again. "You've had a long day, Lili. Rather more adventurous than intended."

"I shouldn't be blamed for that. The bee sting was an accident, and the pickpocketing was entirely beyond my control." She wasn't going to explain the bit with the trash can unless Amelia forced the issue.

"You did very well, all things considered."

Lili blinked. Maybe for once her former nanny didn't *know*. "I did? You really think so?" Her will to please had always been at odds with her will to *par-taaay*, as the Americans said.

"Your father was reasonably satisfied." Amelia sat on the bed and patted the lump that was Lili's knee.

She hunched her shoulders, keeping a tight hold on the covers. "I don't see why we have to report in to him twice a day and *every* night. He's so old-fashioned about everything else, why did he have to get a cell phone? I swear it was only to keep track of me and my sisters!"

"Likely so." Amelia's bristly head inclined, her irises an intense blue in contrast with the oatmeal mask. "Indulge him, Lili. He's concerned only with your well being."

Lili wasn't having it. "That excuse might have worked for the first years after mother's death, when we were still children. But no longer."

"Isn't that why you're here, Princess? Your father has put his trust in you to represent the family. It was a big step for him, letting his baby bird fly the nest." Amelia gave her another pat. "Don't betray his trust in you, my dear."

"Never." *Was enjoying herself a betrayal?*

"That depends," said Amelia, rising. She straightened her robe and repositioned a bobby pin, stabbing it into her scalp without a flinch. "Mr. Tremayne seemed harmless enough, but you shouldn't have flirted so. The poor fellow was too flustered to concentrate on his job."

Lili batted her lashes, smiling at the memory of the baffled but intrigued look she'd brought to Simon's funny, crooked face.

"Although I'd rather you'd stayed with Mr. Tremayne than with that rather tall young chap from the receiving line. I didn't like the looks of *him,* not a whit."

Lili's mouth turned down. Amelia had made that clear when Trey Stone had phoned an hour ago. Without a word, her stern expression had discouraged Lili from agreeing to a date—even though she couldn't have overheard the suggestive banter he'd been whispering in Lili's ear. "Trey Stone? What was wrong with him?" *Was she being warned off by her nanny's sixth sense?*

Mrs. Grundy paused at the connecting doors of their hotel suite. "He reminds me of your old boyfriend, Lars. Too smooth by half." She shook her head. A flake of oatmeal fell off her chin onto her lapel. "I am so very pleased you've outgrown that type of fellow."

Lili swallowed. *I have?*

Darn that Grundy! The woman was a wet blanket. No wonder her father had insisted she accompany Lili to America.

Amelia went on. "Your head may be in the clouds, but your heart's in the right place, Princess. Listen to it and you'll do your father proud."

Lili avoided the woman's sharp eyes as they said good-night. As soon as the door closed, she let her shoulders sag. The bedclothes dropped to her waist. She looked down at her casual knit top and the jeans she'd tucked into her luggage after Amelia had finished packing the fussy matching outfits that gave Lili nightmares of wardrobes to come.

Here she was, twenty-two and still sneaking out past bedtime for a forbidden assignation. But what choice did she have?

Lili crawled out of bed. Annie and Natalia weren't so beholden to pleasing their elders—they'd go their own way, despite what Papa and Amelia had to say about it. And look at Jana Vargas—not even the chief of police intimidated *her*.

Lili put on a pair of sneakers, grabbed a jacket and applied one of her Biore facial strips to the door mechanism so it wouldn't lock behind her. Mrs. Grundy had taken charge of their keys, not even allowing Lili that much control over what was, after all, her own life.

"Time to start living it," she said to herself as she headed for the elevator. Trey Stone, Mr. America in the flesh, had promised to wait for her in the lounge if there weren't any annoying reporters lurking about. Her heart might have wished for her late date to be the more unconventional Simon Tremayne, but he wasn't suited to her present needs. When it came to deflowering a princess, she had the feeling that Trey would be much more amenable to taking on the task, with no second thoughts for propriety.

"IS THIS WHAT YOU WANTED, lovely Lili?" Trey crooned as he snaked his arm around her shoulders and dragged her across the front seat of his convertible toward himself.

Technically, she had to admit that it was. Going for a moonlit convertible ride was supposed to be so Cary Grant and Grace Kelly. Instead it felt more like—like—

Lili cast about for the name of the television serial that had played endlessly on Grunberg's one local TV channel. Oh, yes—*Happy Days!* Or better yet, *Laverne and Shirley.*

Like that lovably wacky duo, Lili had gotten herself into another predicament. It was turning out that, despite his promising first impression, a little Trey Stone went a long way. So did his arm, unfortunately.

She lifted his large hand from its familiar position, fingers dangling within brushing distance of her breast. Trey gave her shoulder a squeeze, apparently quite comfortable to be driving with only one free hand. Lili stifled her sigh.

She looked up at the dark sky, studded with stars to rival the tiny diamonds in her ears. "This is very nice." *Then why aren't I enjoying myself?*

After one quick drink and much smooth talk in the nearly empty lounge, Trey had hinted that they should move their party to a private location. Lili, nervous about being spotted, had rashly agreed. Although Trey was also staying at the hotel, he wasn't quite so bold to invite her up to his room. Not that she'd have gone. She wasn't so stuck on the idea of a madcap fling that she'd throw herself at the first Casanova who came along. It was true that she'd had high hopes for Trey, particularly when he suggested they go cruising in his convertible, but her enthusiasm was fading...for some reason.

They'd driven around for a while, even stopped at the drive-in restaurant that Simon had mentioned. Now they were traveling a country lane outside of Blue Cloud. Lili wasn't sure where, exactly. A needle of doubt poked through her blanket of assurance. The problem with always being taken care of was that she hadn't developed good self-defense mechanisms. Trey had better be trustworthy!

He glanced at her, his face classically handsome in the moonlight. "She walks in beauty like the night of starry skies and cloudless climes..."

"How sweet." *How uninspired.* She smiled up at Trey, locked under his weighty arm. He said all the right things, he really did. He was glib, charming and ever so slightly devilish. Aside from groping her shoulder, he hadn't made a wrong move all night.

Maybe that was it. She was taken with Simon's peculiarities. And the awful, hokey pickup lines he blurted out when he was trying to be charming.

The sporty convertible took the curves like a race car. Fresh, pure country air whistled past the windshield. Lili was a little chilly, but she couldn't snuggle up to Trey without sending him the wrong signal. She wrapped her arms around herself. "This truly is lovely," she said to fill the silence. "Truly."

Trey's white teeth gleamed at her. "We can pull over, if you like."

Lili knew what that meant; the kids on *Happy Days* went parking on Blueberry Hill. It wasn't as popular a practice in Grunberg, where cars weren't commonly owned by teenagers, and princesses on dates were trailed by hot- and cold-running bodyguards.

Trey didn't wait for her approval. When they came to a clearing in the trees that bordered the road, he slowed and drove a short way into the grassy area. A large graceful willow tree hung over the car, its drooping branches rustling slightly in the wind. "This is pleasant," Lili said, keeping her voice unimpressed, even though he probably wouldn't take the hint. She probably shouldn't come right out and say, "Shove it, buster." Princesses were always polite.

"Nice, sweet, lovely, pleasant," Trey said teasingly, shifting his large body around so he was facing her. One arm was draped on the steering wheel. The other had released her shoulders, although now his hand rested heavily on the back of her neck. Lili wanted to shrug it away. But she ought to give him a chance. He certainly *looked* like the kind of man she'd imagined she'd meet in America—tall, dark and handsome.

"I'm a princess," Lili explained with a touch of irony. "I live in a sugar-spun fairy tale where life is beautiful all the time."

"And you come complete with tiara."

She laughed politely. "Sorry to disappoint! I don't wear the tiara as common practice."

Trey's fingertips crawled along her nape. "You must have tried it on at least."

She blinked. "The Brunner bridal tiara?"

He leaned closer. "Yesss."

"Um." Why did men think that hissing in her ear like a snake was seductive? "Actually, no. Even though my sisters and I begged my mother to let us try it on, she never would. There's a legend…" Lili lost track of her words because Trey had dropped his arm around her shoulders again and was drawing her toward his mouth. "Only Brunner brides are supposed to..." Goodness, he had a lot of teeth.

His breath was hot. Minty.

Yeesh, she thought as Trey landed a kiss that consumed the lower half of her face. The kiss was much too wet and loose. She struggled a little, but he held her tightly, applying his mouth to hers like a suction hose. *Slurp*.

She put her hands on his chest and pushed. Still polite, but plenty firm. His mouth left hers with a wet *pop*. She gagged a little and swiped the back of a hand across her lips. Spittle wasn't polite. "Urg. Slow down, big guy."

For an instant, Trey didn't look so pleasant. Then he smiled again and winked at her, a thick lock of dark hair fallen rakishly across his forehead. "You said you wanted a real taste of America."

Yes, indeed she had. "But not all at once, thank you."

He fingered her hair. "You're a cute kid."

She squinted. "Meaning?"

"You're nothing like your sister, are you?"

"Which one?"

"Natalia."

"How do you know Natalia?"

Trey stroked her cheek. "Oh, I don't. I read about her in the tabloids. She's the wild one, right?"

"I suppose there are some who call her that. To me, she's just my sister. I'm the youngest, so she's closer to Annie than I am." Lili tilted her head to get away from Trey's persistent fingers. "I'm surprised you've read about us. We're not all *that* well known in America. Aside from here in Blue Cloud, of course, because my grandmother was born here—''

She stopped, struck by suspicion. Over drinks, Trey had claimed that he was in town to visit friends. She'd asked about his job, but she realized now that he'd evaded the question, leading her to believe, with a few casually dropped comments, that he was independently wealthy. Meanwhile, he'd probed for information about her, the Brunner family, their castle in Grunberg. He'd even hinted around for VIP passes to the grand opening of the jewel exhibit and an invitation to the formal ball. It was pretty clear that he was more interested in the princess than the woman.

In her eagerness for experience, she'd been too trusting. Suppose he was playing her?

Suppose?

"What did you say you do again?" she asked.

Trey grinned. "I didn't."

"You're not a reporter, are you?"

He threw back his head and laughed. "Hell, no!"

"Then why the interest in me and my family?"

"No sinister motives." He leered, his eyes glinting at her from the pattern of light and shadow cast by the moonlight filtering through the branches of the willow tree. "If you must know, I collect pretty girls."

She pushed his hand away. "Some might consider that sinister."

He buffed his nails on his expensive suit. "What can I say? I'm a ladies' man." He was practically boasting. "I assumed you'd had plenty of experience with suave European suitors. And you sure seemed eager enough to partake of the American variety."

"I'm sorry. You're mistaken."

"I can promise you a good time. No strings attached."

Lili wormed her bottom toward the passenger door. "No, thanks."

"Aw, c'mon." Trey reached for her. "Don't be a prude. I know what goes on among you jet-setters. Topless beaches, drunken orgies, wife-swapping. You like to party, don't you, baby princess?"

She slapped his hand away. He reached again, cajoling her with smarmy compliments. "C'mon, Princess. My lovely Lili-Pond." He gripped her waist; she twisted away. "Give me that sweet smile." His fingers plucked at the buttons of her blouse. "Show me your pretty little—"

Lili brought her leg up and jabbed him in the kneecap with the heel of one sneaker. Too bad. She usually hit her targets, but the man's oversized stilts had gotten in the way.

Trey clutched at his knee. "Ahhh!"

She grabbed the bucket-size soft drink from its holder and upended it over his head. Orange soda and a shovelful of ice chips cascaded over his head and shoulders.

Trey shook himself like a dog, spraying the front seat with sticky soda. Lili jumped out of the car.

He clambered after her, swearing so ripely that more spittle flew. *There's a lesson for you,* Lili told herself. *Never trust a man with excess saliva.*

The curses trailed off to whimpers. "Damn, that was vicious. You didn't have to kick so hard. I have a trick knee. And look at my hair. My suit! It's soaked."

"Count yourself lucky. I was aiming higher." She strode toward the road, breathing hard. For all her idiocy, she was high on triumph. She might have gotten into a predicament, but she'd also gotten herself out of it. And all on her own!

Trey got back in the car and started the engine. He backed up toward the road. Lili picked up her pace, trotting along the edge of the pavement. Good thing she'd worn sneakers.

"Don't run away, Lili," Trey called from the car. "I'll give you a ride back to town."

"No, thanks!"

"It's all right. I'll be on my best behavior."

"No!"

"You're going the wrong way."

Lili stopped. *Oh.* She'd been too steamed to notice.

"C'mon, Princess," Trey coaxed. She had to give him a sliver of credit. He hadn't abandoned her. She couldn't even blame him for getting overly amorous; she *had* flirted. "I promise not to touch you," he added.

She was tempted to accept the ride, but decided to hold her ground. Once a fool, and all that. "I'd rather not. There's a farmhouse nearby. I remember passing it. I'll go there and call for a cab." Fiddlesticks. If she hadn't been forced to sneak out, she could have borrowed Mrs. Grundy's handy cell phone. That was what came of relying on others to handle the necessary details.

Trey said, grudgingly, "I have a phone. I can call for you."

"I'd rather not be in your debt," she persisted, although she was beginning to realize that she wasn't entirely out of her predicament. The owner of the farmhouse might not be thrilled to be awakened by a stranger knocking at the door at midnight, even if the stranger was a princess. And the road was extremely dark and deserted. Whether that was good or bad, she wasn't sure.

"Suit yourself." Trey gunned the engine, then peered over his shoulder one more time. His white teeth flashed. "I suppose those VIP passes are out of the question?"

She almost laughed. Kissing Trey was worse than kissing a slimy toad—at least the toad didn't kiss back. But there was something roguishly charming about the guy, for all his crudeness. Maybe…

She wondered if it was possible to accept his cell phone but not his overtures. Trey said, "Well? I'm getting cold," then shrugged and peeled out with a squeal of the tires, tossing Lili a devil-may-care wave.

"Um, Trey?" she said.

It was a minute before the sound of the convertible died in the distance. Lili gathered her courage. This wasn't a problem. No, it actually was, but she could handle it. They must have taxicabs in Blue Cloud, so she had every hope of getting back to the hotel with no one the wiser…except herself.

She'd walked several paces before certain unusual sounds penetrated her consciousness. She stopped, flummoxed. Music—very faint, but carried on the night breezes. In the opposite direction from the farmhouse. Maybe there was another house just down the road, its inhabitants obviously still awake.

Hmm. Lili turned back, her interest piqued. Was that a violin? Accompanied by a guitar? Not a recording. She drew closer to the source, driven to hurry. There were voices, and laughter. It was beginning to sound like a free-form party; exactly the kind of excitement and adventure that she'd wished for.

She smelled wood smoke. Saw the flicker of a bonfire. Tents in a field. Dancers. A Gypsy encampment... Jana's people! Of course. Not unlike the bands of Romany who occasionally traveled through Grunberg and neighboring countries. She hadn't realized until Jana Vargas's appearance at the reception that there were Romany clans roaming America also.

Lili's blood stirred. An evening in a Gypsy camp! What a treat to stumble upon. Jana had seemed sincere about welcoming Lili, even if there was some question about the Vargas diamond lurking between their families.

"AMELIA GRUNDY, HERE."

"Whazzat?"

"Grundy. I'm with the princess."

"Er...right. Lili."

"Her Serene Highness, Princess Liliane of Grunberg."

"That's what I said." Simon scrubbed a hand through his matted hair. He'd fallen asleep with an open book resting on his chest. Bad form for a swinging single bachelor. "Who's this, again?" he said into the telephone, heaving up to switch on the bedside lamp. He righted his twisted glasses. "Grundy, you say?"

Why would the British nanny be calling *him?*

"The princess is missing."

"Missing?" he echoed, suddenly feeling more alert.

"Since ten o'clock. It's now half past twelve."

"But you said you're with her."

"Not literally, Mr. Tremayne. She's vanished."

"For two and a half hours. That hardly constitutes an emergency, does it? The princess struck me as a lively sort of girl. She's probably out having a good time."

"Exactly."

"Ah."

"She shouldn't be on her own," Grundy said.

"Are you certain she is?"

"Evidence suggests she is not."

The book on Simon's chest became as heavy as a headstone. He knocked it aside. "What am I supposed to do about that?" He sounded crabby, but he couldn't help it. Initially he'd thought that he and the princess had shared a moment. An understanding. Apparently not. Lili was cavorting, and it wasn't with him. Stood to reason. The lovely princess was such a distraction that he kept forgetting about his rotten luck with women. Every one of his short list of relationships had ended with him being the chump.

"She's of age," he said.

"Only twenty-two. One mustn't forget that she comes from a traditional society. She's been protected all her life. This is her first time on her own—"

"Poor girl. No wonder she's kicked away the traces."

Grundy carried on as if he hadn't interrupted. "She's inexperienced, our Lili. Naive, one might say." She fell quiet, but her silence was obviously expectant.

Inexperienced? Naive? That wasn't *his* impression of the princess, Simon thought, recalling how she'd teased him with her "innocent" little stripper act. Was he missing a clue?

"I am worried," Grundy said. "Princess Lili plays the flirt, but I do think she'd be susceptible to overtures from the wrong kind of gentleman." She paused significantly. "One who is perhaps planning to 'bag a trophy,' I believe you'd say in the American vernacular."

"Send the bodyguard after her."

"I have, sir. However, I believe reinforcements are

called for. Mr. Wilhelm has discovered from the concierge that the princess left the hotel with a stranger."

"Was it the Tower?"

"Pardon?"

"The man she met at the reception. Tall, well-dressed. Cleft chin. Freakishly hirsute." Simon was feeling around on the floor for his trousers. He found a sweatshirt and put it on instead, right over his pajama top, holding the phone with his chin. "His name's Stone."

"Yes, I do believe that's the one. I have a terrible feeling he's not on the up-and-up."

"Where's Wilhelm now?"

"Searching for the convertible they drove away in."

Simon thrust his arm, and the phone, through a sleeve, then brought it back to his mouth. "I'm going to hang up now and call Henry—Chief Russell."

"My goodness, no. We can't have the police involved. This must be kept discreet, lest the muckrakers get wind of it."

"Henry will keep it off the record, if possible. The man's a bloodhound. He'll probably sniff the air once and know exactly where Lili—Her Highness—is. We'll have her back to you in no time, none the worse for—" He stopped.

Inexperienced? Naive? Susceptible?

Was Grundy trying to tell him the princess was a *virgin?*

"Indeed," said the Brit.

"Huh?" said Simon, feeling damn slow on the uptake. The hair on the back of his neck was tingling. Oddly, he suspected that Grundy had read his mind and responded in agreement.

"Indeed, the princess will return none the worse for the adventure. She always has before."

Now that she'd hooked him, Grundy was sounding less urgent. Even complacent. "The princess has done this in the past?" Simon asked.

"On occasion."

Then why call out the big guns? Simon shoved his left foot into the running shoe he'd found under the bed. He was searching through the clots of dust for the other when it struck him that he *wasn't* the big gun. He was the mild-mannered museum dweeb, not the hero. He didn't rescue damsels in undress.

So why in tarnation had the efficient and spookily perceptive Amelia Grundy chosen to call *him?*

AMELIA HUNG UP the phone, a small smile puckering her lips. Magic had been in the air the instant Lili met Mr. Tremayne—she herself had felt the thunderbolt that crackled between the young couple. But one had to be circumspect about these things, especially when it came to guiding impulsive young princesses. Mistakes might be made.

Not even "fairy godmothers" were foolproof. Look at the Princesses Natalia and Andrea—now there was a pair of stubborn young ladies!

"Patience," Amelia whispered to herself. "Their time shall soon come." Just as Princess Lili's had.

It wasn't for Amelia to force the issue. Better to be discreet, waiting patiently for Lili to blunder about blindly until the perfect moment struck. When it did, Amelia would ensure that the princess's eyes were opened to her intended destiny.

Which wasn't to say that in the meantime Amelia couldn't give a nudge or two to point the reluctant Prince Charming in the right direction....

5

"THANKS A LOT," said Henry. "I'd just gotten home. Didn't even have time to take the uniform off." Minutes after Simon had called, the police chief had driven up in a patrol car, wearing his uniform of a medium-blue shirt with the badge emblem on the pocket, and navy pants, not as crisp and perfectly creased as usual. But still not as rumpled as Simon, who could put a wrinkle in a concrete wall if he had to wear one.

Henry shook his head. "I *knew* all this museum malarkey would be a major pain in my keister. And it's not even the weekend yet."

"Technically, it is." Simon tapped his watch face. "Past midnight."

Henry glowered. "And I'm on baby-sitting duty."

"Princess rescue unit would be more accurate."

"Why do I have the feeling we're rescuing someone who doesn't want to be rescued?" Henry had scanned the streets as they drove through town, but now his attention was mainly on the road. They were traveling north on a wooded lane. Although Simon wasn't privy to the reasons why, there was a dogged look on Henry's face that said he knew what he was doing.

"The princess's personal desires don't seem to be a priority. It's all about her public persona." Simon looked out at the rolling hills, the forests, punctuated by the occasional stately brick house or family farm.

"How are we supposed to find her?" he asked, his voice betraying an edge of desperation. The idea of Lili frolicking with Stone somewhere out here in total isolation did not sit well.

"You'll see."

Simon glanced at Henry's set jaw. "Sorry about this. I thought you'd want to be informed—" In his time in town, he'd learned that the police chief was the repository of all town gossip, accusations and petty squabbles, and Henry seemed to want it that way. "But maybe I shouldn't have called, after the day you had—"

"Nothing I couldn't handle."

"Then you managed to reapprehend your suspect?"

Henry had been more steamed than Simon had ever seen him when he'd returned to the museum to interview Jana Vargas and found the snack shop empty. Although the door was still locked, one of the small second-story windows had been left open—all of a quarter inch. Henry had spotted that at once. Simon obviously wasn't a crime-stopper, but he hadn't needed his college degrees to deduce that Lili was involved. The Gypsy woman had probably crawled out the window, saw it was too far to jump, then got lucky in finding the princess in the next room. Lili had removed her shoes and stood on the trash can to pass over the key, then slipped, crashing into the position he'd discovered her in. This afternoon, he hadn't gotten the chance to explain his theory to Henry. The chief had raced off in pursuit of Jana Vargas.

Henry grunted. "My suspect walked into the station, bold as you please."

"*What?*"

Apparently the chief wasn't fully satisfied by the surrender. He shook his head in disgust. "Not even an hour after she'd escaped."

"Then she's still in custody?"

"Nope." Henry shrugged. "I questioned her, but I had no good reason to hold her. No evidence. Her partner got away with the loot and we haven't been able to pick him up. We don't even have a clear ID on the guy. I couldn't hold either of them for long, unless we can catch them fencing the necklace."

"So why'd she turn herself in?"

"Because she's smart. She knew I knew where to find her, and she also knew I could only question her, not arrest her."

"Then why bother escaping?"

Henry cocked his head. "That's an interesting question. I expect to have the answer before they strike again."

"You think they'll dare? Hell." Simon's stomach churned. After losing his last job over a security snafu— and a woman—it didn't seem right that it could be happening to him again. The gods couldn't be that perverse. "This is going to look bad for the museum. You truly don't believe the jewels are in danger?"

"Naw." Henry slowed and spun the wheel, taking a dirt lane that led to a rambling white farmhouse. While he was being more casual about Simon's concerns than expected, it was always reassuring to know the chief was on the job. No man was infallible—didn't Simon know it—but Henry gave that impression.

"I doubt the Gypsies are that clever," the chief said.

"Gypsies?"

Henry pointed past the hood as they drove by the farmhouse and then the barn, the dirt lane turning into an overgrown trail. He parked when it petered out, and

Simon rose from the car, craning his neck to see beyond a screen of mixed hardwood trees. In the distance, a caravan had been set up in the large pasture that stretched from the trees to the paved road. "Gypsies," he said, belatedly remembering the flyer that Grundy had snatched from Lili. Good thing Henry was in charge. "Jana Vargas is an actual Gypsy."

"Romany is the preferred term," Henry said as he exited the patrol car. "They *appear* to be genuine from the information I've been able to gather so far. I'm checking further back, but so far their record is clean except for a few misdemeanors. No outstanding warrants for those I've been able to ID. But I haven't finished my investigation, either. If trouble's there, I'll dig it up."

Simon almost felt sorry for Jana Vargas. She'd picked the wrong pocket when she'd taken her brazen swipe at Chief Henry Russell's authority. The man was very protective of Blue Cloud and would come down hard on those who threatened its pastoral peace and quiet.

"I don't see Stone's convertible." Simon glanced over the pair of junker-style vehicles that were parked nearby. Even with more pressing duties, Henry had reported that he'd found time to request and read over an initial report on the Tower. He was Trey Stone from Philadelphia. He'd attended Temple University and drove a pricey convertible with a couple hundred bucks' worth of outstanding speeding violations and a lease agreement in arrears. "Lili isn't here."

"Not so fast." Henry strode toward the encampment. Fiddle music carried across the field. "Let's check it out."

A small group of horses and ponies were staked to a

tie-line at the outer perimeter. They moved restlessly when Henry slipped past. Simon stopped to lay a hand on a chestnut's withers. The mare was well-fed and groomed. In fact, none of the equines were the motley hags he'd halfway expected.

Henry had stopped behind a full-height canvas tent with multicolored banners flying from all peaks. He wasn't really hiding, but not showing himself in the open, either. He motioned for Simon to join him.

Simon moved into place. The chief said, "Look."

He didn't have to ask where. There was only one place *to* look.

The fire. The women.

They were dancing.

Simon's face grew hot. The sight was not of this time. It was if he'd been transported back in history, to a scene from a different, more elemental era. As if his veneer of civility had been torn away, leaving him raw, basic, male. Ready to fight for his honor; ready to gnaw on a hunk of meat and bone; ready to grab his woman and…satisfy himself.

A small group of the Romany had gathered around their bonfire. A dark, middle-aged man with a bushy moustache and a bandanna on his head strummed the guitar, sitting beside an ancient wizened fellow who played the fiddle while standing, swaying, now and then letting out a little hop and an enthusiastic "Hup!" or "Ho!"

Several women danced to the lively music. One was Jana Vargas, wearing slim sandals and the extravagant bracelets, her long skirt swirling around her bare legs as she danced. She laughed and shook a tambourine over her head, then brought it down to bang it against her swinging hips. Her hair was loose and wild, flowing over her undulating torso like ebony silk. She was an incredible sight—gorgeous and free. And Simon barely glanced at her, because one of the other woman was...

Lili.

She was transformed. Although Jana was enjoying herself, Lili seemed to be transported to realms of ecstasy. She danced with every fiber of her being, spinning with such joyful abandon that Simon would have feared she'd lose control and tip over into the fire if not for the quick, clever skill of her bare feet. She danced in the dirt as if she'd been born to it, stamping and kicking and twirling. Her face was flushed pink, her dark eyes glittering in the firelight. Lacking Jana's swishy skirts and waist-length hair, she made do with a fringed shawl that she swirled around herself like a belly dancer with a veil. The difference being that her intention was not to entice, even though every move was pure seduction nonetheless. No, Simon thought. She was dancing entirely for herself.

He swallowed the ball in his throat. Flexed his hands. Something in him—the fundamental, one-hundred percent reactionary part—reached out to her. She was provocative and rapturous and vulnerable all at once. He felt as though he'd seen into her heart.

Henry stepped past Simon's line of vision.

The guitarist quit playing. His black eyes flashed. He spoke in a foreign tongue: *"Shawglo!"*

The fiddler's bow screeched across his instrument's strings. Jana brought the tambourine's jangling rhythm to an abrupt stop, slapping it against an upraised palm. "Chief Russell. We meet again." Her voice crackled with ice. "And so soon."

At last Lili realized what was happening and skidded

to a stop midwhirl. She swayed, dizzy on her feet, and Simon rushed forward to grasp her waist before she fell.

She looked at him with unfocused eyes, her dazed smile spreading like liquid honey. "Simon. Have you come to dance with me?"

"Yes." His voice was hoarse.

She blinked. "Truly?"

He didn't know what he was saying. "No. That is, I—" The warmth of her body seeped into his. Her rosy cheeks were dewy, soft even to look at, and he could feel her heart against his chest, pounding with a wild Gypsy beat. Foolish to say he'd come to rescue her.

He smoothed a hand over the dandelion fluff of her hair. "Mrs. Grundy is concerned about you. She sent me to find you."

Lili licked her lips. Luscious lips. "As you can see, there's nothing to be concerned about."

"I wouldn't say that."

She blinked at him, still not entirely clearheaded, going by the half smile and dipsy-doodle expression that flickered back and forth over her face. He kept his arm around her, looking reluctantly for Henry.

A grandly voluptuous woman wrapped in tight black ski pants and a buffalo-plaid blanket was bearing down on the police chief from one direction. Jana Vargas came at him from the other. Although his gaze zipped back and forth between the avenging females, betraying a certain alarm, Henry manfully held his ground.

The older woman flung a hand into the air, barking at the police chief in what must be a Romany dialect. Long dark hair streaked with white spilled from the kerchief wrapped around her head. Her arms churned as she berated Henry for holding Jana without a shred of evidence to prove her guilt. *"Nash Avri."* She spat on the ground. "We have done nothing to be treated this way."

Henry kept his cool, though he maintained moving his eyes to Jana. She stood back, complacently watching the upbraiding with a little smile of amusement.

"That's Baba Magda," Lili murmured. "She's the *Phuri Dae*—the wise woman—of the Vargases, but it's really Jana who's in charge."

Simon was impressed by her knowledge. "And here I thought there was no love lost between you and Jana Vargas."

"We've come to an understanding. A simpatico."

"Trey Stone isn't here?"

Lili's eyes widened. "What do you know about Trey?"

"You were seen leaving the hotel with him."

"Was I?"

"Mrs. Grundy was concerned."

"Yes, you said that." Watching him through her lashes, Lili pushed a hand against his chest. "But were you? Concerned?"

"Of course. I'd be in dire straits if the museum's guest of honor became involved in a public scandal." What he felt for her personally was a private matter, apparently beyond his control. It would do neither of them any good to delve into that when there was already enough trouble to deal with. "You are going to have to come back to the hotel with me."

"With *you?*"

"And Chief Russell."

Lili wrinkled her nose and returned her attention to Henry's heated discussion with Jana and the older, irate woman. "This is so embarrassing. Did you *have* to call out the cops? I've been treated to nothing but kindness and hospitality by these people, and in return they receive this—'' She gestured. "It's a clear-cut case of racial profiling, Jana says. Prejudice against the Roma!''

"You don't know Henry Russell the way I do. He's a fair man. Considering the acts of thievery and the fact that his prime suspect disappeared from beneath his nose—'' Simon paused, looking for signs of Lili's complicity "—I'd say he has plenty of reasons to investigate these people.''

Lili's expression remained stubborn. "I should go and see if I can smooth the waters....''

Simon caught her by the hand before she moved away. "Tell me, Princess. This afternoon, did you give Jana the key?''

"What a question!''

He shrugged. "I notice you haven't answered it.''

She set herself, looking around the camp so she wouldn't have to look at him. She ran a hand through her hair, making the curly fringe stick out even more. Finally she said, "So what if I did? I felt sorry for Jana, getting locked up like that. I wanted to give her a chance to—to—''

"Get away?'' Simon suggested. "Did you know she turned herself into the chief not an hour after you staged her big escape?''

"No.'' Doubt crossed Lili's face. "She didn't tell me.''

"That's because your involvement wasn't necessary. Jana can take care of herself.'' He glanced at the combative couple. "And by the looks of it, she can go toe-to-toe with Henry anytime.''

Lili's shoulders drooped. She was coming off her high. "You're saying I'm superfluous.'' A wry grin. "Strictly ornamental. Story of my life.''

"No, that's not what I'm saying."

"And why are *you* involved, hmm?"

"Ask Mrs. Grundy."

Lili slowly shook her head. "You were jealous, weren't you?"

Simon opened his mouth. Jealous? "Hell, yeah."

The princess raised her brows. "We'll always have hot dogs."

Simon's hopes leaped, but Henry approached them before he could respond. "Listen, Simon. I want you to take the princess back to my car." He cast a quick look over Lili, checking for damage. "Wait for me. I'll be five minutes, maybe ten. Jana has kindly offered me a short tour of the camp." The way he said *tour* clearly meant *inspection.*

Lili sniffed. "I have no say in this?"

"Were you planning to spend the night?" Simon asked, halfway serious.

Her eyes lit up. "There's an idea. I always wanted to run away with the circus. Gypsies will do even better."

"Not on my watch," Henry said.

"Wow." Lili chortled. "You sound just like the cops on TV."

Henry grimaced at her lighthearted comment. The man took police work very seriously. He appealed to Simon instead. "Go on. Get her out of here. Before the next batty idea takes flight."

LILI WASN'T accustomed to being manhandled. In Grunberg, she was almost always treated with respect, occasionally reverence. It was a bore. Even her suitors held back, particularly when they'd been handpicked by her father and subjected to the "My Daughter is a Precious Gem'' lecture. There were plenty of Eurotrash playboys who'd gladly show her a good time, but they weren't the type of men she met in her day-to-day life. Nor the type she particularly *wanted* to give her virginity to, any more than her fumbling schoolboy Romeos had been.

She'd expected that Americans, with their reputation for brash, friendly self-confidence, would be less intimidated by her title. She'd looked forward to that.

Being hustled into the back seat of a patrol car was another matter entirely.

She stopped and looked back at the encampment. Jana had been reserved at first, but had gradually warmed up when she saw how open and interested Lili was about the Romany lifestyle. Her glimpse inside Jana's old-fashioned carved-wood caravan had been more enticing than a display of royal jewels would ever be. It was small and efficient, made luxurious by the hand-painted details and the lush, richly colored beddings and embroidered wall hangings. A strange, wild scent permeated the entire place. Wood smoke, cedar, spice, mixed in with an indefinable aroma of the outdoors. The very scent of freedom.

Simon tugged on Lili's arm. ''I'm coming, I'm coming,'' she said, with one last rueful glance at the dancing flames of the campfire. She'd wanted an adventure. And she'd gotten it. How could she have known that it would only deepen her craving for further experience?

She glanced at Simon as he joined her in the back seat. There were other kinds of adventures. Adventures heretofore unexplored. ''Poor fella.'' She plucked at the shirttail hanging out beneath his sweatshirt. ''I got you out of bed.''

He shifted his hips off the seat and started tucking in. "Mrs. Grundy got me out of bed."

Flirtatiously, she pulled up the sweatshirt to reveal a few inches of gray-and-white striped flannel. "Do you always sleep in a full set of pajamas? How cute. You look like a prisoner."

He took off his glasses and rubbed them on the sweatshirt. "I've never been called cute before."

His cheeks were ruddy. On impulse, she slid her thumb along his cheekbone, feeling the warmth of his blush. In Grunberg, she had to constantly keep propriety in mind. She wasn't allowed to touch men at random, simply because she found them attractive or perplexing or kissable. Especially in public, she had to guard her emotions and actions. If she didn't, she'd hear it from both Amelia and her father.

Not so here. Here, she could dance to the beat of a tambourine, kicking her bare feet in the dirt. She could snuggle in the back of a police car with funny-faced museum curators who'd lost sleep over her.

"You're extremely cute, Simon." She nudged closer. "Like a frog."

He jammed the glasses back on. "Ribbit."

She squeezed his arm. "Now you're mad."

"Ribbit."

"You know what they say about princesses and frogs. We have a very special relationship."

Moonlight flashed on his lenses as he turned his face toward hers. Small brown dots speckled his cheeks— seven on one side, six on the other—and his eyes were green. Lily-pad green. A surprising desire stroked inside her, making her skin prickle with sensation. Hot. Cold. And a lovely, lovely warmth.

"I won't be changing my shape, no matter how many times you kiss me."

"I'm not going to kiss you," she said, watching the gleam in his eyes dim. She took a breath, but her voice still came out whispery and breathless. "*You're* going to kiss *me*."

The gleam sharpened. She sensed his pleasure. "You think so?"

"You must. I'm running a survey."

"I don't dare ask."

"My classmates and I in boarding school used to compare notes on which country kisses better."

Simon chest hitched. "Gives a whole new meaning to diplomacy."

"Which nationality then. I always thought Italy, but several of the other girls swore by the local boys."

"French kisses are good."

She giggled and batted at him playfully, then left her hand on his chest. "American boys weren't even if the running, if you want to know."

Simon's eyes narrowed. "How many of them did you kiss?"

"Me? Or all of us?"

"Just you."

"Hmm." As if she were counting, she tapped her fingers one by one on the faded university emblem on his sweatshirt. "Truthfully?"

"Give me a round number."

She put her mouth to his ear. "Only two."

He pulled back to see her face. The vinyl seat creaked against their backs. "Two?"

"And I'm afraid the second one came a wee bit past my schoolgirl years. So far, my data is inconclusive."

"What does that mean?" Simon asked, all baffled masculine suspicion.

She tilted her head, enjoying herself. "The first was rather memorable. His name was Billy and he was fourteen. I met him in the mountains on a skiing vacation. We kissed only once—behind the ski chalet. He had no technique, but he tasted like hot chocolate and whipping cream. High marks."

"And the second kisser?"

"Not as good as Billy, I'm afraid."

Simon seemed relieved, but not convinced.

Lili sighed. "Yes, Trey Stone definitely brought the American score down."

Outrage flared in Simon's eyes. He had no right, but she was thrilled to see it. "You kissed Trey Stone?" he accused.

She nodded. "In his convertible."

Oh, this was fun! The look on Simon's face was priceless. "Not very far from here, in fact."

His cheeks were getting ruddy again. "You kissed Trey Stone in a convertible on a deserted country road? Have you no sense? What if he was a—a—well, not a gentleman about it?"

"I know him as well as I know you."

"Not nearly. I have a mayor and a police chief who can vouch for me. What does Stone have, beside a head of hair that could double as a pot scrubber?"

Lili shrugged playfully. "Don't forget the convertible," she trilled.

"I drive a Volvo wagon." Simon gripped her upper arms. She nearly melted. He wasn't afraid to touch her, and with passion, too—marvelous! "Would you kiss me anyway?"

She nodded, struggling to keep a serious face. "For

the sake of the survey. But I must warn you, the pressure is on if you expect to up your country's average.''

''What about Stone? How high do I have to rate to better his score?''

She met his stare with an alluring trifle of a smile. ''I shouldn't kiss and tell.''

''It's too late to play the demure card, Princess.''

She leaned into him, letting the silence, and then their rising awareness, fill the car. Outside, the dark trees swayed in the breeze, throwing shadows darker than the starry night across the police vehicle. Except for the distant lights of the campfire and the farmhouse, they could have been alone in the world. Simon was adorable, huffy and bewildered by her flirtatious overtures. As the sparks of attraction that crackled between them deepened into sensual heat, he seemed to change before her eyes, from the rumpled, amusing frog to a romantic Prince Charming, exuding enough masculine charisma to send every girlish cell in her body into a flutter.

And she hadn't even kissed him yet!

''Lili,'' he said, letting his palm hover above her body, as if he didn't know where or how to touch her. She threaded her fingers through his and drew his hand closer, until out of natural instinct he reached for her, clasping her waist to pull her to him. ''Lili,'' he said again, his voice so hoarse he sounded like a bullfrog. She refrained from pointing that out.

''I like the way you say my name. Lili sounds so much nicer than 'Princess.' ''

He searched for words. ''You're the princess of my, uh, heart. Ahh…the royal, the royal ruler of— No, scratch that.'' He grimaced, thinking hard. Deep breath. ''I found your picture in the dictionary. It was listed under *gorgeous*.''

She compressed her lips, not wanting to laugh. That meant she couldn't speak, either, so Simon took that as a sign to go on. "Heaven must be missing a couple of stars tonight, because I see them shining in your eyes."

She blinked.

"Your eyes do shine," he said in a husky, hesitant whisper. "All the time."

"Thank you." Their faces were so close, she felt the puff of his breath on her lips. She pouted them, minutely. Waiting…

His hand pressed the small of her back.

When he opened his mouth again, she stopped him before he could launch into another corny line. "Hush." She slipped off his glasses, let them dangle from her fingertips before tossing them aside. You couldn't get any more obvious than that.

"For the survey," Simon said, and touched his mouth to hers. For a couple of seconds, neither of them moved. No reaction, no response.

Lili's hopes sank; the kiss was so bland she could have been smooching a brother. A father. "This isn't all that I'd expected," she said against Simon's unmoving lips.

And then it happened.

When she spoke, her mouth tilted a little, sliding over his. He ever so softly plucked at her bottom lip. A sweet shiver ran through her body.

Magic. It was magic.

"Oh." Her eyes blinked open in surprise. Simon was already looking at her, sending beams of astonishing sexual magnetism. Heat shot up her throat. She closed her lids again, feeling her eyeballs roll upwards as she melted against him, her hand clinging to his shoulders, their mouths still in perfect, lip-tingling alignment.

He didn't try to deepen the kiss. Only prolonged it…deliciously. The world dropped away as she lost herself in pure, swooning sensation.

Eventually, Simon stopped kissing her. For an instant, her fingers clenched on handfuls of his sweatshirt, then she let go. Took a breath. And raised a mental prayer of thanks to the persons who'd invented kissing.

Simon gulped. "Survey says?"

Her voice came out shaky. "Survey says I have to invent a new category."

"Does that mean I was better than Trey Stone?"

"Trey who?"

"Lili…seriously…" He took her hand. "I know you're a grown woman, but it really wasn't a good idea to hook up with a stranger like that. Maybe in Grunberg, you're always safe, but here, in a foreign country, a woman has to be smart."

"Blue Cloud is a hotbed of criminal activity?"

"No. Not until today. Or yesterday. But there are a lot of strangers in town. Even Henry can't keep track of them all. So be careful. Stick with your bodyguard." Simon's brow furrowed. "How did you end up at the Gypsy camp, anyway? That wasn't smart, either."

Her temper flared. "I felt perfectly safe with Jana and her family."

"But you're a princess—"

"*They* didn't care."

"I do, Lili. I have to. I'm responsible for you being here." He got a stubborn look on his face. "So…what did happen to Trey?"

She made an imperious gesture. "I didn't like the way he kissed, so I sent him away."

"You mean he left you stranded?"

"No. I had a plan. Then I found the Gypsies."

"I guess all's well that ends well. As long as you don't do it again. Henry has enough problems to deal with."

"And you? Do you consider me a problem? Was that kiss simply your way of taking care of business?"

"It was not."

She ducked her chin, suddenly feeling shy. Scooting across the seat, she became aware of a hard lump beneath her. Simon's glasses. She reached down and pulled them free. They weren't broken, but the thin wire frame had twisted into a warped shape.

"Pardon me. I sat on your glasses." She passed them to Simon.

"That's okay." He scratched his cowlick, his eyes veering away from her. The kiss stood between them. How could something so magical become so awkward in retrospect?

She moved even farther away. The police chief had emerged from the trees and was striding toward the car. There was no time to explain herself to Simon. He'd have to think the worst of her—that she was a hopelessly spoiled, foolish, naive, young princess out of sync with the real world.

And maybe she was.

But not for much longer.

6

EARLY THE NEXT MORNING, Simon's doorbell rang when he was still in the shower. Swearing, he grabbed a towel and climbed out, hoping it wasn't Chief Russell or Mayor Applewhite come to report more trouble from their royal visitor. Lili had returned to the hotel obediently enough, but he wasn't convinced by her show of meekness. Her zing-a-ding-a-ling effervescence couldn't be bottled up for long.

Wet soles sliding on the wood floors, Simon hurried to answer the front door, but not before looking through the frosted glass oval inset first. Without his eyeglasses, he had to squint.

All the same, there was no mistaking the big black limousine parked at the curb.

The doorbell pealed loud and insistent. He looked again, peering to the side. Hoping it was Wilhelm or Grundy holding their finger to the button.

Nope. Blond hair. Blurred, but then no one except Princess Lili had corn-silk blond hair *and* a big black limo.

Simon clutched at his towel. There went that damnable *zing* again!

"I see you, Simon." Lili pressed her face to the frosted glass, smooshing her nose into a pink blob. The shape shifted, bringing her cheek and one wide dark eye into focus. "Don't try to hide." She tapped on the glass. "Open up."

"I'm not dressed."

"Excuses, excuses."

"All I'm wearing is a towel." He looked at the puddle collecting around his bony feet. "And I'm dripping wet."

Silence.

Then, "Be a man."

He flicked the lock and jerked the door open a couple of inches. "You're a princess. I have to be a *gentleman*."

She sighed, but her expression was not disappointed. Her mouth puckered. Her eyes glistened like melted chocolate in the morning sunshine. "That's what they all say."

The tousled blond head dipped as she gave him the once-over, from his toes up. He held tight to the clump he'd made of the large bath towel, hoping she wouldn't be able to discern what he'd been thinking in the shower, since you-know-who had been the star of his early-morning fantasies. A breath shuddered out of his lungs, sending a droplet trickling from his collarbone down the center of his chest.

Lili's gaze fixated on it, following the droplet's meandering path. When she lifted a finger, he backed away a step, but she poked him in the stomach, catching the cold trickle before it reached his navel. Her eyes rose to his. She swallowed. "Would you please have breakfast with me?"

Simon hesitated. Her fingertip remained glued to his abdomen, rendering him speechless. Practically thoughtless. But not numb.

He managed a nod.

"I'll let you get dressed then."

"That would be good."

She was still touching him.

"Your finger," he said.

She yanked it away, blushing prettily. "Oh. Sorry."

He nodded toward the limo. Rodger Wilhelm had emerged from the passenger's side of the front seat and was leaning an arm on the roof of the car, staring at Simon's house through slitted eyes. "Are we going to be chaperoned?" Probably a good idea, all things—including his damp towel and his undampened libido—considered.

"Rodger will accompany us, at a distance. I managed to convince Mrs. Grundy to stay behind."

In his head, Simon was rapidly flipping through a mental Filofax. He had a list of items to attend to before that afternoon's ribbon-cutting ceremony, but it was all detail stuff that could be put off for another hour or two. Besides, refusing the princess's breakfast invitation would definitely qualify as bad protocol.

"Breakfast would be a pleasure, Princess Lili. I'd invite you in to wait for me to get ready, but..." He shrugged.

Lili looked at his bare chest. He couldn't remember any woman looking at his chest in quite that way, with an unmistakable, covetous heat in her eyes. Not even his last ex-girlfriend, who'd had reason to keep him distracted from what was going on elsewhere.

"You can invite me inside another day," Lili murmured, reluctantly turning away so he could get dressed.

Another princess, Simon thought, watching her swing down his front steps, her curvy bottom filling out a pair of mannish tailored trousers the way no man ever could.

He lifted his gaze to meet Rodger's glare. The message was clear: Off Limits.

LILI EXPLAINED what she wanted, and Simon directed the chauffeur to The Farmhouse, an old-fashioned home-cooking kind of restaurant that had been converted from a real farmhouse, a white frame structure set on a gently sloping hill. The setup also included a big red dairy barn with white trim, still operable, offering tours and cow-milking demonstrations. Dairy goods were sold out of a small stone spring house tucked into the hillside.

Lili was delighted by the pure Americana of the location. As soon as the proprietors realized who she was—hard not to with the royal limo parked outside the door—they'd wanted to provide her with a private room in back. She declined. She didn't want to be coddled. She wanted to experience a hearty country breakfast alongside the other patrons.

They were given a table on a wide porch that encircled three sides of the farmhouse, overlooking the barn and the green rolling hills dotted with grazing milk cows. The dishes and coffee cups were thick and chunky, the menu was fascinating, the portions huge. Lili wanted to try the rhubarb jam and the sweet-and-sour pork balls, just to see if they were what they sounded like.

She put her elbows on the table and her chin in her hands. She beamed at Simon. "This is exactly what I imagined the States would be like."

He fussed with the bent frame of his glasses. "Is this really your first visit?"

"Practically." She bobbed her head. "My father is very stern, very protective. I was here once as a child, with my mother. I remember only two things clearly. Being scared of the skyscrapers in New York City, because the tallest things in Grunberg are the mountains, and petting a cow.''

"Petting a cow was an event to remember?''

"It happened at a farm—I'm pretty sure it was the farm where my grandmother grew up, here in Blue Cloud. I had an ice cream on a stick and I fed the last bite to the cow. Its tongue was large and rough, I remember that. It slurped out across my hand and I let go. The cow inhaled the ice cream, stick and all. I was afraid to tell my mother what I'd done, so I lived in fear for the rest of the visit, thinking that the cow would suddenly keel over with indigestion.''

"And did it?''

"No. Which was sort of a disappointment, as I remember.''

"They have cows in Grunberg, don't they?''

"Sure. Plenty of them. But since I'm a princess there, I don't exactly get to play the milkmaid.''

"You're a princess here as well.''

"Only if you keep reminding me.''

"Maybe I'm reminding myself.''

"Why—'' Lili blinked at the emotion evident in his eyes, in spite of the askew spectacles. "Oh, I see.''

"You know that we can't have a replay of the past night,'' Simon said, leaning over the table so the nearby diners wouldn't be able to overhear. Thoughtful of him, although Lili was accustomed to being stared at and eavesdropped on. It was a fact of her life, and why she always felt pressed to be on her best behavior. Because the royal family of an obscure principality was not of any consequence to the average American, she'd hoped that she'd feel free to be herself here. Unfortunately, the hoopla connected with the museum had limited her options. But she couldn't make herself resent Simon for that. He was too nice. And one heck of a good kisser....

Any minuscule remaining chance of a fling with Trey or any other playboy had been tossed out the back of the patrol car as soon as Simon's lips touched hers. Between the two of them, they had all the va-va-voom chemistry she could ask for!

She'd decided even before Chief Russell had deposited her back at the hotel what she wanted. All her focus was on Simon Tremayne now, even though he was too set on behaving as a gentleman to take advantage of her availability. A problem, but not one that she couldn't surmount. The bigger problem was that she had only a couple of days to accomplish her first wild fling, when all other attempts had been dismal failures. If only she had some experience with seducing men to go on so that *this* time would be different. It simply wasn't the type of situation where she could go to Amelia for advice.

But her sisters…Annie and Natalia…*they* could help.

A waitress arrived, carrying a tray heaped with their extravagant order.

Lili jumped up. "Excuse me, please, Simon."

He set aside his napkin, rising to his feet. "The food will get cold."

"I'll be only a minute, I promise. I have to…powder my nose." She hurried from the porch, leaving him staring at the steaming stacks of pancakes and waffles and sausage patties in dismay.

Lili went into the ladies' restroom and pulled the cell phone from her purse. After she'd given Amelia the slip the night before, the nanny had insisted that she keep a phone with her from now on. As a safety precaution.

All too familiar with Amelia's omniscient tendencies, Lili hadn't quite dared ask her what she knew about the evening's escapade…or how she knew it. Lili was merely grateful that Amelia hadn't been too dreadfully worried. And pleased that she'd been so agreeable about Lili's breakfast date. Perhaps her old nanny believed that Simon was as safe an escort as a princess could get.

Hah! Not if *this* princess had anything to say about it!

Lili dialed the code for Grunberg, then Natalia's personal line at the castle. Brash Natalia was the sister who'd give her the advice she wanted to hear. The phone rang several times. Lili was trying to figure out the time zones when her oldest sister picked up. *"Ja?"*

Lili tried to sound light and upbeat. *"Guten morgen* from America."

"What? Who? Lili, is that you?"

"I'm sorry, Natalia. You were sleeping, weren't you? I got the time change wrong."

"No, it's afternoon here." Natalia explained that she was sunning by the pool after a hard morning of shopping and wardrobe preparation—major yawn—for her upcoming trip to New Mexico. "What's going on, Lili? Are you all right? Have you gotten into another fix?"

"I'm great. Honestly!" Lili hoisted herself up to sit on the vanity in the empty bathroom, which was decorated in country cutesy style—cherry wallpaper and ruffles at the small window. "I'm not in a fix. Why do you say that?"

"You always call Annie when you need advice and me when you need help, that's why. What is it this time, or should I say *who?*"

Lili giggled. "You know me like clockwork. Except

this time I'm going to surprise you, Natalia, I really am. I've met a different type of man. Not a boy, a *man*. Simon Tremayne. He's a museum director. He's brainy, and so funny and charming…''

''He already sounds better than your last boyfriend, the banker's son from Spitzenstein.''

''That one was more Papa's idea than mine. I wasn't aware of the unfortunate nasal drip until after I'd agreed to see him.'' The doorknob rattled. Lili held the phone away from her mouth and called out, *''Occupado!''*

''Where are you, anyway?'' her sister asked.

''In the washroom of a restaurant called The Farm-house. You should see it, Natalia. It's storybook America, with a big red barn and cows in the fields. Amelia let me out so I could take Simon to breakfast. We're going to eat blueberry pancakes and a breakfast cereal called Cap'n Crunch. Isn't that too cute?''

''Wait a minute, Lili. What do you mean about Amelia 'letting you out'?''

''Oh, that. I guess I was in sort of a fix, but it's okay now. Late last night, I snuck away from the hotel and ended up at a Gypsy caravan, where I danced with a Romany woman named Jana Vargas. *Vargas,* just like the diamond, you know?'' Lili stopped to take a breath. ''It's not as if Amelia truly needed to worry. But she sent Simon after me anyway, and that's when we kissed. In the back of a police car!''

Natalia seemed to have followed the story, up to the end. ''A *police car?*''

Lili nodded, even though her sister couldn't see her. ''I felt so wild and daring. Just like you!''

''I've never been arrested.'' Natalia chuckled; it was probably the only thing she'd never done.

"Oh, I wasn't arrested. The police chief gave me a ride back to town, that's all."

"That's all?" Natalia made a *whew* sound. "So what about the kiss?"

"It was a hundred times better than the American playboy's."

"*Merde.* I can't keep up. *What* playboy?"

"The one I took the convertible ride with. I thought he might be the *one,* but he's not. Simon is. Or so I think. That's why I'm calling…"

"Lili! Are you expecting me to give you permission to boink the museum guy?"

Lili's voice got small. "Would that be crazy?"

"Frankly, yes. You barely know him."

"But you—"

"This isn't about me, Lili." From a young age, Natalia had rebelled against their father's strict rules, and no punishment he could devise or bribe he extended could convince her to conform to royal expectations. As role models went, she was a wayward wild child. Lili had taken in Natalia's "bad" example, wishing with half her heart to emulate it, and with the other half to please her father and keep the family peace by doing exactly as she was told.

"Father and Amelia would die if they thought you were taking advice from me," Natalia said. She chuckled with wicked intent. "What do you want to know?"

"Should I—or, *how* do I let a man know that I'm interested?"

Natalia hooted. "Lili! You two kissed. Trust me, that's all it takes. He already knows."

"I guess so. Then how do I get him to make the next move?"

"Stick out your boobs and pucker up."

Lili slid off the vanity and turned to look in the mirror. Yes, indeed. Her cheeks were as pink as baseball-card bubblegum. "Actually, I already did that," she whispered into the cell phone, making her sister chortle with congratulations.

"If that doesn't do it, you could always make him jealous," Natalia said when she'd sobered up. "Works for me."

The knocking started again. Lili told Natalia she had to go.

"You're irresistible, sweetie. This Simon guy must be a fool if he doesn't take you up on your offer."

"At first he was irreverent, but now he's trying to be a gentleman. You know how it is."

"Princessaphobia," Natalia said with a sigh, using the term the sisters had coined for the young men who were rattled by their royal pedigree. "Seriously, make Simon see you as a real woman, not a hoity-toity, touch-me-not princess."

Lili gulped. "I'll try."

"But only if you're absolutely sure about him. This seems much too fast to me."

Natalia being cautious? That wasn't what Lili had expected, but she supposed Nat was only trying to be a responsible big sister, for once. There'd always been a strong, loving streak hidden beneath her outrageous leather getups and feisty attitude.

Knock-knock-knock-knock-knock.

Lili opened the door and a woman with a small child rushed into the bathroom, begging the princess's pardon. Lili waved her own apology for taking so long. She stepped outside. "I really do have to ring off, Natalia. Simon's waiting." They said goodbye, and Lili returned to the open-air porch, feeling vaguely unsatisfied. Natalia was usually a fling-me-a-love-song kind of girl.

"What was that all about?" Simon asked, once again rising politely as she approached. He came up around the table to hold out her chair. Lili wished that he'd forget his manners and think of her as only a woman he wanted to get into bed.

She took her seat. "I'm sorry for being so long. I had a sudden need to talk to my sisters."

"Tell me about them." He began urging various dishes on her. She chose the ones that looked most unfamiliar. Cereal in tiny boxes plastered with cartoon characters. Pancakes, similar to crepes, but almost like the flapjacks cowboys ate off tin plates in the old Westerns she used to watch with Natalia on rainy afternoons in their drafty family castle.

"You don't want to hear about my sisters," Lili said, her mouth full of sugary cereal that seemed to be exploding in her mouth. She was almost afraid to swallow it. Mrs. Grundy had always fed them thick English porridge in the morning and dense, tasteless scones at tea. By comparison, American foods were a carnival for the tastebuds.

"Sure I do."

She swallowed. No. Regale him with tales of life in the castle and at their *schloss* in the mountains and he'd always think of her as a princess. "What about you?" she asked. "Brothers? Sisters?"

Simon shook his head, then had to catch the unstable spectacles and resettle them on his nose. "No, I'm an only child."

"Where did you grow up?"

"New York."

"A city boy! How did you ever land in Blue Cloud, Pennsylvania?"

"That's a long boring story." He squinted through the crooked glasses. They matched his crooked face, making Lili's heart squeeze tight with emotion. Why was she feeling so tender toward him?

Two bites of the cereal was enough to satisfy her curiosity. She attacked the blueberry pancakes. "Where did you get your degree? I'd hoped to attend an American university, but my father wanted me to stay closer to home."

"New York University. You could have been an exchange student. That's what I did. Spent my junior year at the university in Cairo, studying the Hyskos at the Egyptian Museum."

"Is there an Egyptian collection at the—the—" Lili held up a finger. "Let me get this straight. At the Princess Adelaide and Horace P. Applewhite Memorial Museum?"

"Not yet."

"Then I don't understand why you're there."

Simon managed a level stare, despite his lopsided appearance. Even his collar was uneven—one point of the collar tucked in, the other sticking out from the neck of his green sweater. "Sometimes we have to do what we have to do. You certainly know that, Princess, from personal experience."

She set aside the pancakes; they sat heavier in her stomach than she'd expected. "Let's talk about you."

"Why? You don't have to be polite. I know I'm a passing peon in your life."

Peon? The man definitely had Princessaphobia. "I'd never be so rude! And you're avoiding the subject."

She peered at a bowl of mushy stuff, not sure what she'd ordered. "Which makes me even more curious."

Simon looked away, staring across the fields, but she saw his flush. His voice came out gravelly. "I'm in disgrace, all right? That's why I'm here, curating necklaces and bracelets at Cornelia Applewhite's bidding. No other museum would have me."

Lili winced. "I'm so sorry. Do you—" Oh, this was awkward! When would she learn to be discreet? "Do you want to talk about it?"

Simon looked mortified by his confession. "No, thanks."

"You really should."

"It's a sorry tale that puts me in a bad light."

She tried to look sympathetic.

"I had a girlfriend then, as well as a dream job. But the girlfriend took advantage of my position at the museum, and I'll never make that mistake again."

Lili hesitated. There was wariness in his eyes when he looked at her. She didn't want that. "Which—trusting a woman, or mixing business with pleasure?" she asked, suddenly realizing that she had more than propriety to overcome.

"Both," Simon said. Lili's face fell, but he wasn't looking. He gulped the rest of his coffee and surveyed the half-eaten dishes that littered the table. "Are you finished? There's still enough food here to feed a family of eight."

She nipped at her bottom lip. "I was wasteful, wasn't I?"

"Don't fret. Americans are accustomed to conspicuous consumption."

"Is that what I did?"

His fingertips settled lightly on her elbow as he

helped her away from the table. "Well, I'd say you've got the conspicuous part down cold—" Simon nodded at the other diners as they walked along the porch "—but your rate of consumption needs some work."

She glanced sidelong at his face. Handsome for a frog. And he seemed greatly relieved that the focus was off him. "What about the bill?"

"That's settled."

"But I was going to treat."

"Princesses don't handle money, do they?"

She laughed. "Where did you get such a silly idea?"

He shrugged. "I thought your 'people' take care of all mercenary details."

They descended the wide wood steps into the green yard. Along the stone stepping path, colorful spring flowers nodded in the breeze. "I'm not a helpless baby, you know. I gave Trey Stone a fine wham-bam-no-thank-you-man when he—" She stopped.

The expression on Simon's face turned from bemused to offended outrage. "Then Stone *did* make a try?"

Lili waved away his concern. "Oh, you know. He busted a move on me."

"That's not what—" Simon shook his head, refusing the distraction. "Tell me," he growled. His jealousy thrilled Lili into goose bumps. Her distrustful, mild-mannered museum wonk was suddenly giving off potent waves of testosterone, the way he had last night. "What did Stone do to you?"

"I already told you. He kissed me—badly. When he tried again, even though I said no, I kicked him in the kneecap, dumped a sixty-eight ounce soft drink on his head and jumped out of his car. Then I sent him away."

Simon blew out a breath. "Good job." He paced away from her. "Last night, you left out the part about the kneecap and the sixty-eight ounce soft drink.'' He paused, kicked a pebble, then looked over his shoulder at her, his forehead sweetly furrowed. ''You went to the drive-in? Did he buy you a hot dog?''

Lili wanted to hug Simon. Instead she dropped her chin and said softly, demurely, ''No, he did not.''

Simon came back and took her hand. ''That's good to hear.''

''Why?'' She tilted her head, watching his face as she climbed into the limo.

He ducked in after her. ''Because you promised me—''

She planted a quick kiss on his lips. ''Promises, promises.''

With his eyes behind the cockeyed lenses going meaningfully dark, he put his hands on her arms and gently pushed her back against the car seat. Paper rustled. Styrofoam squeaked. He stopped and said, ''What's all this?''

The back of the limo was filled with take-out containers. ''Oh, nothing. I ordered a few extra breakfasts.''

He peered at her over his wire frames. ''Still hungry?''

''It's for the Gypsies.''

''The Gypsies?''

''That's where we're going next.'' She bounced forward on the seat and rapped at the privacy panel. ''Drive on, MacDuff!'' The limo pulled out of the parking lot.

''Wait.'' Simon reached for the limo telephone. ''I can't go visiting, I have to go to work.''

''You can spare a few more minutes.'' Lili aimed a twinkling smile at him as she carefully moved his hand off the phone. For a brief moment, the attraction between them flared. Then he drew away from her, clearly remembering his Princessaphobia. "Besides," she said, "aren't *I* your work?"

Simon settled back with his arms crossed, creating barriers that would do him no good. "Yeah, being with you is quite a chore."

She kicked off her heels and nestled beside him on the leather seat, legs curled beneath her so the food containers wouldn't be crushed. "You don't mean that." Her palm smoothed a wrinkle from his sweater. "Now...tell me about your life in America. Do you play baseball? Have you ever worn a cowboy hat? We only have two more days, so I want to know everything...."

THE GYPSY CARNIVAL was in full swing by the time Simon returned to the field where they'd camped. Earlier, Lili had persuaded him to leave her there until she had to make her afternoon appearance at the museum for the ribbon-cutting ceremony. He'd stayed for an hour, keeping an eye on her while he helped a young Romany man named Gabriel set up a temporary fence for the pony ride. Seeing that Lili seemed to be safe, welcomed and thoroughly enjoying herself, he'd finally agreed that she didn't need him as an extra chaperon.

Mrs. Grundy had called Simon's office at two-thirty to say that the princess still wasn't back. Again at three. Then three-fifteen. The ribbon-cutting was scheduled for four. "The princess will need time for her toilette," Grundy had said. "She must be fetched." And she'd sent the limo around to collect Simon to do the fetching.

So there he stood amid the chaos and color of the Gypsy fair, feeling somewhat foolish. He'd scoffed at Lili for having a nanny, not realizing how soon he'd be serving in the same capacity. But it was a bright day, the crowd was lighthearted, and he really couldn't complain about being taken out of the office.

The princess was nowhere to be seen. Simon looked for Jana, Gabriel, even the older woman from the previous night—Magda. The pony ride was being run by a kid of about twelve. Simon scouted the other tents, where games of chance were being run by the men, while the women sold various arts and crafts and hand-embroidered goods. An elderly Rom with a purple sash was operating as a tinsmith out of one of the small wooden caravans. He stood on the steps like an old-time carnival barker, shouted to passers-by, sang, played his fiddle and told tall tales. A crowd had collected, but it seemed less to do with pots and pans than with sheer entertainment value. Simon wanted to stop to listen, but the activity around another tent drew him away.

He peered past the shoulders of a jostling, mostly male crowd. A card game was in progress. Young Gabriel was in the middle of it. There came a sudden shout of triumph. A kid in a high school athletic jacket slapped his cards on the rickety table and raised a fist in a victory salute. Boasting to his buddies and taunting Gabriel, he raked in a small pile of winnings.

Simon moved on. He caught up with Jana, who was selling handmade costume jewelry out of her little caravan, and complimented her on the well-run fair. He asked for Lili. Jana hesitated, then directed him to the fortune-teller's tent. Said Lili had been helping out at various concessions all morning, but had finally taken a break because she'd been wanting to have her fortune told.

The fortune-teller's flagged tent was most prominent.

It had been draped with colorful, shimmering fabrics, hung with tassels and beads. The sign outside read:

Madame Magdalena
Fortunes Read And Truths Revealed
Ten Minutes for Ten Bucks

A young girl wearing beads and a head scarf guarded the entrance. "I'm sorry, sir. You have to wait your turn," she told Simon, shyly skirting her large dark eyes away from his direct query. "Madame Magdalena has a customer."

He leveled his palm at chin height. "A pretty little blonde?"

The girl shrugged. "I can't say."

"She's my wife."

"No, she's not. The princess isn't married—" The girl stopped, mortified that she'd given it away.

"I'm not here to cause trouble." Simon took out his wallet and pressed a twenty into the girl's hand. "I'll pay my way inside." He searched through the filmy drapery for the entrance.

"Wait. You have change," the girl said, but he hushed her and slipped inside the tent. The beads rattled softly. He stopped, letting his eyes adjust to the total darkness.

Soft, dreamy music wafted through the tent. A murmur of voices came from nearby, but Simon's orientation was off. He took one step, then stopped when beads rattled again. He reached out his hands, squinting, and parted more of the gauzy scarves. Drooping fringe tickled his face as he pressed deeper.

The velvety tones of the fortune-teller halted his progress. A faint, hazy light shone through the draperies.

"You will have many grandchildren," Madame Magdalena intoned. "I see them, gamboling in the mountains."

"But what about—"

"*Shh.*"

Complete silence followed, except for the soft strains of the background music. Even the air in Simon's lungs froze.

A minute passed. "What is it?" Lili whispered. "What do you see?"

"I see a man."

Simon peered toward the flickering glow. His eyes had adjusted well enough that he could make out two vague shapes hunched near the light. Could the old fortune-telling fraud see him, as well?

"Is he…" Lili sounded breathless. "Oh, please tell me, Baba Magda. Is he *the one?*"

Simon's ears perked.

"He is the one who will cause you much trouble."

Lili's voice shrank. "Oh." Simon edged closer. "Oh, well. What kind of trouble?"

"Mmm-hmm. Mmm." The fortune-teller hummed to herself, moving her hands over her crystal ball prop. The candlelight wavered.

Simon kept to the shadows of the drapery folds, but he was close enough now to see through the last remaining barrier—a curtain of faceted beads.

"Terrible trouble," Magdalena murmured.

"Who is the man? Is his name Simon?"

His eyes widened. Did Lili *want* it to be?

"The name is hazy. It's not what you think…"

Lili's shoulders slumped. "Not Simon?"

He wasn't sure if he should be gratified or not.

"This man…he is…" The fortune-teller lifted her

hands in surprise. "Ah. I see now. He's tall. Very tall. Very handsome. Very dark."

Simon made a face. *Trey Stone. Tall, dark and hairy. Every girl's dream.*

"I know who it is," Lili said, her tone flattened. "I've already met him." She paused. "You're sure you don't see Simon in there?"

"I do see something else."

Big surprise, Simon thought.

The "Madame" went on. "It is small, insignificant." Her mellow voice sharpened. "But rather annoying."

"I don't understand."

"Mmm. 'Tis a tiny creature. Hopping. A leapfrog."

Lili had been leaning over the crystal ball, but now she bolted upright. "A *leapfrog?* You're sure?"

"I'm afraid so, Princess."

Simon rolled his eyes. Lili must have told Jana about both him and Stone, and she'd passed the info on to the fortune-teller. It was the oldest trick in the book.

Lili clapped. "That was amazing! Thank you!" She turned toward the crystal-beaded curtain. "Simon, did you hear that? Come on out, you big oaf. Madame Magdalena will tell your fortune, too."

Busted.

Simon was about to step past the curtain and take his medicine when all hell broke loose. First came the shouts. Then the impact, and suddenly—*whump!*—the tent imploded in a flurry of swirling silks, heavy canvas and a crushing, squirming weight.

7

LILI SHRIEKED.

A tent pole snapped with a loud *crack*.

Simon pushed at the canvas that had fallen on his head and sent him staggering. The two women were also floundering beneath the sagging weight.

"The candles!" Magda shouted. "We'll have a fire."

"Lili—" Simon struggled toward her. "Get out. Crawl if you have to." Something heavy fell against him, knocking him off his feet. Outside the tent, practically on top of him, men grunted and flailed. A fistfight. While grappling, the men must have crashed into the tent, taking it down.

Lili stamped out the candle flames with her feet. "It's all right. No fire."

"Good girl." They moved tentatively in the darkness, reaching for each other. Simon caught her hand by sheer luck; he held on tight. She let out a gasp and came gratefully into his arms.

Voices shouted outside the tent.

"Madame?" Simon held Lili close with one arm and pushed at the canvas with the other. The lightweight scarves were everywhere, impeding his progress.

"I'm here," the fortune-teller said. Simon and Lili pushed toward her voice.

Outside, someone was calling in desperation. "Princess Lili, Princess Lili? Are you in there?" Rodger Wilhelm. Simon hadn't noticed the man when he arrived, but the bulldog must have been on guard nearby.

"One, two, three—*pull*," said another voice, and a section of the canvas peeled back. A sliver of light widened into an uneven gap. Wilhelm rushed inside, tearing through the flimsy fabrics.

"I'm fine," Lili called. The collapsed tent was lifted slightly off their heads and they could see again. She set Madame Magda's chair upright and helped the elderly woman into it. "We're all fine. Just get this stuff off of us before we suffocate."

Simon and Wilhelm worked together to drag the rest of the canvas away, along with others who'd rushed to the scene. A police car was pulling up nearby, the shocks taking a beating as it drove directly across the pasture.

"Thank you." Lili drank in the cool air, squinting into the sunlight. She held out her hand for Simon. He clasped it. "Thank you, Simon."

She looked like a dancer of the seven veils, draped with a panel of sheerest green silk threaded with copper. Pink cheeked, her hair standing on end. Absolutely lovely.

Whatta girl.

"Simon!" She giggled. "I didn't know you're into jewelry. You could be a—what were those girls called? Flappers! You could be a flapper."

He looked down, remembering that in the melee the crystal-beaded curtain had come down around his shoulders. He'd wrenched free, but taken half the beads with him. He lifted a strand and twirled it experimentally. "What do ya think?"

"My tent!" Magda wailed. Her turban had tilted down over her brow. She shoved it back. "My crystal ball!'' She flung her hands in the air. ''This is disaster! What happened?''

''It was a fight,'' Lili's bodyguard said. ''A couple of ruffians plowed into the tent.'' He was shame-faced. ''I'm sorry, Princess. I glanced away for one in-stant—''

Lili patted him. ''Not your fault, Rodger. I wasn't in danger.'' She nosed around the wreckage until she found the crystal ball, which had rolled away, un-harmed.

A crowd had gathered, but they were no longer the center of attention. A portly officer had emerged from the police car. He and Henry were arresting the perpe-trators of the tent collapse. Not surprisingly, they were two of the card players: the blond jock and Gabriel Var-gas, Jana's young, hotheaded cousin, the one Henry sus-pected of being a pickpocket, as well.

It was the jock who fussed and fumed as he was hauled away. ''He cheated me! That dirty Gypsy cheated me!''

Henry had the cuffs on Gabriel, who stood silently, his expression closed and dark. Jana Vargas was round-ing on the police chief, hair and skirts flying, blood in her eye.

Simon caught Wilhelm's attention. ''We'd better get the princess out of here.''

''RESCUED FROM the brink of disaster,'' Lili said, with-out altering the cordial smile that had taken over her face. She nodded and murmured thank-yous as a group of women passed by, congratulating her and Simon on a fine exhibit. ''I told you it would be all right. It always is.''

Simon straightened his tie, a subdued navy silk this

time. He and the princess had arrived extremely late for the ribbon-cutting, delayed not only by the tent's collapse, but by four mysteriously flattened tires on Henry's car. No one except Corny had seemed to mind. Lili had been so very sweet and charming about her apologies. The ceremony itself had gone off with only one hitch—Trey Stone was in attendance. He'd even had the gall to chat up the princess, though he'd made a quick exit when Simon had aimed one of the security guards at him out of sheer orneriness.

"You have extensive experience with pulling miracles out of your hat, I take it."

"Not enough." Lili glanced at Simon, then reached over to give his tie a tug. "My father doesn't trust me on my own that often."

"I wonder why."

Her lips curved as she winked at him. "You cannot blame this latest incident on me. I was merely an innocent bystander."

"You shouldn't have stayed at the Gypsy fair as long as you did."

"But I was having so much fun."

Simon nodded at a thumbs-up from one of the town's bigwigs, a furniture-store tycoon who, by coincidence, wore the world's worst toupee. Thick and curly as a shag carpet. Not even competition with the Tower of Hair would make Simon stoop so low.

Mrs. Grundy peered past Lili's shoulder to put in her two cents; she'd been hovering ever since the princess had returned from the upset at the encampment. "Royal responsibilities must always take precedence, Your Serene Highness."

Lili's smile wavered. "I never seem to remember that."

A rush of sympathy hit Simon. She was a young woman, why shouldn't she act like one?

He touched her waist, moving her toward the lobby. The crowds had thinned somewhat, but he intended to stay to the last and then close the museum himself. What was left of his reputation was on the line; he could afford no slipups at the most important exhibit of his comeback, such as it was.

"I can't leave yet, but there's no need for you to stay, Lili. You've done your duty—and beautifully, if I may say so."

Her serious expression lightened. "Yes, you certainly may."

He glanced at Grundy, several steps away. The nanny was dressed in a charcoal jacket and skirt that was several sizes larger and several shades darker than Lili's conservative, tailored suit, but otherwise practically identical. Almost like matching mother-daughter outfits, except that Lili's vivid beauty couldn't be contained by a few yards of pale gray worsted wool.

He took her hands. "You are beautiful."

She drew in a breath, her eyes shining with pleasure. "And I would be honored if you'd—"

A braying voice interrupted Simon's request. "Hail the conquering hero!"

Simon let go of Lili's hands. "Cornelia."

The mayor descended upon them. "Excellent exhibit, Simon. When you two were so late in arriving, I did worry that there would be another screwup, but it appears that you've come through with flying colors. *This time.*"

Simon winced. *Thanks, Corny.* Everyone within earshot had heard...and with Cornelia Applewhite, earshot was measured in acreage, not meters or feet.

Corny sailed to a stop, grabbed Simon's hand and pumped it vigorously. Her coxcomb's fringe bobbed. "Good job, young man, good job. Horace P., my esteemed grandfather, would be proud."

"As would Princess Adelaide," Lili put in with a tease of a smile.

"Indeed!" Corny shook the princess's hand, then Mrs. Grundy's. "I shall send my gratitude to the palace, as well."

"Report cards for both of us," Simon murmured to Lili, under cover of Grundy's reply to the mayor. Lili's eyes glittered with private enjoyment. His admittedly dented confidence soared.

"I'm about to take the princess back to the hotel," Mrs. Grundy was saying. She signaled to the bodyguard, who'd been extravigilant since the unfortunate tent collapse at the Gypsy fair.

"Ah, but I am hosting an informal post-exhibit gathering at my home. Cocktails and munchies. I had hoped the princess would consider attending...?"

"Perhaps another time, dear woman," Grundy said, going into brisk British governess mode.

At the same moment, Lili spoke up. "Simon, are you going?"

"Of course he is," Corny said heartily.

Lili smiled at the mayor. "I'd love to attend. Although it will have to be a brief appearance. I've had a full day. I'm sure you understand."

Corny bowed her head. "We shall be honored to have you for even a short time, Your Serene Highness."

"Please, I'd rather you called me Princess. Or just Lili. As you may have noticed, I'm not a stickler for protocol." She aimed a big-eyed stare at Simon.

His chest hitched, trying to hold in a laugh at the magnitude of her understatement.

Lili took his hand and led him away, leaving Grundy to handle details with the mayor. "Why did you accept?" he asked. "You have no idea how deadly Corny's little get-togethers are. Picture a couple of dozen dead bores, all of them as lively as a Grant Wood painting."

Lili looked quizzical.

"Do you know American Gothic? The farm couple with the pitchfork and the grim expressions?"

"Oh, yes. The sourpusses. Ever since my first class in Art History, that's how I've pictured my distant Pennsylvania cousins. My grandmother Adelaide came from farm folk, you know."

"Do you still have family in the area?"

"Supposedly there are a couple of elderly ladies, the last of the line. I'd hoped to meet them on this trip, but events have been rather hectic so far. They were invited here today, but I didn't see them."

Mrs. Grundy caught up. "I've made the arrangements, Princess. The limo's at your disposal."

Lili looked at Simon. "Meet you there?"

She was up to mischief; he felt it viscerally. And his blood sang with anticipation, even though he'd meant to approach the remainder of the weekend with utmost caution. However, a command performance was a command performance. He couldn't avoid Lili any more than he could sleep at the museum round-the-clock. At some point, he'd have to trust the expensive alarm system and the security guards to do their jobs, just as he'd have to trust his growing lust not to overtake his resolutions to keep away from females who seemed innocent, but turned out to be treacherous manipulators.

"I'll stop by as soon as I get a chance," he said.

Lili shook his hand, very solemnly, then tilted her cheek at him.

He took the cue and leaned down to kiss it. "Don't forget our date," she whispered. "I'm in the mood for hot dogs."

"How DID YOU MANAGE to ditch the bodyguard?" Simon asked a couple hours later, when he and Lili had escaped from Corny's deadly dull party with their pulse rates intact. Barely.

"I didn't." Lili spoke out of the corner of her mouth. "Check the mirror."

Simon maneuvered his practical Volvo wagon out of its parking spot in front of the venerable Applewhite mansion. Lili also glanced over her shoulder. Sure enough. As soon as they hit the street, the limo glided into place behind them like a sleek black shadow.

"What should I do?" Simon asked. "Give them a chase?"

Lili was tempted, but she remembered Amelia's admonitions in time. "No," she sighed. "Let them trail us. That'll keep Rodger from butting in on our date."

"Do you always take bodyguards on da—" Simon's voice cracked a little "—dates?"

"Frequently." *Always,* if her father had his say.

"That must be the pits."

"The absolute peach pits," she said, then threw in a flirty eyelash flutter. She'd noticed that coquettish tactics made Simon turn geeky, as if he'd been catapulted back to awkward adolescence. He couldn't even say the word *date* without going red. And then there were all those awful pickup lines!

On Simon, though, geeky was cute. She was rapidly

forgetting why she'd ever thought a playboy type was preferable.

"It does put a damper on certain activities," she admitted, giving his leg a not entirely innocent pat. He wasn't as skinny as she'd initially believed. Beneath his baggy suits was firm muscle and the honest-to-goodness washboard stomach he'd displayed in that towel the other morning. She'd gotten to play her fingertips across the hard ridges a second time when she'd plucked at his pajama top the previous evening. And *she* had become a tad geeky herself at the contact, even though she'd mostly managed to contain her urge to blush and giggle like a teenager with a crush.

Simon's fingers clenched on the steering wheel. "Luckily we're only having hot dogs. Can't get more innocent than that."

"At the drive-in movies," she added with an airy insouciance. This should be fun.

His body gave a 90-volt jerk. "The drive-in? How do you know about the drive-in?"

"Didn't you mention it?"

"Don't think so." He sounded wary. "Oh. I remember. What I meant was the drive-in restaurant, not the drive-in movie."

"They both sound like fun, but I prefer the movie."

"Umm, maybe that's not such a good idea."

She turned toward him. There were times it was advantageous to look as pure and unassuming as a pink satin powder puff. "Why?"

"The drive-in—" He tugged at his collar, loosening the tie. "In America, drive-in theaters have this reputation for..."

"Bad movies?"

"Yeah, that, too."

"What else?"

Simon clicked on the car's headlights. "It's getting dark."

"I hear that's an important element for enjoying a drive-in movie." She nodded hopefully. "I've never been, Simon, and I'd really like to go. The entire point of this trip was to experience Americana at its purest."

"I thought you came to be my guest of honor."

She laughed. "That's another way of putting it."

He gave her a look. "You already know about drive-ins, don't you?"

"Yeah, sure," she said in an American accent.

"And you still want to go?"

"Yeah, you betcha."

"Knowing that it's going to lead to..." He started to blush again.

"Heavy petting?" she said with a blink.

He coughed. "I haven't heard that expression in years."

"What's the current lingo?"

"I wouldn't know. I've never been hip to the jive talk."

She stared straight ahead, trying to keep a straight face. "Frankly, I'm intending to enjoy the full spectrum of the drive-in experience."

Simon kept driving, and when she snuck a quick look at him, he didn't appear geeky in the least. He was her handsome prince again. Wings fluttered in the pit of her stomach. Suddenly the interior of the car seemed too small. The air too thick. She certainly hoped that drive-in movies lived up to their reputation.

The sky was dusky as they pulled into the graveled parking area of the drive-in. Lili goggled. An immense movie screen was positioned before them, silent and blank. The lot was filled with a small sea of scattered vehicles. Simon explained that in the early years the movie's soundtrack had been broadcast over speakers hooked to open car windows, which was why abandoned metal poles were arranged in row after row across the lot. Now they could tune their car radio to a special frequency for the show. He parked midway, not too close, but not so far back that they looked as if they had only one thing on their mind.

Even though they did.

Lili had forgotten about her chaperon until the limo pulled in beside them, drawing notice from the restless audience milling around the lot, waiting for twilight. A group of teenagers slowed as they strolled by the car, as if they expected a movie star to emerge. Several jokers tooted their horns. A couple on their way to the concession stand stooped to peer in the darkened windows.

Lili groaned to herself. Discreetly, she waved Rodger and the chauffeur away, hoping that Simon was too involved in tuning the car radio to notice. She didn't want him to inhibited by her escort, as so many of her dates had been. His distrust of women was enough to deal with.

When he looked up, she moved her hand to hair, twirling a short lock of it. The limo cruised by them like a menacing shark, silent except for the gravel crunching beneath its wheels as it circled and parked one row back. No missing *that*.

She smiled bravely. "I'll bet you've never brought a date *and* her limo to the drive-in before."

"I've never even brought a—" His voice halted. "Never mind."

A date?

After her odious spit-take with Trey Stone, lady killer, Lili was rather pleased by Simon's seeming ineptitude. She didn't expect him to be as inexperienced as her, of course, but knowing that maybe he was nearly as thrilled to be here, a little nervous and awed, gave her a very good feeling.

She folded her hands in her lap. "What next?"

He turned the volume of the radio down. It was broadcasting Muzak, with the occasional interruption to urge the customers to partake of the tasty delights of the snack bar.

"I guess it's hot dog time. Are you hungry?"

"You betcha!"

They headed over to the concession stand, joining families and young lovers and rowdy teenagers alike. Rodger followed. Lili tried to ignore him, although she hoped he had plenty of cash for his own junk-food bonanza. The cement-block walls of the concession stand were decorated with bright cartoon blowups of ice cream cones, chocolate bars, hot dogs, popcorn and soda.

Simon saw her eyes widening. "This time, I'm ordering for you," he said. "Remember, I saw you in action this morning."

"But it all looks so yummy!" She stared into the cardboard tray of a passing customer. "Except…what's that gooey orange stuff?"

"Nacho cheese."

"I'll stick to hot dogs." She sniffed the greasy air. "And popcorn, please."

Soon they were loaded up with food. "Now I know why Americans have a reputation for being well-fed," Lili observed. "This stuff is fattening." Simon put the food trays on the car hood and held the door for her.

He'd taken off his jacket and tie and was in baggy pleated trousers anchored by a narrow belt, and a wrinkled button-down shirt with rolled-up sleeves and an unbuttoned collar. As she climbed into the car, she had to make an effort not to balance herself with a hand on his trim midriff.

"You're in shape," she said when he came around to the other side and slid behind the wheel. "Do you work out?"

"Not so much. I have a weight bench at home and I swim at the—" he passed her a paper-wrapped hot dog "—Y."

"Because you look good," she said, munching on popcorn.

"What?" he said.

"That's why I asked."

"Oh. No. I swim at the Y." He drew the letter in the air. "The YMCA. It's an organization with athletic facilities."

"I get it. I was only teasing. The Village People, yes?"

He laughed. "Yes."

They settled in with their food, eating while they watched the small-town crowd pass back and forth, waving to their neighbors, laughing and joking. The sky deepened into twilight; stars began to pop out. A shaft of light beamed from the camera at the top of the concession stand, cutting through the darkness. The screen flickered to life.

While previews played, Lili chewed her hot dog. She'd loaded it with every condiment available. Spicy, tangy flavors burst on her tongue; she couldn't quite decide if she liked it, but it was certainly unique, far bypassing the pale imitation hot dogs she'd tried at various tourist spots in Europe. A long slurp from her soda washed the last bite down. "That was interesting," she said, wiping her mouth with one of the paper napkins Simon had left on the dash.

"Want the rest of mine?"

"No, thanks. I'm full."

"Already? You've barely touched your popcorn. And we have all this candy."

"Later," she said, smiling. "The sugar will sweeten my breath."

Simon looked at the hot dog suspended halfway to his mouth. He set it aside. "Onions."

"Go ahead. I had onions and relish and mustard. I passed on the sauerkraut, though. I can get that at home." She focused on the screen. "What movie are we seeing?"

"Something called *Teenage Wasteland*. I've never heard of it, but I think it's a teen comedy. The second movie, *Midnight Riders,* has a lot of motorcycle stunts and fistfights." Simon scrunched behind the wheel. "Like we didn't get enough of that this afternoon."

"I hope Gabriel isn't in too much trouble."

Simon glanced at her. "Did you meet him?"

"Jana introduced us. She's worried about him getting involved with illegal—oh, I shouldn't say. You're on Henry Russell's side. Jana doesn't trust him."

"It's not a matter of sides," Simon protested, before he stopped midstream and switched topics. "You really enjoyed yourself, hanging out with the Gypsies?"

Lili sighed. "I loved it there. But it's not my life." She scanned the lot, which had grown quieter now that the double feature was starting. "Neither is this…"

"We should remember that," Simon murmured, tapping his fingers on the wheel.

Oh, let's not, she wanted to say, but then she caught sight of the limo in the passenger side mirror. Rodger had a clear view directly inside Simon's car. Unless they fogged up the windows so much he couldn't see inside.

Hmm. She turned her head and blew a big breath directly on the glass.

Opening credits were zooming on and off the screen, red and yellow against amorphous, moving shapes that gradually grew sharper. "I've never heard of any of these actors," Lili was saying, when suddenly a hand came into focus, sliding up inside a cheerleader's sweater. She blinked in surprise. The camera coasted over the cheerleader's shapely leg as it curled around a male's blue-jean clad rear end. The girl's pom-poms rustled.

Simon cleared his throat. He took off his glasses and polished them on his shirt. "I should have warned you that teenage comedies are often...uh...kind of raunchy."

"So I see." Lili couldn't take her eyes from the screen. It was clear now that they were watching a teenage couple make out in the back seat of a convertible. Soulful moans spilled from the radio.

The air inside their own car was heating up even though she and Simon weren't looking at each other. Lili didn't have to look to be as aware of his body as she was of the ones going at it up on the screen. She'd seen explicit movies before. Just not so, well, *large.*

Simon moved restlessly, folding and refolding his legs.

"Would you be more comfortable in the limo?" she asked, still staring straight ahead.

"Hell, no."

"There'd be more room." A warm flush crept into her cheeks. "For you to stretch your legs, is what I meant."

"The only thing more painful than watching this movie with you would be watching it with you and your bodyguard and your chauffeur."

She let out a strained giggle. Her fingers tightened on the box of popcorn in her lap as the action became even more heated. "You're in pain?"

Simon unbuttoned another button at his already open collar. "This is...you know. Awkward. You're a princess, after all."

Thankfully the tenor of the scene changed. The teen-age boy fell headfirst into the front seat while reaching for a condom in the glove box. Suddenly his friends descended, laughing and teasing. The cheerleader stomped away in disgust and the dialogue degenerated into a bunch of dirty jokes about baked goods. Warm apple pie? Lili blushed, clamping her hands on the popcorn box in her lap. Kernels overflowed. "This is dreadful," she blurted. "I can't believe they're talking like that."

"You're too innocent for such crudeness." Simon laughingly put his hands over her ears. "Don't listen." She ducked her head against his chest. Popcorn kernels crunched as she slid closer. "I shouldn't have brought you here," he murmured.

"I wanted to come. But I didn't expect quite this kind of insight into the behavior of the average American male." She squirmed, trying to get a peek. "What are they doing now?"

Simon glanced at the screen. "Still being rude."

Lili had gotten a glimpse from beneath his arm. The make-out scene had disappeared and the story had moved on to a schoolyard location. She had no reason not to watch, except that Simon's arms felt so good around her. She didn't want to move. She took a deep breath and nuzzled against his throat. Her hands crept over his chest, which expanded as he drew in a labored breath of his own. Solid muscle. She inserted a fingertip between his buttons. Warm satin skin. Washboard ripples. Oh, my. Oh, *my!*

He tilted up her chin. "Lili?"

She didn't have to hear the question to know the answer.

Heart swelling with pleasure, she murmured assent.

8

A HUNDRED THOUGHTS ran through Simon's head. Chief among them was that here he was with a princess—a *princess,* for pity's sake!—and that he had no clue what to do next. He knew what he wanted to do. *That* was pure male instinct. But if there was a shred of decency left untouched by his rampaging urges, he could not follow through.

He could not let his hands loose on her body.

He could not press her deep into the seat and climb atop her like a rutting beast, ripping and stripping and flinging away her clothes.

He could not take her. Especially if she was a virgin. Not here, not now...not ever.

Even if she was willing.

And she was.

Lili twined her arms around his neck and lifted her face to his, her rose-pink lips slightly parted. Her skin was fresh and dewy with innocent youth, but her mouth was made for sin. Lush and moist. Velvety soft. Wickedly talented. Every time he looked at her mouth, he became too discombobulated to put more than two words together.

Two words: *One kiss.*

One kiss. He latched onto that thought like a drowning man. Hot need raced through him, raising his temperature to fever pitch, making even his scalp sweat. He could allow himself one kiss.

She was already filling his arms, all soft and curvy and sweet-smelling. Somewhere in between the Apple-white's party and here, she'd removed her jacket to reveal a silk blouse. The collar lay open against the smooth column of her throat and delicate collarbone. Several buttons were undone. A peaches-and-cream vee of skin drew his gaze lower, to where pale blue silk had pulled taut over her breasts. His palms itched to touch them; he tightened his hold on her slender waist instead.

Carefully he lowered his mouth toward hers. One kiss, one fairy-tale storybook magical kiss.

Briefly he thought of last night, in the patrol car.

Okay. One *more* kiss.

Their lips met. This time, there was no moment of awkward adjustment. They moved together in perfect harmony, melting and stroking…soft, wet caresses…a butterfly flicker of tongues. Lili made a purring sound in her throat and he moved one hand to the back of her head, holding her gently in place as the kiss became deeper, richer, hungrier.

So, he thought with a vague sense of satisfaction, *this was rapture.*

He hadn't known.

The windows were foggy by the time he withdrew from Lili's clinging mouth. So were his glasses, blurring the edges of her face. She blinked her dark doe eyes and licked her lips, leaving them glistening with moisture. His lungs constricted at the sight, misty as a dream but still sharply real.

She was panting shallowly. "Please, sir, may I have another?"

"I'm not sure—"

"I am." She lifted off his newly purchased one-hour-while-you-wait glasses and he let her without a second thought because he could always buy another pair, while *this,* being with Lili, was a once-in-a-lifetime experience.

With a small sound of enjoyment, she brushed her mouth over his. His control peeled back like a banana skin, and he took her in his arms with a deep, grateful groan.

"I do so want the full treatment," she whispered against his mouth, an instant before the heat between them escalated into a wildfire. He wouldn't have been surprised if steam came from their pores. No wonder the windows were opaque and cloudy, trickling with moisture.

He brushed a thumb across her nipple and it sprang into a tight bead beneath the silk. "Do that again," she said in his ear, refreshingly open about her desire. Her excitement. Her quest for sensual adventure.

She reached for his hand. "Touch my bare skin."

The buttons of her blouse gave way, revealing a lace-edged ivory satin slip with her small, plump breasts spilling out the top. By then, his mind was a blank. All focus was on the sensation and pleasures of her body pressed to his. The wonder in her luminous eyes.

She closed them when he placed a palm over one breast. He twisted his wrist, sliding his fingers beneath the slip, past a sheer, stretchy bra. Her nipple was small and stiff between his fingertips and he squeezed it lightly, teasingly. She gasped, then moved into the provocative caress, rolling her shoulders like a cat. His fingers spread to cup all of her. She was incredibly soft and warm. And he was hard—rock hard.

Tap, tap, tap.

In one motion, a startled Simon tore his hand away from Lili's breast and jerked his body upright, banging himself against the steering wheel. *Yee-owch.* He dropped down hard, crunching the half-filled popcorn box beneath him.

The knock came again. A persistent rapping against his steamed-up window.

"Damn," he said, as the hot rush of his blood cooled rapidly. But not rapidly enough. "Lili?"

She was making small, frantic squeaks as she buttoned up her blouse. Flushed, she looked at him and nodded, then rubbed her mouth vigorously with the side of her hand, as if that would take away the freshly kissed, slightly swollen look of it.

Ignoring the persistent tapping, he touched her warm cheek, tucked a wayward curl behind her ear. "Don't look so guilty, sweetheart."

She nipped her bottom lip. "That's not guilt. That's delight."

He wanted to kiss her again, but the knocking wasn't stopping. "Mr. Tremayne? Simon Tremayne? Open this window right now."

Simon rolled the window down several inches. Cool air poured into the car's notably heated interior. Rodger Wilhelm's bulldog face filled the space. "That's better." He shot Simon a dagger-eyed look. "Just checking up on you, Princess Lili. Keeping you in my sights. Are you all right? Did you need anything?"

"Like what?" Simon muttered. *"A condom?"*

Lili heard him. She blinked, her blush spreading at the noticeably similar circumstances to the opening scene of the movie. But then she hitched up her shoulders, looked straight at Wilhelm and said, "Privacy," in a rather firm tone.

The bodyguard's face receded. "Sorry, ma'am. Just doing my job."

"Yes. Thank you, Rodger. I appreciate your concern. But as you can see, I'm perfectly safe—" She caught Simon's grin. "Perfectly *fine*." She flicked her fingers at the bodyguard. "Go back to the limo." She glanced at the screen. A group of boys were lurching spastically to peppy music. "Enjoy the movie."

"As you wish, Princess." Wilhelm withdrew, but not without aiming another warning glare at Simon.

He pressed the toggle to raise the glass. The windows were still fogged around the edges, but Wilhelm could see inside if he peered, which he did, circling around the car and bending at the waist, looking through the rear window as he slowly backed toward the limo.

Simon eyed Lili. "Does that always happen?"

"Rodger's very protective."

"Are you—" He stopped. He couldn't be so blunt. *She's a princess, you idiot. She deserves special treatment.*

Which was pretty much the message the bodyguard had wanted to send. Like a splash of cold water. Or a steering wheel in the groin.

Lili handed him his glasses, unbroken and unmangled. "Am I…?"

Holding the spectacles loosely in his hand, he shook his head. He didn't want to know. Either way would be trouble for his future peace of mind.

"Am I pure? Am I untouched? Am I a—*gasp!*—virgin?"

He gritted his teeth.

"Yes, I am." Lili sighed. "And it's quite annoying." She went on, perkily oblivious to his inner struggle. "I've had my chances, but not just anyone will do, you see. I want my first time to be memorable. In a good way.'' She tilted her chin at the movie screen, on which someone was stripped naked and running through a crowded gym holding a volleyball over his private parts. Her lids lowered lazily and he knew she wasn't seeing the movie. "I've dreamed about the qualities I want in a Prince Charming. Handsome, strong, clever and brave, for a start. But most importantly, he must be…'' She gave a girlish shiver. "He must be exceptionally skilled in the art of lovemaking.''

Simon knocked his forehead against the wheel. He couldn't take it.

"I know I'm asking a lot,'' Lili breathed, her voice husky and sexy and as frustrating to his libido as a splinter under his skin. She brushed popcorn bits off the car seat and moved closer. Her floral-and-musk female scent clouded his brain. "Simon…what do you think? Can you help me?''

Holy Tutankhamen! She was going to ask *him?*

He lifted his head, prepared to be a gentleman.

What that meant—yes or no—he wasn't sure.

"Please, Simon,'' she said, with a breathless ardor that went straight to his heart like an arrow. *"Will you help me find my Prince Charming?''*

The soft question was a sledgehammer in disguise. Simon was so shocked that it was not *him* she wanted that his fingers clenched reflexively and he snapped the bridge of his glasses in two.

SIMON DIDN'T SAY A WORD.

He put the broken glasses on the dash. He started up the car and drove away from the drive-in, eliciting several honks and catcalls in his wake. Lili, flustered, hoisted herself off the seat to look behind them at the diminishing screen. Apparently the chauffeur was slow to react; they'd left the limo behind.

Simon's car swerved onto the highway. She dropped down and reached for the seat belt. "Are you angry about something?"

His mouth twitched. "No."

"Because I—"

He trod on the accelerator, throwing her back against the car seat with a *whump*. "You are mad," she said, struggling to sit up again. She checked the road behind them. Lights, oncoming. The limo was chasing them down. Poor Rodger probably thought that Simon was absconding with her for illicit purposes.

Oh, she wished that he were!

Asking him to find her a Prince Charming had been a stupid tactic. She'd only said it because she'd suddenly felt really pitiful to be begging a man to take her to bed, and at the last second had thought of Natalia's advice. Not the part about sticking her boobs out, though that had worked well enough. The "make him jealous" part.

"There's no reason for me to be mad," Simon said, practically spitting, he was so mad. His eyes were narrowed into slits, but that might have been because he was trying to see. "We'd only spent the last fifteen minutes making out at the drive-in movies. That certainly didn't make me a candidate for your—your—"

Secretly thrilled by his vehemence, Lili waited in patient silence. Maybe Natalia had been right about the jealousy thing; she *was* known as the naughtiest of the Three Jewels. There was no end to her male admirers.

"Your ideal Prince Charming," Simon jeered. "After all, I'm only a frog, isn't that right?"

"Yes. That's why I had to kiss you."

"And I didn't oblige with a transformation."

She pressed her knuckles to her mouth, thinking of the way he became more handsome and dear to her heart every time she saw him. She didn't even mind his cowlick and crooked features. He was quirky. She liked quirky. More and more and more.

"Neither did Trey Stone," she said.

Simon's brows angled down. "You're lumping me into his category? I thought we were doing rather well, back there at the drive-in. You didn't have any complaints."

"I'm very polite."

He didn't respond to that, though she thought he might have growled, very softly in the back of his throat. No ribbits tonight.

He glanced in the rearview mirror at the approaching lights, then lowered one of the back windows to clear the remaining vapor. "Where are you taking me?" Lili asked.

"To the hotel, of course."

"Do we have to?"

"I don't see any reason to prolong my mis—the evening."

She didn't want him to be miserable, but perhaps a little anxiety—just a smidgen—would keep him on his toes. If she'd told him his kisses rocked her socks and she couldn't imagine wanting to be with another guy ever again, he'd become too sure of her, even complacent. Men were such complicated creatures when it came to maneuvering them into bed in such a way that they believed it was all their idea.

"This is my second night spent riding in cars with boys," she observed, as he slowed to make the turn into the town. "It hasn't been all that I'd been led to believe.

Could it be the wrong boys, do you think?'' As soon as the words were out, she regretted them. A bit brutal.

Simon shrugged as if he didn't care. "Or the wrong cars." He gestured behind them. "I'm sure your Prince Charming will arrive in a limo."

"Limos are a bore. At home in Grunberg I have a cute little Peugeot, all mine. Bought and paid for with my own—"

"Trust fund?"

"No. My own paycheck."

He frowned. "You work?"

"Is that so surprising? I have two jobs, actually. The one I love is my position as publicity director of the Grunberg Art Society. The one that was thrust upon me is being a princess."

"Tough job," Simon scoffed, but he didn't sound entirely unsympathetic.

"It's not digging ditches, but try it sometime. Put on pantyhose and heels and stand for two hours in a receiving line shaking hands with dignitaries who smell like mothballs, Schnapps and Limburger cheese. I'm just lucky that most of the duties fall to my older sisters."

They'd arrived at her hotel, The Windermere, a modest six-story brick building with a portico out front flanked by topiary urns. Simon slowed, pulling into the open space in front of the door. Their shadow, the limousine, followed closely. Rodger would be at her door straightaway. She'd have to work fast.

"Thank you for a wonderful evening, Simon."

"Are you only being polite again?"

She couldn't toy with him on that point; his eyes were confused even though he was acting as if it didn't matter. "No, I truly mean it. You've fulfilled one of my fantasies. Splendidly."

His brows cocked. "The hot dogs?"

"Those, too." She leaned in to give him a quick peck, but when their lips got close, an outside force took control, urging her to linger, breathing in the fragrance of his skin, basking in his delightful warmth and the feel of his mouth barely touching hers. He wasn't even trying and she was ready to strip off her clothes and jump him!

"Here comes your bodyguard," Simon said, setting her away.

"I'll see you tomorrow night, then...at the ball?" The formal dance would be her last official duty in Blue Cloud.

His expression was pained. "I suppose so."

"There will be all sorts of candidates attending, hmm? And I'll be free to dance and flirt and choose among them...."

It took Simon all of five seconds to swallow that one. "Have a good time," he said, choking on the words.

She prodded him again; Rodger was hovering outside her door. "Simply scads of data for my survey, waiting to be collected...." She puckered her lips ever so slightly.

That did it. Simon jumped in. "I could take you."

"Oh?"

"It's not right, you being unescorted. Just for show, I could be your—" he swallowed "—date. Your date. I'll be your date."

She beamed. "That would be lovely."

Rodger approached, having had enough with the delay.

Simon caught Lili's chin between his thumb and finger and turned her face to his. Her breath caught in her chest; she wasn't intentionally sticking it out again.

"One thing," he said. "If I'm your date, you won't be kissing anyone but me. Put the survey on ice."

Lili agreed with a demure nod.

It wasn't often that she got *exactly* what she wanted.

"SO FAR, SO GOOD," Simon said in his office the next morning, moving back behind his desk after seeing the head of staff-security out the door. "But tonight will be the biggest test of all."

"Whose idea was it to hold this dumb dance in the museum anyhow?" Henry asked from the sofa. His feet were propped up on the coffee table and he was idly scratching the back of one wrist where a bumpy red rash protruded from his cuff. Poison ivy, was his explanation. He'd been grumpy during the entire security consultation, which wasn't like him at all. Partly, Simon blamed the fact that the chief had been forced to release Gabriel Vargas since there was still no evidence he was the pickpocket and the other charge was only a misdemeanor. But the rash and the black eye might have had something to do with it, as well.

"Whose idea do you think? The mayor's, of course."

Henry grunted. "Asking for trouble."

"The Windermere's facilities weren't grand enough for Corny. And we couldn't entertain a princess in the basement of the local Moose Lodge."

Henry's eyeballs swiveled toward the desk; the left one looked very white against his discolored skin. "I hear you did pretty good entertaining the princess at the drive-in movies."

"I hear you got that black eye when Jana Vargas decked you."

"Not so. I walked into a lamppost."

Simon was skeptical. "Is that anything like walking into a door?"

"The very same. Did you get to second base?"

"Fouled out."

Henry produced a rusty chuckle. "I oughta show you some of my better pitches."

"Betcha that Jana's a crack hitter, huh?"

"Enough." Henry frowned while he fingered the tender skin around his eye. "Let's get back to the security detail."

Simon nodded. He needed to put his confusion about Lili aside and concentrate on pulling off the gala without incident. Initially, he hadn't believed that the museum would be a target during a major party, but according to Henry, crowds meant confusion. And confusion was a thief's best friend.

"Your staff is all checked out and fully informed," Henry said. "In addition, I'll be here tonight, along with two of my men—"

"Corny doesn't want uniforms."

Grimace. "Yeah, I know. We'll be in tuxes."

"Stag?"

Henry coughed. "Uh, no. I asked Jana Vargas to go with me—figured it was the best way to keep an eye on her. Strictly a professional duty."

"Right," Simon said.

"And you?"

"I'm escorting Princess Lili."

"Fancy." Henry whistled. "We're talking big leagues."

Simon grinned. "Strictly a professional duty."

"Right," Henry said.

THE DRESS LAY on the bed, shrouded in plastic and tissue paper. Lili, fresh from her bath, looked at it with very little anticipation. If she'd paid sufficient attention beforehand instead of concentrating on peanut butter, hot dogs and dashing American playboys, she wouldn't be stuck wearing a gown chosen by her former nanny. The woman had a kind soul, but she was no fashion maven. If Amelia and Prince Franz had their way, Lili would wear nothing but turtlenecks, tweeds and chiffon ruffles more suited to the mother of the bride than a modern-day princess.

Amelia entered. "Are we ready for the gown?"

"No. There's plenty of time yet." Lili slouched into an armchair by the window. She gazed outside, taking in the tranquil scene as the setting sun threw long shadows over the quaint brick and board buildings of downtown Blue Cloud. The small town had been bustling earlier, festive with banners celebrating the fiftieth anniversary of their hometown girl's marriage to a prince. Lili had wanted to be out and about, just another tourist, but everywhere she'd gone she'd been fussed over. The entire town had Princessaphobia. The best part of the day was when Simon had come by to take her to a baseball game in the park. While they'd chomped on the peanut-butter sandwiches he'd brought along, she'd pretended to ogle the ballplayers, and he'd pretended not to notice. In between they'd talked about all sorts of things—Grunberg politics, Simon's degrees, favorite books and movies, the color of the sky and the shape of the clouds. Chatting and laughing with Simon, she forgotten to be self-conscious. Maybe he had, too.

Lili sighed, needing…something. Reassurance, perhaps. Familiarity. "You knew my American grandmother, Amelia. Tell me about her."

Taking the other armchair, Amelia was as tidy after a full day's activities as she'd been that morning. Never a hair out of place, for the beloved Mrs. Grundy. "Where shall I begin?"

"You know where." Lili smiled. She and her sisters had been raised on stories about their mother and grandmother and the rest of the royal family. Not fairy tales, but magical stories all the same. There was some comfort in their timelessness, even though she now knew they'd been fed sanitized versions.

"Adelaide was only twenty when she met her prince. She was a lovely, gentle girl, with dark hair and dark eyes. Shy and quiet, by all accounts. No one could understand why Prince Rudolf picked young Adelaide out of the swarm of college girls who were touring the castle. It was springtime in Grunberg, and the mountains were were green, fragrant with edelweiss…"

Lili let herself be lulled by the romantic story. There were times Prince Franz blamed his mother Adelaide's American blood for every wayward impulse of his three renegade daughters, but in Lili's memory her grandmother was the most serene woman on the face of the earth. It had been Lili's mother, Marja, a Grunberger by birth, who'd had the fiery temperament. Natalia was most like her. Annie took after their father, athletic and often abruptly outspoken. Lili didn't know where she fit in…except that she tried. She tried very hard, but somehow never quite hard enough. There were too many delightful distractions to stick with a princess's dull duties to protocol and formality.

It was odd to think how she'd initially lumped Simon in with the boring side of her visit to Blue Cloud. When, really, he was the highlight of the trip thus far. She couldn't say she knew him that well, not as well as she'd like to—or *intended* to. After all, it had been less than three days.

Still, he'd become very important to her.

"...and to this day, Prince Rudolf says it was purely a case of love at first sight," Amelia concluded with a bemused little smile. Her eyes were misty. "He knew after one look that Adelaide was his princess."

Lili had reached across to pat the woman's knee—it wasn't often Amelia let her gentler emotions show—when suddenly she stopped.

Love at first sight?

Was *that* why she was so enthralled by Simon? Why he'd transformed from a frog before her very eyes? Why she hated to think of leaving town without reinforcing the bond between them in the most intimate way possible?

Good glory!

And to think, Simon's view of her had frequently been blurred. She did hope he got his glasses fixed for tonight. She didn't want to be in love all by herself.

Lili cleared her throat. "Amelia, do you believe in love at first sight?"

"I believe in the power of magic."

"You *do?*" For all of the sisters' jokes about Amelia Grundy being their fairy godmother, the silver-haired widow had never been given a moment's pause by what she called their "stuff and nonsense." She'd always claimed to be there to attend to the practical matters of the young princesses; spells and enchantments were for witches and little girls whose heads were filled with fairy tales.

"The *power* of magic," Amelia stressed. "Humans can convince themselves of anything."

Lili figuratively fell from her romantic clouds with a

thump. Was that it? Because she longed for a lover, she'd convinced herself that a frog wasn't really a frog?

Amelia rose, brushing away the moment of sentimentality with a brisk clap. "Come sit by the mirror, Princess. I'll begin on your hair."

Lili moved to the vanity and lowered herself onto the brocade stool. "May I have the telephone, please? I need to talk to Annie." She trusted Annie to tell it like it is.

Amelia brought the phone over. Lili dialed, then waited for the overseas line to connect. "I suppose it's three in the morning in Grunberg," she was muttering when her middle sister picked up the phone and said a bleary hello.

"Annie, it's me."

"Nope, it's the middle of the night." Annie yawned.

"I think I'm in love."

Silence. Then Annie said dryly, "Whammo! There's a wake-me-up if ever I heard one. I knew it was a mistake to send you to Pennsylvania on your own."

"This isn't a joke, Annie. I've fallen in love."

"Not in two days."

"It's been three." *Almost.*

Annie chuckled. "Oh, sure. One day makes all the difference."

"It can," Lili said, placing her hand over the mouthpiece to shield her whispered, "Especially if it's one *night.*"

She really had Annie's attention now. "Lili? What does that mean? Last I heard from Natalia, you were having trouble attracting—" She stopped. "Hmm. I guess that problem's been solved?"

"Not fully, if you know what I mean." Lili avoided

Amelia's eyes in the mirror. The older woman picked up a comb and ran it through her hair.

"Listen, kid. You'd better watch out. There are guys out there who think it's good sport to bag a princess. Don't imagine that you're falling in love when it's only lust."

"How do you know the difference?"

"Good question."

Lili let out a little shriek when the comb hit a tangle.

"Is he with you now?" Annie accused.

"Heavens, no! Amelia's doing my hair. Then she's going to torture me with a crinoline and a ball gown."

"There are worse things. Like me in a bridesmaid's dress."

Amelia came at Lili with a steamy curling iron. She ducked and said hurriedly into the phone, "Thanks, Annie. You've been no help at all."

Annie laughed, not insulted in the least. "Any time."

"Don't expect to call *me* for help when you're surrounded by bandits and lawmen in the Wild, Wild West."

"Never gonna happen," Annie said. "And, besides, I know how to take care of myself."

After they said goodbye, Lili meekly submitted to Amelia's no-nonsense hairstyling. While Lili put on her makeup, Amelia went to unveil the gown, which had been delivered wrinkle-free from the hotel dry cleaner that afternoon.

Prepared for the worst, Lili turned to see.

She gasped. The dress Amelia held up by its rhinestone-studded shoulder straps was equal to every fantasy she'd ever had. It was tiny on top, a mere snippet of a lustrous satin bodice in palest blue. Below the nipped-in waist, the skirt billowed out into a ballerina-style extravagance of filmy layer upon layer, each one a different hue, from the underskirt of rich sky blue to seafoam green to the barest whisper of ice blue.

When Lili took the dress and held it against herself, turning to the mirror in awe, the skirt shifted, changing color like the sea. "Amelia, how wonderful! I don't believe it. Where did it come from? Will it fit?"

"Try it on and see."

"Help me." Lili stripped off her robe, revealing her underthings. She stepped into the voluminous crinoline Amelia held out. Once it was fastened around her waist, she lifted her arms to shimmy into the gown as it was gently dropped over her head.

The skirt settled into place like a cloud. Amelia zipped up the back. The bodice was such a precise fit it could have been sewn into place directly upon Lili's body.

She stared into the mirror. "It's perfect. How ever did you do it, Amelia?"

The older woman's eyes gleamed at Lili's pleasure. "I have my ways, young lady. I have my ways."

Lili swished the skirt. "Look! It glistens as if it were sprinkled with fairy dust."

Amelia blinked. She batted a hand at such silly nonsense. "Fiddlesticks. It's only a dress."

"The dress of my dreams." Lili turned and threw her arms around the woman. "Thank you, Amelia. Thank you so much."

After a short while, Amelia excused herself and went to her own room to dress, pausing at the door for one last fond look at the princess in her finery, turning this way and that in the mirror, *oohing* and *aahing* as the dress sparkled.

A fine magic indeed, Amelia thought to herself, smiling with satisfaction as she slipped a tiny vial back into the depths of her worn leather satchel. She straightened, dusted the sparkles off her hands, and set them on her hips with a nod.

If Amelia Grundy had her druthers, her young charge would have an evening that was the stuff of fairy tales.

9

"WHY DO WE SEEM to spend all our time together in cars?" Lili asked once the limo was on its way. The small but stalwart band of media-mongers had descended outside the hotel, seeking a glamorous photo op of the photogenic princess.

Simon glanced at Mrs. Grundy, who sat opposite them. The bodyguard was up front. Lili's companion was looking very librarian-goes-to-the-prom in a long straight navy blue dress topped by a boxy jacket. She sat stiffly with her fingers laced together atop an old-lady pocketbook, the first time he'd seen her without her bulging satchel at hand.

"But they've been nice times, haven't they?" he said, turning his attention to Lili again. Pure and simple, she took his breath away.

She winked. "Maybe even memorable."

It took him a beat to recall what she'd said about how her first lover was required to be memorable, and when he did, it was as if she'd plucked every one of his heartstrings at once. He couldn't help wondering. Did she want *him* to be her lover? A flirty glance, a cozy intimation, and he was a symphony of expectation.

But, no. He was being absurd. She wanted a perfect lover—she'd come right out and said so—and it was terribly obvious that could never be him. A froggy sort of guy didn't go from almost zero success with ordinary women to hitting the jackpot with a princess. It just didn't happen.

Except in fairy tales.

Lili *was* gazing at him with a certain fondness. Her blue gown made a whispering sound as she leaned closer. Her eyes looked deeply into his. His insides stirred. Was she waiting for a kiss?

He angled his head. Her features puckered comically. "What *is* that on your glasses?"

Simon sat back as if he'd been punched in the solar plexus. "Uh...uh...I didn't have time to order another pair of new glasses from the optician, so I—" He pulled off the wire-frames. "It's wire. I wrapped a piece of wire around the nosepiece to hold the two sides together." Sheesh! He was an idiot. He might as well have shown up with a thick wad of tape on his glasses, like the stereotypical nerd. Some date he made for a princess! Even the frogs were going to disown him.

"How clever," Lili said. "It's scarcely noticeable. Is it, Amelia?"

"Not a bit."

Simon shoved the glasses back on. The snipped end of the coil of ultrathin wire pressed into the side of his nose. He'd have a red bump soon. "You're just being polite."

"No." Lili laid her hand over his. She rested her chin on his shoulder, smiling up at him. "I think you look divine."

"Quite handsome," Mrs. Grundy said with a nod.

Simon closed his eyes for a moment. Even trussed up in a tuxedo, he wasn't the kind of man girls dreamed about, he knew that. Lili was being her usual flirtatious self. Tomorrow, she would be gone. And he'd be still be the frog.

"We're here," Mrs. Grundy said as the limo followed the curving road that led to the museum, spotlighted and festooned with its grand opening banners.

Simon looked out the window. The press had beat them, or maybe these were different reporters. It wasn't a teeming crush like the ones he'd seen at Hollywood movie premieres, just a motley band of stringers and freelance photographers, mostly local, hoping for a story or snap that would go national.

Mrs. Grundy departed first, followed by Simon. Only when Lili appeared in her Barbie Dream Gown did the flashbulbs start popping. The reporters called out questions: What did the princess think of America? How was her tongue? Would she sue the museum? Who designed her gown?

Lili stood blinking, her skirts in hand. Although she seemed intimidated, she bravely tried to answer, which only escalated the reporter's fervor. Simon stepped in and took her hand, whisking her away up the broad steps and into the museum.

The party was in full swing. A small orchestra had set up on the open landing of the second floor; strains of a Strauss waltz floated from above onto the small but glittering crowd below. Because of tight space and security concerns, the guest list was exclusive. Platinum Patrons predominated.

"Thank you for rescuing me, Simon." Lili slipped off the satin stole that matched her dress and handed it to Mrs. Grundy, hovering nearby. "I'm not accustomed to that sort of thing."

Simon's mouth had gone dry at the sight of the princess's bare shoulders and arms and smooth, sensuously curved cleavage. "Don't you get the royal treatment in Grunberg all the time?" he rasped.

She touched the tiny diamond that hung from a thin silver chain around her neck, fixing it so it rested in the hollow of her throat. Simon imagined putting his mouth there, feeling her pulse against his tongue, breathing her scent…

"Ah, but you forget," she said. "We're a very tiny country. I'm a little minnow in the large pool of European royalty. When my father isn't on hand, it's usually my oldest sister, Natalia, at the point. I'm mostly overlooked."

"I can't believe that." She was a stunner; not even a blind man could overlook her.

"Believe it." She took his hands, holding them down low as she brought her lips near his. "A little minnow."

His nostrils flared slightly, taking her in. "Meet big toad. Ribbit."

"You see?" She laughed, delighted. "We go together like ham 'n eggs!"

He squeezed her hands. "No more American breakfasts for you, Princess."

Her eyes sparkled as attractively as her dress. "We'll see about that."

Simon was saved from responding by the sweeping arrival of Cornelia Applewhite, in a black gown with a huge bow like a sail at the back. She curtsied. Her solemn, silent escort was whats-his-name Spotsky, who bobbed his head, never taking his mean little eyes off Princess Lili.

"Good evening, Your Serene Highness," Corny brayed. "We are so delighted to have you with us. And looking so gorgeous! All that's missing is a tiara." She nudged Simon. "Shall we crack the display case so our princess can wear the family crown?"

Cornelia saw his stricken expression. "Oopsy daisy! Not a good joke to tell around you, is it? Considering."

Simon attempted a careless shrug. Except for some minor needling, she'd kept the shameful incident from his past hush-hush. Mainly out of self-preservation. She'd been solely responsible for hiring him; his job performance reflected on her.

"You're giving the princess the wrong impression," he murmured, hoping she'd follow his cue and lower her voice.

Corny's head waggled. "I expect she already knows that our curator has a weakness for the ladies."

"Excuse us." Spotsky took her arm. "We've been imbibing on the champagne and it makes us loud."

"Louder," Simon mumbled.

"It's a bridal tiara," said a stern Mrs. Grundy to anyone who was interested. "Only the Brunner brides may wear it. Never, never anyone else. That would be bad luck."

"There's Henry with Jana," Simon said, deflecting Lili's curious stare.

Mrs. Grundy stiffened. "Jana Vargas? What is *she* doing here?"

"Amelia!" Lili was consternated. "Jana has as much right to attend this party as anyone."

Grundy's lips pursed. "I sincerely hope the tiara's safe under lock and key. The Vargases have been trying to claim the diamond for two hundred years."

"With good reason, perhaps," Lili said, arching skeptical brows. "Jana explained their version of the story. They say the diamond was stolen from a Vargas trader years before it was placed in the bridal tiara."

"Poppycock," said Grundy. "The Brunners have always been scrupulously honorable."

Lili shrugged. "Still, there has to be a reason it's called the Vargas diamond."

All the talk about diamonds and thievery was making Simon uneasy. The conversation had cycled out of his control. Should events follow, his career was as dead as a frog floating in a jar of formaldehyde.

He took Lili's elbow. "Let's go see Jana and Henry." *And learn more about the Romany's interest in the diamond tiara.* While Henry had downplayed the pickpocketing incident, Simon feared it was merely the opening salvo of a crime wave. The Romany showing up at the same time as the jewel exhibit was a little too coincidental.

He nodded quickly at Jana and left her to Lili, guiding the police chief off to the side so they could talk out of earshot. "Tell me that we're still secure. Has there been any suspicious activity? What about party crashers?"

"Calm down, man." Henry was as stolid as ever in a tux that strained across his broad shoulders. The instances when he was out of uniform were so rare, even Simon had looked twice at him. "You've got your guard at the door, checking invitations. The alarm circuits are armed. The only thing that could happen now is a natural disaster—"

When had there last been an earthquake in Pennsylvania?

"—and I'm equipped to handle even those." Henry gave Simon's shoulder a manly swat. "You're golden."

"Platinum," he said, watching a couple of the gray-haired donors toddle onto the dance floor, which was simply the central area of the entrance hall, cordoned by velvet ropes.

"Whatever."

"Do you know about Jana's personal interest in the tiara?"

"What?" Henry scowled, clearly unhappy about the slightest possiblity that he was not fully informed.

"Remember? The large stone at the center of the tiara is known as the *Vargas* diamond."

"Yeah, yeah. I knew that." Henry's lids narrowed as he looked suspiciously at Jana. The fresh bruise around his left eye had deepened to purples and blues. "Ms. Vargas continues to insist that she's not after the diamond. I don't believe her."

"That's why you've been hounding her and the cousin and the rest of the Roma…?"

For a moment, Henry looked unsure, which was such a rarity that Simon made special note. He wondered if it had anything to do with Henry's personal interest in Jana, which was as obvious as a black eye, even if the chief was denying it.

Simon was distracted from that train of thought when he sighted a suspicious head off in the distance, moving in the direction of the tiara display. "What about *him?*"

Henry whipped around. "Who?"

"The Tower. Trey Stone."

"I don't see him."

"He wasn't on the guest list," Simon said.

"You're sure of that?"

"You bet." He started off. "I'm going after him."

Henry caught up in a few big strides. "I'll go. I can be less obtrusive."

"I will. I have a bone to pick with him, and I don't give a hoot about obtrusive."

They both went.

"LOOK AT THEM," Jana said to Lili, "racing and pushing like little boys."

"I wonder what's gotten into Simon. As soon as the mayor mentioned the tiara, he froze up on me." Lili stood on tiptoe, trying to see over the crowd. "Should we follow to see what's up?"

Jana tilted her head; she was eye-catching in a unique dress, with an upswept hairdo and long, glittering earrings. "Why not?"

They strolled into the first display room. A bar and buffet of light hors d'oevres were set up to one side of the room. The crowd was thick around it. Not many of the guests seemed to be paying particular attention to the jewel displays, but they stared in appreciation as Lili passed by.

"You're certainly the belle of the ball," Jana said.

"I'd rather be dancing by a campfire."

"Sure."

"It must be wonderful, traveling from place to place, always seeing something new," Lili mused.

"It gets old."

"Does it?" Lili looked closely at Jana, whose embroidered lace dress was vintage. Its cost was probably a fraction of her own ball gown. Likewise Jana's gaudy dimestore jewels and cheap sandals. Yet she was beautiful and confident, equal to Lili in every way. "Would you rather settle down and live a conventional life?"

A startled expression crossed Jana's face. "I never said *that!*"

They paused at the entrance to the inner room. Only a few of the party-goers had ventured this far. Simon and Henry had cornered Trey Stone near the display case that held the Brunner bridal tiara. They seemed to be haranguing him.

Lili swept in. "What's going on?"

"Princess Lili," Trey said gratefully. "I'm so glad to see you. Please tell these two apes where I got my invitation to the party."

Lili fixed Simon with a cool stare. "From me."

He blanched. "I thought—"

She frowned her father's censorious royal frown, an expression of icy, ill-pleased disdain. It had always quelled her and her sisters when they'd been boisterous at inopportune moments.

Simon's jaw clenched. She continued smoothly. "Yes, I asked Trey to attend. After I got a look at the guest list, I knew that if I didn't do something, this party was destined to be as dull as a Grunberg state dinner."

Simon looked sick. He shoved his hands in the pockets of his black pants. "That's the only reason?" he muttered.

Lili almost smiled. *He was jealous.* Served him right! She'd have him begging for the privilege to be her seducer by the evening's end. And then she could finally "submit."

To that end, she turned her attention to Trey instead of cuddling up to Simon the way she wanted. Trey looked like a young Tom Selleck in his tuxedo, complete with dimples and big white teeth. Simon's charms were more subtle. Her gaze slipped away from Trey; she dragged it back again.

"I'm wondering when one of you will wise up and ask me to dance," she said.

Of course, it was Trey who made the first move. He was quick that way. He made a proper gentleman's bow. "Would you do me the pleasure, Your Serene Highness?"

"I'd love to dance with you, sir. But you'll have to remember to call me Lili the way you agreed."

Trey blinked. "Of course."

Lili's gaze wandered toward Simon as she took Trey's arm. He was unhappy. Perhaps even fuming.

Ooh, she loved it when he abandoned his scholarly demeanor to seethe with volcanic manly urges! She hoped it wouldn't be long before he cut in.

"TOOK YOU LONG ENOUGH," Lili said, when Simon finally rescued her from the clutches of the Towering Head of Hair. "Trey was boring me to death with tales of beach volleyball. I thought all tall men in this country played basketball."

"Beach volleyball?" That was odd. Henry's background check on Trey Stone had been as preppy as they came. Beach volleyball was so California. Simon chuckled. "Are you sure you were dancing with Trey Stone from Philidelphia?"

"He lives in L.A., I believe. Said he moved there as a kid after his parents were divorced." Lili cocked her head, her expression amused. "He does have that Hollywood matinee idol look about him, don't you think?"

Simon moved his hand to the small of Lili's back, drawing her closer to him as they danced. Shuffled, really. Even after six lessons at The Howard Bliss School of Dance—"Where Two Left Feet Get Turned Around"—he was no good at ballroom dancing. Although he could do ball changes and jazz hands with the best of 'em.

"Well, Princess, you could always ID him with a kiss."

Lili's lips curved. "You're jealous."

"You betcha."

"Thank you. I was starting to wonder why you left me to dance with Trey for so long. Not to mention Spotsky and a man who trod on my toes every other step."

"Henry and I were going over the updated guest list. You shouldn't have made additions without clearing it with me."

"Nell said I could. And I only added Trey, Jana and Baba Magda, who declined. Oh, and my distant cousins, Jessica and Carlotta Wolf." Lili twisted slightly in his arms, searching the crowd. "Whom I still haven't been introduced to…"

"*You* invited Jana? I thought Henry did."

"Does it matter?"

Simon shrugged. "Probably not. As long as Henry's with her now." He watched the couple in question dance by, locked in each other's arms…and eyes. Damn, even Henry Beer-and-Pretzels Russell knew how to waltz. Simon faltered. This evening wasn't turning out the way he'd prayed. Instead of being on top of the world, he felt exposed and vulnerable. His inadequacies were rife.

Lili had stopped dancing. "Now *both* of you suspect Jana?"

Simon skipped the question. "Tell me about the Vargas diamond. Does Jana's clan have a legitimate claim for ownership?"

"Ohh…not exactly." Lili picked her hand up off his shoulder and waved it airily. "Apparently there's an ancient rumor about the diamond once belonging to the Vargas line. Jana and I talked it over. A few of the Vargases might cling to the story, but they are *not* here to cause trouble. I don't see how you can still believe they came here to Blue Cloud intending to steal it."

"It's not entirely out of the realm of possibility."

Lili set her hands on waist. "You're being stubborn."

"Practical."

"How dull."

"That's me."

"No, it's not, Simon. You underestimate yourself. Is it because of this mysterious incident in your past? What happened? There was a museum theft and you still blame yourself?"

Hot blood rushed through Simon's veins. He took Lili's elbow and led her off the dance floor, skirting the velvet ropes to enter the buffet room. Trey Stone seemed to be following them, but he veered off toward the hors d'oevres when Simon glared.

He focused on Lili's inquiring face. "I told you I didn't want to talk about that."

She gave him a pat. "Everyone makes mistakes, Simon. Good heavens, look at me. Between bee stings, trash cans and kissing frogs, I'm a walking faux pas."

He froze. "It was a mistake to kiss me?"

"Only if you're not the prince."

"I'm not."

She put her hands on his cheeks. Her smile was heartening. "*I'll* be the judge of that."

Suddenly the museum went black—totally, unrelenting black. A chorus of gasps went up from the party guests. In the next instant there was huge crash. Simon couldn't tell if it had come from the tiara room or the buffet tables. A woman shrieked. A man's voice—Trey Stone's?—said, "Hell and damnation."

In the next instant the security alarms went off, a shrill peal that repeated over and over, a piercing assault on the eardrums.

Lili called, "Simon?" She reached for him, her hands patting at his pleated shirtfront for reassurance.

He caught them and enclosed her in his arms. "Stay still. There's a backup power source. The lights will come up in a minute."

A couple of beams cut through the darkness; the security guards had been armed with flashlights. They panned the lights over the stunned guests, crisscrossing startled faces. A frantic babble began to rise as the guests groped and stumbled around the rooms.

"The tiara!" Simon yelled to the guards. He'd dreaded this, but he couldn't leave Lili alone in such chaos. *"Go after the tiara."*

Henry's face suddenly loomed out of the darkness. He was dragging Jana at his side. Rodger Wilhelm also arrived, calling for the princess. The police chief thrust both the princess and the Gypsy at the bodyguard. "Do not let her go!"

Simon briefly squeezed Lili's hand, then followed Henry toward the tiara room. "Where's Stone? Have you seen Stone?" he shouted over the clang of the alarm.

On cue, the backup lights came on. A dim glow, but adequate. "There he is—stealing the canapes," Henry said, somehow finding time for sarcasm as he rushed headlong into the next room.

Simon felt like a fool. Apparently Trey Stone had crashed into the buffet tables when the lights went out, upending a number of dishes all over himself. Instead of ill-gotten jewels, his outspread hands were filled with shiny gobs of black caviar.

A struggle had broken out in the well-guarded inner sanctum. Two of the security guards were wrestling with a black-clad figure. Simon's first concern was for the tiara. Although a couple of the velvet-roped stanchions had been knocked over, the case appeared to be undisturbed.

An icy pit of dread opened inside him. That the tiara was safe was cold comfort. An attempt had been made, and that was bad enough. He was a failure.

Lili rushed into the room, her bell-style skirt sweeping the floor like Scarlett O'Hara's. In a kooky sort of linked chain, she had Wilhelm by the hand, who had Jana Vargas by the hand, who had Mrs. Grundy and two little old ladies by the hand. When Lili stopped abruptly at the sight of the untouched tiara, the rest of her crew piled on top of each other, stumbling and bumbling like Keystone Cops. Trey Stone wandered in behind them, dabbing at his tuxedo with a handful of paper napkins.

Simon approached them, his hands upraised. "You can't be in here. You need to clear out at once—"

A sound from behind made him glance over his shoulder, just in the nick of time. The would-be thief, who'd appeared to be subdued by the security guards who'd surrounded him, had suddenly twisted away when Henry approached from behind with a pair of handcuffs. Running low and fast, he shot like a rocket toward the open doorway.

Which was blocked by the princess and her patchwork entourage.

Simon forgot the tiara. He forgot his career.

He thought only of Lili.

He leaped, making a flying tackle a split second before the thief would have speared into the princess. The two men skidded across the marble floor for a few feet before landing hard in a tangle of flailing limbs. One of the free-standing jewel cases crashed to the floor. It splintered, spilling out a glittering emerald necklace.

The thief was quick and agile. He slid out from beneath Simon, gaining his feet as the two old ladies descended, beating him over the head with their sizable purses. Mrs. Grundy elbowed in between them, pulling the retracting umbrella from her purse. With a flick and a snap, she leveled the weapon at the suspect's midsection, the look in her eyes as sharp as the tip of her umbrella.

Henry stepped over Simon's sprawled form. He captured the thief's hands behind his back and locked on the cuffs. "That's enough. Thank you, Lottie and Jess," the chief said, calmly nodding to the ladies. "Mrs. Grundy."

Lili picked up her skirts and ran to kneel beside Simon. "Are you all right?" she said, her mouth near his ear.

He gathered in his various scattered appendages—still in working order—and sat up. "Uh, sure. I'm fine."

"That was so brave, Simon. You saved the day!"

Snort. "Hardly."

She kissed his cheek. "Has anyone ever told you that you take the self-deprecating bit a little too far?"

He shook his head. It was difficult to be boastful when two elderly women wielding handbags and an ex-nanny with an umbrella were your backup. But if Lili wanted to see him as a hero rather than a frog…who was he to argue?

Simon remembered Madame Magdalena and her prediction about tall men, trouble and hopping toads. "The emerald necklace," he said, rising to his feet. "Where is it?"

The group murmured, turning to search the floor.

After a long tense moment, Trey Stone stepped forward. "Do you mean this?" He held the jeweled necklace in one big gooey hand. "I picked it up for you."

Sure you did, Simon thought.

Henry gripped the tuxedo-clad thief's scruff and tilted his head back so the low-wattage emergency lights illuminated the miscreant's face.

Just then the shrieking alarm cut off. Strangely, the sudden silence seemed equally jarring.

It was Jana who gasped. *"Gabriel."*

10

HENRY RUSSELL had taken charge and gradually, systematically cleared the museum. He'd let Trey Stone go last of all, despite Simon's stubborn suspicions. Which even *he* recognized as having more to do with his feelings for Lili than with actual substantial reasoning.

Meanwhile, the guards had escorted Simon and the tiara upstairs, where he'd placed the precious piece in the museum's safe, followed by a choice selection of the other most valuable or historic items from the Brunner collection. Corny would complain, but until Simon was satisfied that all perpetrators were under arrest and there was no further danger, he was shutting down the exhibition.

He could afford to be cautious…now. His reputation had already sustained a second strike. And he rather doubted that he'd ever get a third chance. Most likely he was down and out for good.

"The power was deliberately cut," Henry said, coming in from outside to meet Simon in the decimated entrance hall.

"That means Gabriel wasn't working alone."

Henry's expression was forbidding as he looked at Jana, who'd been told to wait alongside the princess. She, Lili and the rest of the bumbling crime-stoppers sat on a row of chairs ringing the emptied dance floor.

"I'm about to head out to the Gypsy camp. See if I can roust any suspects."

Simon followed the chief's gaze. Jana Vargas was staring at him, her eyes blazing. Defiant as ever, despite her cousin's arrest. "Lucky for Jana she was at your side the entire night."

"Maybe she was the decoy, as she was at the first reception," Henry said. "After all, Gabriel entered the party with the invitation Princess Lili sent to Jana. We found it in his pocket."

It was possible, but Simon wasn't convinced. He didn't quite know why. "Are you sure Stone isn't invol—"

Henry interrupted. "Give up on Stone, already. I had him checked out, remember? He's nothing but a lazy trust-fund baby, looking to notch one with a princess." The chief nodded at Simon. "Reason to bust the guy in the chops, sure. But not to arrest him."

Simon conceded grudgingly. "All right."

Henry gestured toward the group on the chairs. "I suppose I have to take a couple minutes to interview the Wolf sisters before I leave." They'd been prattling with excitement over the attempted theft, insisting that they must speak to the police chief about their suspicions. Meeting their royal cousin, Princess Lili, had distracted them long enough for Henry and his force to complete their initial crime scene analysis and evidence gathering.

Simon stayed back even when Henry went forward. Jana rose to meet him, insisting that she be turned loose. "So you can interfere with my investigation?" Henry said.

Her eyes narrowed. "Bosh! Your bias is blinding you."

"Gabriel was caught red-handed. I'm sorry, but you'll have to face it." When Jana continued to protest, Henry moved her off to the side, speaking in a low, urgent voice until she had calmed.

Simon looked at Lili. She was serene, her hands clasped atop the glistening puff of her gown, chatting quietly with Jess and Lottie Wolf as if they were visiting at a tea party and not surrounded by the wreckage of a crime scene. Only the troubled look in her eyes when her gaze strayed to Jana betrayed a sense of inner turmoil.

She was admirable, he thought. A true princess: bold, beautiful, kind, generous, honorable. If she occasionally was too flighty, it was only because she was young and impulsive. She had an open heart and a trusting nature.

He realized that there was one benefit to the attempted theft. Lili's silly plan to recruit herself a lover had been thwarted. From here, Wilhelm and Grundy would take over, seeing that the princess was safely returned to the hotel. Tomorrow, she'd depart.

No longer Simon's responsibility.

But not his joy, either.

He should say goodbye now, in front of onlookers. That way it wouldn't get maudlin.

Still, he hesitated.

A sharp point prodded at his back. He jumped, turned. "Mrs. Grundy." She had the umbrella out again. "Put that thing away before the chief registers it as a lethal weapon."

She poked him again. And again. "Go on. Speak to Princess Lili. She's waiting for you."

He pushed the umbrella away. "Only to say goodbye."

"Not all goodbyes are forever, young man. Prince

Franz will be needing a reliable courier to escort the jewels back to Grunberg.''

"After tonight, that would never be me.''

Grundy cocked her head. "You sacrificed yourself to keep the royal family's most precious jewel safe.''

"The tiara," he said, turning his face toward Lili. She glowed. Priceless.

"The princess," Grundy countered, "although I'm quite certain I don't have to tell *you* that.''

Simon hesitated. The tip of the umbrella came up.

"I'm going, I'm going," he said.

"THIS IS GOODBYE," Simon said to Lili, taking her hands. They stood on the steps outside the museum. The night air was fresh and cool on her heated cheeks. Others moved around them, but for Lili there was only Simon. Simon's funny crooked face. Simon's smart green eyes. His soft, deep voice, reaching inside where her heart beat fast and proud. He was not, oh, no, he was *not* saying goodbye to her!

"I apologize for the—the—catastrophes." His brow furrowed, and she realized that by some miracle he'd managed to keep his misshapen glasses in place even when he'd tackled Gabriel Vargas. All the same, it was fortunate she'd asked Amelia to place a special order while she and Simon had gone to the baseball game that afternoon. Even though their time was short, she was sure to ruin at least one more pair before she left.

"The catastrophes weren't your fault," she said with a little squeeze.

"My responsibility, though.''

"One you met admirably.''

His smile was rueful. "You and your nanny are a bit foggy on that point.''

Lili blinked. "It must be the fairy dust," she whispered.

Simon brought his face close to hers. His voice hummed in her ear, an echo of the bumblebee in her mouth, heightening her sensations. "It's been a pleasure, Princess Lili."

Ah, there was the sting. Her chin quivered. "Usually they say I'm a royal pain."

Simon kissed her cheek. He lifted one of her hands to his mouth and touched his lips to the top of it. "You've done your country proud."

Lili's heart was racing. This *couldn't* be the end. She clasped Simon's hand tighter when he tried to let go and step away. She beseeched him, sounding desperate and not even caring. "My country—it doesn't matter—I want—"

"Princess," Amelia admonished. She and Rodger swooped in and gently pulled her away toward the dratted limousine. Lili's last sight of Simon was from the back window: smiling sadly, waving, his tuxedo half undone and missing various pieces, crumpled from head to toe, which made her catch her breath in a gulp.

She bit her lip, fought back the tears, trying to be brave. But then Amelia made a gesture toward her and Lili collapsed into the woman's arms, sobbing her heart out.

SEVERAL OF THE MOST dogged reporters were camped out in the hotel lobby when Lili sneaked down the stairs and hid behind a potted plant. She wore jeans, a gaudy baseball jacket made of blue satin with a B.C.P.D. emblem on it and a matching cap that hid her hair. She was pretty sure she didn't look like a princess, but not so sure that she was unobtrusive. Lucky for her that the reporters were either drinking in the bar or drowsing in armchairs. She might be able to stroll by without alerting them.

"Act normal," she told herself. The best way to hide was in plain sight, so she ventured out from behind the plant, shot the desk clerk a big smile and strolled bold as you please through the lobby.

One of the reporters looked up. "Princess Lili?"

"Who?" Lili said.

"You're Princess Lili." The woman tugged on the sleeve of a sleeping photographer. "Zeke. Wake up. You have to get a shot of this."

Lili wasn't going to wait around to pose. She turned on her heel and ran along an unadorned corridor, banging through a door marked Exit. She galloped down a flight of steps that she thought might bring her to the garage level. They did. She stopped to look around for help. Most of the parking spots were filled, but there were no people in sight. Behind her, the elevator hummed to life.

The reporter was coming! Lili looked around frantically. A narrow, lighted, curved tunnel seemed to be the only way out. Where was her limo when she needed it?

Run for it.

Behind her, the elevator bell *binged*. She raced up the concrete slope as the doors swooshed open. The puttering sound of an engine filled the tunnel. Eerie light washed the curved walls.

Lili flattened herself against the cement wall, closing her eyes tight. If she was about to become a pancake, she couldn't bear to look. Meanwhile, voices echoed in the garage. "Princess Lili? Damn. How did we lose her?"

She opened her eyes. A blond teenage boy on a

moped was staring at her, his mouth hanging open. He wore a shiny red jacket and a matching cap; there was a pizza box strapped to the back of his little vehicle.

"Hi," Lili said, offering her sweetest smile. The boy blushed. "Listen. I'm in something of a pickle. How would you like to earn a really big tip?"

After she and the pizza boy made a deal, it didn't take her long to reach Simon's house. She'd driven mopeds while vacationing in Rome and the south of France. After negotiating the Via del Corso without losing her sun hat, the quiet streets of Blue Cloud were a snap.

A light was on inside, but none by the door. She parked the moped in Simon's driveway, then went and stood on the doorstep like a nervous trick-or-treater, working up her nerve to ring the doorbell. Every time she went to poke the button, her finger started to shake.

Simon threw open the door. "I told you. I have nothing to say—" He stopped, deflating when he recognized Lili beneath the bill of a Leaning Tower of Pizza cap. "Oh, it's you. I—" He ran a hand through his sparse hair. "I didn't order pizza."

"This is my disguise." Wrinkling her nose, she plucked at the collar of the borrowed jacket. "But it smells like stinky feet and tomato sauce."

"You're crazy."

She batted her lashes. "Does that mean you're not going to let me inside? There may be reporters hot on my trail."

"Get in here." Simon grabbed her arm and hauled her over the threshold, then checked up and down the quiet street before closing the door. He locked it.

"Thanks for the kind invitation." Lili shrugged out of the teenager's jacket, looking around her with interest. Dusty wood floors, white walls, a mishmash of unmatched but comfortable furniture. Simon's house was as unassuming as he was. "So this is how the other half lives."

"It's humble, but mine own." He scratched behind his ear. The wire wrapped around his glasses must have loosened, because they were seriously lopsided. He was in bare feet, though he still wore the black slacks of his tux and the pleated white shirt, partway unbuttoned with the sleeves shoved up to his elbows. He looked adorably askew, as if he'd been pacing the floor and fretting.

Was it wrong to hope that he'd been fretting over *her* and not only the botched thievery?

The mere sight of him made her go all warm and melty inside. Especially when she thought of how his mouth had felt on hers. And his tongue, licking, sucking, stroking. She had to look away, before she launched herself into his arms.

"I thought we said goodbye."

"*You* did," Lili agreed. Or disagreed, depending on your viewpoint. A hundred thoughts and words were jostling in her head, but only one feeling.

She decided to go with that.

"I came to tell you that I love you," she blurted. "And I'm pretty certain that in America, love means never having to say goodbye."

"Sorry," Simon said. His eyes widened when he saw the stricken look that came over her. She'd misunderstood. "Never having to say you're sorry, that's what love means. Not—I mean—er, I didn't mean that I was sorry you…" His voice trailed off.

She nodded encouragingly.

He was befuddled, the big lug. "You love me?" he said, comprehension dawning.

She stepped close enough to slide her arms around his waist. "Call me crazy."

He laughed uneasily. "I already did."

She looked up at him with her chin pressed to his chest. "You can't get rid of me that easily."

Simon's fingers spread over her hips. "Lili, you know we can't do this…"

"Why not?"

"For one thing, you're supposed to be looking for the perfect lover. Someone handsome, clever, skilled. *Memorable.*"

She undid the rest of his studs. "I only said that so you'd get jealous enough to volunteer." With her palms gliding over his warm skin, she spread the shirt open. He wasn't skinny at all. Nor pale like a frog's belly. He was perfect. She tickled one of the whorls of hair that clustered between his pecs, then followed the narrowing stripe that led downward.

Simon caught her hand. *Spoilsport.*

"No. Please, Lili." His voice was guttural, telling her what wrenching work it was to dredge up the denial. "I'm not the man for you." He made a sound of frustration. "Much as I'd like to be."

She'd been pressing him backward toward the couch. One firm push and he sat abruptly, giving in with a moan. She climbed onto the cushion beside him, facing the back of the couch with her legs beneath her. Only one small lamp was lit; the room was dim, quiet, private. Not exactly the romantic scenario of her dreams, but it would do. Because it was the man who counted.

"Don't I get a say in this?" she asked, flipping off her cap. She reached up with both hands, ruffling her hair with her fingers, knowing that the motion made her breasts lift and her tiny ribbed sweater ride up to reveal several inches of bare midriff.

He dragged his gaze away. "I don't trust your judgment. First you picked Stone and then you picked me."

Lili leaned toward him, resting her arms on his shoulders. She took off his glasses, tossed them over her shoulder—he didn't even bother to wince when they hit the floor—and then dipped her head for a kiss. *Mmm.* Another. "You really have to get over this self-confidence problem," she breathed, nibbling at his ear. She pushed one of his hands higher, toward her breasts. His fingertips slipped beneath her sweater, grazing her ribs.

"After tonight," he started to say.

She interrupted. "After tonight, it will be obvious that you are the smartest, sexiest, savviest man in the world."

He dragged his mouth away from hers. "You *are* crazy."

She stopped kissing him. "Can't you give me a little cooperation, here? I'm a virgin. *You're* supposed to be seducing *me.*"

"You're not like any virgin I ever knew. Virgins are supposed to be clumsy, awkward and shy. Hell—" his face twisted "—I'm more a virgin than you are."

She sat back into the corner of the plush brown velour couch, bouncing out of frustration, her arms crossed. "How many women have you been with?"

"A—a few."

"More than three?"

"Four."

"Tell me about them."

He gritted his teeth, making a face. "Do I have to?"

"None of them could be worse than Trey."

"Yes, they could. Trey isn't a criminal." Simon frowned, adding, "Much as I wanted him to be."

"Forget him. Which girlfriend was the criminal?"

Simon took a minute to answer. "There's no point to this, Lili. You're leaving tomorrow."

"Airplanes fly both ways. And you're avoiding the question." When he still didn't respond, she tried again. "Tell me about the first one, then. How old were you?"

"Seventeen. She was eighteen. Valerie Wingate. We'd danced once at the prom because she was trying to make her jock boyfriend jealous. Then we ran into each other a few days after she'd graduated and she—" Simon was turning red, but he went on. "This is embarrassing." He took a breath. "She invited me up to her bedroom one afternoon when her parents weren't home. One time, that was all it was. Afterward, she hung up on me when I called. She ignored me in public. Afraid her friends would laugh at her for knowing the class egghead, I guess."

"Hmm," Lili said. "Number two?"

"A sophomore in college. By then, I thought I'd never get a real girlfriend, but along came Debby O'Reilly. A Mata Hari in blue jeans and a ponytail."

Lili tilted forward. "Go on."

"We were together for most of a semester. First love. I thought I was happy. Until I found out that she'd come after me only to get my class notes. And then my help on her term paper. The final straw came when she tried to talk me into cheating on the final exam."

Lili wanted to give him a hug, but he was sending out keep-away vibes. She schooled her expression to genial indifference. "And the third?"

Simon was going by rote now. "Paula Manthey. Grad student. I was working on my doctorate, heading up a research team for a well-known professor of archaeology. Paula wanted a position on the team, by any means necessary. Enough said about that.''

Lili scooted closer and put her hands on his arm. She couldn't help it. ''The fourth?''

''The worst.''

''The criminal?''

His Adam's apple worked up and down in his throat. ''I was only lucky that I didn't get arrested, too.''

''Please tell me, Simon. Once it's said, we can forget it.''

''This one's the kind that stains a guy's reputation forever.'' He sighed. ''Okay. A year ago. I'd worked my way up the chain at an important museum in New York. I was being groomed to take over for the retiring Egyptian collection manager. Traylor Bickett lived across the hall from me in our apartment building. A nice girl from a good family. No connections to my profession, so I thought I could trust her. We got along well. She didn't mind my preoccupations or my long hours.'' He laughed. ''Of course, later I found out that was because the less attention I paid to her, the better. She wanted me around to escort her to various functions, but she didn't want me noticing her addiction.''

Lili inhaled. ''Drugs?''

Simon made a wry face. ''Shopping.''

''Shopping?''

''Yes. Designer clothes. Jewelry. Shoes. After it was over, I learned that her credit-card bills were astronomical.''

''What did she do?''

''She surprised me at the museum late one evening. I don't think she'd planned for it, but while she was there she saw her chance to pocket a rare golden scarab that I'd been asked to evaluate. When we left the building, I vouched for her with the security guards. The next day, the scarab went missing and I was the prime suspect. Rightly so.''

''Oh, no.''

''The police were called in. I was questioned. Even so, I didn't get that the culprit was Traylor until she tried to sell the scarab at a pawn shop for a few thousand bucks. She had no idea what the piece was really worth.''

''How terrible. But I don't see why you were blamed. If you didn't know—''

''I was lax; I used poor judgment. I should never have let Traylor anywhere near such a valuable artifact, but I guess I was showing off or something. The museum board was within their rights to ask me to resign.''

Lili did give him a hug then. He let out a soft moan that sounded like relief and wound his arms around her, holding her tight. He buried his face in her hair, breathing deeply. Gradually, the embrace became less about comfort. She turned her face toward his and he opened his mouth, sliding his lips over her cheek. He kissed her. Deeply, passionately, like a lover. His hands roamed over her, petting and stroking until she was alight with shivery sensation.

She arched her throat beneath his lips. ''These girlfriends of yours…''

''Do we have to keep talking about them?''

''Just this— Oh, that's lovely. Do that again.''

Her sweater had been pushed up to her armpits. He slid his hand beneath her bra and cupped her breast, lifting it to his mouth. His breath was warm, ticklish.

''These girlfriends…Val'rie…Deb-bee…Pall Mall… Tractor Traylor…''

Simon chuckled. Her nipple tingled. "Close enough."

Oh, yes! His mouth was *so* close.

"They all wanted you." *Wanted you bad. Like me.*

"What do you mean?"

"The first one. You danced with her once and she couldn't resist you, in spite of the supposed social stigma. Debby—she didn't *have* to stay all semester. The other two…mmm." Lili shifted her shoulders. "Um, them, too. Treachery aside, they all wanted you." She pressed herself into his hand. "Me, too."

He hesitated. "I've let myself be blinded by sex before."

"But *this* is love."

"It's too soon to be love." He flicked his tongue across her nipple. She stiffened at the lightning bolt of pure electric desire that flashed through her. "See?"

"Just because there's lust doesn't mean it isn't also love."

He lifted his face. "And you're experienced enough to know?"

"I know what I feel." She closed her eyes for a moment, drawing on every shred of poise she'd attained so that she might speak the truest, most important words of her life. "You see, I'm not like those other women. I want all of you, Simon. You're not really a frog to me—that was only a good reason for me to keep smooching on you. You're—you're…" She was panting. She stopped and took a breath, her heart pounding hard enough to knock her clear across the room. "Considering your past with women, I know it's difficult to do, but trust me on this. Because I would never betray you. I don't want anything from you but *you.*"

She clasped his face between her palms. "Simon Tremayne, you're a prince."

He looked at her for a long while, his eyes searching hers. She didn't waver. Finally he said, "Zing went the strings of my heart."

Happiness washed over her. She smiled. "You, too?"

"Me, too."

"Then make love to me?"

"No."

She wanted to scream. Instead she pulled her sweater down. At least *that* made him look disappointed. "Why not?" she asked.

He fingered her hair. "Because if this is love…you deserve to be courted prop—"

"Don't say properly! I hate being proper."

He shook his head, his smile baffled and bemused, but also completely besotted. "You deserve to be treated like a princess. We'll go out together. We'll talk, we'll kiss. A lot. I'll come to Grunberg and meet your father…and your sisters…"

Anticipation bubbled inside Lili like champagne. She nodded, a ridiculously large smile stretching her cheeks. "I suppose we can do that."

"And when the time comes…" He grinned. "Yes, the *proper* time, I'll ask your father for your hand in marriage."

She blinked, awed by the enormity of it. "Marriage?"

"Because I want all of you, too, Lili. Every royal-pain-in-the-patoot inch."

She went blissfully into his arms. But after a while, when he'd stopped kissing her and was simply holding her cozily against his warm bare chest, she thought about what he'd said. She was going to have to study up on the strange ins and outs of American vernacular. "Just one question, Simon."

He made a lazy sound.

She eyed him curiously. "What the heck's a patoot?"

SIMON WAS BEYOND noticing, but Lili had insisted that she needed to wash up and change to get rid of the pizza boy's scent. Afterward, she wandered into the kitchen from the bathroom, wearing only the T-shirt he'd offered. Her legs were bare—something about a spot of grease on her jeans.

The T-shirt was his own. Large and white enough to be nearly see-through, at least on an otherwise naked woman. *Zing.* Hello, Nefertiti! Simon was going to have to talk to her father very soon. Very, very soon. He sure as heck hoped the prince would approve of a museum wonk of ill repute as his son-in-law, who might possibly even be out of a job. Funny thing, the professional failure wasn't as devestating as he'd expected. Maybe because his luck had changed when it came to women.

He kissed Lili. Twice. "I called Mrs. Grundy for you. Didn't want her to worry. But, strangely enough, she wasn't."

"I gave up. She always knows anyway, so this time I told her straight out where I was going. She must like you, because she didn't raise a finger to stop me."

"Ah, but did you know she sent your bodyguard after you?"

Lili's mouth dropped open. "No!"

"He's sitting on the back step. Wouldn't come in, even when I tried to explain that nothing happened—"

She giggled. "Oh, something certainly did happen!"

"But not *that.* So I gave him a cup of coffee and left him to it."

"Why the back step?" Lili asked.

Simon gestured toward the front. "Because of them."

She went to the living room window and peered out. A gabbling bunch reporters and photographers were camped on the lawn, taking pictures of the moped and the front of Simon's house. Lili dropped the curtain and backed away. Something crunched under her stocking-clad foot. "Uh-oh."

"I'm afraid you're in for it, Lili. Unless we can sneak you out without the reporters seeing, your reputation is going to be as ruined as mine."

"They don't worry me." Lili stooped. She came back up with his glasses, mangled beyond all repair. "Sorry. I stepped on them."

"Doesn't matter. I'm thinking of investing in contacts."

"Not necessary." She went to the entryway and searched the pockets of the pizza boy's jacket.

Simon followed, curious about what she was up to now. Life was sure to be an adventure with Princess Lili by his side.

She handed him a familiar black case. "Here you go. We can call it a pre-engagement present."

He snapped it open. "Glasses."

"Superstrength Clark Kent glasses."

Simon lifted them out, squinting skeptically. They looked like Mr. Magoo glasses to him. The lenses were thick; the frames were solid, black and heavy as a brick.

"The optician assured me that they're virtually unbreakable," Lili said with a laugh in her voice. "Try them on."

He did. "I feel like I'm wearing a microscope on my nose."

Lili's laugh overflowed. Pure effervescence.

He struck an I'm-too-sexy-for-my-glasses male-model pose. "How do I look? As soon as we step outside that door, our photo's going to be plastered across newspapers from here to Grunberg. Am I presentable?"

Lili looped her arms around his waist and kissed him full on the lips. "How should I know? It must be the fairy dust again, because whenever I look at you, Simon, I see only a prince."

Epilogue

POLICE CHIEF Henry Russell was in a world of confusion and he didn't like it one damn bit. He'd been up all night, one way or the other, sorting out his suspects and making a hash of his incendiary relationship with Jana.

Gabriel Vargas was clearly guilty. But of what, exactly, was as murky as a swamp. The Wolf sisters claimed to have seen a figure in black running from the back door of the museum, just after the lights went out. They'd been outside with their constant companion, Scooter, rescuing the dog from their car to give him a chance to "water" the shrubbery.

A second suspect fit the scenario. While Gabe was maneuvering into position to grab the tiara his conspirator was cutting the power. Henry figured that the distraction was meant to give Gabe time to swipe the tiara and then slip away in the confusion, but the young Rom refused to talk.

Henry was baffled by inconsistencies. There was no way Gabe could have smashed or otherwise broken into the state-of-the-art case that housed the tiara. Certainly not in total darkness, in a matter of minutes. No, seconds. Was it possible that the young man had been duped into taking part in an impossible theft?

For what purpose?

Officer Sam Blake knocked once on the open door. "Chief, you're going to want to take a look at this."

"What is it?"

"A report on Trey Stone."

Henry waved Blake away. "I already saw that."

"Not this one. I requested more information after Tremayne told us Stone had lived in California. I dunno if it means anything, but…"

Henry rose, strode around his desk and grabbed the fax. "What now?" he growled, feeling uncharacteristically jumpy. No sleep and too much sex and caffeine could do that to a guy.

He skimmed the report. "Well, I'll be damned."

"Trey Stone" was an assumed name.

The Harlequin Reader Service® — Here's how it works:

Accepting your 2 free books and gift places you under no obligation to buy anything. You may keep the books and gift and return the shipping statement marked "cancel." If you do not cancel, about a month later we'll send you 2 additional books and bill you just $5.14 each in the U.S., or $6.14 each in Canada, plus 50¢ shipping & handling per book and applicable taxes if any.* That's the complete price and — compared to cover prices of $5.99 each in the U.S. and $6.99 each in Canada — it's quite a bargain! You may cancel at any time, but if you choose to continue, every month we'll send you 2 more books, which you may either purchase at the discount price or return to us and cancel your subscription.

*Terms and prices subject to change without notice. Sales tax applicable in N.Y. Canadian residents will be charged applicable provincial taxes and GST.

If offer card is missing write to: The Harlequin Reader Service, 3010 Walden Ave., P.O. Box 1867, Buffalo, NY 14240-1867

NO POSTAGE
NECESSARY
IF MAILED
IN THE
UNITED STATES

BUSINESS REPLY MAIL

FIRST-CLASS MAIL   PERMIT NO. 717-003   BUFFALO, NY

POSTAGE WILL BE PAID BY ADDRESSEE

HARLEQUIN READER SERVICE
3010 WALDEN AVE
PO BOX 1867
BUFFALO NY 14240-9952

Do You Have the LUCKY KEY?

Scratch the gold areas with a coin. Then check below to see the books and gift you can get!

PLAY THE Lucky Key Game

and you can get

FREE BOOKS and a FREE GIFT!

YES!

I have scratched off the gold areas. Please send me the 2 FREE BOOKS and GIFT for which I qualify. I understand I am under no obligation to purchase any books, as explained on the back of this card.

311 HDL DNV5   111 HDL DNVT

FIRST NAME | LAST NAME

ADDRESS

APT.# | CITY

STATE/PROV. | ZIP/POSTAL CODE

2 free books plus a free gift   1 free book

2 free books   Try Again!

Visit us online at
www.eHarlequin.com

Offer limited to one per household and not valid to current Harlequin Duets™ subscribers. All orders subject to approval.

Henry Ever After

Carrie Alexander

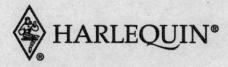

HARLEQUIN®

TORONTO • NEW YORK • LONDON
AMSTERDAM • PARIS • SYDNEY • HAMBURG
STOCKHOLM • ATHENS • TOKYO • MILAN • MADRID
PRAGUE • WARSAW • BUDAPEST • AUCKLAND

"NEVER A CLUE escapes the attention of Blue Cloud's eagle-eyed police chief, Henry Russell," said a stentorian Joe Friday voice, filling the interior of the patrol car. "The man's on the job twenty-four hours a day. No crime is too big for this superlawman to solve. None too small to avoid his stern reprimand…"

Henry caught his own eye in the rearview mirror. He laughed sheepishly. Narrating his patrols was a bad habit. Although more a by-product of sheer boredom than massive ego, he ought to remember that if it distracted him from his assignment for even a moment or two, it wasn't advisable.

But when a guy was the top cop of a bucolic town, where the average crime that reached his ear was "criminy," he had to do *something* to keep himself amused.

Henry continued coasting along the secondary road, completing his midmorning rounds before returning to the station house and the endless joy of paperwork. As usual, all was secure in Blue Cloud, Pennsylvania. Even so, he kept silent and alert, taking in each flutter of the spring-green leaves, every flicker of the blackbird's wing. If so much as a bird's egg was disturbed, he'd see it. Because he was sharp and he was smart and he was blessed with X-ray vision. Damn all, he was hot stuff!

Chuckling again, and forgetting his own reprimand, Henry began to sing along with the radio. The Who was waxing poetic about seeing for miles and miles. Damn appropriate.

Suddenly the lyrics died. *Whoa. Hold up, Eagle Eyes.* Henry stopped singing and started looking. His vehicle slowed.

Hitchhiker ahead.

As soon as the woman spotted the flashers on his roof, she dropped the extended thumb with the casual finesse of long, guilty experience. She began walking toward his patrol unit instead, swinging her arms as if she was only enjoying a stroll along the deserted country road. Dressed in a loose blouse and jeans, her body angled subtly toward the long grass that grew beyond the shoulder of the road. Her face was averted, so he couldn't get a good look at her.

Suspicious. Henry's vehicle crawled by. She kept walking, her long dark hair obscuring most of her face, not even glancing toward him as the average individual would. *Very suspicious.*

Henry braked, then put the car in reverse. She walked on, with serious purpose now, her sandals kicking up pebbles. Still not looking. He glanced in the mirror, saw the road behind him was empty as usual, and let his unit roll along backward, keeping pace with the pedestrian. He opened the passenger side window and leaned across the seats to speak.

"Excuse me, ma'am. Did you know that hitchhiking is illegal in Pennsylvania?"

"Only on the turnpikes," she said, moving briskly.

Hmm. How did she know that? Or, more importantly, why?

"You're in the town of Blue Cloud," he said. "We have an ordinance against hitchhiking on *all* roads."

She paused briefly, then tossed her hair. He saw her profile—smooth lines, Roman nose, full lips, stubborn chin. Exotic. It suited her voice, which was pitched low enough to make him hum inside. "I'm outside of town limits," she said.

"Are you certain?" In preparation for an upcoming event, Blue Cloud's town fathers had posted freshly painted signs on the main road, going in and out of town: Welcome To Blue Cloud, Pennsylvania, Pop. 26,122. Birthplace Of Princess Adelaide Of Grunberg. Unfortunately for her, this stranger was inside the sign, albeit by less than a half a mile.

Her lashes lowered. She kept walking.

"Aren't you going in the wrong direction?" he prodded. She'd been hitchhiking her way into town, not out of it.

"What's it to you?"

Henry didn't like smart alecks. He tapped the gas and zipped his vehicle onto the shoulder, barricading her path. Before he emerged, she'd swung around smoothly and continued in the opposite direction, her hips swinging.

"Hold on, ma'am." He slammed the door and hurried after her. "I want to talk to you."

She didn't stop until he stood in front of her, all six feet, two inches, one hundred ninety-eight pounds of him, blocking the way. When she tried to slip by, he put out an arm to stop her. He made himself look bulky and intimidating, which was a mental process, as well as physical—one he'd perfected. His scowl deepened.

The young woman didn't shrink, but neither did she meet his eyes. He splayed his right hand on his waist, just above his holster, then reached out with his left, and gently but firmly, since she resisted, tipped up her chin so he could see her face.

She jerked away from the touch, hissing foreign words under her breath. Not a language he recognized. Her face stayed up, though, dark eyes flashing with defiance from behind the strands of flyaway hair floating in the pleasant May breeze. "Keep your hands off me, *shawglo*."

He swallowed an instinctive apology, even though something about the woman demanded one. "Who are you?"

"Who are *you* to ask?"

No disrespect to his badge was allowed. He loomed over her, at his most menacing. "Henry Russell, chief of police."

She stood tall, defending her space. Tension strung taut between them. "Jana Vargas."

"Have you got ID?"

Begrudgingly, she nodded.

He waited.

She stared. Liquid eyes, dark blue as midnight. Suspicious and defensive, yet mysteriously attractive.

He held out his hand. "Well?"

"Oh." She blinked with fake innocence. "Did you want to see it? Why didn't you ask?"

Henry drew in a deep breath. *Patience, patience.* "Yes, ma'am, I want to see it. If it's not too much trouble."

"What if I say it is?"

"You'll give it anyway. I was being polite. You might try it sometime. Honey instead of vinegar—they say it works."

"Bah! I don't waste *my* honey on puffed-up lawmen who have nothing better to do than harass harmless pedestrians."

Her honey...

In other circumstances, he'd have made the ready male response. It wasn't only Jana Vargas's smart mouth that was making his blood boil. Her long legs, heart-stopping curves and beguiling air of unfamiliarity had already gotten to him. His uniform slacks felt one size too small. A sip of her honey would have him busting right out of them.

He was more professional than that.

"Keep it zipped, ma'am." *Heed your own advice, Chief.* "Or you'll talk yourself into a hitchhiking citation."

He waited for her reaction. She was fuming, battling her temper, but in the end she only rolled her eyes upward and kept her lips clamped shut. "Good girl," he said. "Now let's see that ID."

With her gaze still pinned to the sky, she reached into her gauzy white cotton blouse. Henry nearly choked on his tongue, trying to keep his jaw from sagging. The low scooped neckline was puckered by elastic, which stretched when she put her hand inside it. Stretched enough for him to see the upper curves of full breasts as ripe as fresh peaches. Or…melons. He'd seen breasts before, of course. Lots of 'em, all shapes and sizes. Another pair—and only the top half of them, at that—shouldn't be sending his core temperature sky-high. Except that there was also movement. Jana leaned forward slightly, reaching deeper, and there was definitely a shifting movement going on in there. The curtain of her rib-length hair had concealed an important fact from him up to now: Jana Vargas didn't wear a bra.

She removed her arm from her shirt. "Were you looking down my blouse, Chief?"

He blinked. There was something in her hand. Not a gun, thank God, or he'd have been a goner. Damn. He was *supposed* to be more professional than this!

He cleared his throat. "I was looking for a weapon."

Her lips pursed. She was one sassy twitch away from a smile. "I'm not a Bond girl. I don't pull telescoping machine guns out from between my breasts."

But you do have a killer body, Henry thought. Her breasts gave new meaning to the word *bountiful,* and he was as low as a basset hound for dwelling on them. He was a lawman, after all. The emphasis was supposed to be on *law,* not *man.*

Jana was holding out a driver's license. He realized that a cord hung around her neck, so she must have fished the laminated card out of a small pouch or purse at the end of it. Why she hadn't simply pulled the cord out of her shirt instead of reaching inside was an interesting question. Maybe she *did* have a weapon in there. Other than her peachy-keen breasts.

He took the license, issued in West Virginia. She was twenty-nine and her address was listed as a P.O. box. More suspicion. Fishy business was often conducted out of P.O. boxes by people who had reason to hide. "Where do you live?" he asked.

"Wheeling, like the license says."

"You don't have a street address?"

She shrugged. "I move around a lot. Wheeling is our base."

Of operations? Henry squinted. "What are you doing in Pennsylvania?"

"Camping."

"Camping?" He glanced around the deserted road. There were no campgrounds nearby. "Where?"

"We have a place. It's legal."

"We?"

"There's a group of us."

"What kind of group?"

Her eyes narrowed. "Human beings."

He counted to ten. "You're here for the festivities?" Blue Cloud was holding a museum opening this weekend, featuring an exhibition of the crown jewels of the royal family of Grunberg. The town was filled with tourists and dignitaries.

"Yes, you might say that."

"And where were you going, just now?"

"Into town."

Until she saw him. Then she hadn't known if she was coming or going.

Henry's instincts told him that Jana Vargas was accustomed to police questioning. The average person volunteered more details than he asked for, but she knew to keep her answers short. Her reaction to his uniform had been both wary and angry.

Yeah, she'd dealt with the law before.

"It's a long walk," he said.

She blew out a breath. "All right. You broke me, Chief. I confess." She looked at him narrowly. "I have a car. It conked out a short way ahead. I was either going to walk back to our campground or hitch a ride into town so I could phone for a tow truck. Are you satisfied?"

"Why didn't you say so from the start? As a general rule, I let first-offense hitchhikers off with a warning."

She shrugged, looking away again.

Silently, he answered himself. *Because she doesn't trust cops.* At least, no more than he trusted her.

He nodded his head in the direction of his vehicle. "Let's go. I'll take a look at your car, and if I can't fix it I'll call for a tow."

"That's not necessary."

"You'd rather stay here, stranded? I won't do that, ma'am."

"But I can take care of myself. I'm perfectly safe."

"Everyone's safe in Blue Cloud," he said with pride. It was his pledge, his job. He'd no more leave a woman alone by the side of the road than he'd let Tommy Finch deliver newspapers in the dark.

Henry took her by the elbow and started walking. "I insist."

She wrenched it away. "All right! I'll go with you." She stomped along the road, matching him stride for stride. "You don't have to manhandle me."

Touchy, Henry thought, holding up his hands. He could concede the point. Truthfully, he'd heard the complaint before. He was a take-charge kind of guy. Even though the more uppity women bristled at that, there was no changing him. He was capable, efficient and maybe even brusque and bossy. The traits had always worked for him, from his days as the oldest child in a single-parent family of seven to his current position overseeing an entire township of needy souls.

Those women who didn't like it—he glanced sidelong at Jana—simply needed to recognize his expertise and be thankful that he was there to fix things for them. Why was that so hard to accept?

Henry shot his gaze front and center. Looking at Jana was a bad idea. Now that he knew what he knew about her lack of undergarments, watching her move was a wicked temptation to see what he could see through the flimsy gauze blouse. Better to focus on his suspicions.

Because of the new museum and its valuable exhibit, he had to be especially vigilant for the next month. He'd breathe a gigantic sigh of relief when the Brunner jewels left town.

"Are you and your friends planning to attend the opening of the museum?" he asked Jana as they reached the patrol unit and he opened the door for her.

She gulped nervously before slipping inside. "I guess so."

He crossed to the other side, wondering what had made her so distrustful of authority. Taking his seat, he glanced at her with what he hoped was a friendly smile. "You like jewels, huh?" All girls did.

"Not particularly."

"Oh?" He stared at the rings on her fingers and bracelets around her wrists. By the looks of it, she'd raided a dime store, grabbing pretty baubles by the handful.

She twisted one of the rings, a gaudy emerald stone too big to be real, set in gold. Then she turned in her seat. Her eyes met his, held them, drew him in. For the first time ever, his world of duty and responsibility shrank to only two people and the simmering chemistry between them. He'd never been *that* distracted by a woman—no matter how hot—before.

"Don't be mistaken by appearances," Jana whispered. Her voice was smoky and seductive, stroking his raw nerve endings until they buzzed. "I'm only an illusion."

He sucked in a breath. He was stunned, but keenly

aware of himself, as if a cannon ball had suddenly
lodged in his belly. "What does that mean?"

Her lids dropped. "Nothing, nothing." She shook her
head. "I was putting you on."

Henry exhaled with a snort. He was the chief, dam-
mit. She was supposed to respect him. Not—not toy
with him!

Breathing hard, furious with himself for falling so
easily under her spell, he turned and gripped the wheel.
Adrenaline pumped through his bloodstream. He
cranked the key, jammed the stick into drive and trod
on the accelerator, trying to mentally block out his passenger until he'd regained his composure. She'd flipped
him head over heels with barely any effort. That just
wasn't...wasn't...*acceptable*.

By George, *he* was the one in charge!

Always.

In a matter of seconds, they'd rounded a bend and
come upon her car. It was a junker, an ancient Ford
Mustang convertible, coated with dust, lacy with rust.
The paint on one of the doors didn't quite match the
rest of the car.

"What's wrong with it?" he asked, pulling over.

"What isn't?" She sighed, wiping her hands on her
jeans. "The car is dead. There's nothing you can do. I
was driving it into town for repairs when it broke down
for good."

"Let me take a look." He was talented with engines;
he'd kept his mother's car running ten years past the
warranty.

"Please," Jana said, reaching for him. "I'd rather you just dropped me off and called a tow truck."

He looked at her fingers. They'd stopped an inch away from his arm. The curly brown hairs on it prickled, as if she'd drawn a staticky blanket across his bare skin. "There's no shame in accepting help, Ms. Vargas."

She withdrew. "I prefer not to be in your debt."

"Look, I made the offer, free and clear. It's part of my job. You won't owe me."

"Even so."

"Don't be so stubborn," he scoffed, climbing out. Lord save him from mulish females who thought that gratitude was a concession that they were the weaker sex! They were, of course. But that was a matter of biology, not character. Men like himself were built to protect females and their babies, and you didn't have to be a caveman to know it.

The convertible was in worse shape, close up. It had been dinged, scratched and dented so many times the chassis looked as if it was made of crumpled tinfoil. The interior floors were grimy and threadbare from hard use. Faded, frayed, but still colorful woolen blankets had been thrown over the seats. Piles of stuff filled the back. He made a quick inventory: several pillows; a bundle of glitzy, beaded, fringed fabrics, maybe clothing—he couldn't be sure; an open box of well-used kitchenware; scattered magazines and books, dog-eared and worn; a folding chair; empty soda cans; assorted trash—wadded fast-food wrappers and even tiny bits of leaves and twigs.

Nothing suspicious, except that the vast accumulation of flotsam made him wonder if Jana Vargas was homeless and if she had money to pay for the tow and repairs. He'd have to insist.

He lifted the hood. "Where did you say you're camping?"

She drifted over, her lip caught between her teeth. "I didn't."

"Do."

She waited until he was bent over the engine. "We set up in a field, several miles east along this road. The farmer who owns it gave us written permission and I made sure we're outside of town limits, so don't even think about running us off."

He fingered a frayed battery cable. "Did I say I intended to?"

"You will." She seemed wearily certain.

"Why's that?" He straightened.

"Wait and see."

Oh, he'd see, all right. But he wouldn't wait for it.

"Well. You're right." He took a handkerchief from his back pocket and wiped his hands. "This engine is deader than a decoy duck. Your gaskets are shot, the fan belt's worn, you've got a corroded battery, and I think the water hose is leaking. Ever hear of maintenance?"

"It's not my car."

"Let me guess. You stole it and are running away

frcm home with all your earthly possessions tossed in the back seat.''

Her chin tilted at a cocky angle. "That's right."

"Give me the real story, Jana."

A gleam of light flared up in her eyes when he said her name. "What happened to Ms. Vargas? I prefer to keep this exchange strictly professional."

He grinned. "I just got intimate with the inside of your engine. That puts us on a first-name basis."

She met his gaze with a measuring stare, then crossed her arms beneath her breasts, pressing them against the thin fabric. "Oh, does it...*Henry?*"

She had him there. Again. He declined to admit it out loud as he deliberately looked away from her bountiful charms. The gauzy blouse was practically see-through and now his tongue was sticking to the roof of his mouth. He pried it off. "The story, Ms. Vargas. And keep to the facts."

"It's my aunt's car. I was taking it into town for her. That's all there is to it."

"I see." Henry rubbed his chin. "So you're camping with your family?"

"Yes. Mostly."

"And all the, ah, supplies in the back seat?"

Jana shrugged. "So my aunt's not a very neat person."

Enough. She'd worn down his patience, to say nothing of his failing self-control. It would be quicker to get his answers elsewhere. "I can call in on my radio and get patched through to the towing service run out of

Spotsky's Garage & Sales. Would you prefer to wait here, or take a ride back with me to your camp?'' *Let me guess.*

''Thanks for the offer, Chief Russell, but I'll wait here for the tow truck. I'll need to go into town to talk with the mechanic anyway.''

''Then why wait? I'm heading that way now.''

She backed off a few steps. ''No. I'll stay with the car.''

It went against his grain to leave her there, even though she was no longer stranded. He told himself that she'd be fine. There were many strangers in town for the weekend events, but they were mostly sweet middle-aged grannies who wanted a look at the visiting princess. No criminal element involved.

''As you like, Ms. Vargas,'' he finally said. He tipped his cap. ''I know Abe Crawley, the tow truck driver. I'll put a rush on it.'' *And convince that skinflint Spotsky to supply a discount.* ''You'll be fixed up in no time.''

After a moment of hesitation, Jana held out her hand. ''I appreciate it, Chief. You've actually been…'' she cocked a brow ''…helpful.'' Apparently that came as a surprise to her.

He clasped her hand in a firm shake, then had to clear the frog from his throat before he could speak. ''Just doing my job, Ms. Vargas.'' The leap of exhilaration he'd experienced at her touch had nothing to do with his desire to help her out. Nothing at all. He'd do the same for any stranded motorist.

Because he was in charge. Yes, indeed, he was in full charge…of *all* his faculties.

2

IT WAS LATE afternoon by the time Jana approached camp, having picked up a ride in town from a couple of elderly sisters and their hyperactive miniature pinscher, Scooter. They were returning from a trip to the greenhouse, the back of their ancient station wagon loaded with annuals. The sisters' family name was Wolf, and they were twittering with excitement about meeting Princess Liliane Brunner of Grunberg, who would arrive tomorrow to cut the ribbon at the museum's opening ceremony. Every time their voices rose, Scooter bounced across the back seat—and Jana—like a ping-pong ball. A ping-pong ball with a sharp bark and even sharper toenails.

"Princess Adelaide was born right here in Blue Cloud," said Lottie, the sister behind the wheel, who claimed to have been a merry widow for thirty-eight years. "She was our cousin. A charming girl. So pretty and sweet. We used to play jacks and ring-around-a-rosy in the summerhouse."

"Then she married His Serene Highness," said the other sister, Jess, nodding and tut-tutting so that she looked like a plucked chicken in bifocals. "And us country cousins were easily forgotten."

"Jess!" shrieked Lottie, making the miniature pinscher cha-cha-cha across Jana's lap on its way to the opposite window. "Adelaide was living in Europe, not on our doorstep. What did you expect her to do? Hop on a supersonic jet and drop by for coffee?"

Wincing, Jana shifted Scooter's paws off her thigh. None of Grunberg's princesses, past or present, particularly interested her. They were far removed from her scope of reality. It was the royal jewels she was dying to see.

Bad luck for her that she'd attracted the attention of the chief of police right off the bat. One glance into Henry Russell's piercing eyes and she'd known he'd waste no time in finding out where she came from and what she was doing in Blue Cloud. Although he hadn't been as crudely provincial about his suspicions as some of the cops she'd battled, he was still the gung-ho type who'd cause trouble for her at every opportunity.

Jana absently scratched behind Scooter's perky ears to keep him settled and sighed to herself as the sisters chattered on. She was used to local police forces coming down on her and the rest of the *vitsa*—family clan; it happened wherever they went. When she'd assumed the leadership role for her little ragtag band of Rom two years ago, she'd learned early on to have all their papers—everything from gaming to campfire permits—in order, so that the police had no easy excuse for running them out of town on sight.

Suddenly Lottie sounded an alarm. Scooter shot straight up in the air and then directly down into Jana's lap, yapping like crazy with his nose pressed up against the window. The stump of his tail wiggled frantically.

"Gypsies. It's Gypsies!" sang Lottie. She slowed the car to a crawl, wavering on and off the edge of the pavement as she gaped at the caravans and tents set up in the roadside pasture. "Look at that, Jess. Aren't they lovely and colorful?"

Jess, who wore a gardening apron, clogs and a perpetually sour expression, adjusted her glasses as she peered past the dashboard. "Dirty creatures, Father said. How dreadful that they've set up camp so close to our home. Shame on Farmer Forbes for allowing it. Shame, shame. I will speak to his wife."

"Piffle! Don't you dare interfere, Jess. Father was a fussbudget with a nasty mouth." Lottie had let the car roll to a standstill as she stared. "I wonder if the Gypsies would mind if I visited. I've always wanted to explore a Gypsy camp. I could bring them my prize-winning snickerdoodles. Ooh, and get my fortune told!"

"You wouldn't dare." Jess wagged her head in disbelief. "You're an old fool, Carlotta Wolf. An old fool."

Jana pried Scooter off her lap. "Right here is fine for me," she said, gathering up her purchases and the bundle of fabric she'd taken from the convertible before leaving it at the garage. "Thanks for the ride."

"Oh, my, no." Jess turned her rancid expression on their passenger. "You mustn't get out here, young lady. Not with those dirty, lawless Gypsies lurking about. It's not safe. Why, they might—'' she lowered her voice ''—*accost* you.''

Jana spoke frostily. ''I'll be quite safe. Though I do appreciate your concern about our hygiene, Ms. Wolf.''

Jess's jaw dropped. ''Wha—''

Jana slammed the door, then ducked to address the other sister through the open car window. ''You're welcome to visit any time, Lottie. The children would love to get home-baked cookies, and I'd show you around the caravans and introduce you to my family.''

Jana's identity had flustered even Lottie. ''That would be lovely,'' she finally remembered to say. Jess poked at her sister, urging her to drive on, while Scooter bounced off the car doors and seat, yipping shrilly. Lottie managed a smile and a hasty wave before departing.

Jana waited until the wood-paneled wagon had disappeared around a curve before she turned toward the temporary encampment, pride swelling in her heart, where once she'd been taught to feel embarrassment and shame. Her father had been a Vargas, descendant of a Romany tribe that had roamed across Europe before migrating to the States a little more than thirty years ago. Her mother was from an average middle-class American family, stuffy Bostonians who'd been appalled when their daughter had taken up with a dirty, dishonest Gypsy man. The young couple had married anyway and lived together in relative bliss for the first eleven years of Jana's life, content to stay with their small group as they traveled the countryside during the summer season. Winters were spent in West Virginia, or sometimes Florida, at a small enclave of mobile homes and dilapidated caravans. Jobs were few. Money was short. When Jana's father had been killed in a construction accident, her mother had collapsed in grief. Soon after, she'd caved in to her family's demand that she return home so they could help raise Jana properly.

The years that followed were not ones Jana cared to remember. She hadn't found her way back to her Vargas relatives until eight years later, when she was nineteen and supposedly heading off to college.

"Jana! Jana! You're back!" called several of the children, who had been floating boats made from bits of bark and twig in the trickle of water that ran in the ditch.

She waved from the road, then tucked her assorted parcels under one arm and clambered through the brush. She leaped from one bank to the other, setting aside her momentary lapse into the past as easily as she shifted the bundle of cloth to her hip. "Hello! Katja, Rudy, Mariella." She ruffled hair, patted cheeks, wiped a runny nose. "Look at you! Your shoes are wet and muddy. Run up to the camp and dry yourselves by the fire, hmm? We'll be having dinner soon."

"Did you get Baba Magda's car fixed?"

"Would I be walking if I had, Rudy? Do you think I'm fool?"

The little boy shook his head. "No, Jana."

She cuffed his thin shoulder. "Go on, then. See if you can beat me to the fire."

She raced him for a few yards, then slowed to a brisk

walk. The May sunshine pooled like melted butter in the dips and hollows of the rolling green pasture. But there would be a touch of spring chill in the air tonight. She must remember to tell the children to take the extra blankets from her caravan. Too many of the adults would be celebrating their first night here with spirits— both high and liquid—to think of their more important responsibilities.

For a moment, the burden of her duty weighed on Jana's heart. But then she saw the tents with their flying flags and ribbons, and heard the twang of her uncle Tito's fiddle and she remembered why she was here, why she had accepted her position as "Princess of the Gypsies."

These people were her family. She owed them for the joy dancing in her feet, for the fire that heated her blood. How could she do any less than care for them and love them with every inch of her heart?

"Jana! *Av akai!* Come, come, sit by Baba Magdalena."

Jana dropped off the cloth bundle and the supplies near one of the tents, then went to join the older woman who was the matriarch of the group. Magdalena Vargas was in her late sixties—give or take a few years, since she was cagey about her exact age—with a comfortably zaftig figure and waist-length hair that was still dark, except for the widening streaks of white that framed her face. With her hooked nose and sagging skin, she was not pretty, but she was revered by the tribe for her great wisdom and skill. Baba Magda had The Sight. Sometimes she was called a witch, and even, in whispers, a bitch, but to Jana she was the queen bee of their little hive. Everything revolved around her. It had been Magda who insisted that the men respect Jana as their leader, at least until Gabriel came of age—and responsibility.

Jana took her place beside the elderly woman. "I'm sorry, Baba Magda, but your car's going to be out of commission for several days. The mechanic says he'll know more tomorrow after he's checked it over thoroughly."

"No matter. We'll have it back soon enough."

"I suppose. But transportation will be a bother, with only *Kako* Tito's truck and the van running. I almost wish Josef was with us. He could have fixed the car." Josef was married to her cousin, Ana. Jana had urged him, as one of their most reliable and able-bodied men, to take the offer of a steady job at an auto body shop in Wheeling. He joined the tribe when he could.

"Ach," said Magda with her usual throwaway flair. "Wishes, swishes. Don't give it a thought, my Jana."

"But we need to advertise our fair. I was able to make copies and distribute some of the flyers while I was in town, but not enough. I'm worried that the townspeople are thinking only of the jewel exhibition and won't be attracted to our little fair."

"Word will spread. The people will come to us even if we don't publicize," Magda said. She was usually complacent, letting life happen as it would. She believed in fate, whereas Jana believed in making her own future. "And we have everything else we need right here. We can get along without my car."

Jana didn't answer, only leaned forward on the camp stool to hug her knees. She was restless inside, more than usual.

"I know, *rinkini*." The Rom word for "beautiful one" had been her nickname for Jana since she was a child. Magda petted Jana's hair, lovingly smoothing it away from her face. "Forget about the diamond for now. We've been two hundred years without it. A few more days means nothing."

Jana looked up, amazed at the way Magda always seemed to know what a person was thinking.

"I only wanted to see it," Jana whispered. "I never have, you know."

"Ach. A diamond is a diamond is a diamond. Too rich for the likes of us."

"I learned in town that Princess Liliane arrives tomorrow. They're having a tea reception for her. I'd like to go."

"Why, Jana?"

"To…" She squirmed. "I don't know. I just feel that I should be there." Fortunately, Baba Magda believed in following instincts. "I can distribute more of the flyers, for one."

"No." Magda's response was firm. "There will be trouble if you go."

"And if I don't?"

Her laugh spilled forth, as rich as any gemstone. "There will still be trouble!"

"Probably from Gabriel," Jana said, brooding over her handsome cousin, who was on the verge of becoming a man. Her eyes sought him, finding him measuring out the horse's evening feed. Gabriel was young, wild and headstrong, racing like a turbulent wind in the wrong direction. She had exerted all her influence over the others to convince them that education and honest trade were the ways to prosperity. Gabe would not listen. He wanted so much from life, yet believed that he'd been given too little. His attitude worried Jana more than all her other problems put together.

If there was to be trouble with Chief Henry Russell, it would be Gabe's doing.

"You met a *gadje*," said Magda. "A *shawglo*." A white man—the law. She chuckled at Jana's startled expression. "Don't look so surprised. One glimpse at your face and it's as obvious as the sun in the sky."

Jana smiled self-consciously. She had hoped to keep her encounter with Chief Russell to herself for the time being. No reason to worry the rest, she'd told herself, though it was not his threat to her family's livelihood that her thoughts had returned to again and again.

It was his…his…

It was *him*. All of him. He was larger than life in her mind, standing there in his crisp blue uniform, looking her over with want in his eyes. Not the leering kind of male interest she often encountered. Henry Russell was a good, honorable man—she didn't need The Sight to sense that, even if she'd be smart to retain her natural suspicion of his profession.

She suspected that he was a lusty man, a man of big, bold appetites. Too conscious of his status as chief of police to act on them when in uniform, but if she should meet him again when he was out of it…*fireworks!*

Stop it, Jana told herself. You know you can't have a fling with a cop. The very idea was laughable.

Except she wasn't laughing. She was *wanting*.

Aside from the handshake, they hadn't touched. Yet when she closed her eyes, she could feel the satin glide of his broad, meaty muscles beneath her palms as if it had actually happened. She knew the scrape of his granite jaw, the hard press of his lips, the deftness of his tongue, reaching into her mouth…

She stole a glance at Magda. The older woman was looking away, smiling indulgently toward the campfire, where two of the women were cooking supper in a Dutch oven and a pot suspended on a tripod over the flames. Comforting scents of smoke, coffee, roasting meat and pipe tobacco drifted through the camp. Once again Jana was reminded that for all her hopes and ambitions, there was much to be said for the old ways. She planned to do everything in her power to protect them, to keep the best of their lifestyle and discard the worst.

Yes. She would do well to remember that, next time she drifted into a reverie about making love with a police officer. Inevitably, her Gypsy clan would clash with authority…and she could choose only one side.

It didn't matter how much her body yearned to receive his kiss. She was a Romany first; a woman second.

Jana took a breath. "The *gadje* was no one special, Baba Magda. He helped me with the car, that's all."

"No one special? Then why is he still on your mind?"

Jana frowned. "I'll forget him soon enough."

"You'll *see* him soon enough," Magda said, chuckling softly. Her gaze was remote, dreaming. Jana's pulse sped up, galloping faster and faster, like the ponies she used to ride bareback across the fields before she was taken away from her Gypsy home, thrust into middle-class America and expected to keep quiet and behave.

Magda was always right. Jana *would* see the police chief again. Not much in her life was a certainty, but another encounter with Henry Russell was.

He would be back.

Causing trouble for her, one way—Jana's heart squeezed tight—or another.

HENRY SAT behind his desk, staring at the accessories and neat stacks of reports without seeing them. Automatically, he nudged his blotter a quarter inch to the right, aligning it with the lamp base. From the time he was fifteen, when his parents were divorced and his father moved away from Philadelphia with his new girlfriend and her children, it had been Henry's responsibility to bring order out of chaos. One harried mother, five younger siblings, ages three to fourteen—he'd whipped them all into shape. He was thirty by the time the youngest, Mike, had gone off to college and his mother had finally remarried, to a portly retired postman from Erie. Henry's obligations had downscaled from all-encompassing to the occasional financial or psychological boost.

Thirty years old and his life had finally been his own.

After fifteen years of hard duty, some men would have revolted. Ditched the career and gone off to live in a grass hut with a nubile native girl. But not Henry. He was a glutton for punishment.

He'd assessed his position and found that the only change he wanted was less stress and risk. So he'd resigned from his post with the Penn State Police to accept the top job in Blue Cloud, where law enforcement was still about maintaining the peace, not containing the anarchy. At the back of his mind had been an idea about finding a good woman and raising a family of his own, but his existence as a small-town police chief had not been as easygoing as he'd expected.

Oh, it wasn't dangerous. Not in the least. But the duties were demanding. Constant. Sometimes irksome.

Henry didn't mind being on the job twenty-four/ seven; in fact, he'd thrived. He was accustomed to being needed. Perhaps he'd even sought it out, now that his family was pretty much set.

He had an entire town to take care of now.

No threats to the citizens' well-being were tolerated. Jana Vargas and her band of Gypsies, included.

"Chief?" Officer Sam Blake poked his head inside Henry's office door. "You wanted me to report in?"

"Is that a question?" Henry barked, slamming shut the manila file folder that contained preliminary background checks from the West Virginia P.D. and one crinkled copy of the bright yellow flyers proclaiming, Come to the Gypsy Fair! that had begun showing up around town.

"No, sir."

"Then report."

Officer Blake cleared his throat, standing front and center before Henry's desk. "The woman's car was left at Spotsky's. Abe says it's a beater, gonna be several days before he gets it running. After she handed out the flyers, the woman did some shopping. Drugstore, a few groceries at the Pick-N-Pay. Then she grabbed a ride out of town with the Wolf sisters."

"Did you take a look through her camp?"

"Yes, sir."

"Ask for their papers?"

"All in order, sir."

"Warn them about fire danger?"

"Yes, sir."

"See anything suspicious?"

"Not that I noticed, sir."

"Fine." Henry waved. "You can go. Tell the officers on duty tonight to keep their eyes open."

Blake shuffled his feet. "Um, Chief?"

Henry scrawled the name *Vargas* on the tab of the folder before raising his face. Sam Blake was a good officer, but not yet seasoned. He was twenty-four, fully ten years younger than Henry, still at the stage where he hoped to impress the girls with his firearm and badge.

"I asked Bethany at the courthouse about the registry and license fees for the fair. She said it was all done by the book, well within the cutoff date."

"Bethany?" Henry echoed, wondering how he could have forgotten to ask about that little item on his checklist. Maybe because the words *Gypsy fair* had conjured up a vivid picture in his mind, one that featured a full-breasted Jana Vargas swaying her hips in a skirt-swishing, pout-puckering, darkly seductive dance directed solely at him?

He shifted in his chair.

"The clerk," Sam explained, "the cute redheaded one with the big bazooms…" His voice trailed off. He winced, obviously waiting for Henry to come down on him for conduct unbecoming an officer.

Instead, Henry said, "Right," as he shifted again.

Sam was blushing. "Sorry, sir. I remember—keep it professional."

"No problem."

"Huh?"

"I said—" Henry blinked. "Right. Keep it professional. No fraternization between departments."

"Yes, sir!"

Henry pushed away from the desk. "Aw, give it a break, officer. Wanna go get a beer?"

3

"Do you know about the Gypsies?"

Henry gazed over the crowd of milling guests, his eyes peeled for trouble. Although a tea-and-cakes tent reception populated by overdressed, middle-aged royalty gawkers was not a venue for major crime activity, he didn't really have the time or patience to spare to go over the same conversation again. Cornelia Applewhite wasn't the first—or even the fifth—to ask him about the Gypsies. Unfortunately, she was the mayor; he had to pay heed to her concerns.

"Yes, I know about the Gypsies." Of course he knew. Even if it had taken him longer than it should have to catch up to speed. "I've known since yesterday. And I believe they prefer to be called Rom or Romany, these days. *Gypsy* is not the politically correct term."

Cornelia glanced at her silent escort, Rockford Spotsky II, the bald businessman whom everyone just called Spotsky. The man shrugged. Corny continued to mull. She was a short woman with a big voice and a matching sense of importance, one of those officious people who believed their presence was a lot more vital to the continuing rotation of Earth than it actually was. While she interfered with Henry's job too much for his taste, her heart was in the right place—with Blue Cloud's continuing prosperity—so he rolled with the punches. He'd become pretty tolerant in his four years as chief of police.

"Politically, I need your word that the Gypsies won't give me any trouble," the mayor said, apparently having decided that since the Rom didn't vote, she didn't have to spare their feelings. "This weekend is very important for our town. If all goes well, the princess's visit will put us on the map."

Spotsky nodded.

Or if all goes bad, Henry added silently. Perish the thought. Wasn't gonna happen on his watch.

"I can't make any promises," he said. "But I'm keeping a look out, Mayor. As are my officers." Well, one officer. With a staff of nine, four currently on duty, he couldn't assign them all to an orderly event like the princess's reception. Not when there were parking citations to write and the mystery of Elspeth Hess's trampled daffodils to investigate.

"See that you do," Cornelia intoned. She was the kind of woman who intoned frequently. Henry was grateful when activity at the museum doors drew her attention away from him. "Ah! The princess! I must run. I *do* hope she's fully recovered."

The mayor took off, leading with her upthrust chin, silk scarf flying. Spotsky followed, his bug eyes glued to the pretty princess.

While the crowd was momentarily distracted by the emergence of Princess Liliane, Henry scanned their faces, looking for anyone out of place. Earlier, he'd caught a glimpse of a dark head slipping furtively among the guests and had gotten the tingle at his nape that meant danger. He always trusted the tingle.

Applause greeted the young princess, who'd come all the way from Grunberg to honor her American grandmother. Satisfied that trouble was not imminent from the direction of the crowd, Henry turned to observe the proceedings. Other than looking somewhat pink in the face, Princess Liliane appeared to be none the worse for the unfortunate bee sting she'd suffered when she'd stuck her nose in the bouquet of flowers presented to her on arrival.

Simon Tremayne, the museum curator, had swept the princess inside to attend to her. He was still hovering at her side. Lucky guy. The princess was a delightful dish—cute, blond, curvy and willing to laugh at herself in the midst of Cornelia's pomp and circumstance.

The mayor was busily forming a reception line. Excellent, Henry thought, motioning for Officer Blake to urge the guests into it. Order was good. Order was easily controlled. Order was Henry's goal in life, and he'd made a helluva good show of it thus far.

Then he saw her. Jana Vargas, skulking at the back of the crowd, hiding in the shadow of the gaily striped red-and-white tent. She did not seem interested in the princess. Her intent was elsewhere.

Henry always kept his hair clipped short and the back of his neck shaved. But damn if his remaining follicles didn't tingle at one fleeting glimpse of the inscrutably sexy woman. Made it hard to tell if he was feeling danger or attraction.

One he could act on, so danger it was.

He worked his way through the crowd, avoiding happy revelers wielding tipsy cake plates. Out of the corner of his eye, he saw the dark head again, slithering in and out of the crush. Long hair. The glint of an earring. Moving in the opposite direction.

Henry stopped. Swiveled his head back and forth. Was Jana that quick?

Or were there two of them? Maybe…working together?

He didn't like the odds. These sort of traveling bands were known for their petty thievery and a variety of con games.

No one worked a scam in *his* town.

He waited for a moment, tracking the more suspicious lurker with his eyes. Despite the long hair and earring, the second person appeared to be a male.

Suddenly Jana's face popped up at the back of the tent again, near her previous position, peering past beflowered sun hats to make a quick survey of the guests. Was she the decoy or was she setting their positions? Planning a quick two-person strike?

Not if Henry had anything to say about it!

A hand gripped his shoulder, halting his beeline for Jana. "Who's that guy?" Simon Tremayne said, indicating the reception line with a nod. A tall handsome man in a tailored blue suit was charming the princess, making her giggle.

Henry spared one quick glance as he tipped back his cap. "Tourist? We've got a lot of them in town this weekend." Which was making his job more troublesome than usual. He didn't want to panic the masses by sending up an alarm too soon.

Simon asked if Henry was sure. Of course he was sure. He knew every person in Blue Cloud, even the agoraphobic computer whiz who lived in Wanda Finch's basement apartment.

Simon insisted. "He doesn't look suspicious to you?"

Well, hell. Henry gritted his jaw, searching for the elusive Gypsies. "Everyone looks suspicious to me."

Simon muttered something about the man being too slick. Clearly, the curator was taken with the princess and couldn't be relied on for an objective assessment. Not like Henry, who never let his personal feelings interfere with his professional duty. He'd arrest Jana Vargas in a hot second. But where had she gotten to?

"The princess seems to approve," he said, knowing it would get under Simon's skin. They'd been working together on a complicated security setup, hooking the museum's state-of-the-art alarm system up to the police station. Simon was the superintellectual type whose immense stores of esoteric knowledge baffled Henry. What good did knowing the lineage of every Pharaoh who'd floated down the Nile do you in the modern world?

"Stone," the curator said. His eyes narrowed with disapproval as he swiped a hand across his high forehead. "His name's Stone."

"Ah."

Simon looked hopeful. "Does that mean anything to you?"

"Nope," Henry said. Jeez. He couldn't be bothered right now by the curator's rivalry for the fair princess's hand. He had bigger fish to fry. But he had to catch her—*them*—first.

While Simon went on about running a check on the "suspicious" Mr. Stone, Henry looked for Jana and her cohort. He saw her moving among the guests every now and then, super casual-like, with an air of detachment. She wasn't fooling him, though. He saw how closely she watched the crowd.

Something was up. Henry could sense it. The pot was being stirred. And Jana Vargas was in it up to her elbow.

"I'll keep an eye on the guy," Henry said to placate Simon, filing Stone's name away in his memory banks for later evaluation.

He glanced at the foreign princess. She had brought along her own bodyguard, but a VIP was a VIP, and Henry was determined that not a hair on Princess Lili's head would be disturbed while she stayed in Blue Cloud. Aside from bee stings that could not possibly be blamed on the Blue Cloud Police Department.

The prickling at Henry's nape was his first sign that he shouldn't have looked away from Jana. His second was the howl of outrage that rose above the chattering crowd.

"*Pickpocket!*"

JANA FROZE as the cry went up again. *Pickpocket*. Fear like shards of ice shot through her veins. Then came the hot rush of anger.

Oh, Gabriel! How could you?

Beneath the tent, the crush of party guests pushed this way and that as they spread apart, then reformed into new, confused groups. Jana took advantage of the melee, slipping unnoticed between the round tables as people abandoned their seats, gaping and gesturing at a woman in a feathered, wide-brimmed hat who seemed to be the center of the trouble. An open purse dangled from her wrist. Her husband, standing uselessly beside her and waving his arms, was hollering about his missing wallet.

Suddenly, another woman screeched. "My pearls!" She clutched her neck as if the missing necklace would miraculously appear.

Jana's instinct was to run.

She stepped away from the tent, intent on a cluster of trees, thick enough to provide her good cover to watch for Gabriel. If she could catch him in time, she could make him leave *without* the goods. She was nearly there when a man's arm snaked around her waist, hoisting her off her feet as he swung her around, up against his body. "Not so fast."

Jana let out a string of colorful swear words. She wrenched at his arm, digging her nails in, but the police chief was too strong. His arm stayed clamped around her waist, pressing her backside tight against his groin. She went limp, waiting for him to ease up so she could slip away.

He didn't relax. "Don't bother trying to fake me out," he said into her ear. "I know a possum when I feel one."

Jana straightened with a snap and stomped her sandaled foot on his toe. His broad chest hitched against her back as he snorted out a laugh at her pitiful effort. The man was a brute...a beast...a bull. *Amria!*

She drew in a deep breath, quieting herself in a belated attempt to regain her dignity. "You may release me. I won't run."

"You already did."

"I wasn't running. I was walking—"

"Very fast, and toward the trees, oddly enough. Didn't you hear my instructions? I ordered everyone to gather under the tent."

"Who could hear over such a babble?"

Henry dragged her toward the stand of lush green elm and chestnut trees. "Shall we take a look at your assignation point?"

Jana didn't waste her breath on denials. Let him look. The more time the chief spent hassling her, the likelier it would be that Gabriel would get away untouched. It might be morally wrong of her to hope for her cousin's escape, but he was family. If he'd had a hand in the thievery—and she was shrewd enough to know that he probably had—she'd deal with the wrongdoing in her own way.

Henry crashed through branches and bushes to a small clearing, pulling her alongside with his right hand locked on her elbow. ''There's nothing to see,'' she finally said, her face flaming with hurt pride. As often as it happened, she should have expected it. But this time, with this man, she'd hoped for the benefit of the doubt. Even if it was only *she* and not her cousin who deserved it.

That he had good reason to suspect her only made it worse for some reason. She couldn't be as angry with him as he deserved.

''You've got nothing,'' she taunted. ''Nothing!''

Henry stared into her eyes, his own as dark as a thundercloud. ''Your partner may have gotten away, but I still have you. That's plenty valuable.'' For an instant, his mouth softened and he seemed on the verge of human decency, but then he grimaced instead. His expression turned hard and unemotional. He pivoted on his heel and towed her back toward the tent.

Well, there you go, Jana scolded herself. You asked for objectivity, didn't you?

She stumbled over a root, stubbing her toe. The chief swung around again, catching her by the other elbow to steady her. ''Are you all right?''

She was ready to make a smart remark, but a slight vibration inside startled her into staying quiet. The feeling began as a fluttering in the pit of her stomach and then moved outward in slow, shivery sensations that brought blood rushing to raw nerve endings. She swallowed, wishing he'd take his hands off her. It was obvious, what was happening between them. He should recognize it and keep away from her before they wound up rolling around on the ground, clawing clothes off each other.

"I'm all right," she said, breathing through her nose. "I'm even innocent, not that you care." *Dinili!* Why had she sounded so petulant?

"I care." He looked at her from beneath the brim of his cap. "Just as I care for the safety of my citizens."

Recognizing the sense of duty, her temper dropped another notch. But before she could respond, he was hauling her across the lawn again, barking orders to the scattered guests, making the disobedient stragglers move away from their cars and back to the tent. Jana stayed at his side, surrendered to his iron grip. She suffered hostile stares without expression, not even able to summon a smile over the chubby woman who was tottering around with the remains of a plateful of cake plastered to her polka-dotted behind, while a friend fanned her pink face with a huge, gaudy sun hat.

Jana closed her eyes. *Thanks, Gabriel.* There went any chance of maintaining good relations with the townspeople.

A man approached the chief and began asking what they should do with the princess. Jana gazed broodingly into the milling crowd until the words *body search* caught her attention. She turned to the men, then, exuding every iota of disdain that was at her disposal. "A body search? Just you try it!" If ever she could achieve high dudgeon, let it be now.

Henry merely looked at her, his face as bland as va-nilla pudding.

"Body search?" she said again, steaming. "I'll give you body search, Chief Russell." *Gadje Dilo!* Foolish white man!

"Thanks for the offer, Ms. Vargas." Sensing his amusement, she reared back. The cocky beast was on the verge of laughing at her.

"I can take care of the search," he went on. "You only have to provide the body."

Jana stared at Henry, willing him to burst into flames. Her body trembled with outrage. "Harassment," she accused. The threat tended to make even the worst of the cops back off.

"Not yet." Henry's voice was menacing, but cool.

"Are you threatening me?"

"That depends on whether or not your cohort slipped away with the goods."

Jana's heart sank. She inhaled, knowing she had to calm down if she was to keep her wits about her. Her voice sounded from faraway. "My cohort?"

"The young man you were looking for in the crowd. Possibly working with." Henry's eyes added the rest: *And intended to rendezvous with in the woods.*

Then he already knew about Gabriel. He'd seen him. Jana heard herself denying it, but it was clear she wasn't fooling the police chief. Henry Russell might be sus-ceptible to her on a physical level, but the man was no dummy. He wouldn't let good chemistry interfere with his job.

A few minutes later, a startled Jana found herself following the royal entourage into the museum. A group of reporters and photographers descended on Princess Lili, but the official group plowed straight through the crowd without stopping, the princess's feisty companion keeping the press at bay with bold thrusts of her umbrella. Jana and Henry brought up the rear. Even though it wasn't Jana the press was interested in, she ducked her head away from the camera flashes, grateful when the chief put his arm around her shoulders, shielding her face from view.

The doors of the museum clanged shut behind them. While the others discussed what to do and where to go, Jana looked around with keen interest, hoping to get a glimpse of the Brunner family jewels. They were in a spacious entrance hall with a stone floor and a wide staircase. Exhibition rooms opened off either side, but they were presently unlit, the doorways barricaded with velvet ropes.

The princess was asking if the jewels would be safe, considering the apparent criminal activity that had disrupted the reception. Henry wasn't ready to guarantee anything, but his manly competence seemed to reassure the princess. Or was it Simon Tremayne, the curator, whom Princess Lili trusted? He seemed quite attentive to her.

Jana watched them from beneath half-lidded eyes. *Petty thieves,* Henry said, glancing at *her*. She was innocent, so it was illogical for her to be insulted. But she was. Why did the man's words rub her the wrong way, no matter what he said?

The entire group was suddenly looking at Jana. She withdrew into her defensive shell, too aware of the contrast between the poised, lovely princess and herself. Intending to drum up business for the caravan while passing out the flyers for the fair—they would be selling crafts and telling fortunes—she'd worn her most wild and colorful Gypsy clothing that morning, and loaded up on the jewelry, too. It was what people expected. She favored brightness and shine, anyway, so she didn't mind. The look was traditional. Compared to the princess, though...

Jana fought back a shudder. She would not be ashamed!

Henry reached toward her. She flinched. He said nothing, only removed his hand, holding between two fingers the small leaf he'd plucked from her untidy hair. Then the princess was holding out her hand to Jana, introducing herself. Henry slipped the leaf into his pocket.

"Hello. I'm Princess Lili of Grunberg."

Resentment surged up in Jana. There was a history between her family and the princess's, but *she* was the only one who was aware of it. The Brunners had been ignoring the Vargas's claims for two hundred years. "Oh, I know who you are," she said, letting her gaze sweep across the blonde. She tilted back her head, reminding herself that *she* was also a princess. "I am Jana Vargas."

Surprisingly, Princess Lili recognized the name at once. "Vargas?"

Jana nodded.

"How peculiar, considering that the Brunner bridal tiara is set with the *Vargas* diamond!" The princess's pert little nose wrinkled. "Have you ever been to Grunberg? Could you be related to someone who owned the diamond previous to my family?"

"No, I've never been to Grunberg. But some of my people were there a long time ago."

"Would I know of them?"

Oh, that was laughable. Jana smiled, disbelieving that even a sheltered, pampered princess could be so naive. "Not very likely. Romany folk don't get invited to the castle for formal dress balls."

"Romany," murmured the silver-haired woman with the umbrella, who'd been addressed as Mrs. Grundy. She appeared to be some kind of companion or chaperon. Jana had barely glanced at her before, but now she inspected the woman more closely. Mrs. Grundy wore sensible shoes, old-lady hose and a woolen suit. Her bearing was stiff, her accent British. She was the type of woman who would have been called "handsome" in her prime, but was now stolid and rather commanding. Something about her tickled at Jana's intuition.

Mrs. Grundy was not as strictly porridge-and-cambric-tea as she appeared. Beneath the starch was…an aura of old-time magic. Suddenly Jana understood. It was the woman's similarity to Baba Magda that was so familiar.

Her eyes met the older woman's. Mrs. Grundy blinked, flustered by their silent exchange—a recognition.

The princess was watching. "Amelia? Do you know how the Vargas diamond came by its name?" She turned to the others to explain. "There's quite a legend associated with the tiara, but I don't recall why it's called the Vargas diamond."

Mrs. Grundy's voice was as stiff as her posture. "I couldn't say."

I'll bet, Jana thought.

She jumped in without second thought. "I could," she told Princess Lili, handing her the last of the flyers that had remained crumpled in her fist all this time. She must have dropped the others in the tent. "If you care to learn the truth…"

The princess blinked, then looked down at the cheaply printed paper. "A Gypsy carnival? Ooh, with fortune-telling!"

She really was young, naive and enthusiastic, Jana decided. Which was refreshing, considering that she'd expected the princess to be stuck-up and aloof.

The princess's bodyguard interrupted, insisting they depart for safer quarters. Mrs. Grundy turned a stalwart back to Jana, dismissing her as she called for their limo. The curator tossed a key to Henry, offering him the use of the museum snack shop to conduct interrogations.

"I'll get the key back to you directly," the chief said.

"I want to stash Miss Vargas, here—" he barely glanced at her, but Jana was more than aware of his hand on her arm "—while I oversee procedures outdoors."

She said a small prayer under her breath, not that it was necessary. Gabriel was as fleet as a deer; by now, he would certainly be long gone. "Stash me?" she said to Henry, intending to distract him even further. "I'm a human being, not a piece of luggage. You can't detain me for no good reason."

The police chief wasn't to be dissuaded. "I have reason. You may be a conspirator in the pickpocketing scheme, which means it's well within my bounds of authority to hold you for questioning. For the time being, consider yourself in police custody, Ms. Vargas. You will remain so until my suspicions are proved."

"Or disproved."

They had ascended the stairs as they spoke. The other princess was being hustled off to Simon Tremayne's office, in her own way as beholden to her keepers as Jana. Lili tossed a small smile of commiseration over her shoulder.

Jana blinked. She hadn't expected to *like* Princess Lili. They were, in a distant way, enemies.

Two hundred years ago, Lili's ancestors, the royal family of the principality of Grunberg, had mysteriously gained possession of a legendary diamond. The diamond had next appeared on the head of a Brunner bride, stunningly mounted on her bridal tiara.

Over the years, Romany folk had repeated a tale that

the diamond had been stolen by the royal family's henchmen from a Gypsy trader named Josef Vargas. He'd died swearing that each royal bride's fate would be cursed until the diamond was worn by a Vargas once again. There'd never been an explanation for how Josef had acquired the diamond in the first place. Given her ancestors' reputations as swindlers and thieves, Jana wasn't sure she cared to know.

That very tiara was here today, in this museum, the first time it had been on public exhibition in years. Not an opportunity Jana could let pass. She wanted—no, she *needed* to see it with her own eyes. Because, despite all the swindles and lies and revisionist history, the valuable jewel had retained its original name.

It was indeed the Vargas diamond.

"I'M SORRY," Henry found himself saying when he was about to lock Jana into the snack shop. He'd examined the place. The other doors were locked and the row of small windows were too high off the ground to be a likely means of escape. "You'll be all right here for a few minutes. I'll be back shortly."

"You should either arrest me or release me," Jana said. Her mouth was set stubbornly. "I don't have anything to tell you."

"I'm not a small-time bozo police chief, Ms. Vargas. I recognized your moves—" His voice caught. *Damn.* One stupid word and the image was back: Jana, dancing, beckoning him with her lips puckered into a sensual promise....

"I don't have moves." Her voice was stony. Unrelenting. Completely at odds with her opulent curves.

Henry shook his head to clear it. "Don't give me that. At the start of my career, I walked a beat in Philadelphia. I got to know every con game and pickpocket maneuver in the street hucksters' repertoire. You were working the crowd with your partner—a young man who looks a lot like you, if I'm not mistaken."

Fear flared in Jana's eyes, then was quickly doused. "You *are* mistaken. Besides, there are several members of my group who might fit that description."

"We'll see about that." Henry looked over the door before he closed it. It was a sturdy door with a heavy-duty mechanism that locked from the outside. No way was Jana eluding his grasp, even though it was extremely likely that her partner in crime was long gone. Blake and the other officers would have been too distracted by the crowd to prevent all escapes, especially one by an experienced pickpocket accustomed to eluding capture.

Jana leaned close, pressing against him as he pulled the door shut. Her lashes flickered. Her lips were soft and pouting. Long strands of hair curved against her cheeks and shoulders, leading his focus downward to the hint of full, rounded cleavage visible between beads and blouse. "Mmm, Henry," she breathed. "I was wondering…"

His eyelids lowered. He took in her scent, felt the warmth of her body, supple and yielding. Oh, yes. He could sink right into her….

"What if I'm claustrophobic?" she said.

His eyes snapped open. She'd put him under her spell—again!

"Deal with it, Ms. Vargas," he said, his voice all gruff because he felt like a dupe. He slipped a quarter from his pocket and dropped it down the front of her blouse. "Go buy yourself a candy bar while you wait." She took the cue and glanced at the vending machines, one hand clutched between her breasts. He walked out and locked the door, pocketing the key.

Henry tried not to think of how, with another ten seconds of bewitchment, she could have lifted it off him with no resistance at all.

The woman was a menace to his authority. And his control.

4

JANA HELD her clenched fist against her heart, feeling its wild rhythm. The man had eyes that could see for miles, deep into her Gypsy soul.

The coin slipped farther between her breasts, at first cold against her skin and then warm. Warm as her thoughts. Fantasies, they were, of being swept into Henry's arms, his lips crushing hers, his big strong hands roaming across her body...

She swallowed, stepping away from the locked door. The quarter dropped past her ribs and she freed her blouse from the waistband of her swishy skirt with an impatient tug, sending the silver coin spinning across the floor.

She watched until it had slowed, wobbled, then fell over flat. *Heads, I boink him. Tails, I keep away.*

Her stomach muscles squeezed tight when she stooped to pick up the coin. *Tails.* Even the Fates were against them. She flipped the quarter in the air, slapped it on the back of her hand. Tails again.

Fate? Bosh! *I don't have to listen.*

There'd always been a push-me/pull-you demon inside Jana, the pragmatic Anglo half warring with her free-spirited Romany blood. Eight years living with her staid New England grandparents in a Boston suburb, of being well dressed, well fed, quieted, disciplined and educated, had a lasting effect even though she'd fought it.

The first years were the worst. Trapped in a house of quiet whispers when she wanted to wail and blubber about her pain and terror, her fear. Her mother, Ann, pale, sickly, grieving. Her gray grandparents, worried for their daughter, alternately mystified and appalled by the fractious, messy creature who was their grandchild.

Even now, when Jana was firmly established in the *vitsa,* there remained a small, unspoken part of her that wanted…stability. Sameness. She'd lived in both worlds, chose one, but still hadn't entirely forgotten what she'd left behind. While Ann had not remarried, she had gradually revived, resuming the quiet life that she, too, had once forsaken. Jana had looked, but there was no sign in her mother that she missed the caravan. Perhaps it was too much a part of her buried past. Where for Jana, being with the Vargases was her only way of remembering the father she continued to miss.

He would have understood. Stephane Vargas had gone against his own tradition to marry the woman he loved.

Not that Jana intended to go so far. She was only attracted, chemistrywise, to Henry. It was a physical thing.

She picked up the quarter. Touched it to her lips.

Then winced at herself. The gesture was romantic, fanciful. No time for that.

She stood. All the doors were secured; she'd watched Henry test them. But the access doors locked from this side. She could probably pick either of the locks, if she needed to...

Tap, tap.

Jana whirled, searching out the sound.

Tap, tap. Tap. Tap.

The window, farthest on the left. A hand was pressed to the glass. Jana rushed over as Princess Lili's face appeared.

"Shh," said the princess, when Jana had climbed onto a chair and raised the sash of the small window. Lili was in her nylon-clad feet, crouched on the decorative brick ledge that ran along the building beneath the row of windows. "Simon's right outside."

Jana gripped the princess's hand, thinking to pull her inside to safety. "How in the world...?"

Lili didn't budge off the ledge. "I crawled out the washroom window. It's right next door. If you'll let go of my hand, I have a copy of the key that Simon gave to the police chief."

"I..." Jana hesitated. She could escape. But did she want to? She shook her head. "It doesn't matter. The door is locked from the other side."

Lili had produced the key from an inside pocket of her fitted pink jacket, a designer original, going by Jana's glimpse of the flawlessly finished silk lining. No better than the needlework some of her Romany sisters did, though.

"What about the other doors?" Lili asked. "You can try it, at least."

"I don't need to escape," Jana said, even as she took the key and tried it on the other doors. The first opened onto a small supply closet filled with packages of paper napkins, plates and the like. The second door led to a kitchen area, which had another exit. She opened that door a crack and peeked into the hallway of the museum. Simon Tremayne stood waiting, running a restless hand through his short light brown hair.

He turned and pressed his ear to the door behind him, a worried look on his face. "Princess Lili?"

Jana carefully positioned the door so it looked to be shut, even though the lock didn't catch, ran back through the lunchroom and handed the key to the princess, who was still crouched in the window. Astonishing. Why would Lili take such a risk? "Simon's calling for you. Can you get back all right?"

Lili tucked away the key, her balance perfect. "Absolutely. Thank goodness for all those boarding-school gymnastic classes I was forced to endure with Mademoiselle Rah-Rah."

Jana's mouth twitched. "Emerson Junior High School. Ms. Barb McClanahan, not-so-fondly known among her students as 'Butch.' Dodgeball was a killer." She shrugged. "You'd better hurry."

Lili rose up, took a step toward the bathroom window, then peered in at Jana again. "If you want to escape in style, I have a limo waiting for me outside."

Jana wasn't sure. "I'll think about it."

"Think quick," Lili said. "You have only a few minutes before we leave."

"I'm not guilty," Jana blurted. Her face grew warm. Why had she felt it necessary to say that? Hadn't she learned not to let others' opinions matter to her?

"I know." The princess smiled. "But don't you want to escape anyway?"

Even before she thought of Gabriel, it was Henry's stubborn, implacable face that flashed into Jana's mind. One-upping him would be a kick. He'd be so outraged. And impassioned. Thrillingly so.

"Maybe," she conceded, thinking secondly of Gabe. If she could reach him before Henry did, she could make him do right.

Lili fluttered her fingers as she crept away. "Then go."

Jana climbed on the chair again and watched until the princess had safely reentered the building. They waved. Jana closed the window, battling the urge to flee. It wouldn't do her any good. Henry would track her down easily enough and then accuse her of resisting…whatever. But she might be able to find Gabe in the meantime, and possibly repair the damage he'd done.

Jana hurried to the kitchen, letting the latch of the connecting door catch behind her. Let the big chief try to figure that one out! She opened the hall door in time to see Simon, followed closely by the bodyguard and the companion, Mrs. Grundy, rush into the ladies' room.

Voices raised. Princess Lili must have created a diversion. Perfect.

Jana slipped away without notice.

GABRIEL FOUND HER. In her bones, she knew he would. He was almost ten years younger, but they had a strong connection. It had been Gabe as a toddler who'd clung to her when her grandparents had arrived at the camp to take her and her mother away. His chubby face and pleading eyes were the last she'd seen of her Rom family for eight long years.

Gabe, now grown tall and wiry with a restless energy that eclipsed Jana's own, intercepted her in a small park not far from the bustling downtown. Nowhere was really safe in a town of this size, especially if you stood out as a foreigner, but Gabe was good at blending in. Even to Jana, he didn't look furtive or guilty.

She grabbed him by the arm and hauled him behind the thick gnarled trunk of an old chestnut tree. "What did you do?"

Gabe grinned, brushing a hank of long black hair off his forehead. His eyes glinted. "Nothing."

"Don't you dare lie to me!"

He grew sulky. "You're no fun, Jana. You've gotten so cautious since Zharko passed—"

She interrupted; Zharko Vargas had been their clan's chieftain, the *Rom Baro*. "And you, Gabe," she snapped, giving him a shake, "you've become a *choro*." A thief.

His devil-may-care grin slipped out. "That's bred in my bones."

"It is not! I'm ashamed of you."

"Don't be. I was like quicksilver."

"*I* saw you, smart mouth. And so did the chief of police."

Gabe shrugged. "He didn't see enough."

"He's going to pick you up for questioning." Jana leaned past the tree to scan the nearby streets. The quaint small town had a celebratory air about it, which was normally good for business. Many would be attracted to their Gypsy Fair. She turned back to Gabe, reproachful. "And me, as well. Henry thinks we're conspirators."

Her cousin's brows arched. "You call him Henry?"

"I have a right." Jana glared. "He dragged me from the reception, in front of everyone. Even the princess saw."

"I did, too," Gabe said slyly.

"Where were you?"

"In the trees—ten feet away from you."

Jana flushed, remembering how she'd liked being held close against Henry's strong body. "Then you're lucky he nabbed me instead."

"Yeah. *I* got lucky."

Her face burned, but she refused the taunt. Better to ignore the implication. She took hold of Gabriel's face, clasping it between her palms so he couldn't look away. His dark eyes met hers, flashing with a familiar defiance. The boy was too handsome and smooth for his own good. The only thing he resented more than the simple but spare Romany lifestyle was the prejudice shown against them, suffering his own conflicting ideas because of it. He wanted better, but he wasn't quite ready to leave the clan to find it. Instead, he'd fallen into bad habits—petty thievery, small cons—following the old Rom belief that the Anglos were fools for the taking. Jana suspected it wasn't only the lure of easy cash; it was also a perverse sort of pride in putting one over on their "enemy."

"Listen to me," she said, clamping her hands tighter. "You are going to return what you stole." Gabe opened his mouth. "Don't," she said, "don't say a word. I want you to gather all of it—the wallets, the money—"

Gabe's thick black lashes lowered. "I dumped them."

"Get them back."

He turned his head forcefully; pulling from her grasp. His expression was dark and resentful. "Should I turn myself in, too?"

She wasn't willing to go so far. "You should go back to camp and hope that I can make this good with the police. Think about what kind of role model you are to the children. Rudy looks up to you. Don't you care what you're putting into his head?"

"That's not my responsibility."

"It should be." Traditionally, a woman did not lead the *vitsa*. Jana had taken charge only in Gabe's stead, deferring to advice from Baba Magda and her uncle

Tito. They were all waiting for Gabriel to grow up and assume his responsibilities.

"And the pearls," she remembered. "Especially the pearls."

"What pearls?"

"Ga-a-abe," she warned.

Reluctantly he met her eyes. "I didn't lift any pearls." He scuffed at the grass. "Wait here. I'll bring the loot to the park."

"Watch out for police cars." There'd be no hope if Henry caught Gabe in possession of the stolen goods.

"They'll never see me before I see them," he boasted. She couldn't deny it. He was as elusive and light-footed as an animal in the wild.

"Bring the pearls," she said, trying again.

But Gabe only shook his head as he moved off among the trees. She watched him wait for a lull in traffic before darting across the street and into an alley. Frequently, he spoke of leaving the caravan, not to attend college as Jana hoped, but for the nebulous adventure and fortune that young men dreamed of. Be it to arrest or the open road, Jana often despaired that she— and the family—would lose him altogether.

HENRY WAS PACING his office when an unnatural hush in the squad room perked up his ears. Activity and noise weren't exactly the bywords of the small station house, but neither was total silence, unless it was the long evening hours, when anyone with a life was home having dinner with their family while Henry did paperwork.

He threw open his door.

Two of his officers, a trio of victims from the museum party, and Mrs. Grace, the station manager, were staring in silence as a woman walked bold as brass past the low-swinging panel gate that separated the public area from the private. Henry noticed two things at once: Jana Vargas still wasn't wearing a bra, and the only sound in the room was the swish of her skirts and the soft jingle of her bangles and beads.

She strode over to Henry, stopped and put out her hands. "I'm turning myself in."

He put a hand over her wrists and slowly lowered them. "You're not under arrest yet, Ms. Vargas. Questioning is voluntary at this point."

She tilted her nose into the air, taking a step back to get away from the contact. His hand had lingered. "You could have told me that when you locked me in the museum."

His fingers closed on sweaty palms. He thrust both fists into his pants pockets. "You left anyway."

With a taunting smile, she looked him over. "There's a vein throbbing in your temple."

He squeezed his eyes shut for a split second. *Concentrate, concentrate.* "How did you manage the escape? The doors were still secure."

She looked mighty pleased with herself. "That's a mystery for you to solve, Chief Russell."

Henry tore away his gaze to focus on the highly interested onlookers, who were gawping at them like a sideshow. He swept a hand toward his office door.

"Shall we, Ms. Vargas? If you don't mind?" he added heavily, more than aware of the throbbing at his temples. The Gypsy woman was a headache, clear and simple.

Not a heartache. Not even close to it.

Jana swept past him. He drew in a deep breath, got a hold on himself, and aimed a glare at his staff. "Get to work. Finish up with the statements and let these poor people go home already."

"Tell her those pearls are family heirlooms," Elspeth Hess warbled. She pressed a hand to her bare throat. Her wattle wobbled. "I simply cannot live without them."

"I'll do my best, Mrs. Hess, but please remember that Ms. Vargas is being questioned as an eyewitness, not a—" Henry's voice strangled. He'd given the victims plenty of reason to believe Jana guilty when he'd dragged her into the museum like a common criminal. For shame, his mother would have scolded, treating a lady that way.

But Jana Vargas was no lady.

She was one-hundred percent woman.

And she'd gotten to him worse than any woman ever had.

Henry turned on his heel and marched into the office. Jana had taken the visitor's seat. Her hands were folded in her lap and her expression was as cool as was possible when nearly every inch of her flagrantly sexy body screamed *fiery temptress*.

"I was about to come after you," he said, lowering himself into his desk chair.

She didn't bat an eyelash. "No need. I am here."

"And your conspirator?"

"There is no conspirator."

Henry counted to ten, three times. Ten bangles on her wrist. Ten inhales and exhales, each one visible in the rise and fall of her breasts. Ten more seconds before she blinked.

"You just called me a *witness,*" she pointed out, narrowing her eyes at him.

"A little white lie."

"Maybe not."

He frowned. "Are you suggesting you saw…?"

"Let's talk about the pearls," she said, waving him off. "It's possible, isn't it, that they were stolen by…an *unknown* party?"

What the hell did that mean? "If you know something, Jana, spit it out."

She shook her head. "I know nothing about the pearls."

Henry let that digest. "And the rest?" He lifted a paper off his desk. "We have two wallets, one money clip and a lady's sterling silver compact missing."

Jana looked at her clasped hands. She licked her lips, hesitated, then spoke swiftly, her voice strained. "I didn't take them, I swear to you. But what if I knew where you might find them? Would that be enough to make amends?"

Henry's honor code demanded full justice, but now

and then he managed to hold his peace and bide his time. He tried to appear amenable. "It would be a start."

"I want you to stop harassing my people."

Amenable faded. "We're not negotiating, Jana."

She leaned forward and grabbed the edge of the desk. "That wasn't a request, Henry."

He also leaned forward, gripping the arms of his chair to hold him back. "When it comes to criminals, I don't make concessions. If you know where the stolen goods are, you'd best confess it now before I—"

"Before you what?" she said, thrusting herself even closer.

"Before I—"

Jana's eyes blazed at him.

He swallowed. Their noses were mere inches apart. He could feel the warmth of her flushed cheeks, see the lighter sapphire flecks in her eyes and the moist sheen where she'd licked her lower lip. Her breath wasn't sweet; it wasn't sour. Hot and spicy, he thought, like her temperament.

"Before I kiss you," he said suddenly. He swore his heart skipped a beat when the words fell out of his mouth.

Her eyes widened, but she didn't retreat. "You wouldn't dare."

Oh, yes, he would. "I've never been a coward." He moved infinitesimally closer.

One, two, three, four...

They were both brash and combative and too stubborn to back down. And they were both breathing hard, fixated on each other's eyes and mouths. Jana's lashes lowered as he covered the last bit of space between them and touched his mouth to hers, catching the soft puff of her involuntary sigh on his tongue. Her lips parted softly against his, then pressed aggressively, meeting his kiss with the full share of sass he'd expected.

Only their mouths touched. Yet it was an astonishing connection—brazen, burning hot. His fingers clenched on the metal chair arms, wanting to delve into her long hair instead. To feel softness, feminine silk and satin and warm, smooth flesh…

His mouth lifted, only to take a breath, but she ducked her face away from his and fell back into her chair with an expression of alarm. She pressed the back of her wrist to her mouth. "What was that about?"

He let out a snort. "Sex?"

"Yes, sex," she said, crossing her arms and biting her lip. Her eyes avoided his. "You realize that I was *not* suggesting a barter." Her brows went up. "No me-for-Gabe deal was struck."

He recoiled. "Do I look like that kind of a man?"

She shrugged. "It's been known to happen."

"If that's so, tell me who, when and where. There are people you can go to. Complaints can be lodged."

"Against yourself?"

"That kiss wasn't about my job and you know it."

Her gaze slid toward his and he saw that she did indeed know exactly what was happening between them, which was worse, in a way. Everything he was about professionally had resisted the attraction, and even that wasn't enough to dissuade him from kissing her. Or planning when he would get the chance to do it again.

"We were in the middle of a conversation," she said.

"Nope. There was no give-and-take involved. You tell me what you know, that's it."

She tossed her hair. "My world's not so black and white."

"Morality is always clear." He slashed the air with his hand. "Right, wrong. They're easy to define."

"Maybe to *you*." She eyed him suspiciously. "Tell me, where does kissing one of your prime suspects fall in these categories of yours?"

"I wasn't kissing a suspect. I was kissing a woman."

"Semantics."

He put on a grin, but his voice was like gravel when he said, "If making love to you is wrong, I don't want to be right." It was too close to the truth to joke about.

She sniffed. "I don't remember saying anything about letting you make love to me."

"There will be no 'letting' involved. You want it as much as me."

"You presume too much."

"Possibly." But he doubted it. He was going to have her in his bed. Or maybe not even a bed. He'd take her anywhere, any time.

He blinked. *Except now, Big Chief. Are you forgetting your dedication to the job?*

Conveniently, it seemed.

Henry cleared his throat. "Back to the matter at hand, Ms. Vargas." *At hand* was a bad phrase to use when she sat no more than an arm's length away from him, looking as self-possessed as before, except for the rosy blush in her cheeks.

He dragged his thoughts away from how she'd feel in his embrace. It was as though he were reeling in a rusty winch. "Tell me what you know about the thefts. If you turn in the goods, the restitution will earn you the department's good favor. That's the best I can promise."

She glanced around the unassuming office, paneled in faux wood and decorated with sports trophies and various citations. "I get the feeling *you* are the department."

"That's so."

Her gaze returned to his face. "I am not the thief. Trust me on that."

"Don't you know that only swindlers and thieves say 'Trust me'?"

"I'm neither." A smile flitted across her face. "Trust me."

He sighed, not sure where his instinct to believe her came from. *This* was why he shouldn't be messing around with her.

She stood. "Are we through?"

He was surprised enough to blurt the truth. "Not on your life."

"For now, we are." She moved toward the door. A

shape melted away, blurred by the pebbled glass, but still recognizable as his biggest dope of an officer, Willis O'Bannion, who'd been twenty years on the job and still couldn't differentiate a fishy suspect from the sardines in his lunch box. Eavesdropping. Whatta sluggo.

Henry got to his feet. "You didn't come here to kiss me, I'm sure. Spill the beans, Ms. Vargas."

She turned, her face a careful mask. "I have no knowledge of the perpetrators, Chief Russell. But there's a chance that you might find the stolen goods in the park on Longfellow Street. Let's say…in a tree. A hollow tree."

"A chance, huh?"

"A good chance."

"And you know this because…?"

"A little bird told me, someone dropped a dime, however you want to put it. I keep my eyes and ears open. But I'm afraid you're going to have to find the pearls on your own. I have absolutely no idea where they are and *I don't expect to get any.*" She tilted her head at him. "*Capisce,* Chief?"

He understood. He didn't like it, and he wasn't sure he entirely believed her, but he understood. More than she knew. "Thank you for the tip, Ms. Vargas. I'll be sure to check it out."

"May I suggest you do it ASAP? Get there before the squirrels."

He nodded. "Yes."

Jana's hand rested on the doorknob. She sneaked a quick peek at him, her dark hair spilling over her shoulder. ''I hope you're satisfied, Henry, because that's all you'll get from me.'' Her voice had dropped an octave, so husky he felt it in his gut again, like a hot spear, except there was no pain. Only desire.

He watched her leave, too poleaxed to reply.

Was she talking about the case?

Or the kiss?

5

OTHER THAN frequent drive-bys of officers on patrol for the Blue Cloud Police Department, the Gypsy camp remained peaceful for the rest of the day. The Rom knew their jobs to prepare for tomorrow's fair and did them with only a little prodding from Jana. Soon the encampment took on a festive air, with colorful wares arranged for display and pennants flying from the tents and makeshift booths. The two old-fashioned wooden caravans were positioned at either end of the row, because they drew the most interest. One was Jana's, and one belonged to *Kako* Tito and Baba Magda, the oldest couple, who acted as grandparents to the entire *vitsa*, most of whom were related by marriage if not by blood.

After supper, which was always a community event, Tito told the children stories by the campfire before sending them off to bed. Jana and one of the younger women, who had married into the clan, got the kids settled into one of the tents. Frequently, Katja, the oldest girl, would ask to sleep in the caravan with Jana, but tonight the children were all about whispers and giggles. Mischief was being planned.

After saying good-night, Jana lurked near the tent for

a while, hoping to catch them sneaking out. She'd been the oldest herself back in those first years at the caravan. Sometimes the ringleader, but just as often the responsible "little mother," riding herd, settling fights and nursing scrapes.

Not much different than what she did now. Jana smiled to herself, thinking of Gabriel. The unrepentant weasel had hidden to watch the police officers recover the stash out of the chestnut tree. He'd told the story after he'd come back to camp at dusk, gesturing and exaggerating it into an outrageous comic event. According to Gabe, the cops had been scrambling, hanging and falling from trees like drunken monkeys before they'd finally found the goods. Uncle Tito had laughed until he was red in the face.

Returning to her little caravan, Jana wondered if Henry had climbed a tree, and if he'd been cursing her when he did.

As the sky deepened into night, Tito took out his fiddle. The adults gathered near the fire. A bottle of homemade wine was passed. Jana sat on the small slanted steps of her little house on wheels. The tension inside her eased. This was the best part of her life with the caravan: the camaraderie of sitting by the campfire beneath the starlit skies, the melancholy music of one lonely fiddle or a strumming guitar sinking into her soul.

From Jana's vantage point above the rest, she was the first to see the stranger crossing the field toward the camp. Her heart leaped. Out of fear, perhaps, but it felt more like a keen anticipation.

It wasn't Henry, though. It was, astonishingly enough, Princess Liliane of Grunberg, traipsing through the long grass without a bodyguard or escort in sight, her short curls shining as pale as the moon.

Gabriel saw Lili next. He stood, letting out a low whistle. Tito drew his bow across the strings with a screech as heads turned, lively conversation fading away as one by one, the others craned their necks to gape at the unexpected guest.

The princess stopped at the edge of the camp, looking nervous, maybe scared. A tentative smile came and went as the Rom continued to stare at her in utter silence, their faces closed and suspicious.

"He-hello?" she said, her voice high as a child's.

Jana stepped forward. She opened her arms. "Welcome!"

The two women met. Jana kissed the princess's cheeks in the European style—smack, smack—holding her firmly about the shoulders, never having read the official guide, *Pomp and Circumstance: How to Meet and Greet Royals.* Not that either she or Lili cared. "Welcome," Jana repeated, "Princess."

Lili blinked. "I don't mean to intrude." She rolled her eyes. "Why do people say that?" She giggled. "Of course I meant to intrude. Just not in a boorish way, if you know what I mean."

Jana faltered. "Um, well, of course. Any time."

"I am sorry. I know it's late and you weren't expecting me…"

Although Jana didn't want to be standoffish, it was ingrained in her. Rom didn't trust the *gadje*—white people. Never mind that her own blood wasn't pure.

However, Lili had risked life and limb to help Jana escape, out of the goodness of her heart, as far as Jana could tell. And she was so obviously a sweet soul without a mean bone in her body. She might be one of the aristocratic Brunners, nemesis of the Vargases for two hundred years, but she was as blameless as a kitten. She didn't even know the story of the famous diamond's theft.

"Don't worry," Jana said. "Truly. As you can see, our lifestyle is free and easy. We play it by ear."

Lili smiled shyly. "I heard the violin. From the road. It was enticing."

Jana squinted across the field. Too dark to see the road. "Do you have a car? You can't be alone?"

"I can't," Lili said with an energetic nod, "but I am!"

"How did that happen?" Jana was wary; she could foresee the police swooping in, accusing her people of kidnapping and other nefarious intentions.

"Long story. I was on a sort of late date—"

"With the museum guy?"

Lili sighed. "No, I'm afraid not. Simon's too restrained for my taste. I was hoping for a more adventuresome escapade. Which I got, but it wasn't quite as thrilling as I'd hoped." She glanced toward the small group, who had remained around the fire, listening with guarded interest. She lowered her voice so only Jana could hear. "Ever find yourself trapped in a convertible with a man whose mouth is like a suction hose?"

"Now and then." Jana thought back to her teenage back-seat fumblings. Her first boyfriend had been as middle-class American as they came: Jason Johnson, who'd read X-Men comic books, wore braces and baggy jeans, and played drums in a tone-deaf garage band called Sound and Fury.

"I decided I'd rather walk," Lili said. She shuddered. "Anything was better than getting sucked into the vacuum of Trey Stone's mouth."

"Jana?" Baba Magda approached, eyeing Lili like a basilisk. "Who is this?"

"Lili Brunner, Baba. The princess from Grunberg."

The older woman made a dismissive sound. Magda had hauteur down cold; she could freeze a snooty mainline socialite at twenty paces. "What's she doing here?"

Lili bit her lip, uncertain.

"I invited her," Jana said.

Magda's heavy black brows arched, but she dipped her head with a conciliatory welcome. "Would you like to join us by the fire, Princess?"

Lili nodded eagerly. "Please call me Lili." Her wide-eyed gaze traveled the group. "All of you. Forget about the princess deal. I'm just Lili."

Jana introduced her to Tito first, explaining that *Kako* meant uncle or old man. Because Lili seemed interested, she added other titles to the names: *bibio, phrala, rom, monisha*—aunt, brother, husband, wife. Her cousin, Gabriel, was *Simensa*.. Except for Tito, none of the group was excessively friendly—that was their way with any stranger—but Gabe was especially rude, standing where the firelight didn't quite reach, staring at Lili with a storm-cloud expression. He barely nodded at the introduction, just continued to glare.

Jana sighed to herself. Gabriel had taken the story of the Vargas diamond to heart. It stood for all the wrongs that had been done to the Rom. He resented not only the Brunners, but all aristocracy. He and a few of the older men were the only Vargases who kept up talk of one day reclaiming the diamond as their own.

Sheer nonsense, after two hundred years. Jana had tried to turn Gabe's passion toward a will to educate and better himself, to no avail, thus far.

Watching him, she decided that it was time for another heart-to-heart talk. Before more trouble arrived.

Princess Lili handled Gabe's surliness with aplomb. She smiled at him once, then ignored His Moodiness as she chatted with the others. She was so genuine and enthusiastic that soon the mood had lightened. The men competed to entertain her. The women brought out some of their handwork and she exclaimed over the artistry of their fine embroidered vests and scarves. Baba Magda asked the princess to attend the fair, and everyone chimed in on the invitation, except Gabe.

Several had offered to give up their chairs or stools, but Lili chose to sit on one of the rugs on the ground.

She accepted the bottle of hearty red wine, gave it a dubious sniff, then swigged, making everyone laugh at her comic expression when she swallowed. She gasped, then held tight to the bottle when Jana tried to take it. "One more sip," she said, and Uncle Tito drew his bow across the fiddle strings in accompaniment. Lili handed the bottle off, batting her lashes. "Whew. My eyes are watering. I've never tasted such a powerful wine."

Jana laughed. "Don't drink any more or you'll wake up tomorrow morning with your eyeballs stuck to the inside of your skull."

Lili asked how long they would stay and where they'd go next. Jana explained the tradition of their traveling lifestyle, begun centuries ago by the Gypsies who roamed Eastern Europe. They talked about Grunberg. Baba Magda remembered traveling there when she was young, hoping that she would get to see the Vargas diamond.

"Oh," Lili said.

An uncomfortable silence fell. The fire crackled. A knot in one of the charred logs popped, sending sparks into the dark sky.

Lili looked around the circle. "Will you tell me about the diamond?"

"Don't you know?" Magda asked, leaning forward on her stool. Flames leaped in her wise dark eyes.

"I don't know why it's called the Vargas diamond."

"That's obvious, isn't it?" Gabe said, stepping from the shadows.

Jana held up a hand. "Gabriel. Please."

"No, I want to know," Lili insisted.

The Rom looked at each other, no one speaking until Gabe broke the silence. "Your family stole it from mine," he said, accusation evident in his sneer. "The oldest story in the book. The rich steal from the poor to make themselves even richer."

Lili looked taken aback, but she did not cower. "How do you know? It was so long ago."

"Gypsies have a long storytelling tradition," Magda said. "The tale of the Vargas diamond has been repeated around our campfires for a very long time."

"Except that time has a way of warping the truth," Jana pointed out. "We don't know for sure—"

Gabe interrupted. "Yes, we do."

"All stories are interpreted over time, colored and, frankly, stretched." Jana shrugged at Lili. "The tale of the Rom who owned the most beautiful diamond in the world is a legend among my clan."

Lili put her chin in her hand and stared at the fire. "The Brunners have their own story."

Gabe sneered. "PR."

Her gaze rose to meet his. "Not entirely."

"The royal family keeps the truth locked up tighter than the diamond."

Lili pursed her lips. "Then you must have been very surprised that the bridal tiara was sent to Blue Cloud for this exhibit, hm?"

Gabe flushed.

"It's no coincidence that you've come here, is it?"

Lili scanned the circle until her gaze came to Jana. "You're here to see the diamond."

"Yes."

She nodded. "I see."

"It's not like that," Jana said, sensing that Lili was thinking of the thefts at the tent reception. "It's only…well, none of us has actually seen the diamond with our own eyes. We didn't come here to make trouble."

"Only to make pennies," Gabe said. "As usual." He thrust a hand through his wild mane of shoulder-length hair, the gesture filled with frustration and scorn. He kicked at a log, rolling it abruptly into the fire. A gout of smoke and flame shot upward, making those closest scramble away, waving and coughing.

"Gabriel, don't go," Jana called, but when the smoke cleared, he had once again disappeared into the black night. She gritted her teeth, muttering, *"Didlo,"* under her breath. Gabe *was* crazed. With wanting, with anger, with impotence at his lot in life. Making him prone to bad decisions.

Lili coughed behind her hand. "I'm sorry."

Jana drew herself up, not wanting to air family problems before a stranger, even if she was on the way to becoming a friend. "It's not your fault. Gabe is still a boy. He speaks rashly."

"Then you don't believe the diamond was stolen?"

"I…didn't say that."

Lili frowned. "I'm supposed to wear the tiara when

I marry. I'd hate to think that the diamond in it is stolen.''

"Then don't." Jana's words were sharper than she intended; she was wondering how Lili would feel if she knew the rest of the story…the part about the Gypsy curse. Of course it wasn't true. Even if both Lili's mother and grandmother had died at relatively young ages.

Lili squinted. "I'll ask Amelia what she knows."

"She won't tell you."

"Why do you say that?" Lili was openly curious.

Jana shrugged, her eyes straying toward Baba Magda. "Women like that…they never reveal too much."

"Women like what?"

Jana made an ancient gesture that was meant to provide protection against wayward magic. "*Dook.* Women who have The Sight." She laughed a little, lest Lili took it too seriously. "You know. Good old-fashioned ESP."

Lili's lips parted. "Ah. But how do you know about Amelia?"

"I could tell, as soon as I looked at her." Jana measured a small space between two fingers. "I have a smidgen of it myself. Just enough to get a feeling now and then."

"My sisters and I call Amelia our fairy godmother." Lili smiled. "Even though we know it's childish."

Jana saw that Magda was listening, nodding complacently to herself. A few of the group said good-night and moved off to the tents. Tito began to play his fiddle again, softly in the background.

"I should go," Lili said, with obvious reluctance.

"It's still early yet. Not even midnight."

"The music is wonderful." Lili's eyes brightened as one of the men got up and did a slow shuffling step around the fire. The fiddler picked up pace. Several began a rhythmic clapping, encouraging the dancer. He waved them off at first, but then saw Lili watching and came over to extend his hand.

The princess looked at Jana, a question in her eyes.

"Go on. Dance." Jana could see she wanted to.

"I will!" Lili jumped up and the unlikely pair began to dance—an elderly Rom with a straggly beard and a young blond princess, whose jeans and sweater couldn't disguise her royal bearing. Lili threw in whatever moves occurred to her, which meant much clapping of hands overhead, stamping of feet and shouts of "Hoy!"

The music quickened Jana's feet. Lili danced toward her, sashaying her hips like a hula dancer, and held out a hand to hoist Jana to her feet. "Dance, *rinkini,*" Magda urged.

"You, too, Baba," Jana said, tugging the old woman up with both hands.

"Not me, not me. My bones are too tired." But she let Jana drag her forward as she wrapped her buffalo-plaid blanket around her middle. Her head rose proudly, and for an instant, Jana saw the young woman Magda had been, all fire and temper and bold, laughing beauty.

Jana felt the tug inside her of the need to live up to the
tradition of her long, proud line of ancestors.

They danced. Others joined them, then dropped
away. Magda's energy gave out, and still Lili and Jana
danced, light and dark, royal and peasant, but so very
much alike.

Lili kicked off her shoes. "It's too chilly," Jana protested, laughing.

"The fire is warm. I've always wanted to dance bare-
foot by a bonfire and this is my chance." Lili stamped
her feet in the dust and flattened grass, so laughing and
joyous she was contagious.

Jana snatched up a tambourine. One of the women
waved a long fringed shawl for Lili, who took it and
danced on, spinning and twining the purple silk around
herself. Tito fiddled energetically; one of the other men
had joined in on the guitar.

Out of the corner of her eye, Jana saw Magda's head
rise questioningly. She threw a sharp glance over her
shoulder toward the trees that bordered the field from
the farmhouse. Gabriel, Jana thought. Or Henry? But
when she whirled again, brushing her hair from her
eyes, Magda was smiling and clapping as normal.

Jana pushed aside her worry. The dance was in her
blood. Nothing else mattered!

HENRY MOVED in a swift crouch toward the tents. He
didn't know why he was being furtive, except that it
was in his training to approach an alien situation with
caution. He and his officers had recovered the stolen

items and the wallets, all contents intact, including cash, after a ridiculous search of the park that had ended with Sam Blake falling out of a tree onto his head. Serious injury might have resulted if Henry hadn't been there to blunt the fall. He'd attempted a catch, but 175 pounds of flailing sergeant wasn't easy to stand up beneath. The bruise on his tailbone bore testimony. Henry winced. He wasn't the star high school center-fielder he used to be.

He whispered, "Look," to Simon, who was creeping over to join him. The museum director had called near midnight, saying that Princess Lili had been reported missing by her British nanny, Amelia Grundy, so that told him all he needed to know. Henry's opinion was that Lili was off enjoying herself, but he wasn't paid to give opinions or advice.

Even though he'd just gotten home and hadn't even changed out of his uniform, he'd climbed back into his patrol car and picked up Simon. When last seen, the princess had been joyriding with Trey Stone, Simon's rival. They'd found no sign of the man's convertible on their ride through town. Didn't matter. Henry's instincts had led him to the Gypsy camp.

No Holmeslike deduction needed there, either.

Henry straightened and moved away from the tent, cautioning Simon not to speak. There was no particular need to sneak, but he wanted to see what he could see when the Gypsies were unaware.

What he saw was more than he bargained for.

He'd found the princess.

Jana, too.

Jana, especially.

They were dancing. Both of them, gyrating and spinning beside a small bonfire, keeping time to the frantic seesawing pace of a spirited fiddler. Princess Lili was deep into it, a blond blur as she spun in circles, a length of purple fabric raised high in one hand. She laughed with delight. No crisis there. The princess was a full participant.

Having decided that, Henry allowed himself to focus on the enticement that was Jana Vargas. Her style wasn't as dizzying as the princess's. Jana dipped and swayed, her hourglass figure moving sinuously to the music while she batted her palm against a jangling tambourine. When she spun, her hair swirled around her like a veil. Now and then she lifted her skirt in one hand, swishing it back and forth, revealing her long bare legs in a way that Henry found utterly provocative. His heart galloped at Secretariat speed.

Simon made a sound of disbelief. He was gaping at Princess Lili like a fanatic who'd received a vision of the Second Coming.

Henry blinked. *Not me. I'm not so blinded.*

He strode into the heart of the encampment.

"Shawglo," someone hissed. The music screeched to a halt, leaving the air discordant with a sudden silence.

Jana turned, saw him, and brought the tambourine down, slamming it against her palm. "Chief Russell. We meet again." Her voice was distant. "And so soon."

Lili danced on, oblivious, until the broken mood reached her brain. She faltered, stumbling over her previously nimble feet. Simon rushed forward to catch her.

Henry stopped and put his hands on his belt. He absorbed the Gypsies' suspicious stares, staring straight back at them. "What's going on here?"

Jana started toward him, her mouth set.

From another direction came an older woman, short and round and formidable, with snapping black eyes and a powerful glare. "You! You're the one who accuses my Jana of thievery." She spoke in a heavily accented voice, making sweeping motions at him as if she were shooing a pesky fly. *"Nash Avri."* She spat on the ground. "We have done nothing to be treated this way."

Henry held his ground. "Ma'am, please calm down."

"Amria!" She took a swipe at him.

Henry ducked. He reached for the woman's churning arms.

Jana had been watching in amusement, her hands on her hips, but now she joined the fray. "Don't touch my aunt, you big ape."

He ducked again. "Tell her to stop attacking me."

Jana spoke in a foreign tongue, a stream of words that alternately sounded soothing and accusatory. Accusatory when she gestured at him.

"Gadje dilo," the older woman said, poking once more at his chest.

Henry shook a finger at her. "Careful who you call a fool, ma'am."

Jana knocked his hand down. "This is Magdalena Vargas, Chief Russell. Our *Phuri Dae*. I expect you to treat her with the respect she deserves."

If she does the same. "I'll try," he said instead, with a conciliatory nod. The woman commanded a certain respect, but even if she didn't, there were several men nearby who looked capable of enforcing it.

But not to him. Henry gave them all his own version of the evil eye until they looked away. Intimidation worked.

He checked on the princess. She was draped in Simon's arms, head flung back, gazing up at him with wonder. Quite compliant, was the princess.

He looked at Jana. She was glaring at him, her color high, her chest heaving. Quite the Gypsy firebrand.

"Listen, Simon." Henry didn't take his eyes off Jana while he edged over to the other couple. "I want you to take the princess back to my car. Wait for me. I'll be five minutes, maybe ten. Jana has kindly offered me a short tour of the camp."

Jana's eyes narrowed, but she didn't contradict him. "We have nothing to hide," she said beneath her breath, while Simon and Lili discussed the plan like reasonable people.

Or maybe not. "I always wanted to run away with the circus," the princess was saying. "Gypsies will do even better."

"Not on my watch," Henry barked.

"Wow." Lili chortled. "You sound just like the cops on TV."

Henry grimaced, deciding he'd better appeal to Simon's good sense. "Go on. Get her out of here. Before the next batty idea takes flight."

With Simon at hand, Lili retrieved her shoes and said somewhat dazed goodbyes to the Romany who had gathered around to offer farewells. They were friendly enough when they cared to be.

Simon took the princess by the hand and led her off into the darkness. Henry had parked near the farmyard, just past a stand of deciduous trees.

"She came of her own free will," Jana said, before Henry could ask.

"I can see that."

Jana's brows tilted loftily. "Are there any other crimes you suspect us of, then?"

"I suspect everyone, Ms. Vargas. Guilty until proven innocent."

She snorted. "I'd expect no less from you, Chief."

Magdalena Vargas had cooled down and was watching the conversation as if she had ringside seats at a tennis match. She sent Jana a significant look that Henry couldn't interpret. "I leave you in my niece's good hands, Chief Russell," the Gypsy woman said, muttering another foreign word as she turned away.

Henry squinted. "What was that?"

"You don't want to know," Jana said with a sweetly acid smile.

He heaved a sigh. "I get no respect."

She shrugged, untroubled. "Not here, anyway."

"The tour?"

"If you insist."

"Nothing to hide, wasn't it?"

"Of course." Jana nodded. She placed a hand on one of the Rom's shoulder. "Please tend the fire while I tend to the chief." She walked away, then turned back when Henry didn't immediately follow. "Coming?"

"Coming," he said. Yeah. One inviting signal and he'd be coming after her like a runaway steam train. Unstoppable. Until the crash.

But what a way to go!

"You see the tents." Jana strode along, surefooted even in the dark. "If you must inspect them, I won't stop you. We can start with the children's tent. They're sleeping, of course, but I'm sure they won't mind being disturbed."

"That won't be necessary. I'd rather search all available hollow trunks."

"As you wish." Her amused gaze slid sidelong toward his face. "I heard you found what you were looking for."

"Except the pearls." *And your young partner.*

"I don't have them."

"What's in here?" he asked, stopping beside the wooden caravan at the end of the row. It was a small house on wheels, quaint and old-fashioned, with a crooked stovepipe and a wood-shake roof. Decorative scrollwork and carved designs covered the caravan. Once brightly painted, they were now faded with age and use.

"Many expensive jewels." Jana folded her arms. "Go ahead and look."

Henry opened the narrow blue door and peered inside. The interior was dim. He climbed a short flight of steep steps and went inside.

The caravan was tiny. His shoes thudded on the pine-plank floor as he crossed it in several steps, inspecting it by the light from the open door and the wan sliver of moonlight that shone through a crack in the tasseled curtains. The jewels Jana had spoken of were laid out on every available surface, arranged on display trays and stands.

"You've found me out," she said from directly behind him. He whirled with one of the bracelets in his hand. "I steal valuables from every town we visit, then reset the gems and sell them in the next town over."

He tossed aside the bracelet. It was made of polished stones and sea glass. All the pieces were. At most, Jana had used a few semiprecious stones. He dangled a topaz earring. "You make these yourself?"

"Yes, and I sell them at our fairs. Don't worry. We have vendor licenses." She stirred the costume jewelry, thrusting a handful of it under his nose. "You see, Big Chief? Not a pearl or a diamond in sight."

He started to brush her aside. He meant to brush her aside. But instead he became aware of how close they were standing, and of the exotic scents of the cozy, tapestry-lined caravan. Earthy, piquant, alluring. Like Jana herself.

She caught her breath, then let it out in a slow hiss, showing a hint of white teeth as her lip lifted.

"Let me smooth your hackles," he said.

She shook her hair back from her face, which was still tinged a becoming pink from her previous exertions. He knew she'd look the same when they made love.

"Keep away from me," she growled. "We had a deal, but here you are, accusing me."

He believed he'd been more than agreeable. "What deal was that?"

"I told you where to find the wallets. You were supposed to leave us alone."

He lifted the handwrought jewelry from her grasp, piece by piece, lightly touching her hand with his fingertips, getting more pleasure than he ought to from such simple caresses, surprised that she continued to allow the contact. "We're alone now, aren't we?"

"That isn't—" She caught her breath as he drew the last necklace across her palm. "You know I didn't want—"

"Yes, this is what you wanted. Exactly what you wanted. You invited me in because you knew that as soon as we were alone I would kiss you."

Her head reared back. "Your conceit is amazing!"

"Not conceit. Confidence." Now that her hand was empty, he traced the vein in her wrist, pushing the sleeve of her blouse higher up her arm as he went. Jana tried to pull away, but he didn't let her.

He placed his lips against her wrist. Her bangles chimed softly. "No," she whispered.

He stopped. "No?"

She shook her head. "Definitely no."

He let go. "Then I wouldn't think of continuing. Even though I'd intended to taste every soft, lovely, naked inch of you."

Jana's eyes glittered, more beautiful than any jewel. "Liar."

6

JANA WAS BREATHING HEAVILY, but it wasn't from the dancing. Her reaction to Henry was all the aerobic workout she needed. He was a commanding presence in his blue uniform with all the official patches and emblems and badges. His biceps were bursting out of the short sleeves, and the navy blue slacks stretched taut across his heavily muscled thighs. Her attraction to him was curious, encompassing both her learned suspicion of anyone wearing a uniform and her innate womanly reaction to the man inside it.

She closed her eyes for just a moment, swaying on her feet as she inhaled. Male animals often emitted a potent musk to attract mates, and Henry Russell was exuding it by the bucketful. All over her caravan. She'd be smelling him for days.

A not unpleasant thought.

"How am I a liar?" he asked, his tone soft but deadly, as if he was setting a trap for her.

Like a dizzy fool, she waded right in. "You're all talk, that's how. You might want to kiss me—" *All over!* "—but you won't. Because you know it's impossible. We can't be together. No way."

He touched a strand of her hair. "For argument's sake, why not?"

She wanted to run, but she was rooted to the floor, riveted by his nearness, the promise of an impending kiss. She wet her lips with her tongue, mentally gathering measly shreds of resistance. "We're from different worlds."

"I don't mind widening my experience. Try again."

That was her main argument. "I'll be leaving in a few days."

"All the better."

Her eyes narrowed. "You have a way of making a girl feel real special."

"This isn't about romance. It's about attraction. The kind that burns hot and fast."

"And short?"

"We can hope so."

She shook her head. No. "Us, together—that would be making a bargain with the devil. I don't care how short the duration is."

He slid his fingertips along the underside of her chin, down her throat, which lifted involuntarily, elongating under the caress. His hand continued its path to her upper chest, where he lingered. Her heart seemed to rise to the touch.

His gaze held hers. "Which of us is the devil in that scenario?"

"Either." Her voice was as dry as parchment. "Depends on your point of view."

"No one's ever called me wicked," he said. His mouth quirked. "I kinda like it."

She was melting toward him, imagining how the smallest movement might send his hand curving downward to cup her breast. The tingling there was acute, needy. She craved his touch, his suckling lips...

Suddenly they were kissing—a mutual seduction. Henry's mouth was hot and greedy and talented. His hand dropped as she'd imagined, pressing firmly against her taut nipple, drawing the breath from her lungs. She said "Ohh," into his mouth and his tongue licked between her lips, bold and impatient. And conquering. She was soft in his arms, willing to be ravished. All the fight had gone out of her. Without it, she felt naked and vulnerable even before he got her clothes off.

He swept aside the bed curtains and backed her onto the bed that was built into one end of the caravan. She had no time to think because he was on her at once, kissing and stroking and squeezing as she twisted beneath him among the heaps of pillows. She welcomed his weight at the same time as she was overwhelmed by it.

The notion was in her to stop before they'd gone too far, but the words wouldn't come. She could only gasp with pleasure when he reached inside her blouse and plucked at her nipple, abrading it with his thumb while his fingertips pressed into her flesh. Kneading it. Making her need him.

His thigh parted hers. She arched, craving the intimate possession.

He dragged his mouth away. "You're sure this is wrong?"

She panted. "I didn't say it's wrong. I said it wouldn't work."

"Seems to be working fine." He moved deeper and higher between her open thighs, a stinging contact. The hot, heavy bulge of his arousal was unmistakable. As was her response.

His mouth dropped to her throat, stringing kisses to her collarbone. Beyond. He nuzzled the neckline of her blouse, undoing the ribbon, working the buttons, each stroke of his tongue more devastating than the last, as the tiny pearl buttons gave way one by one. Her shoulders moved against the pillows, helping him peel open the peasant blouse.

He spread the gauzy fabric, rising up to gaze at her bared breasts. She watched him through her lashes, ready to submit—more than ready despite the knowledge that it was a mistake—until she saw the emotion in his eyes as he touched her and said, "Beautiful." He'd gone hoarse. "You're incredibly beautiful. What's the word? *Rinkini.*"

At that moment, it was clear to Jana that she wasn't the only one who'd been revealed. But she doubted *Henry* knew it. He was so sure they were operating only on a physical level.

"You'd do this?" she said, struggling to sit up with her arm shielding her breasts. She dragged the blouse back over her shoulders. "You'd have wild sex with me, right here, right now, with my family in shouting distance, the princess in your patrol car and you in your uniform?''

He swallowed. ''I'd planned to take off the uniform.''

''You weren't planning anything.'' She ran a shaky hand through her hair. ''Did you bring protection?''

He sat back. ''Uh, no.''

''Are you on duty?''

''Not technically.'' He sighed. ''Fact is, I'm on twenty-four/seven.''

''Then this was a body search.''

''Of course not!''

She offered him a fleeting smile. ''I'm aware of that. It was a joke.''

''I am allowed a private life,'' he said, frowning. ''Not that anyone could tell.''

''Come back and see me when you're out of uniform.'' *And aware of your feelings,* she added silently. Whatever they were, he'd have to figure them out on his own. She couldn't help, because she didn't even know what her own were, except woefully mixed up. And riled up. And, going by the ache inside, frustrated.

Henry pushed off the bed, his gaze skidding across her bare legs. She closed them, pulling her skirt down as she drew her knees up to her chin. It wasn't only an ache. It was a hollow ache.

Henry strode to the door and opened it. ''I still haven't met—'' He stopped. ''What's his name, your partner-in-crime?''

''I've told you and told you. There is no partner.''

''I'll find him, you know.''

She couldn't work up her usual ire. "You have the loot. Isn't that enough to satisfy you?"

Henry filled the open doorway. Even the sight of him did funny things to her, and she was finally beginning to understand that it wasn't only her body that was affected. His touch went deeper than she could allow, since it was a given they would inevitably be pulled apart.

An apt phrase, that. *Pulled apart.* She'd wind up torn to pieces, even though she'd almost fooled herself into believing that a short-term relationship was preferable. Wrong. No relationship at all was the optimal choice.

If only that didn't make her feel so alone.

"Jana, darlin'. There's one thing you should know about me," Henry said. "And remember this well." He waited until she was staring, her eyes gone big, her heart pounding in her throat. Then he delivered the coup de grace: "I always take my full measure of satisfaction."

It was one hell of a parting line. Ten seconds passed before she shot off the bed and hung out the open doorway, watching him stride through the quiet encampment, full to bursting with his male bluster and conceit.

"But do you give it?" she yelled after him. "Tell me that, Chief. Do you give it?"

His laugh carried on the wood-smoked air. "You'll have to wait and see."

THE NEXT DAY was the fair. It opened midmorning and was scheduled to run until dusk. Or as long as the crowds came, according to Jana. Henry had stopped by to exchange a few words with her as soon as he'd arrived late that afternoon. Though he'd had an officer there all day to watch over the Gypsies' activities while he was busy with regular duties, eventually he'd given in to his curiosity and paid a visit himself.

Better to call it curiosity rather than craving. Even if that's what it was—an intense craving to see Jana again. To spar with her, to learn all about her life, to kiss and hold her, if possible. If not, merely being near her would do. She'd engaged his attention like no other woman, even Zoe Burbank, the long-term girlfriend he'd once thought seriously of marrying, before she'd announced that if he left one more dinner date, concert, movie or, worst of all, her gosh-darned bed because of an emergency call, she was done with him.

That had been it for Zoe.

With Jana, he wouldn't have that problem. Although he'd like to. Something told him leaving Jana's bed would be a helluva lot tougher on his willpower.

Damn! He was getting hot again, just thinking of it.

Henry pulled on his collar. While he circulated through the fair, he was careful to keep his game face on. It was vaguely embarrassing to be so besotted, particularly when all his life he'd been in complete control of his emotions. With Jana, he'd been confounded and damn near unbridled from the first moment they met.

''Hey, Chief. You catchin' any cheaters?'' called one of the local men, who was losing quarters at a pitching booth.

"Only you, Larry." Henry flicked a thumb at the booth. "Keep those toes behind the line and aim low."

Officer O'Bannion came by, hitching up his equipment belt beneath a round belly. "You might wanna check out the tent at the back there." He pointed to an unadorned canvas tent set back a bit from the others. "Could be some gambling going on. Poker."

Henry thought it over. He was a regular at Pete Jones's Friday night poker game where some major betting went on. Hell, he'd been known to return home a whopping twenty bucks richer than when he'd left. He couldn't come down too hard on minor games of chance or a penny-ante poker game. Depending on the stakes…

"I'll give it a look-see," he told O'Bannion. "You can take off for a while, but stop by again before your shift is over. Tempers might grow short toward the end of the day."

"Will do, Chief."

Henry made an ambling turn around the booths and displays. The Romany fair wasn't really of enough consequence to warrant two police officers' attention. The women were primarily selling handcrafted items. A juggler circulated through the small crowd, drawing attention with his tricks before stopping to put on a show. There were pony rides and possibly some horse trading going on. The few games of chance available were small-time stuff, typical of carny fare. One woman was reading palms and tarot cards, and in a gaily decorated tent, "Madame" Magdalena had set herself up as a fortune-teller.

"What's the verdict, Chief?" Jana called to him from the steps of her caravan. Though her jewelry displays were well picked over, there was presently a lull in business and no one else was about. "Spotted any lawbreakers? Say, don't look now. Tamara's about to filch a fiver for a faulty palm reading."

He tucked his thumbs in his belt loops and strolled over as if he hadn't been heading this way all along. Jana sat on the steps with her knees drawn up and her long colorful skirts falling around her legs. Her hair was loose again, but she wore a kerchief this time, along with gold hoop earrings and the usual excess of bracelets and beads. Tiny bells were sewn into the front of her vest. She jingled when she leaned forward and said, with a certain saucy lilt that made the back of his neck tingle, "Arrest anyone lately?"

"I've got my eye on your stable boy." The dark young man who'd been tending the horses was his best match yet for the sketchy eyewitness descriptions of the thief the investigation had netted. He had an earring in one ear, was about the right height and age, and he'd disappeared into the crowd after he saw Henry watching him.

The teasing light faded from Jana's dark blue eyes. "And what would the charges be?"

Interesting that she hadn't denied the young man's presence…this time. "You know I don't have unshakable proof," Henry said. "The reception was crowded. None of the victims can be sure exactly who picked their pockets." Ordinarily he wouldn't give away information, but Jana was one sharp cookie. "I can always bring him in for questioning, of course. Maybe he'll let something slip."

"Him."

Henry made a show of taking out the small notebook where he'd jotted down the name...not that he'd forgotten it. "Gabriel Vargas."

"How did you—"

"It's not necessary to ask questions in order to get answers."

"I'm certain none of us—"

"Nope. You're all extremely closemouthed. But I listen well."

"You mean you eavesdrop," she accused.

"Amazing what one learns that way." Turned out that O'Bannion was on to something.

Jana's head tilted. "Such as?"

"You've graduated college, yet you choose to live this way—" Henry gestured at the rough wood caravan, a fine example of folk art, but a claustrophobic's nightmare. He remembered the broken-down convertible with its back seat filled with rubble from their first meeting. "Why?"

Her hands had made fists. "Go eavesdrop some more if you want to know."

"Can't we have a civil conversation?"

"Then you need to work on your manners. I could have sworn this was an interrogation."

Without an invitation, Henry sat on the second step, two down from her. She had to move her legs aside, and still they touched, her knee against his shoulder. Her thigh, if he leaned back a bit. He did.

She wanted to move, he could tell. But she wasn't going to let him run her off.

"You could have a career," he said. He'd lingered nearby while Princess Lili, who'd been at the fair most of the day, chatted up one of the Romany women. In the meantime, he'd picked up all sorts of interesting tidbits, including Jana's background as the child of a Rom and a white woman, and how she'd returned to the clan years later, and basically saved them from indigence with little more than her smarts and a strong sense of leadership.

Jana twitched her skirts. "I'm here because I want to be. And because these people need me. There's nothing wrong with our lifestyle. Not everyone must have two-thousand square feet of overpriced ranch house and three TVs with cable on tap to lead a happy life, you know."

He knocked back his hat and scratched his hairline. "No need to invite you over, then."

She caught her lip between her teeth, uncertain if he was kidding.

"I have digital," he added. "One hundred and eighty channels."

She laughed. "It'd take more than that."

He leaned back a little more, tilting his head so he could see her out of the corner of his eyes. "Picture-in-picture?"

She climbed off the steps as two women approached

to look over the jewelry. ''Picture this—it's not gonna happen.''

''That's not what your thigh said just now,'' he mumbled under his breath. He rose and smoothed out the front of his shirt, still feeling the warm pressure of her body beside his. She hadn't let up for an instant. Maybe it had been a space war, the same way his younger brothers and sisters had fought for elbow room in the back seat of their old car, but Henry doubted it.

Jana wanted him. Bad. But she wouldn't let herself admit it. Because maybe, just maybe, wanting him would lead to wanting a whole lot more.

Thoughts of her filled his head as he strolled away. He forgot all about O'Bannion's mention of possible gambling activity.

Until the brouhaha broke out.

Some of the fair-goers sent up cries of alarm as they hurried away from a spot in the center of the fairgrounds. Other stopped to stare. Several of the Rom were sprinting toward the trouble. Henry joined them.

Two men were fighting, rolling around in the grass as they struggled with each other. Henry was able to identify the blonde one at a glance. Ryan Wells: Big Man on Campus at Blue Cloud Senior High, boastful quarterback of the football team, casual breaker of teenage hearts, all-around bad character and frequent jackass. Ryan had been in various forms of trouble since Henry's first day on the job. The boy needed a firm hand, and Henry was more than willing to supply it, one way or another. Ryan's delusional father wouldn't have it; he insisted his son was only sowing a few wild oats.

The other culprit was a Rom. Gabriel Vargas. Henry had only gotten glimpses of the young man while he tended the horses, but he was fairly sure that Gabriel was the pickpocket from the reception. Especially after Jana had returned the stolen items in her roundabout way.

The pair lurched to their feet. Ryan was bleeding from the nose. He swung wildly. Gabriel ducked to elude the blow. He danced on light feet, easily moving out of Ryan's reach.

Henry pushed through the gathering crowd, many of whom seemed more interested in cheering on the fight than stopping it.

Ryan swiped at the blood dripping onto his letterman's jacket. He swore ripely. "Stupid cheatin' Gypsy."

Gabriel's face darkened, but he didn't respond to taunt, raising Henry's respect a notch.

"I want my money back." With a roar, Ryan rushed forward. Gabriel tried to dodge him again, but several of Ryan's teammates were blocking the way. One of them grabbed the Gypsy's arm. Gabriel pulled away, but the delay was enough for Ryan to land on him, raining blows upon his face.

Henry waded in. He reached out to grab Ryan's shoulders, but the boy was as strong as a bull. "Come here," Henry said, jerking Ryan toward himself by the back of his collar. "You're under arrest."

Ryan flailed at Gabriel. "What about him?"

"Him, too."

"Let me at him," Ryan blustered. By this time, Henry figured the words were more boastful than serious since Ryan seemed to be in the worse shape. When the young athlete wrenched against his grip, Henry let the boy go.

Ryan staggered at the unexpected release. He shook his head, hesitating. A brief surprise flared in Gabriel's eyes before he narrowed them, scowling more at Henry than at his well-built opponent.

Ryan's teammates looked uneasily at each other, then at Henry. Finally one of them said, with fading fervor, "Go on, Ryan. Pound him."

Ryan hiked up his jeans and swaggered forward. He was panting heavily. "You're gonna give me back the money you stole from me."

Gabriel's expression betrayed no emotion. "You lost, fair and square. I outsmarted you, *gadje dilo.*"

"Ya think so?" Ryan sneered. "We're gonna run you thieving Gypsies out of this town. Even the police won't defend you."

Gabriel glanced scornfully at Henry, then put up his fists. "Try it."

Suddenly Jana tore through the mostly male crowd. "What's going on here?" She took in the scene, including Henry standing by, seemingly doing nothing.

He almost moaned at the accusation in her eyes. *Aw, hell.* She was going to misunderstand.

"I see," Jana said. "Nice work, Chief. I'll stop them

if you're not going to." She stalked toward Ryan and gave him a push. "Keep away from my cousin, you big ugly goon."

Gabriel came forward. "Jana, don't—"

"Jana, do," crooned Ryan, looking her up and down. He licked his lips. Crooked his finger at her. "Take me on, lady. I'm ready."

Both Henry and Gabriel descended on Ryan at once, but the Rom was closer. A startled expression passed over Ryan's face as Gabe smashed into his midsection, sending both of them flying head over heels. They toppled like bowling pins, falling into one of the gaudily decorated tents.

Crack. The tent pole snapped. The roof drooped as the canvas walls caved in around the grappling bodies of the young men. In seconds, the entire tent had collapsed. Female shrieks rose from beneath the weighty material as the occupants struggled to free themselves.

"Princess Lili! Princess Lili!" Henry recognized the voice of the princess's royal bodyguard, coming from somewhere in the melee as onlookers crowded in to help. A police car came bumping over the pasture, honking its horn to add to the chaos.

Henry assessed the situation in the blink of an eye. He grabbed Ryan first and shoved him aside. He pulled Gabriel out of the swarm next.

"Magda!" Jana shouted. She tugged at the canvas of what Henry now realized was the fortune-teller's tent. Several people got together and pulled in sync on the canvas, lifting it enough for the inhabitants to step out.

Magda emerged in the draped scarves of her fortune-teller's outfit, her turban tilted over one eye. Jana rushed to her side. Simon Tremayne and Princess Lili came next, covered in crystal beads and sheer silk panels, looking like a pair of belly dancers. The royal bodyguard fussed over her, but she only thanked the rescuers for their quick action and then laughed, irrepressible, looking up at Simon with obvious glee as she teased him about his finery.

Officer O'Bannion had emerged from the patrol car to take charge of Ryan Wells. Henry snapped the cuffs onto Gabriel Vargas, who was sullen but unresisting. He gave him a quick pat-down. "Sorry, kid, but I have to take you in—"

"He cheated me! That dirty Gypsy cheated me!" Ryan hollered as he was being led away.

"Shut up and take your medicine like a man," Henry muttered.

Jana, apparently satisfied that Magda was unharmed, returned her attention to Henry and Gabriel. She stormed up to them, brushing past the princess, who was being led away by Simon and the bodyguard. "How dare you let that musclebound jock loose on my cousin!" She flicked hair out of her eyes. "Were you going to stand by while Gabe was beaten to a pulp? Is that what passes for law and order in this town?"

"I had no intention of letting it go that far," Henry explained. "All the fight was gone out of Ryan and I knew it."

Jana flung a hand at the flattened tent. "Then what do you call that?"

"Wouldn't have happened if you hadn't busted in, calling names."

"So now it's my fault?"

"He's right, Jana," Gabriel said. "You should have stayed out of it. You don't have to protect me."

Jana stamped her foot. "Someone has to keep you out of jail!"

"Calm down," Henry said.

"Don't tell me to calm down."

He rolled his eyes. "Do all Gypsies have such tempers?"

She sucked in a breath, her anger flaring even higher. "You don't know anything about Gypsies! Except stereotypes!"

He chuckled, hoping that would ease the tension. "Look, I didn't mean anything by it…"

"Sure you didn't."

"Just let me do my job, okay?"

"That would be a nice change." She set her hands on her hips, throwing darts with her eyes. She was one pugnacious woman, but her ethnicity had little to do with it. The attitude was part and parcel of her firecracker personality, and, truthfully, it turned him on something fierce. She was far too distracting for his peace of mind.

"*Scummade igenom.* You haven't even tried to solve the theft," she accused. "You've focused only on the Gypsies, because *all* Gypsies are thieves, right? Just like we're all filthy crooks who cheat the good townspeople out of their money, steal their babies and curse on anyone who crosses us!''

Henry held up a hand. "Now, hold on. I never said—"

"I can curse you, if that's what you want." She straightened with a snap. The crowd that had gathered around them hushed as she made a forking gesture with her hand. Her voice came swift and low. "You will suffer bad luck for the next seven days. If you're fortunate, after seven days the Gypsies will *all* be gone from this town—" she flicked her gaze at Gabriel "—and then it will be over for you, sorry white man."

She drew herself even taller, regal and haughty with every speck of her being. She said, *"Enkelt!"* then grabbed up handfuls of her skirt and swept away, leaving Henry dumbfounded.

He did *not* believe in curses.

7

THE NEXT MORNING, Henry sat behind his desk, filling out a form and scratching himself. His hands and arms were the worst off, but he itched around his collar and behind his ears, too. Jana's curse kept springing to mind. He dismissed it time and time again.

Coincidence. Nothing more.

Unlike the flat tires. And the mixed-up files.

The past evening, he'd had O'Bannion bring Ryan Wells in for booking, and had taken Gabriel Vargas himself. Problem was, when they'd reached his patrol unit, he'd discovered that most of the air had been let out of his tires. Four flats at once wasn't coincidence— it was vandalism. He'd even caught three of the Gypsy kids giggling in the underbrush nearby and had chased them back to camp. The Vargas boy had held his tongue, of course, but there'd been a small light of satisfaction in his eyes when Henry had stomped back out of the bushes and called in a ride from the station.

The itching had started during the night. By morning, the rash had been evident, but he didn't have time to stop by Doc Welch's for a prescription because Henry had already received a call to come in to work. Apparently, there were problems worse than poison ivy at the station house.

It had turned out that every paper in the place had been mysteriously misfiled overnight. When Mrs. Grace, the station manager who'd been with the B.C.P.D. since 1962, had arrived early to get a head start on the day, she'd pulled a 698-Triple E and found herself staring at a 277-84b instead. She'd checked every drawer of the filing cabinets before panicking and calling Henry at half past seven, when he was in the middle of his first application of salve. According to Mrs. Grace, the old case files and the various forms in all their triplicate glory weren't actually missing, they were simply…rearranged.

Incomprehensible.

The doors had still been locked and nothing else had been disturbed, so it seemed unlikely that a break-in had occurred. All Henry could figure was that they either had a prankster on the staff or they were…

"Cursed," his men had whispered. Soon after, Henry had given up consoling Mrs. Grace and retreated to his office to brood over Jana's angry prophecy.

His discretionary office fund was shot to hell for the month. Mrs. Grace—who'd been wearing a powdered-sugar moustache at the time, a bad sign indeed since only extreme upset called for extreme doughnut ingestion—informed him that she'd need a hundred hours of overtime to set things straight. She'd even put down the doughnut and called in two emergency bottom-of-the-barrel part-time workers from Stop-Gap Solutions, the only temp agency in town. When the ''calvary'' arrived, one had fuchsia hair and a nose ring. The other had apparently dropped out of kindergarten before learning the alphabet. The outer office was heaped with files and would be for the foreseeable future.

If Henry hadn't already had a rash, the upheaval would have given him one. He liked things neat and clean, black and white, open and shut.

Jana Vargas was turning out to be a veritable rainbow of distraction.

A knock at the door made him look up. Speak of the devil. He'd been expecting her, of course. She'd be bailing her cousin out. Henry had booked Gabriel and Ryan on a basic charge of disturbing the peace, a misdemeanor. No sense trying for more, like destruction of property, when the Gypsies were sure to leave town now that they'd held their carnival. It wasn't as if he meant to do them any favors. Simple reasoning said that they wouldn't be around to testify, which worked to both culprits' benefit.

''Are you decent?'' Jana said, peering inside.

''Guess so.'' *Regrettably.* Henry bobbed to his feet, scowling even though he was glad to see that she wasn't holding too big a grudge. He motioned to the visitor's chair. ''You're perky this morning.''

''Placing curses always puts me in a good mood—'' She broke off, staring at him. ''Ooh. What happened to you?''

He rubbed at the traces of pink liquid still visible

beneath his jaw line. "It wasn't your curse, if that's what you're thinking."

She came closer to examine the rash. "Poison ivy?"

"No doubt."

"You might want to put something on that."

"Have you got a special Gypsy potion for me?"

Jana crossed her arms, looking at him skeptically. She was wearing jeans and a bright yellow blouse this morning, with a scarf, folded into a wide band, holding back her hair. The scarf was striped in purple, blue, green, yellow, orange, red. All the colors of the rainbow.

"As a matter of fact…" she said.

"Never mind." He coughed, shifting papers around on his desk. "I'll go see the doc as soon as I finish my meeting at the museum." He sent Jana a warning look. "Simon and I are going over the security plans."

"Good luck."

"What do you mean by that?"

She shrugged. "There's still a thief on the loose, isn't there? Simon must be nervous about protecting the Brunner bridal tiara."

Henry let a silence stretch between them. "You're certain of that? Gabriel's still in jail, you know."

Her fingers folded around the small pouch purse hanging from her neck, *outside* her blouse, this time. "I've come to bail him out. But he's not the thief I meant. Someone stole those pearls, and it was neither Gabriel nor me."

Henry considered that; he was still inclined to believe her. "I owe you an apology."

Jana's brows bobbed.

"You're right about me failing to look for suspects outside the band of Gypsies. I know better. I should have done—" his throat twisted; it wasn't often he had to admit to a professional fault "—better."

She dropped into the chair. "I guess I owe you an apology, too. I *did* lose my temper with you. I saw you refereeing the fight between Gabe and that—idiot—"

"Scum-sucking ignoramus, wasn't it?"

She let out a nervous laugh. "*Scummade igenom.* It means 'white man from town.' Or 'ignorant scum,' depending."

"Interchangeable terms?"

Her full lips curved. "Depending."

He got up, checked the activity outside the office, then sat on the corner of the desk on one haunch, out of some basic male urge to be closer to her. He swung his leg. "So we're both sorry."

Her lips parted with a soft, feminine sound as she stared at his flexing thigh. His blood turned warm and thick, pooling in his groin. Still staring, her eyes bright, she edged closer to the opposite arm of her chair, clearly reacting to his presence without thinking or she'd have been pressing closer. Rising to the challenge. The way he was.

"Um," she said faintly. "Yes, sorry."

He bent forward slightly, leaning his elbow on his knee to distract from his growing…problem…

attraction…whatever. Jana's hands were pressed between her denim-clad thighs. Her lips made a prim line. The frilly neck of her blouse had gaped slightly to reveal a smooth curve of cleavage. His fingertips curled, itching to caress her. He already knew that her skin felt as satiny as it looked.

"I wasn't going to let Ryan beat up your cousin. I doubt that he could have. He's bigger, but Gabriel is faster." Henry's voice was gentle, coaxing. He didn't know where his reassuring attitude came from, except that seeing the vulnerability in her eyes made him feel more than responsible and protective—he felt that way with everyone. Jana brought out a certain chivalry and a desire to impress her that he was flummoxed by, frankly. Usually he did what was needed exactly the way he wanted, for the good of all concerned. He rarely had to explain himself.

"I was hoping that when they faced off and Ryan realized he wasn't going to prevail with either fists or threats, they could settle the dispute without official interference by the law."

"Oh." Jana's nose crinkled. "So then it *was* my fault, in a way. I stepped in and escalated the situation."

"Right." Henry believed in calling a spade a spade. "After they'd crashed into the tent, I had no choice but to arrest them."

"Sorry. I should have listened to you." The admission came a bit grudgingly because she was stubborn, but also fair. She understood.

"That's right. But there's no real harm done. It'll probably do Ryan good to have spent a night in jail."

Jana pursed her lips. "He didn't get bailed out last night?"

"Nope." Henry laced his fingers together over his kneecap. "Contrary to appearances, I don't normally play favorites. When Magda asked, I told her it was too late to bail Gabriel out. Same went for Ryan's father, even though he put up a fuss about it. He even had the mayor and her boyfriend, Spotsky, on my back."

Jana looked up at him with what might have been admiration. "But you didn't budge."

"I didn't budge."

Her lashes lowered. He felt the warmth of her gaze as it trailed across his body. "I misjudged you."

He leaned down and touched her knee to get her to look him in the face. "Likewise."

She made another small, purely feminine sound when she caught her breath. Her smooth, golden-tinged cheeks took on a rosy glow as she scooted farther back in the chair. "About that stupid curse…"

"Don't worry. I didn't take it seriously."

"Oh, you didn't?"

He chuckled. "How could I?"

Her eyes went to the rash on his hands. "Poison ivy," he said. "Remember? I had to chase through the underbrush after a couple of kids who'd let the air out of my tires. Must've run through a thicket of poison ivy."

"Yes, I'm sure that's all it was," she said demurely,

although her eyes were dancing with wicked humor. "Too bad about the flat tires."

"That was petty vandalism. You might want to give those kids a talking to. Along with Gabriel. He shouldn't have been playing cards for money in the first place."

Jana's chin tilted. "I can take care of my own house, Chief."

"So can I."

"Not by the looks of the mess out there." She rose and moved restlessly around the office, picking up trophies and pictures and putting them down again. "We're at an impasse."

"I prefer to think of it as an understanding." He put his hands around his knee again, tightening them until his knuckles were white when she bent slightly to peer at one of his family photos. Her bottom, cupped by faded blue denim, was a sight to behold.

"Is this your family?"

"Yes. That's my mom, Lynda, and my five brothers and sisters. Jack, Angela, Sarah, Laurie and Mike, from oldest to youngest."

"Nice family. You're the oldest? I should have known."

"I came by my bossiness naturally. What about you?"

She smiled over her shoulder. "Are you calling me bossy?"

"You're in charge, aren't you?"

"Temporarily so. When Gabriel takes over, I'll be..." She shook her head, not finishing.

"We're not as different as it would appear," Henry mused.

"Oh, I wouldn't say that!" Jana laughed and tucked a strand of hair behind her ear as she moved on to the group photos of the B.C.P.D. Straight Shooters, the department baseball team. Next she studied a couple of his commendations. "Heroic actions in the line of duty," she read. "Very impressive."

He stood and circled the desk, uncomfortable with her interest. It felt a little too intimate, but not in the way he'd fantasized over. "Just doing my job."

She turned to face him, sliding her hands into her back pockets. "What exactly did you do to earn the commendation?"

"Nothing much." He slid a finger beneath his collar where it itched. "There was a woman with two young kids who showed up in town a couple of years ago. I started keeping an eye on them...."

"Because they were suspicious characters?"

"Coulda been, but no." He shrugged. "Turned out they were destitute and living out of their car. I, uh, found them one night, parked in an alley to sleep. The mother had been running the car to keep warm, but her carburetor was faulty and they'd been inhaling the fumes...."

"Heavens," Jana said, concern coloring her voice. "You saved them."

"Like I said, it's my job."

"What happened to the woman and her children?"

"They were fine. A little dopey and headachy when I roused them. One of the kids was sick to her stomach. After they got clean bills of health, I helped—that is, *several* of us helped find them a place to live. The mother got a job at the school lunchroom, but six months ago she qualified for a small business loan and opened up a little stationery store downtown."

Jana breathed in and out slowly as she stared into his face. She had a quizzical, faintly bemused expression, one he couldn't quite figure out. All he knew for sure was that he'd like to kiss the small frown away.

"You'd be a good father," she said at last.

He gulped. "Pardon?" Jeez, he hadn't expected that from her, of all people.

"It's obvious. You like to take care of people, and you do it well. You should have lots of kids."

"So should you." As soon as the words were out of his mouth, he knew they were truer than he'd assumed. He could see Jana as a mother, the young, fun type of mother who laughed a lot. She'd shriek over the children's mischief, maybe even give them a swat on the behind, but she'd be quick to forgive and to distribute hugs and kisses and lots of love.

Damn. What was he thinking? She was a Gypsy; a stable family life was the last thing she'd be interested in.

"Not me," she said, alarmed. "I'm not settling down anytime soon."

''Me, neither,'' he said, not as alarmed, but trying to be.

''I have enough on my plate as it is.''

''Yeah, so do I.''

Jana chewed her bottom lip. Somehow, they'd drifted closer and closer until they were mere inches apart. Which seemed to happen frequently when they were around each other. He moved one of his hands to her slim waist and let it rest there, just above her unbelted jeans. Her body was warm through the fabric of her shirt. He wanted to do more than touch her so innocently. He wanted her in his bed, naked. He wanted her begging him to make love to her, and begging while he took his time about it, exploring every precious nook and cranny of her, finding the places where she tasted the sweetest and where he fit the best.

No overnight project.

''We've gotten off track,'' she said, her voice pitched low and sexy enough to draw a shudder out of him. ''I came here for Gabriel. I brought bail money.''

''Right. No problem.'' Henry had a hard time focusing. ''I'll take care of it. You'll want to see Mrs. Grace about the paperwork....''

''Paperwork,'' Jana repeated dubiously.

His mind sharpened. ''Do you know anything about that?''

She blinked. ''Red tape's not my favorite thing in the world, that's for sure. Gypsies have an aversion to official records.''

''You wouldn't have...'' He shook his head, silently

calling himself an imbecile. There was no curse. Jana had nothing to do with the mixed-up paperwork. He'd find a logical explanation if it killed him.

"I wouldn't have a lot of things," she said, brushing by him. He inhaled the wood-smoke scent of her hair. "That's how I like it."

Henry turned. "What about an invitation to the museum gala?" he blurted.

Jana froze. "What do you mean?"

He plopped himself into his swivel chair and started flipping the triplicate pages of the requisition forms. He hadn't been this nervous since he was fifteen and asking a girl out for the first time. He'd taken Mandy Donahue to the movies. She'd had blue eyes and dark hair and a quick tongue—which hadn't been only verbal. Apparently that was the type he went for.

"I thought we could go together. I'll be on duty, but not in uniform. You said you wanted to see the tiara."

"They had the ribbon-cutting yesterday. The exhibit's been opened to the public. I can look at the tiara anytime I want."

"Oh." He glanced up and was startled by Jana's look of utter amazement. "Then you're not interested?"

"I just—" She blinked several times. "I can't imagine that I'd be welcomed."

"No worries. You'd be with me." And that way, he could keep an eye on her, though he had to admit that security hadn't been his first concern in asking her. The manly part of his lawman identity was coming closer to taking over each time he saw her.

"Is that all it takes to make me acceptable?" she asked in a hurting voice that surprised him into seeing how insecure she was beneath the scrappy attitude. The amount of injustice and insult she must have suffered in the past made him want to go out and knock together a few heads. Including his own.

"Don't waste a moment of worry on that. You're more than acceptable just the way you are."

"I'm not sure about this." She looked both wishful and fearful, as if she'd been handed a Christmas stocking and was afraid that all it would contain was a lump of coal. "I thank you for the invitation, Henry, but I'll have to think about it."

"All right," he said evenly. Let her get used to the idea. Him, too.

It was a minute before he was ready to get back to business. Consternated by his extended state of distraction, Henry set his mind to handling Gabriel Vargas's release with alacrity, despite a lengthy holdup while Mrs. Grace searched for the proper paperwork. Jana paid fifty bucks in bail, and with a phone call, Henry arranged for a court date the next week. Since there were few crooks in Blue Cloud, even the small-time sort, justice was meted out quickly. He assured Jana that it would probably be a matter of a small fine and possibly a few hours of community service. At the back of his mind, he was aware that perhaps this meant she and her band of Gypsies would be staying around a while longer. The mayor would harangue him about that. But he didn't care. The thought of keeping Jana nearby was so enticing that he started adding up other misdemeanors the Vargases could be charged with and ended up late for his meeting with Simon Tremayne.

Rubbing his chin in thought, Henry had left the station and was walking toward his official car with the blue-and-black B.C.P.D. emblem on the door, when a honk from the street made him look up. Jana and Gabriel were driving by in the rundown convertible.

She tooted again and waved. He lifted a hand in response, staring at the astonishingly pretty picture she made. Her long hair streamed in the breeze, as liquid as a mermaid's. She was laughing, bright and boisterous in her sunshine-yellow blouse, driving with one-handed, carefree abandon. The uncertain young woman from his office was long gone.

"Yes!" she shouted to Henry as the car careened around the corner. "Yes, I'll go with you…!" The engine roared, drowning out her voice as the car accelerated. In the passenger seat, Gabriel Vargas cast a gloating look over his shoulder as they sped away.

What was that about? Henry felt dazed by their sudden appearance. Were the pair of them up to something after all?

He was so busy watching the diminishing convertible and puzzling over where Jana's joyful yes had come from that he didn't notice the cast-iron lamppost.

Until he walked straight into it.

THE TIARA was beautiful, in a remote, fairy-tale sort of way. Nothing in Jana's life made her feel connected to its icy glamour, not even the name of the large blue-white diamond at the center. She wasn't sure she fully believed the legend about the Vargas diamond. Sometimes she could even convince herself that it was only a good story to tell around the campfire.

But then there was that little something else…

A twitch, a feeling…

Magic, a voice whispered in her ear. The voice sounded a lot like Baba Magda's.

Jana leaned closer to the glass-domed case, pushing just a little against the barricade of velvet ropes. If she could really see it, maybe touch it—

"Careful," a masculine voice said in her ear. A real one. "You'll set off the alarms."

She straightened, throwing a quick glance at Henry. He was motioning an "it's okay" signal to the security guard who'd stepped forward from his post. There were two of them in the room and another at the entrance to the museum. Jana had little doubt that she was on their Suspicious Faces to Watch For list.

"What are you doing here?" she asked Henry, keeping her gaze glued to the Brunner bridal tiara.

"I just finished a meeting with Simon and the security staff. Didn't I mention that to you before, in my office?" He was looking at her again, the way he had earlier, the way that made her aware of every inch of her skin. And every inch of his. "What are *you* doing here?"

She spoke lightly. "Looking at the tiara."

"What do you think of it?"

"It's very beautiful." He followed her as she circled the case. It was set up in the center of the room so that visitors could examine the famous tiara from all angles. Several spotlights beamed from the ceiling, making the tiny diamonds in the delicately wrought piece shimmer and sparkle.

"Spectacular," said a young man as he arrived before the domed case. He spread his hands, speaking too loudly where others had been hushed. "Don't you agree? Isn't it spectacular?"

Jana looked at him, annoyed. He was tall, dark and too handsome, the type of man who wouldn't leave home without styling gel and a hair dryer. He wore pleated trousers with a sweater tied around his neck, and he was barely looking at the tiara.

"Trey Stone, isn't it?" Henry offered his hand.

"Yes, sir," Trey said, showing all his teeth. There were many of them.

Henry gave his name. They shook hands.

Jana sidled away, using Henry's bulk as a buffer. She wasn't getting a good feeling from Trey Stone. Partly the feeling came from Princess Lili's less-than-flattering description of their date, but Jana also had a vague suspicion that she'd seen him before. Maybe he'd attended the fair.

"Wait a minute," Henry said to her, grasping her hand. "I want to talk to you."

"Outside." She pulled on him. The pit of her stomach was fluttering; she had to get out of there.

Henry said a quick goodbye to Stone and followed

her through the museum. She breezed past the security guard in the entrance hall and pushed hard on the double doors. They swung shut as she stood on the broad stone steps, taking deep breaths of the spring air.

"What was that about?"

"I don't know. Just a feeling."

Instead of scoffing, Henry asked gently, "About the tiara, or about Trey Stone?"

"Both," she admitted.

"Want to tell me about it?"

Her head shook. "Not really. It's nothing…tangible. Baba Magda says I have The Sight, but that's wishful thinking for her part. I don't *know* things, the way she does. I only get…um…" She waved a hand, making her bracelets jingle.

"Hunches?" Henry supplied.

"I suppose you could call them that."

"I get them, too." He rubbed the back of his neck.

"Oh?" Amused, she turned to see if he was teasing her. Her eyes widened. "Oh, no! What happened to you now?" Sporting a fresh, tender bruise, his left eye was painful-looking. Add the incipient black eye to the angry rash and he was one down-on-his-luck cop. A rush of sympathy replaced her uneasiness, pushing Trey Stone out of her mind. Henry was as rugged as they came, but he didn't look so tough now.

"I walked into a lamppost, but no one believes me. They think you decked me."

"Me?"

He loomed over her. "No one else has given me the grief you have."

She tipped back her head, not budging an inch. "Is that what you call it?"

"Yeah, when I'm feeling frustrated." His voice dropped. "Which is all the time, lately. You're hell on my body, sweetheart."

She had to smile. "Don't blame this on me. Blame it on the curse."

"I'm cursed all right. Cursed with wanting a sassy, spicy, sexy woman like you."

She rose to her tiptoes and kissed the end of his nose. "Come with me."

"Where?" he said, lacing their fingers.

She gave him a smoldering look. "To my caravan. I'm going to make you all better."

8

HENRY LET OUT a groan as Jana hovered over him, applying herself to his care. "This isn't what I had in mind," he complained, even though she could tell that the heat felt good. Really good. Too bad about the goopiness, but he'd just have to put up with it.

"Hush," she said. "Let me take care of you."

He struggled to raise himself off the bed. "I don't do passive very well."

She pushed him down and even crawled on top of him to see that he didn't get up again. "Stay put. Don't move. This might stink, but it's going to feel great. You'll thank me in a few hours."

He groaned again and laid his head back on the pillow as she applied the messy green poultice to his eye. "What's in that thing?"

"A few herbs, but mostly plant matter that's been stewed down to extract the natural healing properties. I got it from Tamara, who is a *drabarni.* An herbalist."

"She's the one who was reading tarot cards at the fair. You *are* treating me with a magic Gypsy potion."

"Don't be such a baby. It's one-hundred percent natural. Completely safe. Shut up and enjoy it, Chief."

"Mmm." He smiled to himself, moving ever so

slightly beneath her. Enough to tell her that he'd been putting her on a little, with all his complaining. Also enough to make her insides shiver with awareness. The outsides, too, when he spread his hand over her hip, his palm warm, his fingertips touching her hipbone. He adjusted himself a tiny bit and she sucked in a breath, suddenly intensely aware of their intimate position. She hadn't meant to seduce him. It was just that tending to him was awkward with her bed being enclosed on three sides the way it was, and the fringe from the drooping drapes tickling her face every time she leaned over to minister to him.

She started to move off his thighs, but his hand tightened on her hip. ''Don't forget the rash.'' His good eye was closed and his mouth was as sober as ever, but she had the sneaking suspicion that he was smiling all the same.

''I'll have to take off your shirt.''

Sigh. ''Oh, all right.''

She almost laughed. Oh, sure, he was being agreeable enough, *now*. Well, she could still make him suffer.

''Here we go,'' she crooned, slowly unbuttoning. She parted the heavy cotton uniform shirt, revealing the sexiest chest she'd ever seen. He was a slab of pure muscle, covered with dark, springy hair that became more downy as it arrowed down the center of his flat, hard stomach and disappeared into the waistband of his slacks. As she worked his arms out of his sleeves—and he let her, lying there like a deadweight with that determined non-smile on his face—she tried not to notice how the rash on his arms, neck and upper chest didn't distract from his masculine beauty one bit.

She shifted her leg and slid off him. He made a sound of protest, but she couldn't stay, especially when she'd felt his body's quick response through their clothing, which had only contributed to a nice friction between them.

Judging by the self-satisfied expression on his face, he wasn't at all embarrassed by his obvious state of arousal. So much for suffering!

She retrieved a small tube of salve from one of the built-in cupboards, then stopped and closed her eyes for a second, telling herself to stay objective. Nurses did this kind of thing all the time.

Yeah, sure. Especially in porn films...

"Ahem. I have a salve." She approached the bed warily, her gaze drifting over his sprawled body. The man had no modesty at all, but *her* face was flaming. So much for objectiveness!

He made no answer.

"Um, can you scoot over a little so I can sit?"

"There's room." He turned partway onto his hip, looping an arm around her waist and dragging her down beside him, fitting her derriere snugly against his groin. The fire in her face spread quite a bit lower.

"Give me your arm." She grabbed and yanked it into position, trying to be brisk. But spreading the salve into his bumpy, pinkened skin wasn't a particularly good way to stay detached. Especially when he moaned pleasurably under his breath.

She dropped his left arm onto the bed, then squeezed a dollop of the clear, gooey salve across his upper chest, working it into his skin with her fingertips. His muscles were firm, but not as rock-hard as she'd expected. There was some pliancy, and his skin was like warm velvet. She could easily imagine sleeping curled up beside him, cozy and safe.

"Better?" she murmured, greasing his neck and jaw.

Lazily, he opened one eye. It had gone from brown to darkest black, the pupil dilated in the dim light of her caravan. Although it was still only midday, with the curtains drawn on the one small window, it might as well have been midnight. "If this is Gypsy magic, I'm all for it."

She showed him the tube. "Only $2.98 at the pharmacy."

"Then the magic must be in your fingertips."

"I never thought you'd be such a sweet talker."

He moved his head against her pillows. "Spend much time thinking about me?"

"Of course...not."

"Me, too."

"Egotist." She slapped his chest.

He caught her by the elbow and drew her down to him. "I've spent a lot of time thinking about you. Not only about how you smell so fine and the way you taste so sweet, but about how you live. Where you're going, what you'll become..."

Jana's lashes lowered. Not a good idea, because that

meant she was staring at his gleaming chest. "You're worried about my future?"

That was a new concept. Strange, and a little frightening. But a comfort, too. The Rom were a tight-knit family with an unbreakable bond, but they weren't much into security and planning for the future. However, she had a little too much staunch New England blood running through her veins to be completely carefree.

"Do you ever think about settling down?"

"Ohh…maybe. Sometime."

"One day in the future? When you're no longer in charge?"

"Yeah," she said softly, dropping her palm against his chest. Mindlessly she pattered her fingers on his skin. "I might try it."

"You'd leave the Gypsies?"

"Not altogether. I can't imagine breaking away completely. I don't want to. But…well, sometimes I think about being a full-time schoolteacher. I'm certified. I even do substitute teaching during the winters. That way, you see, I'd still have my summers to travel with the caravan."

"Sounds like a plan to me."

She slipped her fingertip over his cheek, wiping up a dribble from the poultice. "Maybe one day."

"I could put in a good word for you with the Blue Cloud school system. They have openings for the next school year."

The feeling between them had grown too comfortable. She pushed away. "There's that bossiness again! Henry, I don't need you to fix my life. I'm not ready for a change, so please don't force one on me." She flung her hair aside. "Besides, I can imagine what people would say about the police chief taking up with a no-account Gypsy. Or is that why you wanted to find me a job? To make me respectable?"

"Jeez, Jana." Jaw bulging, he levered himself up on his elbows. She had to look away from all the flexing and clenching muscles in his chest. "There you go again. Doesn't my asking you to the dance tonight prove anything?"

"For all I know, you want to take me just to show off how tight security is. What better way to prove it to people than by bringing a wild Gypsy, right?"

Scowling, he caught the poultice as it slid away from his eye.

Her mouth dropped open at the guilt she read on his face. "You did!"

The left side of his face was streaked with green goo and wet shreds of leaf matter. "'Course not. But why did *you* say yes, so suddenly? *After* you'd talked to Gabriel?"

She shot to her bare feet. "He had nothing to do with it. I accepted because after I left the station, a courier handed me a personal invitation from Princess Lili and I—I didn't want to go alone!"

"I see." Henry slowly climbed off the bed. Standing, his chest seemed even more massive. His dominating personality matched it well. But, by God, she was no

pushover. Even for the Creature from the Green La-
goon.

"Are you still willing to go with me?" he growled,
advancing on her. The poultice fell to the wood floor
with a *plop*. He grabbed a small hand towel and vigorously scrubbed away the remaining green goop.

She set her hands on her hips. "Yes!"

"Good." A look of satisfaction came over his face
in the instant before he pulled her gracelessly into his
arms and brought his mouth down hard upon hers. She
managed to suck in a quick breath and was glad for it
a minute later, because she was lost in the overwhelm-
ing, red-hot, black-as-sin, swirling world of his kiss. He
ravished her mouth thoroughly. And she was helpless
to resist.

Even if she'd wanted to.

HENRY STRIPPED OFF his clothes right where he stood.
For a man who looked as if he'd been dragged through
the underbrush backward, he was feeling pretty damn
good. He still had his suspicions about Gabriel Vargas,
but Jana was looking more like an innocent bystander
with every piece of information he collected. From what
he'd been able to gather through official channels—and
some not so official—she'd been nothing but a boon to
the band of traveling Rom.

He looked at himself in the bathroom mirror. Not a
pretty sight, even after Jana's cures. While the rash
hadn't disappeared, the itchiness was now tolerable. The

skin around his eye was tender and faintly purple, but not as floridly bruised as it might have been.

He touched his bristly jaw. Yup, he'd have to shave. The museum shindig was a formal affair. He didn't care for the fuss and bother with tuxes and all, but he had to admit that he was looking forward to dancing with Jana.

An hour ago, he'd finally been put in touch with a cop in Wheeling who'd dealt with the Vargases in the past. Though Gabe had several black marks on his juvenile record, he'd been clean since Jana had taken over after the death of Zharko Vargas. She was apparently keeping a firm hold on the group, helping them find permanent jobs, good medical care, even completing the paperwork that qualified one of the Gypsy couples and their children for a house from a helping-hand organization. In fact, the entire clan had joined in the building of it, along with two more houses for other disadvantaged families.

Jana had also told the truth about teaching as a sub. Every principal who'd hired her gave glowing reports. Her degree was in order, her college record impeccable.

While none of this contradicted what Henry's gut had been telling him even when the facts looked suspicious as hell, it was nice to have solid, incontrovertible facts to rely on. Feelings were unreliable, but you could take college transcripts and employment records to the bank.

For just a second, Henry paused to consider whether or not he'd still want Jana if she'd turned out to be the ringleader of a gang of pickpockets and swindlers. He'd always been a straight arrow, so the answer should have been no. But…

He wasn't sure.

Didn't matter now, did it? He yanked aside the shower curtain. He had a fancy ball to go to with Jana Vargas, Gypsy princess, on his arm. The latter kind of made up for the former.

He turned on the taps. The pipes shuddered and clanged, then blatted out a spurt of dirty water. "Ugh." Henry opened them up full blast. The water that gushed out was green, putrid green, smelly as the moldy cantaloupe he'd once left in the bottom of his refrigerator for an entire summer. He let the water run for as long as he could stand, hoping it would clear.

It didn't. In fact, it got worse. Now it stunk like a high-school chemistry experiment gone terribly wrong.

Breathing through his mouth, he reached in and twisted the taps to the off position. The green water kept gushing. *Hell.* Now he'd have to put on a towel and run down to the basement to turn the water off at the source.

Swearing at the inconvenience, he backed away from the foul soup filling his tub.

Blast that curse!

"MY HOUSE IS A TRIPLEX," he told Jana an hour later while they stood in line with the Blue Cloud version of beautiful people outside the new brick museum. The Princess Adelaide and Horace P. Applewhite Memorial Museum—The Addy-Appy for short—was lit up like a Hollywood movie theater on opening night. There were even photographers and reporters on hand, all for Princess Lili, who'd yet to arrive.

Henry and Jana could have bypassed the wait and gone straight into the museum, but he wanted to see what kind of a job the guards were doing as they checked invitations. No one was supposed to get inside without one.

"Yes?" Jana said, extremely cautiously. He'd already told her why he'd been late. Because of the blasted green water, he'd had to shower and change into his tux at the station house. Which had meant parading before Mrs. Grace and the two temps, one of whom had pinched his butt. The other, the boy with the pink hair and piercings, had slipped his phone number into Henry's cummerbund. A case of either wishful thinking or really bad gaydar.

"My tenants share the basement with me. Mrs. Peevey was doing her laundry. When she saw me coming down the stairs in a towel, she got so flustered she dumped bleach on her brand-new Ralph Lauren sheets. Now I have to replace them. Do you know what those things cost?"

Jana blinked. "That's, um, ter-r-rible."

He peered at her through his good eye. "You don't seem sorry."

She blinked again. Didn't make her look innocent at all, if that's what she was hoping. "Should I be?"

"You're the one who cursed me, so, yeah. You should be real sorry. So sorry you're offering me anything to make up for the trouble you've caused."

"That *I've* caused?" she scoffed. "But that would mean you actually *believe* in the curse."

He couldn't swallow that, so he avoided it. "That's not the point. I just want to know how to get rid of it."

She smiled. "They say the first step is admitting you have a problem."

"I have a problem." He twined his arm around her waist as they moved up in line. An elderly women looked back at them and tittered as he said into Jana's ear, "It's you. What you do to me. Do you have a cure for that?"

"Suffer." She gave him an elbow in the ribs, then fluttered her fingers at the women ahead of them. "Hello, ladies. Lottie, do you remember me? Jana Vargas. You gave me a ride…"

"To the Gypsy camp!" Lottie Wolf said. "Dear me, yes, I remember. I so wanted to go to your fair, but Jess wouldn't let me." She rolled her eyes at her sister, standing rigidly beside Lottie in a black dress that looked as if it had been unearthed from a trunk full of mothballs. Lottie patted her freshly blued hair. "My land, Jana. Aren't you the prettiest thing!" She eyed Henry. "Do I know your young man?"

"Henry Russell, ma'am. Chief of Police." The Wolf sisters had known him since he first arrived in town and solved the Case of the Missing Birdbath. The butler did it.

Lottie's expression cleared. "Chief Russell! I didn't recognize you, out of uniform and so…afflicted. You poor dear."

"You ought to slap a raw steak on that eye," Jessica Wolf said. She let out a huff and turned her back on Jana. "It appears that they'll let *anyone* into this party."

"Don't mind the sourpuss," Lottie said, forestalling Henry's ill-advised comment. "We received our invitation directly from Princess Lili herself, so now Jess is putting on airs."

Jess shot out a hand and gripped her sister by the arm. "Come along, Lottie. We're off to meet the princess." The two sisters handed over their invitation and were waved into the museum, past the courtier who held the door.

"How's it going?" Henry asked the security guard. "Any party crashers?"

"We caught a couple of reporters trying to sneak in. That's it, sir."

"I didn't bring my invitation," Jana blurted. "I, uh, didn't realize I needed it."

"No problem," Henry said. "She's with me," he told the guard. "Jana Vargas."

The guard checked a master list. "Got her. Go on in, Ms. Vargas. But you'd better stick with the Chief. Don't wander off alone. We can't let you back inside without the invitation."

"I'm not used to this," Jana murmured to Henry as they stepped inside the museum. "I don't know the protocol."

He gave her a squeeze. "When you want to be, you're as regal as Princess Lili." He ducked his head near hers. "Don't tell Simon or Lili I said so, but you're also twice as beautiful."

FROM THAT POINT ON, the evening became a magical fairy tale to Jana. The museum shone like a jewel, from the gilded ceiling to the gleaming instruments of the orchestra on the second-floor balcony, to the golden glow of the sconces and the polished stone floors. The guests were lustrous and rich in formal gowns and stately tuxedos. Champagne flowed, glasses tinkled, laughter sparkled.

Princess Lili arrived to a chorus of *oohs* and *ahs*. She was stunning in a blue-green and sparkly silver ball-gown, as storybook lovely as a princess should be. For one instant, Jana felt like the poor country cousin in her hand-me-down lace dress and simple sandals, but then Lili swept toward her, lavish with compliments, and Jana knew that those who mattered accepted her as she was. It helped a little to see Jess Wolf's jaw drop when she realized that the lowly Gypsy was the first person the princess greeted.

Jana suspected that Henry wasn't having as good a time. He tolerated numerous comments on his black eye and seemed to be in constant touch with either Simon, the mayor, the security guards or a fellow officer. There was a minor incident when Henry and Simon descended on Trey Stone as if they suspected him of ill intentions, but the princess explained that she had added Trey to the invitation list at the last moment. Simon wasn't too pleased about that—which had nothing to do with security and everything to do with jealousy—but Henry was only relieved.

With the evening half over, Henry finally relaxed his vigilance long enough to ask Jana to dance. She was surprised by his agility as he swirled her around the dance floor beneath an elaborate glass chandelier.

"You know how to waltz!" she said, breathless.

"Not by choice. I had to learn for my sisters' weddings."

"Three sisters," she remembered. "They're all married?"

"Yes. I found a poor slob from the police academy to take Laurie on last summer."

She shook her head at the fondness in his voice. "*You* found the husband? So now you're a matchmaker, too."

"If I didn't get them married off, I'd be taking care of them forever."

"Isn't that an archaic attitude?"

"No. I'm an equal-opportunity big brother. After Mike graduates from college, I'll see that he finds a wife to take care of *him.*"

"And who takes care of you?"

Instead of giving the expected answer, he said, "You did a pretty good job of that this afternoon."

Jana caught her breath, but she couldn't look away. Henry's eyes darkened as he watched her watch him. Her admiration probably showed in her face, along with her attraction. He held her exactly right in his arms, letting her find her own flow with the music because it must be obvious that she had no experience with waltzes. Astonishingly, he knew that to lead didn't always mean to take control. Another good point to add to the growing list of reasons why he was so much more than an untrustworthy *shawglo* for her to keep away from.

He was, simply, a wonderful man.

Henry pulled her a little closer. "You should talk." His voice dipped low, beneath the music. "How many people are you responsible for?"

Enough. But she wouldn't mind adding him to the list. Because she knew that he'd also take care of her.

With an effort, she tore away her gaze and rested her cheek on his shoulder. "Let's just dance." Her eyes drifted shut.

By then, they were no longer waltzing. He was holding her too close for that. She could feel his body heat through her dress. It was easy to imagine being naked with him, having the broad chest she'd uncovered earlier pressing against her, solid as a brick wall, while his hands moved across her skin. And his lips…oh, his lips would be hot, so very, very hot and possessive…

She lifted her head, intending to brush a kiss across Henry's cheek. Instead, when her eyes opened, she caught a glimpse of a face that put all thoughts of sex out of her mind. Gabriel! How could that be?

She straightened to better see past Henry's shoulder, but Gabriel was gone. If it had been him at all. The room was full of people and all the men wore similar tuxedos. It didn't seem possible for Gabe to be here, in a tux, mixing with the gray-haired scions of Blue

Cloud's upper crust. He didn't have an invitation for one thing.

Jana froze inside. She'd left her invitation in her caravan. Gabriel *could* have found it.

But why would he want to attend the party? Normally, he scorned such events. He'd even tried to talk her out of going, when she'd mentioned that the princess had invited her. He'd tried very hard.

Henry was watching her curiously. "Jana, is there something wrong?"

"I don't know." She spun on her heel, frantically searching the other dancers. Simon Tremayne was leading Princess Lili off the dance floor, into the first display room. Lili looked very happy and lighthearted. Trey Stone meandered after them, quite dashing in his tuxedo. There was no sight of Gabriel.

She must have seen wrong.

But I wasn't. And I'm going to have to tell Henry.

"Jana?" Henry's voice had sharpened with suspicion. Her stomach dropped, regretting the doubt that he still held concerning her. But, really, could she blame him?

They moved off the dance floor toward the open doorway that led to the jewel displays, passing the lady mayor, sans her usual escort, along the way. "Henry," Jana began, "I might be wrong, but I think—"

The lights went out before she could finish, and the museum was plunged into total darkness.

Several horrified shrieks went up. Guests gasped in alarm, some of them calling to each other through the darkened rooms. A loud crash came from the area of the buffet tables, followed by a man's oath.

Jana clutched Henry's hand, then his lapel, even though he hadn't let go of her for a second. "Henry? What's happening?"

A shrill alarm went off, cutting out his reply. She let go of him and put her hands over her ears.

Several flashlight beams shone through the vast room, revealing groups of guests huddled together, looking about with startled eyes. Two of the security guards converged, illuminating a path toward the tiara room with their lights. Henry grabbed hold of Jana's hand and pulled her into the next room, where Simon was yelling for the guards to look after the tiara.

Jana found herself thrust toward Princess Lili and her bodyguard, a jowly middle-aged man. "Do not let her go!" Henry shouted above the alarm, and then he and Simon dashed away.

The guard put his hand on Jana's arm, but she shook him off. Henry's words were ringing in her ears louder than the security alarm. *Do not let her go?* Then she was still considered a suspect! He *had* asked her to the ball in order to keep an eye on her!

Finally, the backup emergency lights came on. They shone at a low wattage, but it was enough to see. Jana looked over the crowd. Henry had disappeared. Gabriel was nowhere in sight. The only person she recognized was Trey Stone, standing by an upended buffet table with his tuxedo smeared with food.

Jana turned to confront the princess and her bodyguard. "I'm not staying here!" It was hard to know for sure over the noise and chaos, but she believed that something terrible was happening in the next room. For certain, Henry was involved.

"Yes, you will, miss," the bodyguard shouted at her over the continuing alarm.

"Nonsense," Lili said. She grabbed Jana's hand, then the bodyguard's. "Let's go."

Amelia Grundy arrived, putting out her hands to stop them. She had Jess and Lottie Wolf with her. "No, Princess, you mustn't. It's too dangerous."

Jana broke away. "I'll go alone!" But the bodyguard caught her again, holding on even when she wrenched at his strong grip.

"Come on!" Lili pulled at the bodyguard's other arm. Between them, they got him moving. Mrs. Grundy grabbed Jana's free hand as she rushed past, linking her with the Wolf sisters, as well.

All together, they arrived in the inner room where the tiara was displayed in its shatterproof case. Jana gasped. The tiara was untouched, but a struggle was ensuing in a dim corner between Henry, a man in a tux, and a couple of the security guards.

Simon approached them, his hands upraised, his glasses askew. "You can't be in here. You need to clear out at once—"

Suddenly the apparent thief broke away from the guards who'd subdued him and darted for the doorway they were blocking. Simon spun on his heel and tackled the man an instant before he ran head-on into the prin-

cess. Lili stumbled backward a few steps; her bodyguard caught her by the elbows.

Simon and the tuxedo-clad crook went down in a
tangle of flailing limbs, sliding several feet on the polished floor. They crashed into a jewel case, breaking the
glass and upending the sparkling contents across the
floor.

The crook leaped to his feet like a cat. Jana backed
off a step, horrified by the familiarity of his movements
even though she hadn't gotten a good look at his face
in the dim light. She barely noticed bumping into Trey
Stone as he darted past her. Dread had filled her. She
was too stunned to react.

Meanwhile, Henry was closing in on the crook from
behind. Before he could apprehend the young man, the
Wolf sisters descended, beating him about the head and
shoulders with their purses. Mrs. Grundy stepped in,
wielding the sharp tip of an umbrella at the thief's lean
midsection.

Henry snapped on the cuffs. He was disheveled, but
quite calm. "That's enough. Thank you, Lottie and
Jess." He raised a brow at the British nanny's lethal
umbrella. "Mrs. Grundy."

The princess let out a breathy exclamation and ran to
Simon, who was still sprawled on the floor. They em-
braced.

Jana looked closely at the suspect, dreading what she
would see. His head was down, but she knew. The room
began to spin and she closed her eyes, growing sick to

her stomach. *This isn't happening,* she said silently. *Please, please, don't let this be happening.*

Simon was asking about the necklace that had spilled out of the broken case. No one seemed to know where it was, until Trey Stone stepped out from behind Jana again, proffering a handful of emeralds. "Here it is." She eyed him distantly, remembering how he'd rushed forward, obviously to "rescue" the necklace off the floor. "I picked it up for you," he added, shooting a glance at Jana.

She was too sickened to care.

Especially when Henry tightened a hand on his captive's collar and pulled his head back.

The alarm stopped, thrusting the room into a tense silence.

Jana broke it, inhaling in shock as the truth hit her, dead-on and undeniable. "*Gabriel,*" she said, his name torn out of her throat with deepest regret. There was nothing she could do to prevent this.

Not even the worst curse in the world would help Gabriel now.

9

"I'M SORRY, JANA."

In Henry's estimation, the words didn't fit; Gabriel Vargas didn't look sorry in the least. Perhaps he was regretting the scheme now that he was caught, but he wasn't sorry about the attempt. Not one bit. Tough luck for Jana, who was shattered.

Henry rubbed his jaw. A lump was forming where he'd taken a punch from Gabriel's fist during the initial struggle. He should have saved himself the trouble and let the old ladies loose as soon as the alarms went off. Was this part of the curse against him, or merely misadventure as usual?

Jana took her cousin by the shoulders. Henry couldn't tell if she wanted to hug him or shake him. He'd have hugged her if he had the option, but he didn't. Not on the job.

"Why did you do this?" Jana demanded of Gabe.

"You know why."

Henry's ears perked. Normally he wouldn't let a suspect converse with *anyone,* but he was interested in what Gabriel had to say for himself. He might offer a motive to Jana that he would never reveal to the law.

"That stupid, stupid story," Jana hissed. "I curse the

day Zharko planted ideas about the Vargas diamond in your head.''

''We have a right to it—''

''*Shesti!* That's pure nonsense and you should know it.'' She gave him a little shake. ''Too much time has passed, Gabriel. The Vargases should have forgotten the diamond long ago.''

The young Rom thrust his chin at Princess Lili and her entourage, standing nearby, exchanging the occasional word of reassurance, but mostly listening to Jana and her cousin, shaking their collective heads in disapproval. ''It's cursed for them. Why should they get to keep it?''

''Cursed?'' Princess Lili's voice wavered.

Mrs. Grundy's blue eyes sharpened. ''The royal family doesn't believe in such balderdash.''

All eyes went to the Brunner bridal tiara, sitting atop a pouf of blue satin inside the glass dome, glistening beneath the spotlights. Beautiful. Cold. Untouched.

Lili glided toward it, her full skirts sweeping the floor in a lovely swirl of gleaming blue-and-green layers. ''We believe the legend that says no one but a Brunner bride should ever wear the tiara, don't we?'' She raised her brows at Mrs. Grundy.

Gabriel's head rose proudly. ''Ask yourself why all the Brunner brides die young,'' he boasted.

Jana kicked him with the side of her foot. ''Hush.''

Lili stared at them. ''My mother, Princess Marja, was killed in an avalanche when I was nine.''

''But your grandmother lived until she was sixty-one," Mrs. Grundy advised, taking the princess's elbow. She led Lili away, who was saying, "But that's not so old." The Wolf sisters followed, murmuring reassurances.

Jana sighed. "Gabriel. You shouldn't have done that. There is no curse."

"You know better, Jana. Remember your *dook*."

Henry had had enough of the curses and legends. None of this was factual information he could build a case with. He motioned Officer Blake over and told him to take the prisoner away to the station house. Gabriel would be held there until Henry could interrogate him.

"I'll go, too," said Jana, a stubborn look on her face.

"No, you will not. I want all eyewitnesses to wait here in the museum. We need to go over the evening, moment by moment."

"Why? Obviously, you've apprehended your suspect."

Henry looked her square in the eye. "Do you think Gabriel is a fool?"

"Hotheaded and impulsive, yes. But not a fool."

"Then why would he make such a hopeless attempt to steal the tiara when his plan clearly couldn't work? And who cut the lights?"

Either Henry was mistaken, or a tiny hope flared to life in Jana's eyes. "What are you saying?"

"He has a conspirator…and it isn't you."

She caught her bottom lip between her teeth and went very still. "Are you certain, Henry, even though I've been telling you that all along?"

He was as solid as ever. It was a good front for the times when he questioned himself. ''This time, yes, I am.''

''I don't believe that's so. When the electricity went out, you handed me off to Lili's bodyguard like a common criminal. At least for a moment, you thought I had a part in this...'' She gestured at the disarray of the broken display case and the milling bystanders, whom the security guards were attempting to corral. In the next room, platters of upended hors d'oeuvres were being crunched underfoot. The mayor was arriving to view the disaster area, by the sounds of the verbal hand-wringing going on. Silent Spotsky was back at her side, slipping in the spilled caviar.

Henry furrowed his brow. Jana was right. He didn't trust her—not entirely. He didn't know if he ever could. ''Jana...''

She shook her head, her lips compressing. ''Don't.'' She made a shooing motion. ''Go on. Do your job. Leave me be.''

Henry was frustrated by her dismissal, but he knew that now wasn't the time. Especially when Lottie Wolf was bearing down on him in ruffled green chiffon, warbling his name. ''Oh, oh, oh, Chief Russell? Jess and I simply must speak to you! When we went to get Scooter from our car to take a wee, we saw something quite curious....''

JANA HATED WAITING. She was too impatient and nervous, accustomed to showing trouble her back rather than sitting still and staying quiet like a good little girl, waiting for a pat on the head from the *skummade igenom*. Her Boston grandparents' training hadn't taken.

She glanced at Princess Lili. The princess was good at waiting, so serene and calm. Even Gabriel's bald statement about the curse of the tiara hadn't ruffled her too badly, aside from a hasty recounting of her ancestor's lives and deaths. Mrs. Grundy hadn't liked it, though. Probably because she believed in the curse a lot more than Lili did. As the princess said, Amelia Grundy *knew*.

So did Jana.

She knew that she needed more in her life than duty and responsibility. She needed the thrill, the sparks, the comfort and joy that she'd found these past few days. She needed Henry Russell.

How could that be when neither of them trusted the other?

She was afraid to believe in any *shawglo*, even one like Henry, but too much in love—or getting awfully close—not to want to. The push-me/pull-you demon was back, and this time it was her very heart that was at stake. She studied Henry as he consulted with Simon, telling herself that this was happening too fast, doing her best to be angry with him instead of in love. She couldn't love him. It would be the end of so much for her.

Too soon, too soon, she thought, as he left Simon and walked toward her across the emptied entrance hall of the museum.

She rose to meet him, insisting that she be allowed to leave, even before he began issuing his typical commands. "I can't be forced to stay here all evening," she said. "I have to get back to the camp—"

He put on his best scowl. "So you can interfere with my investigation?"

Her eyes narrowed. Was the Big Chief planning to barge into the Gypsy's encampment and roust them all out of bed to be interrogated? "Bosh! Your bias is blinding you again."

"Gabriel was caught red handed. I'm sorry, but you'll have to face it."

"I have. He's guilty. But that doesn't mean we all are."

"Listen to me, Jana." Henry dropped his voice and took her by the elbow to move her off to the side, away from the earshot of the last few witnesses. She prickled at the presumption of being moved about like a chess piece, but was too disheartened to put up her usual front.

"I want you to keep away from your camp for tonight." Henry raised a hand when she started to protest. "I know, I know. No assumptions. I'm looking at everyone who was here tonight. But it's natural that your cousin's most likely partner, or partners, would come from among the Gypsies. You must see that."

"No. I don't. I know them. There have been times, I'll admit, when they pulled a few...well, they didn't always follow the letter of the law. But now, we're straight up. I promise you."

"Then you have nothing to worry about."

"If I can't be with Gabriel, I want to go home."

"You can go to my house," Henry offered. "And wait for me there, okay?"

She frowned. "Your house? Would you trust me there?"

"I have no other choice."

"That's not exactly flattering..."

"But you agree?"

She was still devastated by Gabe's arrest, and a little confused, so she nodded. "I agree."

It was only later, when Henry had left her standing in the middle of his bland beige living room with a 32-button high-tech remote control in hand—why did men think TV was a cure-all?—that she began to wonder what she'd agreed to.

"Is YOUR TV BIG ENOUGH?" was the first thing Jana said to Henry when he came home, hours later, dog tired.

He threw down his wrinkled tuxedo jacket and the long-abandoned cummerbund. He'd lost the bow tie somewhere along the way and popped one of the shirt studs; a gap had opened in the center, which widened when he removed his shoulder holster and shrugged off the thin black suspenders. "Are you casting aspersions? Or suggesting my big screen was a Freudian choice?"

"Both." She shrugged. "Neither. But that thing is a monster. Still, I couldn't find anything interesting to watch, so I cooked instead." She smiled rather shyly. "It was nice to use a real oven for a change."

He sniffed. A hot, spicy, meaty scent had permeated the house. The smell was close enough to heaven to make him groan. "Food."

"Hungry?"

"Starving."

Henry could see that she was dying to ask about Gabriel and the investigation, but she went into the kitchen instead and opened the oven. The wafting scent of hot food made his eyes roll back in his head. He staggered after her like a thirsty man in the desert.

"You're wearing my clothes." *And they look better on you than me.* He looked at her curvy bottom as she bent over the open oven door, carefully lifting out a heavy casserole dish he hadn't known he owned. Every now and then, his mother or one of his sisters would show up and stock his freezer and fridge with home-cooked meals. They taped instructions to the foil: Reheat at 375 degrees, 55 minutes. No Microwave!!!

Jana removed the cover, then slid off his matching cow-print potholders. Matching cow-print potholders were definitely another woman thing. He just hadn't expected them to be a Jana Vargas thing.

"I wasn't going to sit around watching TV in an antique lace dress. So I went through your closets." She flipped her hair over her shoulder, glancing back at him with a serving spoon in her hand poised in the air above the casserole. "Do you mind?"

Considering she'd chosen a large white T-shirt and

plaid boxer shorts that showed off her long, smooth legs, he wasn't about to object. Even the thick white socks that she'd scrunched around her ankles looked cute. If the casserole was no good, she looked good enough to eat. "Did you find my stash of *Playboy* magazines?"

"I thought men grow out of that phase when they graduate college."

"Give up on naked air-brushed beauties? Not to mention the incisive articles." He chuckled. "Besides, I only keep the collector's editions."

"Oh, I'll bet." Her answering chuckle was hollow. "Boys will be boys."

She set a dish on the small round table in the breakfast nook, then went back to the kitchen to find utensils and pour a glass of milk. "You've been drinking coffee all night," she said, when she saw his nose wrinkle. "Milk is good for you."

"You've made yourself at home." He sat in one of the heavy pine chairs that outweighed the little table. Man chairs. He'd bought them after one of the set of matching chairs had folded under him as if it had been constructed with toothpicks.

"Just following orders." Standing uncertainly by the table, she watched while he leaned down to lift his pant leg and reveal the gun that had been strapped above his right ankle. Velcro ripped as he removed it. "Is that the last of the weapons?"

Nodding, he unloaded the bullets and laid the gun on the table, next to the tall glass of milk. She shuddered.

Her eyes were large and abnormally bright. "Would you have shot at Gabe if he'd escaped instead of being attacked by the Handbag Brigade?"

"No. Too dangerous with that many people around." He picked up a fork. "What is this?"

She pronounced an unpronounceable word with lots of consonants. "It's Hungarian. Halfway between a casserole and a stew. I found potatoes and beef chunks in your freezer, and a carrot that wasn't too limp…" Her voice ran down and she sat across from him, looking dejected. "Can I go home now?"

"If you want," he said, eating.

"They'll be wondering where I am."

"Baba Magda knows. I was at the camp, asking questions."

"Oh, God." Jana buried her face in her hands. "This is a nightmare. Did Gabriel confess?"

"He's a stubborn one. Won't say a thing, except to insist that he was working alone."

"He wouldn't talk." Her voice was bitter. "It's a matter of pride. Misplaced pride."

"And loyalty?" Henry prodded.

"Not to the Rom. This was a separate thing, I'm sure of it."

"What about the pickpocketing?"

"Are you charging him for that?"

Henry shook his head.

"That was…" She took a deep breath, dropping her limp hands to the table. "He's done it before. I thought

I'd convinced him to stop, but it's like a game to him. To put one over on the *gadje*."

Henry touched her arm. Stroked it. "Have you ever done it?"

She shivered, then whispered, "A couple of times. When I was very young."

"Then it wasn't entirely a bad thing, you being taken away by your grandparents."

"In some ways, no."

She twisted on the chair, brushing away Henry's hand. He went back to eating the spicy stew, keeping a careful eye on her. She had a lot to deal with. He'd protect her if he could, but there was no way to undo her cousin's mistake.

After a while she cleared her throat, determined to hear the worst. "What's going to happen now?"

"We'll continue to look for Gabriel's partner. In the meantime, he'll be charged with attempted burglary. It'll go better for him if he confesses."

Jana's head came up. "What about the Wolf sisters? Didn't they say they saw somebody?"

"That's a strange thing. I'm not sure what to make of it. They were outside with their dog, Scooter. They claim that a bald man in a tuxedo was lurking around the back of the museum, only a short time before the electricity was cut, but it was too dark for them to ID him."

"There you go—there's your suspect!"

"Maybe, maybe not. It could have been someone

sneaking a smoke. Half of the men at the party were balding.''

''True.'' She sighed. ''The only one it lets off the hook is Trey Stone.''

Henry waggled his fork. ''Why does everyone suspect Stone? Simon's been on my back about him from the start. I checked him out. He's just a playboy from Philly with an attraction for royalty. The only connection I could find was that he leased his spiffy car at Spotsky's.''

''He was odd about the emerald necklace tonight,'' Jana said, lost in her own suspicions. ''For a second, I thought he was going to pocket it rather than give it back. If Simon hadn't asked...'' She frowned in thought. ''And besides, he reminds me of someone, or I've seen him before. I just can't think who or where.''

''A bargain-basement Tom Selleck?''

She offered a bleak smile.

''Whoever was involved,'' Henry said, ''it was a weak attempt. There was no way the plan could work, and I'm surprised Gabriel didn't know it. When I told him about the tiara's display case being alarmed, he looked shocked for just an instant. I have to wonder if he knew what he was getting into.''

Jana's face clouded. ''His mystery partner could have been using him as a dupe.''

''But why?''

''Isn't that what *you're* supposed to figure out?''

''Honey, I'll do my best.''

She blinked at the endearment. ''I know you will.''

For a moment, it seemed that she wanted to say more. Her eyes had gone soft when she looked at him. But then she got up and began to move restlessly around the kitchen, letting off steam as she ranted about Gabriel, waving her arms, spouting Rom words Henry didn't understand. He couldn't help notice how her breasts moved beneath his baggy T-shirt, how her hips swayed, the way she bit her lush lower lip. Her eyes were a stormy midnight blue, full of passion.

"I should go," she said suddenly, catching what must have been a look of lust on his face.

"You can stay the night. If you want."

She hesitated, a mix of emotions crossing her face.

"I have a spare bedroom," he explained, giving her the option.

She set her hands on her hips. "You don't want me to share your bed?"

"No." *Yes.* "I mean, I'm sure you're not in the mood—"

She stopped him with a raised brow.

He sputtered. Hot fun in the summertime! He'd *never* figure out this woman's moods. She was as mercurial as a thermometer in the Sahara. Heating up in two seconds flat.

A slow smile spread across her face. Her lashes dipped, making her eyes look exotically slumberous and sexy. "Haven't you heard? I'm hot-blooded. A wild Gypsy passion runs through my soul."

Henry stared. They were certainly on the same wavelength.

Even so, he couldn't tell whether she was kidding. But he knew that when a woman looked at him the way Jana was, he'd be a *gadje dilo* indeed if he didn't make some kind of move.

He shoved back his chair. "Jana, if you're not serious, tell me now."

She gazed straight at him, her excitement betrayed only by the rapid pace of her breathing and the rising color of her face. "I've been wanting to make love with you since the first time I saw you."

His throat tightened. "Me, too. We must be crazy."

"Probably." She shrugged a little, but it was enough to do interesting things to her body. That was more than he could take.

In one swift movement, he swept her into his arms and carried her to the bedroom.

HE PUT HER DOWN on the bed, but she didn't stay down. Jana rose up to her knees, her hands pressed to his chest, fingers spread. His hair was tousled and he was attractively mussed with his suspenders hanging down and his shirt half undone. As handsome as he'd been in his tuxedo, black eye and all, she liked him even more this way. A little out of control, with his labored breathing matched her own. She could feel his heartbeat, too, pumping fast and strong.

"I guess this means I'm not a suspect," she said, undoing his tuxedo shirt. He wore a white T-shirt underneath, tight enough to hug his muscles.

"You're not a suspect."

"You'd agree with anything I said right now, wouldn't you?"

"Just about." He nipped at her mouth, catching it and deepening the kiss until she felt the velvet slide of his tongue on her lips. The need inside her spread, sending sweet shudders racing over her fevered skin.

"Is there something you wanted to ask for?" he said, stopping with her face cradled between his hands.

She closed her eyes, knowing what he asked, but what was happening between them was only about him and her and no one else.

She plucked at his shirtfront. "All I want is you."

"Good." He kissed her again, one of his hands slipping up the back of her loose T-shirt. He stroked her spine, a tickling caress, then lifted the shirt off in one motion, making her catch her breath. Her hair crackled against the cotton fabric, full of electricity, then fell across her naked breasts.

Henry touched her nipples with careful fingertips. Her flesh drew tight. She didn't want him to go slow and careful, but if he needed to approach her with reverence, she was willing to get a good grip on his arms to withstand the exquisite torture. He palmed her breasts, cuddling them with tenderness, lowering himself to sit on the bed so he could take one aching bud into the wet heat of his mouth. She swooned then, clinging to his shoulders. Pressing kisses into his hair.

They toppled onto the bed. "Up you go," he said, settling her astride his supine body. She peeled his T-shirt up over his head, leaning into the solid wall of muscle. His palms covered her breasts. She threw back her head, ridden with a wild desire.

Her hips rocked against his. "We're going to do this."

He panted. "You bet."

"It's against all the rules."

"You don't have rules, and I can break as many as I want without being arrested."

"I have rules." Her stomach jumped as his slid his hands inside the legs of her boxer shorts. "Staying away from the law is number one."

"Right now, I'm not the law."

His fingers found her, slipped inside. She rose up, then sank onto all fours, hovering above him with her hair falling in his face. He looked at her with love in his eyes. She lowered her head, searching for his mouth, his kiss. "Then who are you?"

"Your lover."

"Not yet…"

"Yes. Now. Right now."

"I can't debate the…issue." She licked soft kisses over his mouth, down his throat. "Not when you're doing—" his fingers speared deeper, playing inside her "—*that*. Oh, please." She opened and closed her mouth against his heaving chest, her bottom up in the air, moving slowly from side to side in a sensual dance. "Please don't stop."

He rolled her onto her back, not stopping, somehow not stopping. She dug her heels into the bed and reached for his fly. "I think you need to be naked."

"You, too."

"Don't stop."

"Then how—"

She arched. "Umm." Shoved his pants down as best she could. He worked one hand around to the small of her back and yanked the boxer shorts over her derriere by the stretchy waistband. Both of them were too eager to delay much longer.

"Protection," Henry said.

"Don't stop," she said. "I can reach the drawer."

"You really did search my house."

Her eyes closed in bliss. "I was bored." Really, she'd made an educated guess.

His mouth sought her breasts again. Exquisite. "I'll have to find ways to keep you busy."

She sighed, reaching for him. "This will do."

He pressed a palm to the inside of one thigh. "Open for me now."

Suddenly she was stricken. The intimacy was too much. Deeper than anything she'd experienced. "I don't know if I—"

He cut her off, saying "Shh," against her mouth. "Do you trust me?"

She looked into his eyes, breathed his scent—pure arousal. Finally she nodded.

"Then let me in."

His hands were large and hot, touching her, teasing her, but not forcing, or even persuading her to surrender. That was her own choice, and she'd already made it. Her thighs parted wide, wider, and he moved between them. He entered her slowly, filled her completely. "Trust me," he said, pushing deep.

She trusted him. Yes. Oh, yes. She did.

His flat belly flexed against hers. The muscles in his chest rippled. She wound her arms around him, pressing her thighs tighter against his hips, the soles of her feet riding his bunched calves.

The bed creaked beneath them. The pleasure built to an unbearable degree.

She smoothed her palms over his face, startled by the stark desire in his eyes. "Trust *me*," she whispered.

He said, "Yes, always," and the pleasure burst inside her like heavenly starfire.

10

PRIKAZA.

The next morning in camp, Jana heard the word everywhere she turned. Sometimes it was in her head, but often it was not. The family whispered it behind her back. Some used it loud enough for her to overhear.

Prikaza. Bad luck. The kind that came from becoming to close to the *gadje.*

Jana had *prikaza* in a bad way.

So, she feared, did Gabriel.

They were packing up camp, preparing to move to the next destination. Blue Cloud had gone bad for them, and no one wanted to stay. There was worry over Gabriel, but they knew that eventually he would be released. He could jump bail if it came to that, though Jana would do everything in her power to come up with a solution, including the first step of hiring a legitimate lawyer. If only she could talk to Gabe, figure out why he'd been so shortsighted and reckless....

Henry had said that she should be able see her cousin, probably later today. He'd been getting ready to leave for work, and she hadn't had the heart to tell him that the caravan would be moving on as soon as possible.

They both knew the other night hadn't been a lasting commitment.

Tears sprang to Jana's eyes whenever she paused in her packing to think about Henry's offer to help her get a teaching job in Blue Cloud. She wanted it more than she'd ever suspected, especially after discovering how right she'd felt, making love with Henry. The idea of leaving so soon—leaving at all—was a pain inside her that no family bond, however meaningful, could soothe.

Late that morning, Baba Magda stepped into Jana's caravan and caught her dabbing at her eyes. "Dust," she said, blinking. A glimpse in the mirror was enough to drop the pretense. Her eyes were red-rimmed and her nose was slightly swollen. She didn't look much like a woman in love, unless you knew that love with a *gadje* always led to heartache.

Magda, who could be so fierce, held out her arms, clucking with sympathy. "Poor child."

They hugged. Jana closed her eyes tight, refusing to let the tears come again. "I knew I would have to choose," she muttered, stepping away. With a sigh, she leaned against the doorjamb, watching as the last tent was packed away. The remaining horses were fractious as two of the men loaded them into the rickety trailer. They missed Gabriel's special touch.

Magda sat on the bed. "Your father chose a white woman."

"And he had *prikaza,* too."

"No. His destiny wasn't changed by the marriage. I knew he would go at a young age."

"You *knew?* And you let him—"

"I let him live, Jana. Live every minute of his life. Knowing Fate doesn't alter it."

Jana's stomach flip-flopped. Her parents' deep love for each other had endured, even with their vast differences.

Could it be the same for her and Henry?

The sun had grown warm. She stuck her bare foot into a patch of sunshine, wiggling her toes. Henry had promised that he would do what he could to assist Gabriel's case. That didn't mean he would get him off, of course. Henry's sense of justice didn't bend, unlike the rather flexible code the Rom lived by. But if there was any chance at all to find the mastermind of the senseless crime, he would do it, even without Gabe's cooperation.

Magda sat, as tranquil as a Buddha, watching Jana's turmoil.

She went to kneel by her aunt, taking the woman's plump, careworn hands into her own. "What should we do about Gabe?"

"Gabriel will be fine. It'll all work out." Magda patted the top of Jana's hand. "Trust me."

Jana almost smiled, remembering what Henry had said about *that* phrase. But then last night, he had asked her to trust him and she had agreed. Did she, or didn't she?

She looked into Magda's eyes. "Do you *know* it?"

"I give no guarantees, *rinkini.*"

Jana licked her lips. Her voice had dried in her throat.

"What about me?" she rasped. "How do I make the right choice?"

"When the time comes, there will be no mistake. You will open your mouth and the right words will rise up from your heart. And you'll be happy, my Jana. Very happy for all your life." Magda took Jana's chin in her hand and squeezed it, her own face creasing into a generous smile. "This I know for a fact."

Jana closed her eyes, drawing a deep breath. "I can't leave with you."

Magda wasn't surprised. She made a sound of agreement.

"I must stay. To help Gabriel."

Magda nodded, encouraging Jana to go on.

"And for...myself. For..." She swallowed, finding the strength to speak her choice. "For Henry." The pain inside her wound impossibly tight for an instant and then released to a dull ache. It hadn't been about leaving Henry, because she couldn't do that any more than she could cut out her heart. The pain had been about leaving her family.

HENRY'S MORNING had been spent in a world of confusion and he didn't like it one damn bit. He'd been up all night, one way or the other, sorting out his suspects and then complicating his incendiary relationship with Jana by taking her to bed. After that, he should have told her there was no way he'd let her out of his life. She'd have to accept that she was stuck with him for good. But for some reason, women—especially sassy, independent women like Jana—reacted badly to being told what to do. So he'd prepared for work as usual, calming her worries about Gabriel as best he could, fighting the urge to throw her over his shoulder and carry her back to the bedroom, where at least he knew he could keep her happy.

Because the case he was building against her cousin surely wouldn't do it.

Henry gulped the cold remains of his fourth cup of coffee, then crushed the cup and threw it toward the trash can.

Gabriel Vargas was clearly guilty. But of what, exactly, was as murky as a swamp. There were several inconsistencies, any way Henry twisted the pieces of the puzzle. The missing pearl necklace was one. Then there were the Wolf sisters, who hadn't swerved from their claim about the bald mystery man in a tuxedo lurking near the back door of the museum. If their annoying little dog, Scooter, hadn't had an urgent need to "water" the shrubbery, they'd never have seen him.

A second suspect fit the scenario. Gabe was the inside man. While he was maneuvering into position to grab the tiara, his conspirator was cutting the power. Henry figured that the distraction of darkness and the ensuing chaos was meant to give Gabe time to swipe the tiara and then slip away in the confusion, but the young Rom refused to talk.

What baffled Henry was the obvious stupidity of the plan. Gabe had done nothing to avoid setting off the alarm the instant he touched the case that held the tiara.

Perhaps he'd been told that the alarm would be taken care of? Certainly Jana was ready to believe that her cousin had been duped into taking part in an impossible theft. If he was to be fair, Henry had to admit that could be so.

But for what purpose?

Officer Sam Blake knocked once on the open door, wearing his hat tipped to the back of his head because of the big red knot on his forehead. Between Henry's black eye, Sam's noggin and Willis O'Bannion's fresh case of hives—which popped up whenever he had to make an arrest—the B.C.P.D. was looking the worse for wear. If Henry didn't solve this case soon, his men would be qualifying for combat pay.

Sam cleared his throat. "Chief, you're going to want to take a look at this."

"What is it?"

"A report on Trey Stone."

Henry waved the sergeant away even though Trey had been at the scene of the botched theft. The big buffoon had been the one who'd overturned the buffet table in the dark. "I already saw that."

"Not this one. I tracked down more information. I dunno if it means anything, but…"

Henry rose, strode around his desk and grabbed the fax. "What now?" he growled, feeling uncharacteristically jumpy. No sleep and too much sex and caffeine could do that to a guy.

He skimmed the report. "Well, I'll be damned."

"Trey Stone" was an assumed name.

JANA'S CARAVAN had originally been built to be pulled by horses. That was no longer practical, so the little house on wheels had been converted so that it could be towed by a vehicle. Jana had wanted the family to take the caravan with them, but Magda refused. She'd even handed over the keys to her convertible, saying that Jana would need her own place to live, at least for a while. The comfortable familiarity of the caravan and the good memories it contained would help her through any bouts of restlessness or homesickness she should suffer.

Slowly and carefully, Jana drove the caravan toward the town of Blue Cloud. She was thinking that *homesickness* was a funny word, when it was really "family-sickness." Part of her thought that she'd feel a lot better about the move when she got to know Henry's family and began to feel at home here, but then the other side of her, the wary side, said she was crazy. She'd known Henry for only a few days. Yet here she was, betting her future that he'd want to take her on, lock, stock and caravan.

"Talk about leaps of faith," she said to herself, squinting into the sunlight as she followed the curved road that led past the tree-shaded museum. The oncoming sign caught her eye: The Princess Adelaide and Horace P. Applewhite Memorial Museum.

The Addy-Appy she'd heard it called by the townspeople. The nickname was a bit of a joke, seeing as how Blue Cloud's mayor, Cornelia Applewhite, was so proud of her family name and was appalled to hear it shortened.

Jana had tried to stay out of the mayor's way during her stay in town—mayors tended to frown on Gypsy visits—but she supposed that wasn't always going to work. If she wanted to become an upstanding citizen, eventually she'd have to be introduced to Mayor Applewhite and her constant escort, that creepy bald man named Spotsky.

Bald.

Nah. Not possible. Spotsky was a respected businessman.

Jana frowned, braking her car. She looked back at the museum, remembering where she'd seen Spotsky before. It had been her first day in town, when she'd brought the convertible in for repairs at the business called Spotsky's Garage and Sales. She hadn't actually met him, but she'd seen him in his office, talking to a younger man. A younger man who was tall, dark and handsome, at least from behind. She hadn't seen his face, and Spotsky had slammed the door shut as soon as he'd seen her looking, but now that she thought about it, the young man could have been the princess's admirer, Trey Stone.

Didn't mean a thing.

Unless it did.

HENRY WAS HUMMING under his breath as he sped toward the Gypsy camp. He was back on top. He could see for miles and miles and miles again.

The deserted field came as something of a shock.

He slammed on the brakes and his patrol car skidded over the country road, fishtailing over the center line. The previously bustling pastureland was barren. Other than the trampled grass, not a single sign of the Gypsies remained. Not even a piece of trash or a crumpled yellow flyer, rattling in the breeze.

Vacant. Desolate. Bleak.

As was his heart.

Jana had gone? Just like that? No notice, not a single goodbye?

He'd wanted that, for a time. Back when he thought that making love with her once would be enough to get her out of his system. Now he knew that wasn't how it worked when you fell head over heels in love with the one woman in the world who was your destiny.

Henry swore. That was some kind of wicked curse she'd put on him. Bad luck until she and the rest of the Gypsies left town. Didn't she know that her leaving would be his worst luck of all?

The back of his neck was prickling. A little late. He'd already fallen face-first into a world of trouble.

He reversed the patrol car and tromped hard on the accelerator. He had all available officers on the road, hoping to pick up the man known as Trey Stone before he skipped town in his fancy leased convertible. Why not tell them to be on the lookout for the Gypsies, as well? Jana wouldn't like being brought to him, fussing and kicking, but at least she'd be back. He'd find a way to persuade her to stay.

Henry picked up then put back the radio mike. Dumb idea. Real dumb.

He'd have to come up with a better plan than to arrest her. His mind whirred as he drove by rote, barely seeing the trees and country houses as he sped by. Nearing town, he took a turn at the dairy farm that had been converted to a restaurant called The Farmhouse, deciding at the last moment to take a run by the museum. His tingle was bothering him, particularly since he no longer knew if it was connected to Jana or the job.

As he drove, he rubbed the back of his neck with irritation. The song he'd been humming kept floating through his head. He was no good with lyrics other than the "miles and miles" part, but there was something about crystal balls and seeing through a haze, wasn't there? How appropriate.

He hummed, filling in the words when he could. "Mmm, mmm, you've deceived me...blah, blah, blah..."

Stupid song.

He saw Jana's face. She smiled knowingly and whispered husky words that sounded as clear as if she'd been sitting in the front seat right beside him: "There's magic in my eyes."

Henry slammed on the brakes for the second time that day.

He turned his head to the left.

The Addy-Appy.

Jana's caravan was parked in front.

AFTER SHE'D TRIED the front doors and found them locked, Jana remembered that Simon had moved the tiara and a few of the other most valuable pieces to a safe the night before, saying that the exhibition was temporarily closed down. Mayor Applewhite had complained loudly, to no avail.

Jana stepped away from the doors. Several cars were parked in a lot at the side of the museum. Simon was probably inside, along with a staff of security guards. She had no reason to be here.

Forget reason. Follow your instincts.

She went around the side of the brick building, looking for other entrances. There were the small, high windows that Princess Lili had crawled in and out of. Crazy.

Jana couldn't reach them, anyway.

She spotted a back entrance and went to try it, not expecting it to be open.

It wasn't. But she could pick the lock. Zharko had taught her the skill as a child. She'd found it quite useful when her Boston grandparents had confined her to quarters for her frequent infractions of their rules, but she was bound to be rusty now. And the doors were certainly alarmed.

Didn't hurt to try, though. She and Gabe could share a cell.

HENRY CHECKED the cars in the lot. Simon's was there, plus those belonging to several members of his security staff. No unidentified vehicles, save one sedan that certainly wasn't Trey Stone's flashy convertible.

Henry parked beside Jana's caravan and went to check inside. Empty, at least of her, and that was as empty as it got. Next, he trotted up the stone steps to the tall double doors of the museum. Locked. There were no sounds to be heard when he pressed his ear close to listen. Not even a mystical whisper from Jana to tell him what to do.

He walked around the museum and found the back door.

Standing wide open.

Jana had gotten in. Did he trust her?

Henry drew his gun and approached cautiously. He knew every inch of the museum's floor plan. The place was dark and deserted. Simon would be in his second-floor office. The security guards…

Nowhere to be seen.

Henry slipped silently through the exhibition rooms. Every nerve ending in his nape was jittering. Even his rash was tingling as if a hundred spiders had dropped down his shirt.

Jana. Trouble. Jana. Trouble. The two were permanently intertwined in his mind.

The first floor was unoccupied, the tiara case empty.

Henry paused at the bottom of the steps, listening before he ascended. *There*—a man's voice. Simon.

Instinct told Henry to stay quiet and keep back. He moved off into the deep shadow of the curved staircase, looking upward as footsteps sounded on the second-floor balcony.

"You won't get away with it," said Simon.

"I have so far."

"Henry's going to figure it out."

"That big, dumb cop's easy to fool. He looked right at my son and didn't notice a thing. In the end, this will all be blamed on the Gypsies."

"Maybe so. Except for me."

Laughter. "*You* won't be talking." Henry heard the telltale sound of a gun being cocked. "It's a shame that you didn't eat any of the doughnuts. You'd be sleeping as pretty as you please, along with your guards, if you had. And I wouldn't have to…take care of you. But you were helpful in opening the safe."

Silence from Simon.

Henry didn't breathe. *Where the hell was Jana?*

"Look," Simon said. Henry had to hand it to the curator; he was keeping his cool. "Through the window above the doors. See the caravan? We're not alone."

The other man swore. "Why's she here?" After a moment, he chuckled. "Maybe this is even better. I'll leave the door open when I leave; the Gypsy woman will wander in and find your body…. The cops will think she's guilty as sin."

Henry said a silent prayer, hoping that Jana would remain hidden. Maybe his luck wasn't *all* bad. He'd parked the patrol car on the opposite side; Jana's caravan blocked it from view.

More laughter. "That's perfect. I couldn't have

planned it better if I tried. Come on, let's get going. Down the stairs. Take it easy with that tiara.''

Henry pressed closer to the wall as the pair started down the steps. As long as Jana stayed out of sight, he'd get a clear shot at the thief as soon as they stepped into the open space of the entrance hall.

Simon appeared, carrying the tiara in his outstretched palms. Spotsky was right behind him, pressing the barrel of a gun to the middle of the curator's wrinkled shirt. The bald businessman carried a satchel that was probably loaded with the rest of the jewels from the safe.

Simon had hesitated at the bottom of the steps when he saw the foyer was empty. "Where's Trey?"

"I sent him out of town. The boy did his part, even though he almost blew it by lifting the pearls too soon. All I wanted him for was to lure the Gypsy boy into taking a shot at the tiara." Spotsky chuckled. "I knew all about the security system from old Corny. That woman never shuts up. I couldn't get to the tiara as long as it stayed where it was, so…"

"You set up the botched theft."

"Exactly. Simple but brilliant." A prod of the gun. "Keep moving."

"Trey's your son?"

"The hair fools 'em every time."

"The name…"

"Trey Stone, aka Rockford Spotsky III. Used to call him Rocky, when I was still married to his mother."

Simon stepped into the patch of sunlight shining

through the arched window above the doors. "Trey Stone, three stones. Clever."

That's right, Henry thought as he eased forward. *Keep him talking.*

"Yeah," Spotsky boasted. "But the fourth rock is the one that really counts." He'd let Simon get ahead of him as he waved the gun at the large diamond at the center of the tiara. "That baby is worth millions." He stepped toward Simon again. "Hand it over."

Henry leveled his gun at the thief. "Police! Freeze!"

Everything happened at once. Spotsky whirled, clutching the tiara in front of himself as if it were bulletproof. He started to swing his gun around in Henry's direction.

Every move was in slow motion to Henry. His pulse slowed. His trigger finger tightened. At the same moment, a whizzing sound ascended on them from above.

Spotsky looked up, his eyes bugging out.

Jana whooped, and suddenly it was all happening too fast for Henry to believe. She was a blur, sitting astride the long, curved bannister, sliding down it with her hair flying behind her. There was no time for any of them to react. She zipped downward, momentum launching her into the air, arms and legs outspread.

She hit Spotsky smack dab in the tiara.

The tiara went flying in one direction, Spotsky's gun in the other. Simon was closest, and he kicked it away, sending it spinning across the polished floor into one of the darkened exhibit rooms. Henry rushed to pull Jana away from Spotsky, but he needn't have worried. The man's bald head had smacked into the stone floor. He lay unconscious beneath Jana's weight.

She ground her sandaled foot in the middle of the thief's gut as Henry helped her stand. "Are you hurt?"

"Nope." She put a shaky hand to her brow. "But I've got a wicked head rush."

"That was the dumbest, bravest thing I've ever seen. What were you thinking?"

"I—" She blinked. "I didn't see you until it was too late, or I'd've let you handle it. Trust me." She stepped off Spotsky, making a sound of pleasure as her arms wound around Henry's waist. She leaned into him. He holstered his gun so he could hold her tight with both arms. She'd be lucky if he ever let go of her again.

"I wasn't going to let him get away with stealing the tiara and blaming the whole thing on Gabe," she said, glancing back at Spotsky. Simon knelt beside him, testing his pulse. He gave a thumbs-up.

"What about Simon? You saved his life."

Jana blinked. "I guess I did."

"I'd have the mayor present you with a medal for bravery if there wasn't the small complication of Spotsky being her so-called boyfriend."

"That does put a wrinkle into my culpability," Simon said with a lopsided grin. Corny had been threatening him with all manner of dire consequences since the first attempted theft.

"What happened before I arrived?" Henry asked.

"The security guards were drugged," Jana said with a shudder. "I saw them all upstairs in the lunchroom, sprawled here and there. That was when I knew for sure that there was something strange going on."

Simon ran a hand through his sparse hair. "Spotsky had keys he'd lifted from the mayor's purse, along with the alarm codes. I'm not sure how he managed the drugs. All I know is that he walked into my office with a gun and forced me to open the safe." He looked at Jana. "Where were you? And how'd you get in?"

She bit her lip, then glanced up at Henry. "Um…"

He rolled his eyes. "Don't ask."

Simon looked askance. "Same way you got out of the lunchroom the other day, I imagine. Thank God Lili wasn't here this time, or she'd have slid down the bannister right behind you."

Jana shrugged. "It was the only thing I could think of."

Simon nudged a foot into Spotsky's midsection. "I suppose we should call for an ambulance." He remembered the guards and sprinted up the stairs. "Right away!"

Henry released Jana so he could double-check the unconscious man, in case Spotsky was a pro at playing possum. "This should be good for Gabe's case," he told her, lifting Spotsky's head a few inches off the floor. No reaction. He pulled an eyelid back. Oh, yeah, the man was out. "I'm not saying he'll get off scot-free, but his sentence should be fairly light, considering the circumstances."

He looked up when there was no response from Jana. She'd wandered off.

"Jana," he said, watching as she knelt to pick up the tiara, which had skidded quite a ways across the floor. She hadn't even heard him; she was completely absorbed by the legendary tiara. With a small catch of her breath, she ran her fingertips over the tiny rows of diamonds and platinum filigree.

Finally she raised her head. Her glistening eyes sought out Henry's. "Isn't it the most gorgeous thing you've ever seen?"

Not even close.

He left Spotsky and went to join her. "Why don't you try it on?"

"Oh, no, I couldn't. It's not for me." She held it out to Henry, turning her face aside. "Go on, take it. It's caused more than enough trouble for us."

He wouldn't let her hand it off. "Do you believe in curses?"

She looked at his bruised eye. "Not—not really."

"Suppose you did. Wouldn't you, as a Vargas, be the perfect person to remove the tiara's curse? I have a feeling that Princess Lili will be a Brunner bride before too long. You don't want her to walk down the aisle in this tiara, afraid that her happily ever after won't last, do you?"

"No," Jana breathed. "But I don't know how..."

"Sure you do. The right words will come."

She smiled at him. "How is it that you're so smart and that you can trust me so completely?"

He grinned. Gave a wink of his bruised eye. "Just lucky, I guess."

She looked down at the tiara again. "It's not words that will stop a curse. It's…knowing. Belief. Trust. Love." She touched a fingertip to the center diamond. "And perhaps a little bit of old-fashioned magic."

Henry took the tiara from her and placed it on her head. She squared her shoulders and lifted her chin, her lively blue eyes outshining the Vargas diamond by a thousand facets. She had nary a drop of royal blood, but she was a princess nonetheless.

"If the Brunner brides were ever cursed, they are no longer," Jana pronounced grandly. "Now that a Vargas has worn the tiara, we'll all have happy endings forevermore!"

Henry couldn't speak; his heart was stuck in his throat. He knew that Jana was offering him his own happy ending. And he knew that in whatever form it should come, he—*they*—would handle it just fine.

"*Ves'tacha,* may I have this dance?" He held his arms open.

Jana glided into them. "Beloved, hmm? Where did you pick that up?"

"On the side of the road," he said grittily. "She was hitchhiking." And then he waltzed his beloved Gypsy princess across the floor. No music was needed. They had magic…and love.

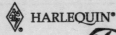

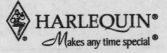

The latest continuity from Harlequin Books continues in October 2002 with

STRANGERS WHEN WE MEET
by Marisa Carroll

Check-in: Radio talk-show host Emma Hart thought Twin Oaks was supposed to be a friendly inn, but fellow guest Blake Weston sure was grumpy!

Checkout: When both Emma and Blake find their fiancés cheating on them, they find themselves turning to one another for support—and comforting hugs quickly turn to passionate embraces....

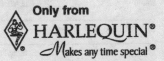

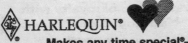

Princes...Princesses...
London Castles...New York Mansions...
To live the life of a royal!

In 2002, Harlequin Books lets you escape to a
world of royalty with these royally themed titles:

Temptation:
January 2002—*A Prince of a Guy* (#861)
February 2002—*A Noble Pursuit* (#865)

American Romance:
The Carradignes: American Royalty (Editorially linked series)
March 2002—*The Improperly Pregnant Princess* (#913)
April 2002—*The Unlawfully Wedded Princess* (#917)
May 2002—*The Simply Scandalous Princess* (#921)
November 2002—*The Inconveniently Engaged Prince* (#945)

Intrigue:
The Carradignes: A Royal Mystery (Editorially linked series)
June 2002—*The Duke's Covert Mission* (#666)

Chicago Confidential
September 2002—*Prince Under Cover* (#678)

The Crown Affair
October 2002—*Royal Target* (#682)
November 2002—*Royal Ransom* (#686)
December 2002—*Royal Pursuit* (#690)

Harlequin Romance:
June 2002—*His Majesty's Marriage* (#3703)
July 2002—*The Prince's Proposal* (#3709)

Harlequin Presents:
August 2002—*Society Weddings* (#2268)
September 2002—*The Prince's Pleasure* (#2274)

Duets:
September 2002—*Once Upon a Tiara/Henry Ever After* (#83)
October 2002—*Natalia's Story/Andrea's Story* (#85)

 Celebrate a year of royalty with
Harlequin Books!

Available at your favorite retail outlet.

HARLEQUIN®
Makes any time special®

Visit us at www.eHarlequin.com

HSROY02